For Brian and Avril, my ultra cool nephew and adorable niece. Love you loads, guys! Love is the Reason is for you.

Chapter 1

In a studio apartment in New York City, Matt Ardle stretched his full six feet five inches on the double bed, one muscular, tanned arm behind his head, the other loosely around Heidi's shoulders.

"Happy?" he asked, flipping on to his side to face her.

Her response was prefaced with a breathtaking kiss. "Ecstatic! I can't believe we're actually living in The Big Apple, a ten-minute walk from Times Square! It's everything I imagined it would be."

Jumping from the bed, she ran to the window, pushed up the lower sash with all her might and stuck her head out into the chilly New York air. Allowing the noise from nearby 57th Street to filter into their modest 7th Avenue studio apartment, she stretched as far as she could, excitement fizzing inside as she looked to her left toward Central Park and then at the opera lovers queuing for tickets outside Carnegie Hall on the opposite side of the street – the Box Office opened mid-morning.

"Have you called home yet?" Matt asked tentatively, getting up and crossing the floor to join her.

She shook her head, her long mane of auburn hair shielding her face and masking her expression. A silent response that spoke multitudes.

"Don't leave it too long, Heid. You don't want your parents putting out an SOS for you." He held his breath, watching for a signal to indicate she'd heard him. And hoping more than anything that she would heed his words.

Calm before a storm. The whispered words arrived uninvited in Matt's head, forcing him to contemplate the inevitable, pouring cold water on his short-lived escape from reality. He hated being the responsible one, ironic as it seemed under their circumstances. But Matt wasn't one to shirk doing the right thing. Probably down to his mum's ability to instil a conscience in her sons, he thought, a warm feeling flooding through him as his mother's sound words of advice rang loudly in his ears. His pulse quickened as an unexpected rush of heat surged along his neck and into his cheeks. Secrets – he hated secrets, hated not being able to share this important event with his parents. Or anybody else for that matter. Instantly, he qualified his latest actions by convincing himself he was saving his family from worry and what they didn't know couldn't harm them. His pulse slowed in pace but his nagging conscience refused to be placated.

He leaned his shoulder against the wall, tracing the old-fashioned floral wallpaper-pattern with his index finger, reminded of the time he'd scribbled on the walls of his grandmother's hallway. Gloria had scolded him at the time, yet many years later he'd heard her bragging that she'd been the first to discover his artistic talents. Comical really, seeing as his graffiti efforts on the wall of the basketball court got him a severe reprimand from the local gardaí at the time. His granny, of course, found a positive amidst the shame of having the gardaí ringing on the doorbell. She had pointed out the quality of his drawing to anyone prepared to ignore the fact that he'd been defacing public property!

Would Heidi's parents be so forgiving when they discovered she'd absconded to New York without saying a word, he wondered. With him? Matt didn't think so and in the absence of any response from Heidi on the matter, he tried again to get her to rethink her decision and at least let her family know she was safe.

"It'll only take a moment to make contact, Heidi. Tell them you have a new number. Even a one-line email to put their minds at ease. You won't have to disclose where you are unless you want to. What if they've been trying to call your mobile? Or they need to get in touch with you urgently?"

Not for the first time, he fretted about the consequences of Heidi's decision to follow him, fearful of the determined lengths she was capable of going to (and not only in geographical distance), hating the distasteful fact that he too was party to her deceit.

Packing his things with his mum, he'd been really careful to continue the charade that he was setting out on a big adventure alone. Well, the big adventure part was true. But alone? He'd barely spent a moment alone since he'd met Heidi at JFK airport.

When he'd accepted the offer as a gym teacher and basketball coach at NYC College, Heidi had instantly conjured up plans of her own. Back home, he'd been caught up in the fizz of her excitement. Extricating himself from arrangements he'd made with college friends, he'd welcomed her suggestion with open arms and a big smile on his face. But now that they'd arrived and their web of lies was spinning wider and wider, he had serious reservations about the wisdom of their decision.

Heidi half-turned towards him, raising an eyebrow and shrugging her shoulders. "In another few days, I'll call them and give them my new number. It's no biggie, Matt!"

His persistence matched her obstinacy: "But what's the worst thing they can say, eh?"

He watched as she slowly withdrew from the window, tugging on the frame to get it back into place. Once she'd secured the old-fashioned latch, she drew the heavy velvet drapes together, shutting out the city and isolating them from the rest of the world.

"Stop fussing, Matt. I'm not expected back from Cyprus for another few days so they won't be even thinking about me yet. Anyway, in case you haven't noticed, I *am* a consenting adult!"

"Oh, I'd noticed," he deadpanned, looking deep into her eyes, then slowly allowing his gaze to rove the length of her svelte body, the deep physical attraction he felt for her causing his breath to quicken.

Heidi's soft, seductive voice cut into his fantasy.

"Don't you want to be alone with me?"

Matt moved a step closer and nodded, drinking in the outline of her firm breasts, her tiny waist and legs that went on forever.

She ran her tongue over her lips. "Can't we savour

where we are for now? Being away from it all without having to hide from interfering and disapproving families? We deserve this bliss. Allow us to enjoy it. Please?"

Her words hung in the stuffy room, the mood between them intensifying, their anonymity paramount and their location immaterial once they were together.

Unable to resist her tantalising, Matt reached out and pulled her into his arms. He inhaled the lingering scent of the latest YSL fragrance she'd sprayed from a sample bottle in Macy's, his tongue flicking gently against her earlobe, his body tingling with lustful anticipation.

"Cold?" she asked when he shivered in her arms. "Maybe it's time you put on more than your boxers." She tilted her head as she looked up at him, her bright blue eyes twinkling mischievously, her finger trailing over his chest, circling his belly button, her hips swaying gently against his thighs. She was expert at distracting him and expert at getting her own way, making it impossible for him to refuse her anything.

"Or maybe it's time you took off yours, you little minx," he said, feeling her warm breath on his ear, submitting to her advances and entwining his fingers in hers. Guiding her towards the wall, childhood scribbles and family issues were the furthest things from his mind as their lips met. Their rented space in Midtown Manhattan was a safe haven from the world's demands and the chain of events about to unfold. At least for now.

Chapter 2

Lucy Ardle curled up on the couch in her sister Delia's conservatory, oblivious to the magnificent sea view, the uncertainty of her future stretching before her, a brand-new chapter in her life about to begin.

Earlier that afternoon she'd been fraught and distracted, her mind on the other side of the Atlantic with her son, Matt. He'd left for New York a few days previously, excited and apprehensive. Watching him walk through the departure gates of Shannon Airport reminded her of his very first day at nursery school when he'd clutched his teacher's hand and waved Lucy a solemn goodbye. This time his wave had been cheery, his bright eyes holding hers until he'd disappeared beyond the security gates. The lump in her throat threatened to choke her long after he'd disappeared from view, a dark cloud of loneliness slipping around her.

Danny didn't understand. But husbands seldom did, Lucy thought, fiddling with the collection of bronze figurines on the table beside her, remembering Danny's sorry attempt at comforting her when she'd tried to explain how she felt. She wasn't a fool and had known full well he'd been watching the Sports Channel over her shoulder while she poured her heart out. Irritated by his nonchalance, she'd stormed from the house, telling him in no uncertain terms how inconsiderate he was being.

She drove furiously to their entrance gate where she braked sharply, scattering gravel. Then she nosed out onto the narrow byroad, glancing up the road to her neighbour Carol Black's lavish house, Hillcrest, wondering if she was there. But a chat and a coffee with a neighbour wouldn't remedy this situation. Only a heart-to-heart with a sister would do.

As per usual, Delia was on hand in a crisis, her home not far from Lucy's by car, living as they did on opposite sides of the seaside village of Crosshaven in County Cork.

Lucy's lips shaped into a sudden smile as she remembered her younger sister's shock when she'd arrived on her doorstep, babbling incoherently, tears rolling down her cheeks.

"Anyone would think there was a death in the family and not a bit of upheaval over a graduate leaving home!" Delia had blurted out, ushering Lucy inside Bracken, her split-level home on Strand Hill.

Once Lucy's sobbing had subsided, Delia went to the kitchen to make coffee.

"It's a lot tougher than you expected, eh?" she said as she returned with a laden tray: steaming coffee, a bowl of whipped cream, a plateful of the chunkiest chocolate-chip cookies Lucy had ever seen and two enormous mugs.

"The emptiness is surreal, Del, not to mention the

dread of endless boring days with nothing to do. As for the stillness in the house . . ." Lucy shuddered. "I find it impossible to stay there any length of time. And I know I was forever shouting at him to lower the volume on his rock music but I'd do anything now to hear the thudding bass guitar bringing the house back to life."

"Come on, this isn't like you. I thought you were delighted for Matt to spread his wings?" Delia went for reinforcements, returning a moment later with a large box of chocolates – an essential accessory in any crisis. Unwrapping the cellophane, she took the lid from the box and gave Lucy all four of her favourite Turkish delights from the top layer.

Popping one in her mouth, Lucy lined the others up like soldiers on the table in front of her. Thinking hard about Delia's question, she sucked on the mixture of milk chocolate and soft gelatine, enjoying the rich taste as it slid down her throat, reaching for the second one before she'd even finished the first. "Of course I'm happy for *him*. It's me I feel sorry for."

"You weren't nearly this bad when Stephen left for Oz, Luce," Delia reminded her, filling both of their mugs.

"I know but this is totally different, a complete wrench. I missed Stephen like crazy. But at least Matt was still at home then. And I was busy. It's so damn orderly in the house now. No sports gear lying around, no mess in the kitchen and nobody clearing all the nice stuff from the fridge in record time."

"Surely that's not all bad?" Delia ventured carefully, scooping a generous helping of cream into her coffee and pulling her feet under her as she made herself comfortable on the couch for a marathon sisterly chat.

Lucy shook her head. "For the first time in years, I can hear myself think. And I can honestly tell you I don't like one word of what I'm hearing." Loneliness expanded inside her like an inflating balloon, overwhelming her with its severity, making it impossible for her to look forward.

Delia reached out and took a truffle from the box, nibbling at it as she outlined her sister's predicament aloud. "So the boys are settling into new lives, Danny's happy to leave them to it and that leaves you where exactly? Disgruntled? Lost? Bored? As far as I can see, Luce, it's time to give yourself a kick up the backside, step out of your comfort zone and take your spare time in a new direction."

Lucy's eyes misted. "Look at the state of me. I'm pathetic. I can't even think straight, never mind anything else. Being a mother and wife, organising school runs and PTA meetings are all I've known for the last twenty years."

"That's the most ridiculous thing I've ever heard," Delia shot back, popping two chocolate hazelnuts in her mouth, her patience and tolerance wearing thin, annoyance speeding up her chocolate consumption. "It's a hell of a long time since you've done a school run! For God's sake, Matt is twenty-one! It's not like he was hanging around your feet every day. He was barely ever home. Get a grip, sis!" She crunched the chocolates loudly, running her tongue around her teeth to extricate tiny pieces of hazelnut, refusing to indulge Lucy's self-pity.

This time her sister couldn't disagree. "Maybe not, but he was always coming and going, generally with a few others in tow."

"To pick up his laundry and get fed no doubt," Delia muttered under her breath, instantly remorseful when her sister's face crumpled. "Ah, I didn't mean it like that, Luce, but he's a grown man and he wouldn't want you pining after him. Give yourself some time to get used to things. You'll soon find your feet again."

"I hope so, Del. I really do. But, right now, it's a shock to my system."

Munching on chocolate after chocolate, they managed to eat their way through to the second layer, discussing Lucy's dilemma in great detail and coming up with a few suggestions to ease her into the next phase of her life. Surprise November sunshine filtered into the conservatory as the sisters chatted amicably, the unexpected warmth – along with Delia's reassuring words – brightening Lucy's spirits and encouraging her to look forward once more.

"Next week, Del," she promised her sister determinedly, allowing herself another day or two to wallow, "next week will be the start of something new, a time to find myself again. And who knows what adventures will come my way?"

Carol Black breezed in the front door of her luxury three-storey home, more than satisfied with her Saturday afternoon. Eric was due back from his business trip the following day and had promised they'd have reason to celebrate. And knowing how her husband liked to do things in style and have her looking her best, Carol hadn't left anything to chance. Her platinum bob gleamed after her trip to the hair salon and the dress she'd spotted in Lily & Clara's boutique window in

Ballincollig was now safely wrapped in tissue paper and rightfully hers.

Flicking through the post sitting in the box since the previous day, she soon realised it was all bank stuff and dropped the envelopes on the hall table for Eric to deal with. He'd made it clear from the early days of their marriage that he didn't like her opening his post so now she never dreamt of doing so, in any case finding his wheeling and dealing complex and impossible to follow, something she'd have lived quite happily without. But the rewards were fruitful, and the lavish lifestyle something she'd become accustomed to, so she was happy to turn a blind eye to the intricate and possibly suspect detail.

Feeling suddenly weary and pleased at the thought of having their large sleigh bed to herself, she craved an early night with the plasma TV and her fashion magazines for company, but unfortunately her daughter Isobel would need a lift to the airport in a while.

At present Isobel was locked away in the study on the third floor, knee-deep in prep work for yet another project she was co-ordinating for her high-level IT position. Amazed by her daughter's hunger to succeed in such a male-dominated environment, Carol often worried that one day Isobel would look back and weep, regretting spending her Saturday nights wrapped up in the latest software development instead of a handsome man's arms. A stickler for perfection, she had a flight to Dublin that evening, adamant she'd need Sunday to set up her conference room and get everything exactly right (including burning mood-sticks to induce the exact atmosphere she wanted to prevail) so the first of her presentations, on

Monday morning, would go without a hitch. Isobel left nothing to chance.

Definitely inherited the ambitious gene from her father, Carol thought with a smile, grabbing her Lily & Clara bag and her bundle of glossies, anticipating a perfect end to her day once she'd dropped Isobel to the airport.

Chapter 3

Matt pulled on a chocolate-coloured T-shirt, khaki combats and a grey sweater. Sitting on the bed, he laced his Timberland boots. "Come on, Heidi, we haven't travelled all this distance to stay cooped up indoors."

"You weren't complaining a while ago!" Heidi, who was also getting dressed, turned and gave him a cheeky grin.

"Yeah, well, I've worked up a hunger now and I'm ready for New York and its millions of delis." He was ravenous after their energetic lovemaking. "I can already taste chocolate donuts. Or should I start with pancakes doused in maple syrup? And I'm definitely going to follow that with a huge portion of chocolate-chip ice cream." He grinned at the horrified look on Heidi's face.

"Sounds disgusting!" She patted her flat stomach. "I'm not ruining all I've been through with this body! It's taken me long enough to get to a point where I'm happy with it. But," she added, slipping a sweater over a long-sleeved shirt, "I will have one of those *Sex and the City* margarita cocktails later today if you're offering?"

"Anything your little heart desires, m'lady." His green eyes were full of mischief, his good humour infectious as he grabbed his keys from the breakfast bar and led the way from the apartment. He entwined his fingers in hers once they were on the bustling street outside. "Are you up for walking to Times Square or will we hop on a tour bus?"

"Eh, doh! Why do you think I'm wearing flatties?" She pointed at her feet. "Of course I'm up for walking! I want to breathe the same polluted air as every other New Yorker. And skip along the streets like Sarah Jessica Parker and Kim Cattrell and see the steam rising up from the manholes like I've seen happen a million times on *NYPD*. And hear the sound of the underground . . ."

"You're such a baby," he interrupted, amused by her unashamed enthusiasm and lengthy wish list. He'd no idea New York meant this much to her.

Heidi slapped him playfully on the arm.

Matt smirked, ducking his head just in time to avoid walking into a shop canopy. They continued along the street and it wasn't long before they came upon the first deli, tempting aromas wafting onto the street and assaulting Matt's nostrils long before they'd reached the door.

"Cinnamon donuts!" he cried, sniffing for a moment and punching the air with his fist when he knew he couldn't be mistaken. "At last I get to live the real New York dream!"

Dragging Heidi over the threshold of the shop, his jaw dropped as he surveyed the magnificent selection in stock. Manna from heaven! All my Christmases have come at once, he thought, his mouth watering as he scanned the array of delicacies laid out in glass cabinets, a treat for every day in the year. He'd happily sample every single one.

Beside him, Heidi's eyes were fixed on the luscious chocolate brownies, her personal downfall when it came to piling on calories. But she'd learned to resist temptation, considering the sweet chocolate taste too small a reward for the hours of guilt and empty retching afterwards. I need to get out of here fast, she thought.

"Matt, I'll run back to the apartment and get a jacket. It might get a lot chillier later and these air-conditioned shops are freezing!"

His eyes never left the laden counter as he passed her his apartment keys. "Take your time. I'll be still here drooling over sugar-coated donuts, trying to make up my mind which one to get first! Want anything?"

"Something small – and low-fat," she said after a moment's pause, gambling on just one treat.

"And I'll get some coffee to go as well. We can sit outside while we're munching. Who knows? There might be a celeb or two passing by."

Heidi snorted. "Like you'd recognise one if they stood in front of you and asked for the time!"

Matt shrugged and smiled. "Can't help it if they don't impress me much!"

"You're going to be wasted here! And did you see the giant M&M shop? Amazing, to say the least. If Alex . . ." She stopped, realising too late what she'd been about to say, the little she'd said already too much.

Matt stiffened, the memory of Heidi referring to Alex as "the love of my life", and her tender expression as she said it, filling him with uncontrollable jealousy. He shoved away his childishness, forcing himself to pick up the conversation as though nothing was wrong.

"Yeah? About Alex? You were about to say?"

"Doesn't matter," she muttered.

Despite the hum of ovens and the hiss of steam from the nearby coffee machine, a distinct silence fell between them. They stood looking at each other.

Heidi spoke first, her words hurried, her tone a forced brightness that lacked the teasing they'd been enjoying only moments before. "I'd best get that jacket. Sooner I'm back, sooner we're on our way to the shops."

Matt also made an effort to get things back on an even footing, his jealousy ebbing away as quickly as it arrived. "We could take a stroll through Central Park. Or go boating on the lake instead of going shopping?" *Again*, he added mentally. She'd already dragged him around Macy's and Bloomingdales. He'd had no idea what he was letting himself in for when she'd promised they'd only visit two stores on their first morning out. She said nothing about each store being the size of Cork city – in his eyes anyway. But seeing as he wanted their first day to be as much her thrill as his, he hadn't ruined it by complaining. It's not as if they were only on vacation so Matt knew he'd have plenty of time to explore Madison Square Gardens and hopefully get tickets to a game. Or visit Ellis Island and Wall Street and the other "boring historical sites" as Heidi referred to them when he'd read out the chief attractions from his tattered edition of the *Lonely Planet* guidebook.

"Your turn to decide," she said generously as if

reading his thoughts. She reached up and planted a kiss on his lips before hurrying from the cool air-conditioned deli and along the street in the direction of their apartment.

Matt sighed, wishing he'd handled her mention of Alex better. Still, he thought, we seem to be okay now. There's no point letting it ruin my appetite.

"One glazed cinnamon donut and one chocolate donut, please, and some of those butter-shortcake cookies," he said.

He glanced along the glass display cabinets, eyeing a section labelled low-fat and going to check it out. A gingerbread man! Heidi will love that, he decided, smiling at the coloured M&M eyes and mouth. He wished she wouldn't obsess about food, watching every morsel she put in her mouth, logging her daily carb intake on her mobile phone. Hell, he'd love her no matter what shape she was. But she didn't believe him when he told her that and constantly argued that he'd only taken real interest in her when she'd taken control of her pear-shaped figure. In reality, she couldn't have been further from the truth.

"Will that be all, sir?"

"I'll take one of those low-cal gingerbread men, a large full-fat mocha and a regular skinny latte," he said. "That should do for starters," he added, laughing, his eyes opening wide at the sight of what seemed like fifty containers of ice cream – each one a different flavour. Taking a step nearer the refrigerator, he realised there were flavours and mixtures he never knew existed with an array of toppings on the side that would put Christmas decorations to shame.

Within moments the deli guy, a lean silver-haired man, had packed Matt's purchases into a brown-paper bag and passed them across the counter to him. "You on vacation?"

Matt laughed. "Feels like that right now but we're actually here for a long stay."

"That your girl who came in with you?"

Matt nodded, meeting the other man's eyes, his face breaking into a grin. "Indeed she is. Beautiful and charming. But she watches her waistline so you'll more than likely be seeing more of me than her."

"Ah, the pretty ladies! They pay a high price for their figures!" He turned around to get the coffees, talking as he worked. "You, on the other hand, have to return some morning and try our breakfast pancakes. Workers walk blocks to get them, sometimes fighting over them when stocks are running low. Greatest recipe in New York City. It's our secret ingredient that makes the difference."

Matt grinned at his typical New York confidence. "Sounds good. Although I'll have to get back training if I'm popping in here on a regular basis."

"Bah! Worrying about how many kilos you weigh! Much more important to enjoy your food and live an active life. You staying nearby?" He passed the coffee over the counter.

"We couldn't be nearer – we're in the apartment building just a little way down the street. The name's Matt, by the way."

"Roy," the deli guy introduced himself, shaking his outstretched hand. "You've come all the way from Ireland, I take it, Matt?"

Matt nodded. "No disguising this accent!"

Roy rang Matt's money up in the till and handed him back his change. "We get them from all over in New York City but we love the Irish best of all." His face broke into a smile, revealing a chipped front tooth in an otherwise perfect set of white teeth.

"Yeah, yeah. Heard it all before. And you? A native New Yorker?"

"Ah, now that's a story I don't share very often but, hey, you come back to my store a few times and tell me what you think of my food and I might regale you with a tale or two."

"I'll look forward to that," Matt laughed, balancing the hot drinks in one hand and carrying the brown bag in the other.

"You have a nice day now. And don't forget to come back and try our pancakes, y'hear?"

Matt smothered a grin. He didn't need reminding. "Oh, I hear you alright!"

He was still grinning when he stepped out into the bright sunshine. These New Yorkers could really talk the talk, he thought, imagining how long it would take to get that much information from an Irish shopkeeper. And yet for some inexplicable reason (other than the delicacies he carried in his brown-paper bag) he was glad he'd met Roy. For an American sales person, he had a rare authenticity about him. And after only a brief few minutes in his company, Matt deduced that this tall, lithe, silver-haired Latin American had indeed an interesting story to tell.

He could imagine Heidi's reaction when he told her he'd befriended the local deli guy in the space of time it took to buy a few cakes! He knew it wouldn't surprise her but neither would it appeal, the notion of exchanging personal details with a total stranger an abhorrent invasion of privacy for Heidi.

As men, women and children of all ages and races strode along the sidewalk, he wondered what was keeping her. Don't tell me she's changing her clothes again, he mused, taking a seat at one of the bistro tables outside the shop while he waited. He couldn't wait to sink his teeth into one of his donuts, imagining the soft gooey centre melting in his mouth. But he didn't want to tuck in without Heidi. His grumbling stomach would have to wait a while longer.

He sipped his coffee, his attention drawn to three Japanese tourists with heavy-duty cameras who had decided to photograph the deli. Amused by them, he failed to notice the flurry of activity near a payphone on his side of 7th Avenue past the location of the apartment.

By the time he'd drained his coffee and, despite his good intentions, nibbled halfway through a donut, he decided it was time to find out what was delaying Heidi. He searched his pockets for his phone. "Damn," he muttered under his breath, "I must have come out without it." Grabbing the brown bag – but leaving Heidi's cold coffee behind – he strolled the short distance back to their apartment building. Pressing the door buzzer, he waited patiently for her to release the lock. But the doorbell went unanswered and much to his chagrin, seeing as Heidi had his keys, he had no choice but to stand outside and wait.

Three minutes later, despite another few assaults on the buzzer, Heidi still hadn't released the latch to let him in. His stomach rumbled. The deli goodies he'd been so looking forward to were losing their appeal. Just as well I didn't get the ice cream, he thought. It'd be running along the pavements to Broadway and Times Square by now! He put his ear to the large solid door, positive he could hear the bell ringing each time he pressed the buzzer. But why isn't she letting me in?

And then the catch was released. Quickly he pulled away from the door.

"About time, Heidi –" he began, but stopped abruptly when an exceptionally tall, shaggy-haired man in his early thirties ambled out. His black shirt hung open over a faded printed T-shirt and loose-fitting faded denims. On one shoulder he had a guitar case and on the other a shabby rucksack.

"Hey, man! You coming in?" He kept a hand to the door and held it open for Matt, a broad grin on his face, showing off even white teeth.

"Sure. Thanks," Matt said, very grateful to get inside the building. He presumed the guitar player lived in one of the other apartments and nodded at him as he began to move away.

"You have a nice day now!" the other guy called before closing the door.

Matt got into the little lift and impatiently waited for it to make its slow way upwards to the fourth floor.

Arriving at his apartment door, he paused and took a deep breath to calm himself before he knocked.

"Heidi!" he called, knocking a little harder than he intended, startled when it swung open at his touch. He stepped inside. "What's keeping you? How long does it take to get a jacket?"

Kicking the door shut behind him, he went and

dropped the brown bag on the counter top, then grabbed a container of milk from the fridge.

Her perfume lingered in the open-plan room. Her handbag was upended on the couch, the keys she'd let herself in with thrown casually beside it. My untidy ways must be contagious, he thought with a smile.

"I've got you a surprise!" he called, taking a long slug of milk. Still no response. He was getting fed up waiting around for her. Women – why did they have to spend so much time checking and rechecking their appearance? "Heidi! What's going on? I thought we were all set to head up to Times Square again? Is everything okay?"

A gentle breeze aired the room, drawing his attention to the open window.

That's odd, Matt thought, moving to the window to stare out at the activity on the street below. Why did she bother opening the window if she'd only popped back to get a jacket? He couldn't make sense of it. Running a hand through his short fair hair, he pushed away the fleeting thought that he'd have been better off exploring New York alone. *If you want to know me, come live with me*. The wise old saying worried its way into his mind, his eyes following an enthusiastic jogger breaking into a sprint on the street below. Matt itched to get into proper training, his gear-bag already packed and ready to go. But he'd promised Heidi his undivided attention for the two weeks before he started work. Getting such an attractive – and lucrative – job offer had come as a result of his successful stint training the UCC basketball team while he was a student there. Leading a number of teams to international standards, he'd made quite a name for himself on the basketball circuit.

This is ridiculous, he thought, getting another drink of milk from the fridge and calling her again. "Come on, Heidi! Shake a leg!"

He bit into his half-eaten donut, downing the second one in quick succession and then moving on to the shortcake cookies.

The 7th Avenue sounds filtered in from the street below: voices carrying in the breeze, passing traffic beeping horns and sirens wailing in the distance.

"Heidi, I need to use the loo!" he called, giving advance warning before knocking and pushing open the bathroom door. He'd expected to see her sitting on the toilet engrossed in a glossy magazine. Or maybe at the mirror reapplying her make-up. But the last thing he'd expected was not to see her at all. She wasn't in the bathroom. And seeing as it was the only other room in their studio apartment, it was obvious he'd been talking to himself for the past few minutes.

Grabbing his mobile from the bedside locker, he dialled her number, unaccustomed to the single American ring tone instead of the ring-ring he was used to back home. He waited patiently for her to answer, clenching his jaw in irritation when it rang out. In the absence of voicemail – she'd obviously omitted to set it up when she'd changed SIM cards – he sent her a curt text: wher r u? call me asap

Sitting on the edge of the bed waiting for the familiar beeping of his phone, he couldn't shake the feeling that something was terribly wrong, although, other than the open window, her upended handbag and the fact the door had been off the latch, nothing else jumped out at him as being odd.

He stared at his silent phone, watching the minutes ticking over on the time display, each one reminding him that she still hadn't replied.

Should he go back to the deli? Maybe she had turned up there and was waiting for him? He went to the open window. Leaning out at a perilous angle, he could see the deli further along the street, its outdoor chairs and tables now occupied. But not by Heidi. He stared fixedly at its door for a while, willing her to emerge. Then he shook his head in exasperation and pulled back into the room, giving up on that notion. She'd come back to the apartment if she didn't find him at the deli, wouldn't she? Surely she wouldn't think he'd gone off sightseeing without her?

Flopping on to the couch, he put his head back and closed his eyes, his phone on the tan velour cushion beside him. His concern grew, his unfamiliarity with the city gnawing inside him as myriad possibilities fought to be heard. What if Heidi had been abducted? It was New York after all. What if someone had followed her to the fourth floor and barged in the door to the apartment to attack her? Or worse? He shivered as the thought flashed through his mind. Could that explain why the door was unlocked? Perhaps, he thought, but he doubted an intruder would be considerate enough to leave the rest of the place untouched. His eyes shot open, the white kitchen presses directly in his line of vision. For the first time, he noticed the old-fashioned décor and wondered about his choice of living accommodation. Their budget had been limited, this building being one of the few they'd been able to afford close to Midtown. Matt buried his face in his hands, wondering if the minimal deposit and low rent reflected something about the building, or perhaps the neighbourhood.

He tried to ring her again and left another text message – less curt, more anxious – then returned the phone to its place on the cushion and threw himself back on the couch again.

Reaching out to touch her discarded handbag contents, he fingered through them absentmindedly. Apart from her diary, low-carb diet sheets, a packet of tissues and a few well-thumbed photos of her family, he could only find a tube of concealer (which he squeezed out of curiosity and squirted a blob of the 'Barely Beige' all over the leg of his combats), a tube of fuchsia lipstick (he opened that with more care, mystified why the manufacturer didn't simply call it pink) and the trial size of perfume she'd picked up in Macy's. Uncomfortable at this invasion of her privacy, he pushed the bag and its spilled contents away from him.

Then he thought of her wallet. She always kept it in a secure inside pocket. It wasn't there now. Matt sat up straighter on the couch, his imagination going into overdrive again. Did that mean they'd really had an intruder? Or had Heidi herself removed the wallet, deciding the bag would be an encumbrance walking through the city?

Swiftly he pulled his rucksack from under the bed and checked the hidden compartment his mother had sewn into its interior, breathing a huge sigh of relief when he found his passport, travellers' cheques and spare cash still safely tucked away there.

What about Heidi's passport? It wasn't in her bag. He began to rummage through her suitcases, checking zip pockets, inside pockets and even the pockets of her cream knee-length mac, the one she'd boasted about buying in the Brown Thomas summer sale at a fraction of its original price. He remembered her wearing it as she'd walked into the JFK Arrivals hall, her auburn hair striking against the delicate cream. Receipts for two cappuccinos and one still water, all purchased at Cyprus Airport on her outward journey, did nothing to ease his worry.

She might have taken the passport with her – for safekeeping or as ID – in her jacket pocket together with her wallet. That made sense.

Restless and uneasy, he sat down again on the couch. As he did, his eye fell on her leather-covered diary. He took it from the couch, swinging it between finger and thumb. Maybe she had jotted down something she wanted to see today, something she hadn't mentioned to him? He sat there hesitating, chewing on the inside of his cheek before finally whipping it open where she had the cord marking the page.

Scanning the entries, some indecipherable in her illegible scrawl, he sat up straighter when Alex's name jumped up from the page.

"*Boston!*" he said aloud, his mouth dropping open in shock.

He stared at the latest entry, scrawled in red ink – from a leaky red pen too if the smudges on the page were anything to go by.

But even her careless handwriting couldn't disguise Heidi's intentions.

The diary shook in his hands, the colour draining from his face. She had booked a seat on a New York to Boston flight from Newark Airport with Continental Airlines. On Monday morning – two days' time. There was no mention of a second seat, no mention of him. Just the large clear '*Alex!*' underneath that had caught his eye.

He stared at her handwriting, the large loops and joined letters coming in and out of focus as he tried to make sense of it, anger bubbling inside him. "Lying bitch!" He threw the diary on the floor, pulling back his foot and kicking it as far away as was physically possible in the meagre floor space.

He'd hung on her every word, believed everything she'd told him and sacrificed spending time in Australia with Stephen in favour of bustling New York because Heidi wanted to be able to visit him there. And though he'd applied for jobs all over – Boston, New York, Chicago and San Francisco to mention a few – he'd decided fate was intervening when an offer too good to refuse came from NYC College. Heidi had jumped into his arms and wrapped her legs around his hips when he'd told her the good news.

But now, he couldn't be sure of anything. The ease with which she'd lied to her family crept into his mind, giving him a hollow feeling in his stomach. Although he couldn't judge her for lying, seeing as he'd omitted a large amount of the truth himself. Her drastic decision to change her number and distance herself from family against his better judgement attached itself to the red ink in her diary – at least in Matt's puzzled mind. Had she been using him as a stepping-stone, he wondered? But why? It didn't make sense. Matt ran a hand over his stubbly chin, unable to unravel her reasons. She could have left for New York or Boston without his involvement.

He picked up the diary, squirming inside when it fell open on the same page. He stared at the evidence, the unquestioning belief he'd held in their relationship teetering dangerously close to the edge. She's lying to me too, he thought, keeping secrets. But why? The pages were made of light paper, his sweaty hands blotting the red ink even more. Of all the things Matt hated, dishonesty was top of his list. He snapped the book closed and flung it onto the couch, furious that she'd duped him in this way.

He strode to the wardrobe and pulled open the doors. Her suitcases were still there, stacked high. The charge on her luggage excess had almost cost as much as her flight ticket and though he'd lifted every single one onto the luggage trolley, he couldn't tell whether there was one missing or not. There'd been so many when she'd landed, he'd lost count, his enormous rucksack paltry by comparison.

He wasn't thinking straight. Even if she had taken one of the suitcases, why would she go without her handbag? And he knew she wouldn't go anywhere without her low-carb diet sheets.

He stood motionless, confused and angry. None of the pieces of the jigsaw fitted together. Nothing made sense. Except that she was jerking him around.

Pulling off his T-shirt and combats, he changed into his running gear and grabbed his door keys. He was damned if he was going to waste another moment doing things her way if this was how she was going to repay him. He'd travelled all this way to experience the New York way of life and he was going to start right now. But despite his strong intentions, in his heart he knew he wasn't ready to give up on her. Not yet. And the miniscule percentage of him that wasn't boiling with rage had every intention of keeping his eyes peeled for a beautiful auburn-haired lady. *His* beautiful auburn-haired lady.

Forgoing his usual pre-run stretches, he left the apartment in a blur, the door already closed tight when the phone beeps he'd been waiting for finally sounded on the mobile he'd left behind him.

Running for an hour had released Matt's frustration and confusion. He had slowed his usual pace considerably, taking the opportunity to appreciate the autumn foliage in Central Park. Jogging past the boating enthusiasts on the lake had brought a smile to his face and the hive of activity around the Boathouse reminded him of Heidi and the thrill she would have got from dining there, its normality forcing him to believe he'd overreacted. There had to be a simple explanation, the airline details he'd uncovered no doubt some sort of mistake. He missed her suddenly, wanting to share every new experience with her, have her at his side as they mingled into the New York way of life, revelling in the freedom of being a proper couple for the first time.

Slowing his pace on the last block before home, he'd strained to see her long auburn hair as he neared the apartment, his heart sinking when she wasn't sitting on the steps waiting for him to let her in. He'd been convinced he'd misinterpreted the situation, the risks they'd both taken to be together flashing through his mind, reminding him of how real their love seemed.

He rested his hands on his knees and tried to catch his breath, wondering if true love for one person could be no more than a bit of light-hearted fun for the other in a relationship.

Chapter 4

Eric Black stepped out of the hotel-room shower, shaking the water from his mop of dark hair and rubbing it dry with a towel. Nothing like freezing cold water to get my brain functioning again, he thought, his skin still tingling from the forceful power-jets, his energy levels reviving. It had been a long, hot, stressful morning. He pulled a luxurious dressing gown from the heated towel-rail and wrapped it around him.

As he sauntered into the large double bedroom, he suddenly felt different, a strange, inexplicable sensation he couldn't explain. A moment passed before it dawned on him what had changed. For the first time in longer than Eric could remember, his shoulders weren't weighed down and his gut wasn't knotting with stress. He felt lighter than he had in ages.

Excited by the prospect of his luck changing – particularly if the next few hours worked out as he hoped – Eric exhaled deeply. The photocopy of the contract he'd thrown on the round oak table caught his eye. He grabbed the pages, flicking through them until he came to the important few lines at the end, the few lines warning about the serious legalities associated with what he was about to do.

"This deal could make such a difference," he mumbled, scanning through the text and memorising some of the detail of the luxury apartment complex he'd purchased at a knockdown price that morning. Marble throughout, air-conditioning, twenty-four-hour concierge and reception service, balconies with southerly and westerly aspects, offering residents luxury living and full advantage of the Floridian sun. And, he realised as he turned page after page and took note of the detail, so much more. He mentally listed its attributes, planning his best approach on selling it on at a handsome profit at his next meeting, obviously omitting the unfortunate issue of it being located on the seedier side of town, an area becoming more and more pronounced for its ghetto lifestyle.

In a lawyer's office in the next town, the first part of the transaction was moments away from being signed and sealed, leaving everything hinging on the second part going through as quickly as possible. He brought his fingers to his mouth and chewed on his already bitten nails, the pressure of preparing a winning sales pitch making him twitchy. But the thought of not giving the project his all agitated him a whole lot more.

"Hold it together, Eric." He spoke aloud to himself, closing his eyes and clutching the pages until the paper crumpled in his hands. When did I become weak, he wondered? When did I become someone who has to memorise a sales pitch and stand under a cold shower to shock myself into doing what I've been doing all my life? "The first day you used your gold pen to sign a dishonest and dodgy property deal, you moron," he reproved himself, shrugging the dressing gown from his shoulders and leaving it on the floor where it fell.

Staring at his nakedness in the full-length mirror didn't do much to improve his mood so he pulled a pair of Calvin Klein boxers from his travel case and stepped into them, continuing to check his reflection as he did so. His tan was fading, he noticed, and he'd gained a few pounds, his recent absence from the gym evident. He'd spent every spare moment that summer chasing business deals, securing one to overcome the losses of another but missing out on several sailing weekends in the process. Fabricating a tale for his fellow yacht-club members, he had boasted that he was on the cusp of making his next million and too busy to take a Sunday off. In reality, he was wrestling with bankruptcy.

Turning sideways, Eric patted his paunch, regretting the alcohol binges he'd indulged in, yet knowing too well he'd needed the numbing effect of whiskey to help him through long nights of wakefulness. His gaze strayed to the enormous bed at the far side of the room. All going according to plan, the next few hours could change his poor sleeping patterns and he might actually get a good night's rest tonight. Housekeeping had already been in and turned down the sheets, leaving two wrapped chocolate liqueurs on the bolster pillow, even if it was still only afternoon. Partial to quality, he was tempted to peel the paper off and pop them in his mouth now. But first he needed to secure a good reason to celebrate. And loitering around this hotel room wasn't getting him any nearer to that goal.

"Carol, where are you?" he muttered after he'd dialled his wife's number three times. He hated answering machines, paranoid about their lack of privacy. "Damn woman is never where she should be." He tossed his phone onto the dressing table beside his wallet – a wallet holding five maxed-out credit cards – another of his financial disasters depending on the success of this upcoming deal.

Snapping out of his trance, he dressed quickly and splashed his favourite cologne on his cheeks, applying fixing gel to his hair and giving one last glance in the mirror. Approving his slate-grey shirt, pink and white striped tie and dark navy Tommy Hilfiger jeans – a look Carol regularly told him was a bit young for him – he was satisfied his recent slovenliness was cleverly disguised beneath his loose-fitting shirt.

I'll try her number one last time, he thought, sighing in exasperation. "Pick up, Carol," he said in vain, disgusted when once again the automated message minder hollered in his ear. He disconnected the call, pocketed his phone and wallet, grabbed a zip-up cardigan – slate grey to match his shirt – and left the room.

Eric heard the commotion in the bar long before he reached the door, a group of rowdy thirty-somethings causing a stir. Not the ambience he had envisaged for his meeting but something that was outside his control, like a lot of things recently.

Pushing his way through the crowd, he noticed the person he was looking for in a secluded cubicle at the opposite end of the bar. On closer inspection, he realised he wasn't alone. Two red spots stained Eric's cheeks. A third party witnessing their deal hadn't been part of his arrangement. With a heavy feeling in his chest, he pressed on, a false smile painted on his lips and his intuition bellowing that something was very wrong about the scenario ahead of him.

"Eric Black," he said by way of introduction, recoiling when his offer of a handshake was met with disdain. "Let me get another round before we settle down to business."

The other man put up his hand in refusal. "A slight change of plan, Mr Black. I'd like to introduce you to a good friend of mine: Zeb Dowling from Zebedee Holdings. I don't believe you've met?"

In a matter of seconds, Eric's high complexion faded to a sickly greyish-green pallor.

"Eh, no, I don't think so." Eric didn't look at Zeb, his gaze fixed firmly on the other man instead. "I didn't realise you had an involvement with Zebedee's?"

The other man laughed, a laden sneer.

Eric unzipped his cardigan and loosened his tie, struggling with the top button of his shirt as he got his words out in a rush of self-defence. "There's nothing illegal here. It's all above board."

"Did you ignore the small print?"

Eric swallowed and gave a brief nod, a magnified version of the contract appearing in his mind's eye.

Zeb intervened at this point. "You're selling something you haven't taken ownership of. I suggest you find another buyer for that wrong-side-of-town complex you took off my hands today, Eric. But best leave my brother-in-law out of it. Eh, dude?"

"Buying and selling is how I make my living." Eric struggled to salvage his reputation, seeing no other way apart from giving in.

"Swindling is what we call it here in Florida," said Zeb. "But just to advise you, there's a very strong network of property dealers in St Petersburg so you might need to find your buyer in another state. And a word of caution, Eric . . ." he paused for effect, draining the last of his whiskey, "check your facts before you buy next time. We've had that apartment complex on our books for a very long time. Got very close to a sale on a few occasions too but unfortunately," he rattled the ice cubes in his glass, bestowing a smug smile on Eric, "we never found a mug to sign on the dotted line. Until now, that is. So you've done us a very big favour." He pulled back his sleeve to reveal a diamond-encrusted watch. "Oh, perfect timing! We'd best be off. The ink should be dry on that contract by now."

Without further delay, the duo banged their glasses on the table, got up and left.

Eric watched with his mouth open, blotches of colour returning to his cheeks, a dart of pain causing his chest to contract. He clutched the edge of the table, bringing a hand to his chest and rubbing it ferociously. Damn heartburn, he thought, swallowing the acid taste in his mouth. What on earth have I got myself into now? Invested in the final nail for my coffin? Why didn't I listen to my accountant when he advised me to steer clear of this one? Or any more deals for that matter.

He checked his watch, the noise in the background disturbing his concentration. The lawyer representing him in Florida would have submitted the papers to the vendor's legal team ten minutes before. If Zeb's last words and sarcastic grin were anything to go by, they'd double-crossed him. They'd got one over on him before he had the chance to do it to them. They'd seen right through him and he'd fallen for it.

His hands shook as he took his mobile from his pocket to dial his lawyer. His chest contracted more and more with every unanswered ring.

Leaving the cubicle, he staggered through the overbearing crowd, turning around sharply when he felt a hand gripping his shoulder. "Yes?"

"Your bill, sir? Will I charge it?"

"What bill?" Eric snapped. "I didn't order anything."

"But your friends said you'd cover their drinks." The bartender waited expectantly.

"You have got to be joking! They're no friends of mine."

"But, sir . . ."

Find some other loser to pay their bill, he thought, pulling out of the bartender's grasp.

He hurried to his hotel room to pack his few belongings and get out of there as quickly as he could. He flung the chocolate liqueurs against the wall, resisting the temptation to hurl several other objects after them.

He didn't bother to check out, the irony of punching in a PIN for a credit card that would undoubtedly be cancelled by the bank in the days that followed making it a waste of time. With the risk that somehow it might have been cancelled already. Securing a quick profit had been his last opportunity to avoid bankruptcy and now he'd gone and messed it up. It's only a matter of time, he thought, before they repossess everything I own. At least everything I have in my possession. Truthfully, I *own* absolutely nothing.

The overwhelming humidity caught in his throat as he ran onto the street, the buzz of leisurely holiday-makers mocking him. With shaking hands, he entered whatever coins he had in his pocket into the nearest public payphone and tried his wife's number again. It rang and rang. Eric stared absent-mindedly at the variety of passing vehicles: open-backed trucks conveying construction workers, convertibles with star-struck lovers, family saloons and jeeps filled with tired children after an exhilarating day of theme parks and sandy beaches.

Carol's voicemail cut in on his thoughts, her chirpy tone serving to irritate him further. But this time, out of necessity, he left a message.

"Carol, get your car and your jewellery," he instructed, the numerous notification letters he'd received from the bank weighing heavily on his mind. By now he was struggling for breath, his palate like cardboard, his tongue feeling as though it didn't belong in his mouth. He forced himself to keep talking. "And anything else of value that can be shifted from the house. Leave them with somebody who won't squeal. And for God's sake, call me back as soon as you get this message. I need you to book me a flight urgently. Get cash somewhere instead of using your credit card. I'll go to Tampa Airport now and wait there until you let me know my flight number." He was about to hang up when he remembered something else. "And Carol, tell the girls immediately. Their credit facility won't –"

The phone beeped in his ear, an automated robot requesting more coins if he wanted to continue his call. Eric hung up. He didn't have the money to continue.

Chapter 5

Carol searched in her handbag for the anti-ageing face-mask she'd purchased, the flashing screen on her mobile catching her attention. Damn, she thought, remembering she'd put it on silent mode while the hairstylist had worked her magic that afternoon.

Putting the phone on loudspeaker, she hit the voicemail button, deleting blank message after blank message, wondering what the hell was going on. She interrupted the playback to check the call log, surprised when Eric's number and an international one showed up on her screen.

"Why on earth is he ringing and hanging up?" she mumbled, annoyed that he'd soured her good mood and interrupted her leisurely evening. She moved through the empty messages until finally his voice came on the line. She was very tempted to press delete but his panicky tone stopped her in her tracks, forcing her to grab the phone and put it close to her ear. His words were hurried and tinged with fear. Carol could make no sense of what she was hearing. Checking the call detail, she realised he'd left the message some time before.

Leaning against the cold windowpane, she slid down the floor-to-ceiling glass onto the heated bedroom floor, listening to every detail in both that message and the one that followed. Repeatedly.

Her heart pounded in her chest, her body was rooted to the floor. Oh God, she thought, I've already wasted so much time. The repossession company could be here any moment. But it's Saturday night, she thought then. Surely we'll be safe until Monday? But she couldn't be definite and she sure as hell didn't want to wait to find out. Bile crept up her throat, forcing her to make a dash for the ensuite bathroom.

The coldness of the bathroom wall refreshed her warm, clammy skin. Staring around at the lavish detail – ornate marble tiling, high ceiling with a stained-glass window filtering coloured light onto the white walls, ornate plasterwork and top-of-the-range bathroom fittings – she memorised every tiny detail like someone waving goodbye to a loved one. Glancing through the open door to her bedroom, her eyes rested on the crystal chandeliers she'd imported from New York, the polished wood they'd chosen in Germany, the gigantic sleigh bed she'd coveted at an auction . . . It hurt too much to look. She buried her face in her hands, hot angry tears flowing on her cheeks, heart-wrenching sobs coming from deep inside. Why now? Why now? Damn him, damn him, damn him.

Carol pushed her long blonde fringe back from her pale face, struggling to grasp how Eric could have jeopardised everything, her head racing as she tried to remember his exact words. She couldn't bear to sit through his panicked instructions again, the scanty recorded message echoing around the bathroom: move as much out of the house as she possibly could, warn the girls about their credit, organise a flight for him, pay with cash. A living nightmare. If only he had quit while he was ahead – well, maybe he hadn't been ahead as such but at least he was keeping his head above the brink of bankruptcy.

She dried tearstained cheeks with her pale-blue sleeve, the angora soft against her skin.

How could this have happened to us? How did I not pay closer attention, she wondered, her face flushing guiltily as she recalled her endless spending. Anger raged inside. Whatever amounts she'd indulged on fashion and beauty, he'd been downright ridiculous when it came to buying a yacht (only the biggest one docked in Crosshaven!), not to mention the must-have top-of-the-range Mercedes and of course elite membership to the Golf Club, the Yacht Club and a couple of gyms – depending on what businessman he was trying to impress! But, as he regularly announced to anyone prepared to listen, he considered himself worth it.

"Damn you, Eric," she cried. "God damn your greed!"

Before she tried to figure out the best way to book him a flight home – using cash no less, a commodity Carol seldom handled – she dialled her youngest daughter's number as she moved toward the third floor. *The O2 customer you are trying to call* . . . She'd have to keep trying.

"Isobel!" she screamed, needing to hear her voice,

needing to hear her usual pearls of wisdom and discuss this latest travesty. God damn Eric, she thought. He's ruined us all.

Isobel burst through the study door, her inky black hair pulled back in a tight pony-tail, her Chanel reading glasses resting on the bridge of her nose, a perplexed look on her face. "What on earth, Mum? You scared me half to death."

"Oh, Iz," Carol cried, "it's your dad, he's lost everything!" She noticed Isobel's raised eyebrow, the way she shook her head as though she'd heard it all before. "This time it's serious, Iz. Very serious."

Chapter 6

Lucy beeped the horn as she pulled away from Delia's house which glowed with light in the darkness. Pushing her Michael Bublé CD into the player she hit the random-play button. She drove through the village and set off along the Owenabue Estuary, humming along to the easy tune of 'Home', smiling wryly at the coincidence in song choice. For the first time since Matt left, she *was* looking forward to going home. Visiting Delia had made a huge difference, her heart noticeably lighter even if her stomach was laden from an exorbitant amount of chocolate!

"*I wanna go home,*" she joined in the chorus, stopping abruptly when the lyrics were drowned out by the sound of screaming sirens.

Her dark-brown eyes instinctively shifted to her rear-view mirror, all thoughts of empty-nest syndrome forgotten as flashing blue lights approached, their urgency chasing her, daring her, insisting she move out of the way. Responding immediately – her left hand reaching for the gear-shift, her right foot applying pressure on the brake pedal – she swerved into the hard shoulder and yielded to the urgent warning, the high-pitched wail reverberating in her ears long after the imposing red fire engines had disappeared from view.

Keeping an eye on her mirror, she eased the car onto the road once more, the expanse of woodland on her left looming under a black sky, the estuary of the Owenabue River gleaming darkly on her right. The sense of danger lingering in the fire brigade's wake brought a disturbing image of frantic victims to Lucy's mind. She pressed harder on the accelerator. Delia's right, she thought, I shouldn't complain. I'm luckier than a lot of parents and wives out there. I have the opportunity to take my life in a new direction. But first I must apologise to Danny and reassure him – if he allows me – that the person at the altar rails twenty-five years ago hasn't been abducted by aliens.

Minutes from home, she was already looking forward to sinking into a hot bubble bath as soon as she'd made her peace with Danny. A bottle of her favourite chardonnay was chilling in the fridge. Definitely a large glass for me while I'm in the bath, she thought, imagining its fruity taste. She was two thirds through a gripping crime novel and planned on topping up her bath water until she'd reached the last page. Impatient now, she increased her speed as she approached the junction for home, catching a glimpse of flashing lights as the cumbersome fire engines swerved to the left and on to the same byroad she'd be taking.

Now she couldn't prevent her body from trembling, a feeling of dread hovering around her, the threat of impending danger intensifying, her earlier concerns trivial in light of the emergency wail thumping loudly in her ears. She tightened her grip on the steering wheel and made the left-hand turn, reducing speed as she rounded the sharp bend. Fear gripped her, part of her craving to find out what family was in trouble, another part of her – the part that made her heart thump – wanting to put on blinkers and drive right by.

But blinkers wouldn't disguise the smell of smoke filtering through the partially open car window, concrete evidence that trouble was near. Far too near. Suddenly there was silence. The sirens had stopped. But where? What entrance had the fire engines taken? The last remaining bend before her home shielded her from the truth. For Lucy, it was still a guessing game. Could it be at one of her neighbours' houses?

Selfishly, she willed the emergency to be anywhere except her house. But despite her best efforts to mentally transport the problem onto somebody else's shoulders, the truth was waiting for her as she careered around the right-hand bend. The time for guessing was over. Reality was staring her in the face. She shook her head in disbelief. Thickening black smoke and a kaleidoscope of sparks billowed in the sky directly over Sycamore Lodge. Directly over her home.

"Agh! No! Not our house!" Lucy banged the palms of her hands against the steering wheel, the feel-good music emanating from the CD player mocking her. She hit the switch to turn it off. Time slowed to a crawl. She stared without seeing. Nothing made sense. How could their house have caught fire? Danny was a builder, a perfectionist. He'd installed every available safety precaution to protect their home. Her blood ran cold. Danny . . .

She screamed, the high-pitched sound reverberating in the car. He'd been at home when she'd left. Thoughts flailed wildly in her head, nothing comprehensible. She needed to get inside the house, an image of him sleeping on the living-room couch flashing in her mind. Before she'd left for Delia's, he had been on the couch watching the sports channel on telly and more than likely he'd have eventually fallen asleep, a regular occurrence on a Saturday afternoon or early evening. She'd often have to wake him up for dinner.

Pressing her right foot heavily on the accelerator, she willed the car to move faster and cover the short distance to her home. But the Opel Vectra's engine seemed to have taken complete control, refusing to bridge the gap between Lucy and the disaster ahead, shielding her from seeing Sycamore Lodge crumble before her eyes.

"Oh please God, let him be okay, don't let him be still in there," she pleaded aloud, her voice unrecognisable as she felt everything skewing out of control.

Her blood turned icy, her body shaking. She clenched her teeth together to stop them chattering. Her heart pounded so hard she was convinced it would burst right out of her chest. She continued to stare through the windscreen, jolting forward as the car shuddered when she shifted it into a lower gear, forgetting to depress the clutch properly.

Her foot slipped off the accelerator pedal. The car stalled. Every second stretched like an hour. But she valued those stolen moments while her view of the house and garden was obstructed by the mature conifers lining the avenue. The image of her beautiful home collapsing to the ground and a lifetime of memories being destroyed in a torrent of smoke were distinct possibilities, yet for a few moments more they remained unconfirmed. For that brief interlude, she indulged in the pretence it was a dream and any minute now she'd wake up in her own bed and laugh at it all. If only, she thought, her stomach churning as she stared at the bizarre sky ahead.

"Danny, Danny, please, please be okay!" she pleaded again, unchecked tears coursing down her cheeks.

The mood she'd been in as she'd stormed out of the house, she hadn't even said goodbye. She ached to reach him, desperate for proof that he was safe, desperate to make amends for her earlier truculence. More than anything, she needed to feel his arms around her, protecting her from harm, being the man of the house, being *her* man. She tried to reason with her exaggerated thoughts, struggling to breathe as pressure built in her chest, repeating to herself over and over that Danny must have already left the house. She willed him to appear before her – with his broad shoulders and muscular arms from years of heavy manual work, his permanently tanned face from the outdoor life, his rotund stomach the result of his healthy appetite and penchant for a few beers at the weekend. He was the strong, reliable type, those green observant eyes of his never missing a trick. He wouldn't have allowed their house to burn down. Danny wouldn't. He just wouldn't.

She turned the key in the ignition once more, inching the car forward, now in full view of the house, her eyes fixed on the angry red and orange flames dancing from her bedroom window on the first floor, the glass already shattered from the intense heat, the ground below covered in debris. She strained to see more, noticing the crowds of onlookers gathered on the road, jumping in her seat when a garda banged on the window, signalling her to pull over immediately. He was blocking her pathway to Sycamore Lodge, refusing her entry to her home.

Jamming on the brakes and shutting off the engine once more, she released her safety-belt and scrambled from the car, the driver's door swinging open in her wake as she ran past the garda through the entrance to her house. She began to cough, billowing smoke polluting the air in thickening black clouds, stinging her eyes.

Two fire engines were parked near the house with several firemen directing water hoses at the exterior, working diligently to control the blaze. The fire-chief's van was parked further back from the house.

She halted, bringing her hands to her face, peering between her fingers like she did during the gory scenes of hospital dramas.

The young garda stepped in front of her, blocking her pathway and gripping her shoulders. "I'm sorry, but I can't let you through. The fire officers are doing everything they can. Allow them to get on with it. We don't want an injury on our hands."

Lucy jostled with him, attempting to move around him, refusing to listen to his words of caution. She used all her force to get away from him, trying to release her shoulders from his grip, but to no avail. "My husband could be in there!" she screamed, her dark-brown hair sweeping across his face as she pushed against him with all her might. "I have to tell the firemen! Please let me go . . . please!"

But her pleading fell on deaf ears, the garda's firm hold on her shoulders preventing her from moving a step closer to the house.

He spoke slowly and calmly. "You have to understand. We don't know what ignited the fire. There's a risk of explosion. I can't let you any nearer – it's for your own safety."

"But my husband –" She broke off, sobbing now, tears continuing to roll freely down her cheeks, her gaze fixed on the blazing building.

"Why do you think he's in there?"

"He was there when I left!"

"How long have you been gone? Could he have gone out?"

"I'm telling you he's inside!" Lucy screamed at him, frustrated that he wasn't responding quicker. "He was lying on the couch watching telly when I left – it was hours ago but he'll have fallen asleep and, believe me, when he falls asleep there's no waking him! What if he's suffocating right now while you're standing here refusing to let me past?"

"I'll speak to the fire chief. But you must promise me you'll stay right there, okay?"

He maintained his hold on her arms, fixing her with his gaze, until she nodded.

Finally relenting, she had no choice but to stand and stare as he went to talk to the fire chief. Watching the fire dancing she imagined it laughing hilariously, licking her home with a forked tongue, each movement sweeping another bit of it away. Her shoulders were hunched, her eyes glued to the house, her knees squeezed together as she was overcome by a sudden desire to pee.

The garda was back, catching her by the arms again as she swayed before him. "I told them but they were already doing a search of the house," he assured her. He sympathised with the distraught woman who was no longer fighting against him, the hold he had of her arms probably her only means of support. Without it, he was convinced she'd collapse at his feet. "I didn't catch your name?"

"Lucy Ardle," she responded between chattering teeth, her voice barely audible.

"Lucy, the fire officers are doing everything possible to get the situation under control and they're in there searching for your husband. If he's there, they'll get him out. Is there anybody you'd like me to call? A family member or friend to be here with you?"

"The only person I need is my husband," she whispered. She dragged her gaze from the house, gazing at the garda instead, her dark-brown, tear-filled eyes pleading with him for help.

The garda turned to look at the top floor, shivering slightly as he contemplated any man's chances of getting out of the house alive. He involuntarily stepped backwards as yet another window exploded, pulling Lucy with him. They watched as slivers of glass flew in all directions, flailing through the smoke-filled air before finally landing on the ground below.

Lucy yanked her arms from his grasp, bringing both of her hands to her mouth as she watched flames lapping against Sycamore Lodge, scorching it bit by bit, destroying Danny's careful construction work. Their beautiful Tudor home was already unrecognisable, already an ugly version of what it had once been.

Without warning, a sweeping wind circled around them, leaves rustling in loud angry whispers over their heads, large drops of rain plopping on to the ground.

The heavens opened and sheets of rain pelted angrily on the watching crowd, forcing some of them to run for shelter. In a minute, Lucy's long brown hair was a sopping mess, her black trousers sticking to her legs, her jacket drenched. But she was oblivious to her soaking body, rooted to the spot in a trance-like state. She watched as the harsh rain battled against those same dancing flames, forcing them to recede marginally but failing to overpower. Again the fire seemed to blaze for her, showing her who was boss, reminding her who had control.

From what she could see amidst the rain, smoke, mess and debris, the right-hand side of the house was still structurally intact. But looking to the left told a whole other story where the fire still blazed in their bedroom. The living room, where she had left Danny, was directly underneath the area worst affected.

Pain sliced through her as she stared at the scorched exterior walls. The trademark Tudor frame disintegrated piece by piece on to the sodden ground. Watching its demise, she wept pitifully. She'd chosen it to brighten up the white exterior, never once imagining it would end up like this. She continued to pace over and back in front of the gate, unable to stand still. Tudor framework can be replaced, she thought, but Danny can't. How will I get through life alone if anything has happened to him? She chewed on her thumbnail, another loud crash dragging her attention to the attic windows. Glass exploded onto the roof in front of her eyes, scaring her even more. What hope had Danny got if the toughened windows were collapsing like a house of cards? The cold hand of fear squeezed her heart, clenching it in a vicelike grip. In that moment, she imagined her husband dead, visualising a slow funeral march through the streets of Crosshaven as his body was brought to his final resting place and she was left alone to grieve. She dropped her eyes to the wet ground, another explosion forcing her head up sharply in time to see glass from the ensuite window fly through the air.

Despite the heavy rain, neighbours and passers-by were still present at the scene, some out of curiosity, more out of genuine concern. Pushing their way towards Lucy to offer support, they shared snatched pieces of information over the noisy fire engines, each speculating on what had happened, refusing to budge until Danny's fate was resolved.

Lucy didn't care about the crowd, their presence more of an irritant than a comfort. In truth, she wished they'd all disappear. She edged away from them, inching slowly forward until she was inside the entrance pillars, the garda instantly at her heels like a loyal puppy. There she dropped to her knees on the filthy ground. Too much time had elapsed. Every passing second increased her dread.

The rain stopped as suddenly as it had begun. Struggling to her feet once more, Lucy wrapped her arms around her soaking body and stared blindly ahead.

"Danny . . ." she whispered into the dark night, jumping out of her skin when she felt a hand on her shoulder.

Daring to hope for a moment that by some miraculous turn of events it was her husband appearing from somewhere, she quickly turned around. But her face crumpled when she recognised her nearest neighbour.

"Lucy!" said Carol. "I wasn't here when you arrived. I had to go back to the house to tell Isobel to call a cab

– she has to go to the airport and I was supposed to drive her there but –"

"Oh, Carol, I think Danny might be in there. I think he's . . . what if he's . . ." Her voice was hoarse from smoke inhalation, her eyes red and swollen.

"Danny might be in there? Oh my God! No!"

"I left him watching telly . . ."

"But his van is gone!"

"It's in the garage. He'd already loaded it up for work on Monday. It was the last thing he did before coming in to watch the football . . ." She couldn't go on, the normality of what she was saying far removed from the nightmare exploding around her.

Carol pulled a sobbing Lucy into her arms, holding her tight. "I've been ringing your mobiles . . ." Her sentence trailed off as she realised what silence from Danny's mobile might mean.

Lucy froze in her arms as the same thought struck her.

"I was the first to see the smoke," Carol went on, "and I ran over to check . . . I couldn't believe it . . . flames and smoke everywhere . . . I called the fire brigade . . ."

Lucy nodded, too overcome to speak. She clutched her neighbour, not sure which of them was trembling most but immensely grateful that she'd been there to call for help and that she was here with her now.

"I begged them to hurry," Carol continued. "I even ran as close as I could to the house, shouting and calling your names, but it was useless. The flames were already bursting through your upstairs bedroom. I presumed the house was empty. The car and van weren't there. I've been ringing your numbers ever since."

"Thanks for making that call, Carol," Lucy stammered,

finding it difficult to get the words out between chattering teeth. She remembered leaving her mobile phone thrown carelessly on the sofa beside Danny. After their argument, she'd been too stubborn to go and get it. How could I have been so pig-headed, she thought, the rough wet tweed of Carol's jacket scratching against her cheek as she buried her head in Carol's shoulder. Would Danny live to survive this and ever drive the van again, she wondered, an image of him invalided flashing in front of her eyes. A lifetime committed to a wheelchair or worse. What if he died? What if he already had?

"What if . . . what if it's too late, Carol . . .?" She gasped in fear, straining to see if there was any sign of movement from the house. But she could barely see whether the door was open or closed, never mind if there was anybody coming out of it. How could she tell the boys if Danny didn't make it?

"Danny's strong. You can't give up on him . . ." Carol wished there were words to comfort Lucy. Holding her neighbour as tightly as she could, she stared ahead and waited, praying silently for Danny's safe recovery.

Suddenly, a flurry of movement caught Carol's attention. She remained tight-lipped until she was sure her eyes weren't playing tricks on her. She'd been staring at the house for so long she wasn't sure if the activity was real or something she was imagining because it was what she wanted to see. But the longer she watched, the more convinced she was that her eyes weren't deceiving her. They were carrying somebody out.

"Lucy, look!" she exclaimed excitedly, pointing towards the house. "They're bringing him out. Can you see? They have him. They have Danny. Oh thank God!"

Lucy hardly grasped what Carol was saying, understanding only when she spotted the uniformed men carrying her husband. Freeing herself from her neighbour's arms, she ran towards them. She didn't call. She didn't shout. She just ran as fast as her legs would carry her.

Right at that moment an ambulance swung through the entrance gates, sweeping past Lucy and coming to a sudden stop in front of the fire-officer's van. The driver and a female paramedic jumped from the cab. Swinging open the back doors, they dragged a stretcher and portable oxygen tank from the back and made their way to meet the firemen who were carrying Danny between them.

Lucy hurried after them, slowing her pace to watch them transfer Danny's lifeless form on to the stretcher. She dreaded to think how much damage he'd suffered, clinging to the relief that for now he was still breathing. At least he must be, she thought, if they're fixing an oxygen mask on his face.

"What are his chances?" She reached out to touch him, directing her question at nobody in particular and anyone who'd listen. Only his face was visible, his body completely covered by a thick red fire blanket. By the time the paramedic had fixed an oxygen mask to his face, securing it with white plastic straps around the back of his head, obscuring his nose, mouth and chin, all she could see were his shut eyelids, black forehead and singed eyebrows.

At least he's out of the house, she thought. At least he's out. Now they can help him.

"He was unconscious on the upstairs landing," the fireman who'd carried him out explained.

"At a guess, his oxygen levels have dropped considerably

and that's our first priority," said the ambulance driver. "The next few hours will be crucial but, judging from what we've seen, he's miraculously escaped burns to exposed skin though there is some singeing and scorching on his arms. That in itself is a bonus and will improve his chances, such as they are. It's difficult to say how much smoke he's inhaled until we get him to the hospital."

"Thank God he hasn't any burns," Lucy whispered.

"You'll travel with him?" the ambulance driver enquired kindly, helping to push Danny's stretcher back into the van.

Lucy didn't need to be asked twice. She forgot about her waiting neighbour, forgot about the car she'd abandoned at the side of the road, and climbed into the ambulance as soon as the stretcher had been pushed into place. She sat in silence, unable to fathom or make sense of the enormity of what had happened to them. All she wanted was for Danny to open his eyes and speak to her. She'd have been grateful for any sign, however small. But, alas, there was nothing.

They travelled the shortest route at the highest speed possible to Cork University Hospital, the sirens screaming urgently as they sailed through every red traffic light. Lucy clutched the edge of her seat with tears flowing freely on her cheeks as the ambulance sped around the final roundabout. Moments away from the Accident & Emergency entrance, when she breathed a sigh of relief that they'd arrived in one piece, Danny's heart stopped beating.

The hospital was jammed. Lucy refused to sit down in the waiting area.

"Won't you please let me call somebody to be with you?" asked a kindly middle-aged nurse who'd been assigned to stay by her side. "It's not good for you to be alone. Not now. Your children perhaps?"

Lucy shrugged indifferently. Alone. Not alone. It made little difference. It wouldn't turn back the clock. It wouldn't change a thing. "Even if our sons were here, things would still be the same. Danny would still be on the critical list." Her voice broke. She lifted her head and looked through bleary eyes at the nurse.

"His vital signs are positive. You have to hold on to that."

Lucy nodded. "But is that enough?" *His heart stopped. His heart stopped.* The words kept going around and around in her head. She was terrified it would happen again, her confidence in Danny's physical strength well and truly disappearing. Watching the ambulance personnel working flat out to kick-start his heart had shattered any illusion she had about him being invincible and able to withstand any situation. *He's human,* she thought, *and as fragile as anybody else I know.* The scene had haunted her ever since, compounding her worst fears, forcing her to imagine his funeral.

"What age are your sons?" the nurse broke into her daydream.

"Twenty-four and twenty-one. Matt – he's the youngest – only left home a few days ago." She sobbed quietly, wiping salty tears from her cheeks with the back of her hand.

The nurse eased an arm around her shoulders. "Travelling around the world like so many students?"

"New York." Lucy stared into space for a few moments,

the planning and packing for his departure seeming like an eternity ago now.

"And your other son?"

"Stephen." Lucy gulped as she mentioned her eldest son's name. An ache filled her heart as she thought of him, overcome by how long it had been since she'd held him in her arms. "He's been in Australia for the last two years."

"You should let them know," the nurse suggested, glancing around the waiting area and noticing the growing crowd. Yet another hectic evening in the emergency department, she thought, another shift that would leave her dead on her feet.

"I can't call him. Not yet."

"What about other family or friends? Or your husband's family? Shouldn't they be told? You could give them a call."

Lucy checked her watch, surprised at how late it was, struck by the unfairness that the world was still spinning on its axis while her life was being ripped apart. She wanted to rip her watch from her wrist and smash it on the cold white tiles, deny the passing of time, react to the blow they'd been dealt, cause a scene. But, meeting the nurse's gentle gaze, she realised she hadn't responded to what she had said and knew that the only scene she'd be causing would be a mental one. Quite honestly, she was having difficulty remembering the nurse's question.

"I'm sorry, what did you ask me?"

"Danny's family? Your in-laws? Would you consider calling them with the news?"

"His parents live in West Cork – Clonakilty – his sister in London. It wouldn't be fair to disturb them at this hour. Tomorrow will be time enough." She took a tissue from her pocket and held it against her flaming cheeks, wishing she could soak the three-ply material in ice-cold water and then reapply it to her face.

"And your own family?" the nurse persisted.

"Mum's in a retirement home in Kinsale." Lucy bit her lip, stifling a groan. Mum, she thought, the last person on earth I can cope with right now. The thought of telling Gloria about the fire brought her out in goose-bumps but, noticing the nurse's expectant expression, she knew she couldn't dither much longer. The poor nurse was probably dying to get away from her long miserable face. "I'll phone my sister in a little while," she promised.

As timing had it, the nurse was called to help a fainting patient and Lucy was relieved to be left alone with her thoughts. Oblivious to other waiting families around her, oblivious to the fact that her clothes and shoes were still damp and her long brown hair a knotted mess from the earlier downpour, she closed her eyes and escaped inside her head. The austerity of the hospital surroundings allowed her a temporary reprieve, a period of numbness where she could stand in a trance with her head against the wall, indulging in the delusion that their life would somehow find its way to somewhere resembling normality, anywhere resembling normality.

Carol drove Lucy's car into her driveway. Luckily the keys had been in the ignition, making it possible to move it from the side of the road. Ensuring it was locked, she took Lucy's handbag and hurried to her front door. She couldn't wait to get indoors and have a shower, wrinkling her nose at the stench of smoke from her clothes and hair. Getting soaked in the rain had made matters worse and she was full sure her tweed jacket would never recover. Definitely an item for the next charity collection, she thought, flinching inside as it dawned on her that she'd be a charity case soon. Her hands shook as she searched her bunch of keys for the front-door one.

After the ambulance had left, she'd remained at the scene for a while, watching the firemen battle with the blaze before finally drifting away with some of the other spectators. Another neighbour had invited a few of them for coffee, the small group shaken as they dissected the shocking house-fire piece by piece, analysing how the Ardles would recover and throwing all kinds of suggestions into the mix as to how it could possibly have happened. The range of theories was wide, a handful realistic but for the most part absurd. Refusing the third cup of coffee, Carol made her excuses to leave. The conversation had digressed at that point, no longer holding her interest enough to keep her sitting in wet clothes.

The phone rang in the hallway as she pushed open her front door.

"Isobel? Damn it!" she exclaimed, when the phone went dead as she put it to her ear. She wondered if her daughter had already checked into her Dublin hotel. She'd ring her later.

Catching sight of her reflection in the hall mirror, Carol leaned in to take a closer look. She hadn't realised the rain had taken such a toll on her appearance. Her normally pristine silver bob stuck out in all directions, her thick fringe a mass of frizz, her face grimy, the mascara she'd applied earlier that day smudged under tired hazel eyes. She imagined her husband's horror if he saw her in such a state. But she presumed, her heart filling with bitterness, his pretentiousness would now be part of their past, just like their cherished home.

Overcome with exhaustion, her brain numb as the events of the evening whirred continuously, Carol could barely function. She thought fleetingly of Eric's request – or demand – for an air ticket. That would have to wait. For tonight at least she'd try to get some sleep, because there was little doubt it could be her last night in a warm bed for a very long time. She dropped Lucy's bag into a drawer and, making her way into the utility room, peeled off her wet clothes, pushing what she could into the washing machine and shoving the tweed jacket into a bin where she stored her dry cleaning. Seeing Isobel's favourite mohair inside brought a tug to her heart. She'd been shattered leaving for the airport, the situation Eric had landed them in hitting her really hard and the fire still raging in their neighbour's house – though of course they had both thought the house was empty at that point. Unaccustomed to seeing her oldest daughter freaking out, her face contorting in alarm, her habitual self-control absent, Carol was forced to look at the bigger context of Eric's foolishness.

Replacing the lid on the bin, Carol exhaled a long slow breath, the familiar throbbing of a migraine beginning to take hold. Dry cleaning would be an unaffordable luxury from now on, she thought, knotting a fresh bath towel tightly around her.

She filled the detergent and fabric-softener compartments, turned the dial to the hottest wash her discarded clothes could survive, shuddering at the memory of the fire. The speed at which it had spiralled out of control was too surreal to comprehend. Leaving the ground floor in darkness, she grabbed her handbag from the hall table and dragged her weary body up the sweeping staircase, the whirr of the washing machine echoing through the otherwise still house.

The hot water was running, she had her shower gel and shampoo ready but just before she stepped under the water, she grabbed her phone to text Lucy and enquire about Danny. Whatever about parking financial worries for one more night, she found she couldn't do the same with the fate of her neighbours. Automatically hitting the shortcut key to write a text, the screen displaying Eric's multiple missed calls disappeared from view. She stopped punching the keys, remembering Lucy telling her she'd left her phone in the house.

"Not much point sending a text to a phone that's burnt to a crisp," she muttered, tossing her mobile onto the window ledge and stepping under the hot cascading water to scrub the memory of that Saturday from her mind.

Chapter 7

Lucy waited anxiously as the Intensive Care nurse approached.

"Good news, Lucy. You can see Danny in just a few moments."

She closed her eyes in grateful appreciation that he'd survived his horrific ordeal. So far at least. "Is he responding to treatment?"

"It's hard to say, to be honest. They've sedated him to give his body a chance to cope. His blood-oxygen levels are erratic and it's much easier to stabilise him under sedation."

"But will he pull through?" Lucy interjected, craving reassurance.

"His temperature's on the high side and his lungs are congested. So he's not exactly out of the woods yet but the doctors are very hopeful."

"And his heart?" Lucy held the nurse's gaze.

"Still beating," she responded.

The seriousness of Danny's condition walloped Lucy like a slap in the face. Then she let out the breath she'd been holding and inhaled again, trying to achieve calm.

"Has he shown any glimmer of consciousness?"

"Nothing major, I'm afraid," the nurse answered as honestly as she could. "But that's not unusual," she added, noticing Lucy's face contorting and her eyes filling up once more. "Of course that doesn't mean he's unable to hear so make sure you chat to him."

'Unable to hear'. . . her words set Lucy's mind in a spin . . . he had been unable to hear the smoke alarm . . . but how on earth could he have missed its warning? She wished she knew. It certainly shrilled loud enough whenever she had a sneaky cigarette out the bathroom window. In fact it was only a couple of days since she'd had to wave a towel to silence it . . . and then . . . oh dear God.

The blood drained from her face. She remembered every detail of what she'd done next.

The smoke-alarm battery was low. And even after she'd silenced it, the irritating beep sounded periodically. In bed that night the noise had interrupted her sleep and, unable to stand it any longer, she'd crept out of bed, dragged her bedroom chair onto the landing and removed the battery to kill the noise. And that was the last thought she'd given the smoke alarm. Until now.

The nurse mistook Lucy's silence, suspecting she needed to pull herself together before visiting Danny. "Take a moment, Lucy, and I'll be back to you."

"It's my fault," Lucy whispered to herself as soon as the nurse had left her side, oblivious of the strange looks she was getting from the other people waiting around her. She paced the corridor, guilt and remorse filling her with shame. How can I live with myself? All this occurred because of a simple AA battery and laziness and carelessness on my part! She felt herself recede inside her own skin, psychologically regressing from the reality going on around her. She stopped pacing, joining her hands to prevent them shaking, her eyes riveted to the emblazoned *Exit* sign over the entrance doors. Her head told her not to move but her heart screamed like a team-mate waiting for her to move in a relay race, shoving the baton into the palm of her hand and ordering her to run like hell.

Lucy sat by Danny's bedside, thoughts of fleeing her responsibilities forgotten. The reality of her husband's injuries was something she couldn't run from. Danny's face – what she could see of it under the huge oxygen mask – was deathly pale, needles and tubes sticking out of him, a spider-web of wires attaching him to a machine and adding to his vulnerability. Reaching out, she grabbed his limp hand and clutched it tightly, brought her lips to his ear and prayed.

"Don't die on me now, Dan. Hang in there."

She sat for ages staring at him, jumping forward in her chair when his mouth moved ever so slightly behind the mask and a muffled noise escaped his lips, his brow wrinkled, his hands clutching the sheet.

Lucy turned and caught the nurse's eye, relieved when she came straight over. "Is he okay? He seems rather agitated." She made to get up from her chair to allow the nurse enough room to work.

"Stay where you are," the nurse said, slipping in behind Lucy's chair. "I'll check his blood pressure and temperature."

"Is there something wrong?"

"The sedation is wearing off a little but there's nothing new to worry about. He's a fighter, your husband."

Lucy smiled weakly and for the first time since she'd rounded the corner to Sycamore Lodge that evening, she let out a sigh of relief.

"I'm just going to ring my sister and then I'll be right back to him." Impulsively, she clutched the nurse's hand. "Thank you for looking after him and keeping him comfortable. Thank you so much."

"There's no need for you to stay all night," the nurse added. "We'll have him under close observation. You should really get some rest."

"I can't leave him, not yet, and that's as much for my sake as his," Lucy admitted.

The nurse smiled, her refusal to leave coming as no surprise.

Lucy took coins from her pocket and dialled Delia's number from the hospital payphone, the absence of her mobile already a huge inconvenience. Waiting for her to answer, she mulled over what Danny would need, her shoulders drooping seconds later when it dawned on her that their possessions were most likely a heap of ashes by now. The clothes on their backs could well be all they had left. And in Danny's case, she realised, it amounted to a hospital gown!

She was worried about her handbag which she had abandoned in the car – there were credit cards in it. Would the gardaí have taken it? Or, not noticing it, have locked it into the car? She must get Delia to find out.

As Delia's phone rang and rang, Lucy's thoughts strayed from their clothes to their home. Her breath caught in her throat as she visualised the potential loss. Her kitchen table and chairs – what better wood than ash to ignite and blaze, sparks rushing around the room and spreading to the customised sideboard she'd had specially made? And what about her bedroom? That was a definite disaster. How she'd enjoyed redecorating it only a couple of weeks earlier, choosing new pastel colours and novelty bits and pieces to give it a modern look, copying it right out of a magazine and going to great lengths to source the exact fitted furniture. Finishing the second coat of paint, she'd stood back and admired her toil, delighted she'd refused Danny's offer to get in the professionals. She clutched the receiver tighter, remembering the snow-white satin covers and soft lavender cushions she'd put on their bed that morning. Gone up in a puff of smoke.

She hung up and tried again, listening to the ring-tone, willing her sister to be there.

Furniture and soft furnishings could be replaced, she thought. Rebuilding a lifetime of memories was her real concern. Could they ever fix this mess and resurrect the keepsakes and mementos lurking in every corner of the house, the chips and scratches on walls and doors, memories of unruly toddlers and rowdy teens? Digging into the recesses of her mind released a torrent of happy memories.

How much of their life was already destroyed, never to be captured again? And the practicalities, like where would they live in the meantime? Lucy clutched the receiver so tightly she thought the plastic would snap in her hand.

"Hello?"

Her sister's chirpy voice burst on to the line, dragging Lucy back to the present with a sharp tug. "Del," she began slowly, coiling the phone flex around her little finger and taking a breath. She dreaded having to say the words out loud but knew she couldn't put it off a moment longer.

"Something's wrong," Delia instantly picked up on her hesitation. "What's happened, Lucy? Is it Matt?"

"There's been the most awful accident, Del," Lucy babbled, one word tripping over the other when she found her voice, getting them out as fast as she could before she clammed up again. "There was a fire at home and Danny . . ." But uttering the horrible words brought torrents of tears again and though she could hear Delia begging her to tell her what was wrong, she simply couldn't go on.

But Delia was already piecing things together. "Oh my God! I heard something on a news bulletin. That was your house? I didn't think it could be – I was sure you'd have rung me right away. It said a man was pulled to safety. That was Danny! Are you at the hospital?"

"The University Hospital. We've been here a couple of hours."

"A couple of hours. Oh my God! Why didn't you call me before now? I'm on my way. What ward?"

"Intensive Care."

"Oh crap."

You said it, Lucy thought, wiping away her tears with the heel of her hand. 'Crap' just about described her situation.

"Del, one thing – could you swing by Sycamore Lodge on your way? I left my handbag in my car which

I didn't even lock when I left in the ambulance and I don't know if the gardaí –"

"Don't worry – I'm on it."

"Thanks, Del. See you shortly."

"Luce, once you and Danny are okay, that's all that matters. Don't worry about anything else. Your insurance company will get you back on your feet."

As she hung up from her sister and made her way back to the Intensive Care Unit, Lucy tried to remember the insurance company they'd renewed with. But try as she might, the name wouldn't come to her. The renewal notice had sat in the messy 'to be dealt with' pile of letters on the kitchen windowsill for ages, the premium request arriving weeks in advance of its due date. She definitely remembered calling a few competitors and being appalled at how much the amounts had increased during the previous twelve months. And still not satisfied that she was getting the most competitive rate, she'd devoted an entire afternoon to surfing the net for a better quote, the rain pelting against the window outside and the wind howling down the chimney. The memory of that afternoon made her realise that she'd abandoned her quest midway when her mother rang for one of her marathon complaining sessions. Her main complaint that day had been about the lack of insulation in the nursing home, the rattling glass in the window and how afraid she was that it would burst in on top of her bed.

Lucy stopped abruptly before re-entering the room where Danny lay, her heart missing a beat, a cold feeling washing over her. She had no recollection of receiving confirmation documents or writing a cheque and posting it off as she normally did. Her mind drew a complete blank. *Surely I didn't forget to follow it through?* Cold sweat ran down her back. Her feet stuck to the floor. A loud pulse pumped at the side of her neck, a ringing beginning in her ears. The nagging worry took hold, the urge to charge home and check her unruly box of documents overwhelming. *What if I never renewed it? What if our policy has lapsed?* Her hand shook as she pressed the bell to get in, her mind in freefall as the evening went from bad to worse, something she hadn't thought possible.

First the smoke alarm – crazy, dangerous and utterly irresponsible – but now we've no insurance cover! That's a whole new dimension, a dimension that could finish us for life, a dimension we may not survive.

She covered her face with her hands and leaned her forehead against the door for a couple of seconds, jumping out of the way when the nurse pushed the door against her. The gentle hum and erratic bleeping of medical equipment echoed in her ears as she made her way back to Danny's bedside, grateful he was still sedated and unable to see the shame on her face. *Where on earth are we going to get the money to rebuild? The banks aren't lending, Danny's assets are all tied up in unfinished projects and now, into the bargain, he's going to be physically unable to work!* This thought fed into another. *Has he serious-illness insurance to cover that eventuality,* she wondered, suddenly realising how ignorant she was regarding Danny's business affairs.

Arriving at his bedside, she stared at him for a moment, his sleeping form a shadow of the larger-than-life character he actually was.

The nurse approached as Lucy sat back down. "Lucy, I'm sorry to disturb you."

"Yes?"

"Inspector Phelim O'Brien would like a word with you."

"With me? Why?" Lucy snapped, jumping up from her chair and leading the nurse away from Danny's bedside. It wasn't a conversation she wanted him hearing in his current medicated state.

Taken aback by Lucy's sharp tone, the nurse put her hands up in defence. "I'm only passing on a message. My job is to look after your husband not act as your legal rep."

She made to step away but Lucy, instantly ashamed, put a hand out to stop her.

Biting the hand that's feeding me, metaphorically speaking of course, Lucy thought, is not the way to go. "I'm so sorry, Nurse," she said, her expression softening as she yearned to make amends, "I shouldn't have snapped but I'm scared and confused and, to be honest, I'm totally out of my depth."

"I'm sure the inspector's questions will be routine, probably nothing at all to worry about, just ticking a few boxes."

Lucy gave a cautious look towards the door where Inspector O'Brien was waiting. Thoughts raced through her head, none of them making sense but all of them convincing her that Inspector O'Brien didn't waste valuable time ticking boxes. He'd come with a specific mission in mind and, unfortunately for her, she was his target.

Chapter 8

Eric paced Tampa Airport, ignoring the rumbles from his stomach each time he walked past Wimpy bars and buffet counters. He'd failed to contact his lawyer to cancel the purchase agreement he'd initiated and had no other option but to make straight for the airport, hoping Carol would have already booked a ticket for him. But Carol hadn't, nor had she returned his calls, and fear had become his closest friend. His eyes darted around the crowded airport, his paranoia making him jumpy and irritable as he walked the length of the floor. I have to get out of this city, he thought, looking over his shoulder, expecting somebody to pounce on him and drag him away in cuffs. Or worse still, expecting a call from Carol telling him the finance companies had already impounded their home.

The noise level was intrusive, his thoughts and concerns struggling to be heard. He checked his phone again, the plastic casing hot in his sweaty hand. The battery was still alive but dying. With empty pockets, he had no choice but use it, despite his concerns that he was leaving a trail for the authorities to track him. He was afraid to use his credit card or withdraw funds from the ATM, expecting even the smallest transaction to cause bells and sirens to ring, singling him out like a soloist under the beam of a spotlight.

More than anything he craved the safety of Irish soil. His heart beating fast, he pressed redial to call Carol's mobile for the umpteenth time. Yet again, his efforts were fruitless. He glanced over his shoulder, tensing when he saw two policemen walking briskly in his direction. Keeping his eyes fixed on the floor, Eric shrank inwardly, making himself as insignificant as possible. He was giddy with relief when the officers breezed past him without as much as a second glance.

American law terrified him, an intricate maze with as many loopholes as legalities. The small amount he knew about it did little to console him. His stomach lurched, the possibility that the contract he was running away from would put him behind bars weighing heavily on his mind.

He dialled the landline at home. The phone rang and rang. He imagined the shrill tone echoing around an empty house, the thought of his home lying vacant sending a shiver down his spine. Had the banks already taken ownership? Would another family shortly invade the house he and Carol had cherished? Heat rushed through his body, his shirt clinging to his back. Using our home as collateral against high-risk business loans wasn't very cherishing, he admitted to himself, ashamed he'd betrayed his family's trust, owning up to his stupidity for the first time.

The phone continued to ring. Glancing upward at the

flight board, the green lights blurred out of focus as his past mistakes rolled through his mind, like the credits at the end of a film where, unless you kept a very close eye on the screen, the names disappeared too rapidly into the ether.

An urgent and repeated passenger call interrupted Eric's meandering thoughts, snapping him back to the present and reminding him with clarity that the past was irrevocable.

With the phone clung to his ear, he looked around him, totally removed from the blur of activity in the airport. A shadow of the hard-nosed businessman he'd prided himself on being – the guy who pulled an ace from the deck where others folded – Eric was suddenly reminded of Monopoly, his favourite Santa present of all time.

Seeing the comparison between his current situation and the rules of the game, he gave a wry smile, realising too late that he'd wasted his final '*get out of jail free*' card, didn't have the funds to purchase another and had little option but face the banker and declare bankruptcy. Regardless of his excellent track record at Monopoly, beating the bankers he'd become involved with was a whole other story.

Listening to the continued sound of the phone ringing hundreds of thousands of miles away, he willed Carol to pick up so he'd get one final throw of the dice, the opportunity to get all around the board and land on *Home*. Then hearing the beeps of his dying battery, he cut the connection and flopped into the nearest seat, accepting there was nothing he could do but sit and wait for his opponents to decide if he could still be part of the game.

Eric slumped against the uncomfortable departure-lounge seat. He had never felt more alone in his life.

Chapter 9

Carol woke from a deep sleep, memories of the fire and the calls from Eric swirling through her brain. It was twenty past ten.

She'd tossed and turned for most of the night, going downstairs twice to get a hot drink in the hope it would help her sleep. By five o'clock she gave up and switched on her bedside lamp. As her eyes adjusted to the light, she pulled herself up a little against the pillows and lay there, drinking in every detail of her bedroom and trying to imagine life without her home. Without her beautiful Hillcrest. Tears flooded down her face, heart-wrenching sobs making her body ache until eventually exhaustion won and sleep overcame her.

But now, wide awake once more, she tried to concentrate on what needed to be done. Organise Eric's ticket for a start. "Without using a credit card," she muttered to herself as she made her way to the bathroom to brush her teeth. Her eyes stung from crying, her skin was blotchy as though she'd drunk too much wine the night before. If only. Sipping wine and giggling with friends was a memory from another lifetime, way down her list of priorities.

"Bloody mobiles, they never work when you want them most," she muttered to herself a few moments later when she failed yet again to get through to her youngest daughter. Sighing heavily, she dialled Isobel's number instead.

"Hi, Iz, are you okay?" She listened attentively as her daughter detailed how she'd been working flat out since six that morning. "I wish you had somebody to help you, Iz – you take on too much alone." But her concern fell on deaf ears. "Well, at least promise me you'll break for lunch and get some rest. I can't imagine you've anything left to do at this stage. And you have to pace yourself to get through the next few days' talks. Please, Iz, promise me."

"Just get Dad home as soon as you can, Mum. There has to be something he can do to salvage this mess."

But responding to her daughter's request and getting Eric home was more difficult than Carol had realised. Finding a travel shop open on a damp Sunday in November was a mammoth task in itself but eventually – after combing all the shopping centres on the outskirts of Cork City, pausing only to gulp down a coffee and muffin for lunch – she pushed open the door of a holiday shop on Patrick Street and flopped into a chair in front of a bored-looking travel agent who seemed none too pleased to have to deal with her.

Leaving the premises 800 poorer, Carol wasn't surprised by the sudden downpour of torrential rain. It seemed fitting and, as well as matching her mood, it camouflaged the tears on her cheeks, self-pitying tears for the lifestyle she hadn't appreciated until it was gone. She thought of her grandiose house, with its three storeys, large windows and Georgian front door reached by a flight of wide steps, and shivered. She felt as though the house already belonged to somebody else and she was returning to a stranger's home, somewhere she no longer belonged.

Tampa airport was a hive of mid-morning activity. Travellers scurried around, dragging luggage, clutching valuables, queuing impatiently and scanning monitors searching for flight details. Police scoured terminals, watchful and suspicious, in their liaisons with security.

Eric, meanwhile, was locked in a toilet cubicle, paranoia getting the better of him, convinced his name was on a wanted list all over North America. He had passed the night dozing fitfully on benches, chin on chest, terrified of arousing suspicion. His phone-battery dead, his contact with home severed, he was afraid to enquire again if a ticket had been booked for him – he had already checked at the Traveller's Aid desk three times, sweating with nerves and embarrassment. He could only conclude Carol had not got his message.

But once he'd got over the initial sense of panic, the severance brought surprising temptation. Temptation to flee. Feeling lighter and giddier than he had in a very long time, Eric dropped his phone into a nearby dustbin, picked up his overnight bag and left the bathroom. On his way out the door, he spotted a fifty-dollar bill on the floor, pouncing on it as though it were a winning lottery ticket. He held it tightly in his hand and left the airport.

Glancing around him, he spotted a bus pulled up nearby. Hurrying to it, he jumped on – not even checking its destination – and handed over the money to pay his fare. Judging by the change from the fifty-dollar bill, he was travelling long-distance. And long distance was what he wanted.

Unzipping his cardigan and taking it off, he rolled it in a ball and turned it into a makeshift pillow, staring out the window as the bus moved away from the kerb. He was tired of stringing the pieces of his life together, tired of juggling balls in the air and tired of pretending everything was okay when it was anything but.

Eric closed his eyes and allowed the motion of the bus lull him to sleep.

The warm Pacific lapped around him while Carol and the girls (only little then) watched him from the beach where they were on their knees making sandcastles. Their shrieks of laughter made him smile. He floated on his back, staring up at the clear blue sky without a care in the world, the warm water trailing through his fingers and toes. He could have stayed there forever . . .

If only that person shaking him would stop!

"Sir, sir, this is the last stop. You've got to get off here now."

As the dream slipped from Eric's grasp, he watched it fade away, refusing to open his eyelids and leave his family or that glorious blue ocean and soft golden sand, until finally it was gone and he was back on the bus with a crick in his neck, cramp in his legs and diesel fumes stinking the air around him.

Taking a few moments to adjust to the glaring

sunshine reflecting against the grubby window, he finally pulled himself up in the seat and gazed through bleary eyes at the bus driver staring down at him.

"Are you on vacation, sir?"

"Eh . . . yes," he agreed, wiping drool from his chin with the heel of his hand. He looked around him, sitting up straighter and grabbing the cardigan that fell from behind his head. He was the only passenger left on the bus. He looked through the window, searching for a clue as to his location. But he could see nothing but buses on every side. He daren't imagine what he would do next. Where would he sleep? He put his hand in his pocket for his phone, remembering as his fingers reached the empty lining that he'd dumped it at the airport.

He got to his feet, pulling his small holdall from underneath his seat and clutching both handles in his sweaty palm, arching his back to ease his stiff limbs.

Where the hell was he? He vaguely remembered changing buses at some stage of his journey, again without registering the destination.

Suppressing his panic, knowing better than to insult the American standing in front of him, he chose his words very carefully. "What's the name of this town again?"

"Sarasota. Our last stop." The driver paused, then added gently, "Where are you going from here, sir?"

Eric was taken aback. He tried desperately to recall any facts he might know about Sarasota, eventually coming up with, "Where's the nearest beach around here?"

Eric stepped out into intense heat again, the door of the bus from Sarasota snapping shut behind him. He looked around, wiping dust and grime from his eyes, convinced he'd landed in some forgotten outback until a glimmer of blue ocean caught his attention. There was barely a width of roadway and some marshy ground separating them.

Eric picked up his bag and crossed the road, the blue ocean seeming like an extension of his dream. When the soft golden sand came into view, he began to undo the laces on his shoes, ready to relive his vivid dream. Moments later, he was trailing his feet through soft warm sand, ignored court appearances and frightening debt a million miles away.

Chapter 10

Delia spooned an extra large amount of coffee granules into her mug as she waited for the kettle to boil. She was exhausted. It was mid-morning on Monday and it felt like the fire had happened two weeks rather than just two nights ago. She had spent the best part of the previous day and two nights at the hospital with Lucy, managing to grab a few hours' sleep that morning before the shrill of her alarm clock awakened her from haunting nightmares.

Staring through the French doors as the kettle came to the boil in the background, the sight of the picturesque garden shed at the end of her garden made her smile. Danny had built it for her, labouring over it at weekends and evenings, roping in tradesmen where expertise was required, refusing any form of payment except her speciality: Bailey's cheesecake. Lashings of it. Insisting a proper brick shed would hold a lot more than the poky wooden Barna she'd had since she'd first bought the house on Strand Hill, he'd custom-built it to include ample shelving and units where she could store the delicate raw materials she used in her jewellery design.

Startled out of her reverie, she hurried to answer the phone, hoping against hope it was Lucy with some good news.

But her nephew's voice came down the line instead. "Delia, it's Matt!"

"My God, you're up early! What time is it over there? How lovely to hear from you! Are you settling in? What's your apartment like?" Shit, she thought, cringing at her silly rambling, reminded of her mother and her inquisitions. But how am I going to hold a conversation with him without mentioning Lucy and Danny? Her sister had been adamant that the boys shouldn't find out about the fire. She didn't want either of them to come rushing back, being determined to get things sorted as much as possible before concerning them. A lot easier said than done in Delia's opinion.

"Eh, Del, one question at a time, please! I can't get a hold of Mum and Dad. Any idea where they've disappeared to? Gone off on a luxury cruise to celebrate getting rid of both of us?"

"Ha, ha. As if!" Delia cursed under her breath. She'd told Lucy something like this would happen but had never expected to be the one receiving the call. And certainly not so soon after the fire. She searched for a plausible excuse, the first words she could think of spilling from her lips. "We had flash lightning," she improvised, pouring boiling water over the coffee granules and tipping in a drain of milk.

"What has that got to do with anything?"

"Lucy's phone line was hit on Saturday night. Not sure about their mobiles though. Could well be that the mobile masts were affected as well . . ."

"Oh? I s'pose it could happen alright."

Delia leaned her head against the wall and groaned inwardly. She'd got away with it. For now at least. But sooner rather than later, Lucy would have to rethink her decision about keeping things quiet. "Do you want me to pass on a message, love?"

"I need Mum to call me as soon as she can, please, Del. My reference from the Fitness Centre in Rochestown Park Hotel is in my room. NYC College already received a detailed reference from the university but asked me for supporting documents from any relevant work experience. So my part-time job there should cover that. And I'll need my long birth cert too. Just in case my passport's not enough ID out here."

"Sure, sure, I'll pass on the message. How's your apartment?" She steered away from the subject of his parents.

"Small but serviceable is probably the best way to describe it."

"The location's good though?" Delia took a long gulp of coffee.

"Yep, smack central."

"Ideal for Lucy and me to go shopping then?"

"Shopper's paradise, Del. No invitation necessary. You're always welcome."

"Thanks, love." Delia blinked back unexpected tears. He sounded so happy. If he knew what was really going on!

"Ask Mum to send them express post. Tell her to have a root around in the mess and she's bound to stumble across them."

Delia wanted to howl at the unfairness of what was happening, the mess in Matt's room a whole lot worse than he could ever imagine. She'd no idea if his room had even survived, never mind anything in it! But she kept her tone bright. "Knowing your mother, it's already pristine!"

"Come to think of it, Del, my reference is on the PC. Maybe Mum could email it to me instead? I'll give you my address."

"Sure, just hang on a sec, Matt," she replied, grabbing a pen and notepad and taking a gulp of coffee from her mug to calm herself. Accessing the computer might prove impossible too. But she wasn't going to try and explain that to her nephew. They'd deal with it somehow. "OK, Matt, call out the address."

Delia's brain was on overdrive as she wrote down his details. His birth cert, she thought, I can pick that up in town. Biting on her bottom lip, she wondered about the reference. I suppose we could explain the situation to the Rochestown Park Hotel. They'd surely have saved a copy. She'd call them herself and see. It would be one less worry for Lucy.

"I'll get your mum onto it straight away, Matt. And I'll get her to call you."

"Yeah, that'd be great. There's something else I wanted . . ." he began, but let his words trail off. "Actually, forget it. I'd better wait until I'm talking to her myself. It's nothing that won't keep."

When they'd said their goodbyes, Delia dropped the

receiver into its cradle and sat staring into space. At this time most Monday mornings, she would have already tended to the tedious part of running her own jewellery design business: processing on-line orders, stocktaking, invoicing and sending Internet mail shots to potential customers. And once she'd sorted all that, she'd be swimming lengths in Carrigaline Court Hotel Leisure Centre, treading the water and stretching her limbs before a long day cooped up indoors soldering metals and shaping stones to suit her latest designs. But not that morning. That morning, her heart ached for her sister and she couldn't muster either energy or inclination to plunge into chlorinated water.

She jumped in fright when the phone shrilled again. What now, she thought, lifting the receiver once more, holding it away from her ear when her mother's unmistakable screech came down the line.

"What the hell is going on, Delia? I've just seen Lucy's house splashed all over the morning *Examiner* . . ."

Delia listened to Gloria's aggressive tones as she spat her accusations in quick succession.

". . . and the piece reported that a man was rushed to Intensive Care suffering from smoke inhalation. It's Danny, isn't it? Don't lie to me!"

Delia put her head in her hands, desperation flooding over her. When had the media jumped on the bandwagon?

"Delia, will you answer me? Please?"

She could hear the distress in her mother's voice, her frustration turning to sympathy. "Yes, Mum. It is Lucy's house and Danny is recovering in hospital." The pause on the other end of the line worried her. Should she have concealed the truth? Waited until she could sit her down and tell her face to face?

"And as per usual, I'm the last to know."

Gloria's harsh accusing tone dismissed Delia's concerns that the news was too much for her mother's ageing heart. "Mum, please, I didn't want to worry –"

"Worry me? Bah! When were you going to tell me?"

"I've had little or no sleep. I've been at the hospital for the past two nights –"

"Get down to Kinsale this very minute and get me out of this decrepit retirement home! I'm coming home to my family whether I'm wanted or not!"

Damn, damn, damn! Delia feigned a bout of coughing, stalling for time. Despite their differences and Gloria's ability to rub Delia up the wrong way, she actually felt sorry for her mother. Of course she'd had a dreadful shock seeing her daughter's house blazing on the front page of the *Examiner*. She and Lucy had thought that wouldn't happen. They had even talked about how 'lucky' it was that it had happened on a Saturday night as it wouldn't feature in Sunday's news and would be forgotten about by Monday.

Her breath caught in her throat. If it had been in the *Examiner*, then no doubt it was splashed on the Internet too. What about Stephen in Australia? He scanned the national papers on a daily basis. She'd have to talk to Lucy as soon as possible but first she needed to calm her mother. If she herself had found out like this, she'd be screaming down the phone at someone too!

"Take a breath, Mum. Danny had a comfortable night. The important thing is they're both going to be okay. Now wouldn't you be more comfortable staying where you are than coming back in the middle of all this chaos?"

"Huh! Have you been thinking I'd disappear here in this home? Well, you can think again, Delia O'Leary. Get down here now to collect me because, if you don't, I'll be outside your door before you can spell the word *fire*!"

"On the way," Delia mumbled, hanging up the phone. How am I going to convince her to stay where she is and leave us alone, she worried, the promise she'd made Matt going completely out of her head as she grabbed her keys and left the house.

Chapter 11

Matt felt marginally better when he got off the phone from Delia. Hearing a voice from home had consoled him a little, made him feel less alone. And less anxious.

This was the morning Heidi was due to fly from New York to Boston. And he was more confused than ever.

She had sent him a text, a text that shut him out more than before. Seeing his phone flashing had made his heart leap when he'd returned to the apartment that first day, his fingers burning as he fumbled with the keys, sweat dripping from his chin onto the screen. He couldn't open it fast enough, his heart sinking to the floor when he read the brief text.

need time out. please don't worry. talk soon. Hxx

He'd lain in the Manhattan apartment for the past two nights, unaccustomed to the sounds both inside the building and on the street outside, the two kisses at the end of her text the only positive he had to cling to. After reading the message, he'd responded instantly, begging her to tell him where she was. But other than a return text with just one kiss, he'd had no other contact from her.

For two long nights he'd strained to hear her return. Leaving the window open for a bit of air, he'd heard every car horn, voice, howling dog and squealing cat in the early hours of the morning. New York truly was the city that never slept. He'd jumped out of bed on several occasions, convinced he'd heard her footsteps on the landing outside his door. But each time he was met with an empty corridor or late-night stranger passing by. There had been no trace of his flame-haired Heidi. During the day he had kept busy and away from the apartment – he couldn't bear the waiting.

He'd contemplated contacting the police but each time his fingers hovered over the phone, he'd changed his mind. Considering Heidi's parents thought she was holidaying in another country, he didn't fancy having to explain that to NYPD. Hours of soul-searching later, he'd decided reporting her disappearance would implicate him in something he knew nothing about. And then he might never find her. It also occurred to him that he'd no idea what type of visa Heidi had travelled on.

And, in the last analysis, considering her missing passport and obvious impending travel plans, his gut instinct screamed that she'd left of her own free will. She was not a missing person.

Storing the flight details as a draft text on his mobile, Matt dressed quickly and left his apartment, doubling back a few moments later and taking his passport and spare cash from the hidden compartment in his rucksack. Better to be safe than sorry.

He flagged down a yellow taxi-cab. "Newark Airport please," he said, allowing his gut instinct take the lead.

Chapter 12

Lucy was finding it impossible to keep her eyes open. Sleep had evaded her ever since the fire, followed by her informal 'chat' with Inspector O'Brien which thankfully had been brief and not too gruelling. But by midday on Monday her body was in meltdown and deciding it just had to have sleep. When she'd refused to leave Danny's side, the nurse had brought her the most comfortable armchair she could find, encouraging her to at least catch forty winks while Danny slept.

To make way for other emergencies, he'd been moved from the Intensive Care Unit to a high-dependency observation ward. But he was still under very close scrutiny.

Lucy pulled her knees up on the chair, staring at his chest moving rhythmically up and down. Closing her eyes with the intention of resting a moment, she slipped into a dreamless sleep and was completely disorientated when she woke with a start to feel somebody shaking her shoulder.

"What?" she asked grumpily, wiping drool from her mouth and rubbing crusty sleep from her eyelids. Unable to figure out why her body felt so cramped and why she wasn't at home tucked up in her large king-size bed, it took her a moment to get her bearings and remember where she was. But despite her confusion and blurred vision, she couldn't mistake the big smile on the nurse's face.

"I didn't think you'd want to miss this. Take a look," the nurse urged Lucy, pointing a finger at Danny. "I think somebody's finally ready for a chat now. I'll leave you both to it." She crept away to see to the patient in the next bed.

Instantly, Lucy was wide awake and sitting bolt upright in her chair. "Danny! Oh my God, I thought I'd lost you," she said, bursting into uncontrollable tears.

"Not this time," he croaked, his voice husky and muffled behind the oxygen mask. "How long have I been here?"

"It's Monday. You've been asleep for nearly two days." Lucy didn't care how husky or hoarse he sounded. He had pulled through and it looked like he was going to be okay. Thank you, God, she whispered, instantly feeling energised and better able to deal with the rest of their problems now she knew for certain he'd survive. With tears in her eyes, she leaned gently over him and kissed him tenderly on the cheek. "I'm so sorry, Danny," she blubbered. "The whole thing . . . it was all my fault. I never replaced the battery in the smoke alarm . . ." She pulled her sleeve over the heel of her hand and wiped her nose. It was impossible to hold back her anguish. Guilt had weighed heavily on her for the last two days, a dragging ache straining across her chest, a tight knot in an otherwise empty stomach.

Danny shook his head and tried to pull himself up a little in the bed, pushing away her offer of help. "I can do it myself," he said, always one to manage things alone. And then, as if he hadn't heard a word of her last admission, he seemed to be processing what day it was and fretting about work. "Monday. But I had a job booked in ..." He spluttered and coughed into the mask. Gripping one of the side-rails, his knuckles whitening with effort, he tried to pull himself up once again, reaching out and grabbing Lucy's hand for support.

He struggled to talk. "The fire . . . it was upstairs . . . I tried to . . ." He gasped between every few words, stopping to draw breath, then giving in to his congested lungs and flopping back against the pillows, the exertion of speaking wearing him out.

Tears streamed down Lucy's cheeks, her heart constricting. How could this have happened to us, she wondered, raging against the unfairness of it all, hating the terrible uncertainty dumped upon them.

"The . . . house?" Danny spoke very slowly, the mask over his nose.

Lucy stared ahead, not knowing what to say, unable to find words to describe the state of their home. Terrified that the truth would set him into immediate relapse, she pulled at a loose thread in the white starched sheet. "I haven't been back to examine it but it didn't look great from outside."

"Insurance . . . assessor?"

Lucy held his hand tightly. He has no idea of the extent of the damage, she thought. But his recovery was her priority and if that meant closeting him from the truth for a while longer, well, so be it.

"Yes, yes, don't worry . . . I'll attend to all of that. You must rest now."

She'd forgotten to contact his employees. All local lads, she could only presume Danny's staff would have heard about the fire. Being honest, she hadn't given a thought to anything or anyone for the last forty-eight hours. Except Danny. Keeping the news from family was pricking her conscience slightly but now that he was awake and able to make his own decisions, there would be plenty time to let everybody know. Cocooned in the hospital without a mobile phone, she'd found it easy to avoid the outside world. And avoid making a statement in Carrigaline Garda Station as she'd promised Inspector O'Brien she would.

Danny wrinkled his brow in concentration. "I fell asleep . . . on the couch . . . I'd watched a couple of matches . . . and then dozed off . . . Water, please . . ." He pointed at his throat, his voice barely a croak at this stage. "Sandpaper."

Lucy stood up from her chair and poured him a small drink, moving the oxygen mask aside to allow him take a sip. Not surprisingly, his forehead was hot and sticky, the slightest exertion making him break out in a sweat.

"How did I get out? Who . . ." He paused mid-sentence when Lucy moved the mask again to hold the cool glass to his lips, tilting it gently to help him take another sip.

She filled in the gaps, keeping it simple. "The fire officers found you collapsed on the landing. You were out cold. Smoke inhalation."

Danny laid his head against the pillows. "The fire extinguisher . . . was upstairs . . . I tried to get it . . ." He paused again, this time to try and wade through his hazy memory and recall what happened next. In the lengthening silence, his breathing intensified, his reading on the heart monitor jumping about at a furious pace.

"Leave it for now, Danny. It'll come back to you in time, I'm sure." Lucy pulled her gaze away from the monitor, afraid he'd catch the worried look on her face.

"I think I'll sleep now. Come back when . . . you've checked the damage . . . I need to know," he told her, feebly waving her away.

She stared at him for a moment, taking in his bloodshot eyes, the purple hue of his lips and his blotchy complexion. A distant clanging registered in her mind, the sound of a medical apparatus falling to the floor, all other sounds fading in the distance as she focused on Danny's brusque manner, the coldness in his tone. The speed with which he was encouraging her to leave was hurtful and confusing. After hours of waiting, praying and watching, Lucy was struggling with her emotions, every ounce of her wanting to lash out at him, unleash her fear, let him know the excruciating terror she'd been through. Using every grain of self-control she possessed, she held it together for just a short while longer.

"I'd really rather stay with you until you're a little stronger. Everything else can wait."

He shook his head and again gestured with his hand for her to leave, closing his eyes.

Hurt and disappointment jostled around the pit of her stomach. "What about your parents? I haven't let them know yet. Should I call and tell them?"

He kept his eyes closed. "Call Jenny . . . on her mobile. She'll find the best way . . . to tell them."

Shocked by his steeliness and blatant exclusion tactics, Lucy's head reeled. His words were barely audible, his concern for his parents evident. More than any he's shown for me, she thought, with uncharacteristic spite. She inhaled deeply, her face blank of expression.

"And Stephen and Matt?"

"No!" Danny's eyes shot open. "Why upset them?"

Lucy sighed. "At least we agree on something," she muttered, unable to mask the bitterness in her tone.

The thought of calling Jenny filled her with apprehension. Danny's only sister – the sister-in-law she'd never connected with – lived an indulged life in the centre of London, barely making the time to come home and see her ageing parents, never mind remember her brother and his family at Christmas or birthdays. For the most part, this arrangement suited Lucy well. At least it reduced the number of times she actually felt like stabbing somebody in her own living room! But this was one occasion where she couldn't avoid making contact with her arch-enemy.

She forced a smile on her lips. "Okay, Dan, I'll try and get through to Jenny when I leave. And when I come back I'll be able to tell you how badly burnt the house is."

Danny nodded, adjusting the mask on his nose, frowning when Lucy came up against yet another problem.

"Oh God, I don't have her number. My phone was in the fire, as was yours I presume. The address book was in our bedroom, so we can kiss goodbye to that too . . ."

"Find a way," Danny hissed, rushing the words out in practically one breath. "The Insurance Company. Chase them up too."

Lucy blanched. "God, Danny. Where am I going to start?" It's a nightmare, she screamed inside, then glanced away from him, taking in the seriously ill patients around her and measuring the one thing still intact – her health – against all the odds stacked against her.

She looked around again to find Danny's bloodshot eyes searching hers.

She let out the breath she'd been holding. For the first time ever, he's depending on me. I can't let him down.

"Sorry, Dan. It's all such a shock, that's all." Lucy planted a kiss on his forehead and turned to leave the ward.

As she pushed through the doors, she bumped into a nurse coming in. "Can I ask you . . ." she began, stopping abruptly when she looked over the nurse's shoulder and noticed Delia standing behind her. But it wasn't the strained expression on her sister's face (or the fact her cropped hair seemed to be standing up in all directions, a sure sign she'd been running her hands through it in frustration) that cut Lucy off mid-sentence. It was the glowering look on the face of the person accompanying her. Oh God no, she thought, clenching her fists and digging her nails into the palms of her hands. I can't deal with this now.

"Lucy?" the nurse prompted. "You were going to ask me something?"

Lucy shook her head. It would have to keep. She'd have to wait for a more private moment to ask her about Danny's behaviour, the side of him she'd seen today – accusing and aloof.

But now she stared into the face of a much more pressing problem. Her mother.

The nurse pulled Lucy to one side. "Carrigaline Gardaí were on again. They want to interview Danny but I told them his condition was still critical."

"Thank you."

"They said to remind you to call in to the station though."

Lucy nodded, unable to stop her cheeks flushing, tremors of inexplicable guilt flooding through her. "It's on my list of things to do," she responded, noticing her mother's eyebrows rising.

Chapter 13

Matt dashed through Newark Airport like a headless chicken, his eyes searching the crowds for Heidi while scanning every arrival and departure screen for the Boston flight. Realising it was delayed, he sighed with relief, grasping the breathing space that gave him. He stormed around the cafeterias in the area, pushing through crowds, trying to catch a glimpse of Heidi's auburn tresses, cursing and apologising every time he mistook somebody else for her and made to swing them around. He was in a dilemma: he knew he should plant himself at the entrance to Departures but his only hope to talk to Heidi was to locate her well before her boarding time. No good trying to accost her as she dashed past him into Departures. Especially under the noses of a bunch of security staff.

"You're acting like a crazed lunatic," he muttered to himself, jumping out of the way of a motorised luggage buggy and wondering what on earth he hoped to achieve even if he did find her. He wasn't about to hold her against her will. And if she thought so little of him that she couldn't even offer him a proper explanation for her sudden disappearance, well, shouldn't he accept that said it all? Leaning against a pillar, he took off his baseball cap and wiped the sweat from his brow. If the lads at home could see me now, he thought, visualising them around a table in the local pub laughing their heads off to see him running around an airport looking for Heidi when New York was full of hot women!

"Can you point me in the direction of the international check-in please?"

Startled when he felt his sleeve being tugged, Matt looked down at the tiny brunette standing next to him. "Excuse me?"

"The check-in for international flights? You know where it is?"

He quickly looked at the overhead signs and pointed her in the right direction. "Eh, that way."

"Great. My glasses are somewhere in my luggage, you see, and I can't read the signs without them," she explained, laughing at the look of embarrassment on Matt's face as she made a joke of her poor eyesight. She hiked a large rucksack on her shoulders and clutched the handle of her suitcase. "Thanks so much for your help. You have a nice day now!"

Matt watched her hurrying off, the weight of her luggage slowing her down, her tiny footsteps adding to her delay. Surprising himself, he ran after her. He was a sucker for women in distress, a huge part of the reason he'd become the focus of Heidi's affections in the first place. It would only take a few minutes to help her out.

"Let me take that for you," he offered, lifting the

rucksack from the girl's back and flinging it over one shoulder while she happily handed over the case and attempted to match his pace towards her check-in.

Matt's concentration on the job in hand took his mind off his real reason for being in Newark Airport. It also took his eye off the mêlée of people he was hurrying past and prevented him from recognising a familiar face in the crowd, a face that would most certainly have halted him in his tracks.

Chapter 14

Lucy followed Delia and Gloria into the Waterfront café in Crosshaven, hugging her arms around her body, the biting salt air slicing through her light clothing. The village was quiet, the amusement arcade still, the boatyard bereft of activity. But instead of finding this dreary, Lucy found the normal routine comforting. At least some things are as they should be, she thought, joining her mother and sister at a window table.

"Have you had lunch, Lucy?" asked Delia, picking up the menu and scanning it.

Lucy shook her head. "No, actually but –"

"You must be starving! You haven't eaten properly since the fire. We had a quick bite in Kinsale but you should order something now."

Lucy inhaled the aroma of rich roasting coffee beans. "Honestly, Del, I'm too tired to face food now but I can't wait to get a decent cup of hot coffee. I've been surviving on machine coffee for the past couple of days and how the suppliers get away with serving that muck is beyond me."

Gloria pursed her lips together, folding her arms across her chest. "Will one of you just go and get the damn coffees and then sit down here and tell me what exactly has been going on. I've been kept waiting long enough as it is. This is no way to treat your mother after the shock I've had this morning."

Much to her mother's disapproval, Lucy had nodded off to sleep in the back of Delia's car on the way from the hospital to Crosshaven. Gloria had already dragged as much information as she could from Delia and was itching to interrogate her eldest daughter to try and fill in the gaps in what she knew was a deliberately sketchy explanation. Despite her best efforts to get her to swing by Sycamore Lodge so she could see the damage for herself, Delia had adamantly refused. "No, Mum. The Gardaí still have it cordoned off. Soon enough poor Lucy will have to survey the damage. Anyway, that's her call. Not mine."

Lucy could feel the stares of the customers at the other tables, most of whom she knew from the locality, their eyes shifting uncomfortably when she turned to salute them.

As Delia rose to go for the coffees, Lucy clutched her sleeve. "Delia, I'll give you a hand," she said.

"Okay."

"I feel as though I've got two heads," Lucy whispered as they stood at the counter.

"They're curious, that's all," said Delia. "I'm sure they don't mean to be rude but who can blame them? We'd probably be just as nosey ourselves."

Lucy looked down at her wrinkled outfit and made a face. "I've been wearing the same clothes since Saturday. It's no wonder they don't want to come anywhere near me!"

Delia brought her nose nearer to Lucy and sniffed. "So that's where the pong is coming from. I thought the sea had been polluted!"

The sisters shared a smile.

"Lucy, I'm sorry about Mum. She wouldn't take no for an answer." Delia glanced around to check Gloria was still sitting by the window and not standing behind them eavesdropping.

"I can only imagine. I'm sure she means well but . . ." Lucy broke off and yawned widely.

"What would ye like, girls?" said the assistant who came to serve them.

"Three white coffees and three of those luscious éclairs please." Lucy pointed to the cream pastries in the glass display case, hoping one of them would give her an energy boost. If she didn't get some sugar into her soon, she honestly felt she'd be asleep at the table in a matter of seconds.

"Your house," Delia explained in a low whisper, "was splashed across the front page of this morning's *Examiner*. Mum called me. She was in a right state . . ."

Lucy bit her lip. "Oh cripes!" She stole a look at her mother, a pang of sympathy flashing through her as she imagined how awful it must have been to see that. And be all alone into the bargain. "No wonder she's reacting like she is," she conceded.

"Underneath the bad mood, she's worried sick about you both. But you know Mum, Luce. She wants to know every gory detail from what started the fire to –"

Lucy threw her hands in the air. "I don't know how it started – nor does Danny! Honestly, what am I supposed to say?"

"You could cry?"

Again, the sisters shared a smile, knowing only too well that tears and heartfelt sobs were wasted on Gloria. Always had been, even when they were little girls squabbling over the last marshmallow.

"That will be twelve euro fifty, please," the counter assistant said.

Lucy turned to Delia. "Sorry, Del, can you? I'll pay you back as soon as I can. I used up all the change I had on the payphone."

Delia waved away her explanation and settled the bill.

"It was good of Carol to take care of my car and rescue my handbag," said Lucy. Delia had tracked car and handbag down to Carol's house the night of the fire. "I really should have contacted her. Only for Carol, who knows what . . ." Lucy sighed, but didn't finish the sentence. "Come on, let's get the interrogation over with and get Mother back to Kinsale."

Delia hadn't the heart to tell Lucy that Gloria was refusing to go back. When she'd collected her from the retirement home, her cases were packed. She'd told the surprised care assistant that she wouldn't be back. "I'll be staying with Delia, so you can send my post there. I'm needed at home," she'd announced, before walking out the door, her step as sprightly as a twenty-year-old's.

"I've a to-do list as long as my arm, including making a blooming statement at the Garda Station." Lucy was thinking aloud as they strolled back to their mother.

"Why do you have to make a statement when you weren't even there?" Delia questioned, balancing the tray as she followed Lucy to the table.

"God only knows but I suppose there's procedure to follow. I'm not in any rush to call in there, I can tell you."

"Surely they can leave that to the insurance assessor? Particularly with Danny being so ill?"

Lucy stopped abruptly and turned around to face her sister, heat rising in her neck and spreading to her cheeks. "That's the problem, Del. I'm not sure there is an insurance assessor. I have no recollection of renewing the policy."

Delia opened and closed her mouth, clutching the tray in case she dropped it and its contents on the floor. "You're in shock, Luce. Not thinking straight. Of course you renewed it. You'd never be that careless."

Lucy fervently hoped her sister was right. Back at the table, she took a seat across from her mother and lifted her coffee cup to her lips. She drank and held the liquid for a moment in her mouth, appreciating its succulence, then felt the caffeine hit as it raced through her veins.

"Now, Lucy, no more stalling, tell me everything," Gloria instructed, frowning in disapproval as Delia bit into her chocolate éclair and proceeded to lick the cream that oozed from the sides.

"Oh, Mum, do I have to go over it all again? You've no idea how exhausted I am." Lucy leaned on her mother's sympathy, willing her to ease up on the questions and leave her alone.

But Gloria wasn't having any of it, clucking her tongue and taking a quick sip from her coffee cup. "You and me both. Traumatised is the only word to describe how I'm feeling right now. And I can only say that you're not helping. If you can't let your mother support you . . ." She allowed her sentence to trail off, the emotional blackmail in her tone enough to make Lucy break her silence.

Trying to find the best words to start, Lucy stared through the window, the events of Saturday rushing at her in a torrent. "I'd spent the afternoon with Delia. Danny was on the couch watching telly when I left. I knew he'd doze off eventually as he usually does on a Saturday afternoon . . ." She omitted to say she'd left the house on bad terms with him. Or why.

Gloria nodded, impatience replaced with anticipation.

Lucy resented this trait in her mother but restrained her desire to scream. She pulled a hand through her lank hair, wishing more than anything she could just go home and immerse herself in hot water. Ironically, she recalled the scented bath she'd never got to take on Saturday evening. Best-laid plans.

"The first clue I had that anything was wrong was when the fire engines overtook me on the road and I saw them take the turn-off to Sycamore Lodge . . ."

She continued with the story, drifting into a daze as she remembered every detail.

Gloria sat up straighter in her chair, her chin jutting out in obstinacy. She pushed her silver hair behind her ears, her Helen-Mirren-style bob in need of reshaping. "But how did the fire start? Did you leave something plugged in? Or a saucepan on the boil?"

"God, Mum, what on earth are you insinuating? That it's Lucy's fault? Don't beat around the bush, will you?" Delia cut in, wiping around her lips with a serviette before screwing the tissue paper into a tight ball and bouncing it on her empty plate.

Lucy rubbed her throbbing head. Sitting at the same table as her mother and sister was always the same, one sniping at the other, trying to outdo each other in the nastiness stakes. Acting as referee was her usual role. But today she was in no mood to entertain their bickering.

"Stop. Both of you. Please. I have a thumping headache."

"Not surprising considering the speed you drank that coffee!" Gloria said accusingly.

Lucy ran her finger along the rim of the cup, tempted to pick it up and fire it through the window. Or across the table at her mother – making sure to miss her of course! But with that venomous thought came instant guilt and remorse. "I've barely slept in two days, Mum. Danny's heart stopped beating in the ambulance. I was sure he was gone, that I'd lost him . . ."

Delia reached over and squeezed her sister's hand. "But he came through it, Luce. And he's on the road to recovery now, however slow . . ."

Gloria turned away from her daughters, staring at the grey sky merging with the water as she delivered her next accusing blow. "I wanted to visit him but you made sure I didn't get anywhere near him! You couldn't get me out of that hospital fast enough. What about the boys? Do they know yet? Have you told Danny's parents or that stuck-up sister of his over in England?"

"Not yet," Lucy admitted, keeping Danny's instructions to herself for now. Otherwise her mother would have her on the phone that very second. And she needed to build herself up to making that call.

Another tongue-clucking from Gloria. "So you're keeping them in the dark as well, leaving them to get the shock of their lives like I did when I read it in the paper?"

"Mum, it wasn't like that –"

Gloria pursed her lips and spoke over her daughter, taking umbrage and using it as an opportunity to be heard (as if she ever waited for opportunity). "Those people have a right to know that their son is fighting for his life, Lucy, whether you like it or not. Or whether it suits you to have them visit or not. Imagine if it was Matt or Stephen? Wouldn't you want to be the first to know? How I reared such selfish daughters, I'll never know."

"Look, Mum –" Lucy began, trying to appease her mother and reduce her dramatics. She noticed the people at the next table discreetly peeping at them and lowered her voice. "Danny wasn't able for visitors. He only woke up properly this morning. And the reason I didn't ring his parents was because I didn't want them to have to go through what I was going through." This wasn't the whole truth – far from it. In fact, she hadn't the strength to face telling them – had hardly the strength to hold herself together. "And Delia and I thought there was no danger of any of you seeing it in the newspapers – because of Sunday intervening, you see. It never occurred to us the papers would pick it up this morning. It's hardly a matter of national interest." She pushed away her plate, her half-eaten éclair no longer appealing.

"Hmm." Gloria still wasn't convinced. "Telling them is your responsibility, Lucy."

"This is my first time to leave the hospital since

Saturday evening. It's unlikely Jenny will get her hands on the *Examiner* where she is."

"But she could read it on the Internet . . ."

Lucy couldn't believe her ears. What did her mother know about the Internet? Obviously they had a lot more recreation in the retirement home than Gloria had been letting on. "She could come across it, Mum, but I'm hoping she won't. At least not before I get a chance to tell her myself."

"Well, go and ring her now then! Here . . ." Gloria searched in her brown-leather handbag for her phone, "I've plenty of unused credit. Take it. Call her."

"Stop putting pressure on her!" Delia's words were sharp. "Lucy's in shock, Mum. Look at the state of the poor girl! She's barely eaten in two days, has only had about an hour's sleep in total. It's her you should be worried about, not anyone else. It's always the same with you. Worrying about everyone else and forgetting about those who should really matter." She picked up Lucy's leftover cake and popped it in her mouth.

Gloria put a hand to her chest and shook her head as she watched Delia munching, raising an eyebrow as her gaze rested on her daughter's hips for the briefest moment. Long enough to show her disapproval of Delia's recent weight gain. "I hope that spare bedroom is aired for me, Delia O'Leary? I don't want to end up getting my death of cold like poor Greta when she went to stay with her daughter. And don't put me upstairs. The steps kill my chest lately."

Lucy looked from her sister to her mother and back again, dread registering on her face. What was going on here, she wondered? The night she'd come to the hospital, Delia had offered her and Danny a roof over their heads for as long as they needed it. But had she heard correctly now? Had her mother just announced she would be staying in Delia's too? She was afraid to even contemplate any kind of future for the three of them if they were all going to be under one roof. They'd kill each other.

Lucy's brain was working a mile a minute. She couldn't nurse Danny back to health with her mother dictating from the side. God no! What could they do instead? She'd have to find somewhere else. Should she try and organise rented accommodation? Would she be able to get a short-term lease? Or perhaps Danny had a free unit in the last development he'd built? She'd been so absorbed in Matt these last few weeks she'd forgotten to ask whether he'd shifted the last of the terraced houses. Anywhere would do just so they could have a place to call their own.

Delia, meanwhile, was concentrating on stirring what was left of her coffee, working up the courage to challenge her mother. "Mum, why did you rent out your own house if you didn't plan on staying in the retirement home? Can you not ask the tenants to leave or something? Surely you can see that Lucy's needs come first?"

"Indeed I will not break the terms of the lease! You've an empty house, Delia, and of course Lucy's needs are a priority. Isn't that why I'm suggesting we pull together?"

A politician couldn't have delivered his closing argument better, Lucy thought, pushing back her chair and standing up. Her fight was gone. Inspector Phelim O'Brien and Sycamore Lodge were waiting for her and no doubt she'd need every bit of energy she had left for both ordeals. Her mother, she realised, was the least of her problems.

Chapter 15

Matt couldn't put his finger on it but there was something very familiar about the guy a few places ahead of him in the queue. His exceptional height put him head and shoulders above most others, on a level with Matt who was accustomed to being one of the tallest in any group. But that was in Ireland. In New York, everything from fries to humans seemed to come in supersize. But it wasn't only his height that attracted Matt's attention – his shaggy hairstyle triggered something in his memory too. Craning his neck to try and glimpse his face, all Matt captured was a side profile. And that in itself didn't sound any fanfares as to where he'd seen him before. He inched ahead, his attention drawn to the menu board as he got nearer. Coffee or beer? No contest. He needed a beer. And soon.

Hovering around the terminal where the Boston flight was boarding had proved a waste of time. Heidi hadn't appeared. As time ticked by and last call came for passengers to board – and her name wasn't among those called – he'd begun to feel foolish for dashing to the airport in the first place. At last he had to admit defeat and had abandoned his post, wondering whether the Continental Airline desk would be able to tell him if Heidi was on the flight or whether that would be classed as confidential information. He'd give it a go – but first a beer.

And that notion led him to the beverage kiosk. And put him in the queue behind the familiar-looking guy.

"Who's next, please?"

Matt made his way to the counter, finding himself standing right beside 'Tall Guy' as he'd begun to think of him. And his shabby guitar case.

Fanfares finally hollered trumpet-style. Now he remembered.

"Sir, can I help you today?"

But Matt didn't reply. He couldn't concentrate. 'Tall Guy' had let him into the apartment block the day he'd been locked outside when Heidi disappeared. And now he just happened to be at the same terminal detailed in Heidi's diary at the very time she had noted down. Coincidence? He couldn't be sure but he didn't think so. There had to be a connection. But what? Surely this guy wasn't the mysterious Alex? The love of Heidi's life? His gut instinct said no.

How was he going to investigate without appearing like some kind of psychotic stalker?

Matt was no fool. He was in a strange country with an unfamiliar policing system, a policing system that thought nothing of carting someone off in the back of a squad car for the slightest misdeed. He wasn't about to have himself arrested for harassment in New York City. And yet he couldn't ignore the nagging suspicion building inside him. He couldn't walk away. His mind raced. There has to be something I can do, he thought.

"Sir, can you please move on if you're not ordering. We've got a long line behind you."

The assistant's irate tone didn't perturb Matt. What did disturb him greatly was the dilemma he'd just found himself in. Approaching a complete stranger and accusing him of being party to his girlfriend's disappearance was hardly appropriate. But letting him get away without as much as having a word was out of the question. His relationship with Heidi – obscure as it was – deserved that much effort at least. Matt moved to the side without ordering, his thirst for beer replaced with a hunger for answers.

He watched from a nearby table, closely following Tall Guy's every move, waiting – like an animal stalking his prey – until he'd finished at the counter and picked up his guitar to move on.

Matt rubbed his stubbly chin, his craving for alcohol returning as he contemplated his next move. Dutch courage would have helped, taken away that edge of fear, the edge of apprehension that generally made his voice squeak, made his confidence plummet, made his throat close each time he tried to string a sentence together. His senses were alerted as Tall Guy sloped past his table. Matt could no longer see where he was going but strained to hear every sound, using his imagination to create a picture of what was going on behind him. Hearing the distinct twang of a guitar case being banged against a table, the rattle of a glass as Tall Guy dropped the tray down in an effort to save his guitar from falling on the floor was as good as satellite navigation, giving him an exact location. Hearing a grunt of satisfaction after a long pause gave Matt reason to guess he'd taken his first slug of beer.

Matt drummed his fingers on the table. He couldn't wait too long, couldn't afford to miss his opportunity, yet for optimum results timing had to be perfect. He waited. And then, as though his senses were magnified, Matt heard the scrape of a chair and another thump of the guitar case against the table. He knew that Tall Guy was on his feet.

Grabbing the edges of the table, Matt feigned a fit of choking, coughing and spluttering to the best of his acting ability, his awareness on high alert as he waited for the inevitable slap between the shoulder-blades. And right at the point where Matt's face was purple from effort, came a thump from behind, just as Matt had wished for: his excuse to enter into conversation with this stranger, his opportunity to challenge coincidence.

Matt exhaled dramatically, nodding his head to let Tall Guy know he was feeling much better after being clouted between the shoulder blades.

Now, would Tall Guy recognise him? He had only seen him for a few moments on Saturday. Would he remember? Or would he pretend he didn't?

"You gave me a scare there, man. You okay now?"

"Thanks to you I am! Can I get you a beer as a thank-you?"

"Nah, I'm on my way now. Doing an audition in a few hours." He patted his guitar case.

This information threw Matt slightly. Had this guy

just flown *in* to Newark? He had assumed he would be flying out to somewhere. Boston, to be precise.

What could he do to engage him in conversation a bit longer? "Broadway?" he asked.

Tall Guy snorted. "Ah hell, why not aim a bit higher? Somewhere like Madison Square Gardens for instance?"

Matt found it impossible to read this last comment. Is he being serious, he wondered, disliking his superior attitude. "You're not waiting for a flight then?"

Tall Guy shook his head. "Hey, what's with all the questions, man?" He hitched his guitar on his shoulder, pushed his hair back off his face and made to move away.

"Curiosity of the Irish, I guess," Matt responded hastily. "I'm new to the city. Over-enthusiastic, I suppose."

Tall Guy stopped and turned around. "Ah, best make an exception then." He raised one sharp eyebrow. "So tell me, is it true?"

Matt frowned. "Is what true?"

"That there's a pot of gold at the end of every rainbow?" He gave a loud guffaw, an exaggerated wave and walked away.

Matt stared after him, his dislike intensifying. Not satisfied to be dismissed as abruptly as he had been, however, he hurried after him, breaking into step beside him and matching his pace. He *had* to find out what his name was.

"I didn't catch your name," he said. "It'd be nice to know the name of the guy who saved my life so I can tell my grandkids in years to come."

Tall Guy continued walking with his characteristic swagger, bunches of people breaking apart to allow him through. "Julian Ebbs."

Not Alex. Matt felt a flood of relief.

"And yours?" said Julian. He glanced at Matt, making full-on eye contact.

"Matt Ardle."

Matt saw Julian's expression darken slightly, his eyes flickering beneath his hooded gaze. So he did remember. Or at least the name 'Matt Ardle' was significant to him.

"Where you heading, Matt Ardle? Manhattan?" Julian asked, his sarcastic grin returning. "Maybe we can share a cab?"

Matt's heart-rate quickened. Julian had reacted to his identity. Without doubt, there could be only one plausible explanation: Heidi. He wasn't about to look a gift horse in the mouth, concentrating on moving nearer to reconnecting with her and considering Julian his best chance to do so. Ignoring the gut instinct he relied so heavily upon and the reservations rising inside him that he was entering unchartered waters, he moved purposefully towards the exit doors.

"Yes, Julian, I'll gladly share a cab to Manhattan with you."

Matt felt uncomfortable. And not only because his long legs were cramped in the tiny space in the back of the black cab. Julian's close proximity was unnerving, his near-black eyes boring across at Matt, making him wish the American cabs were ordinary saloon models instead of vintage-style Mercedes where passengers sat facing each other. His smugness was overbearing, the tension in the air palpable, both passengers playing cat and mouse and diverting the conversation away from the real reason they'd jumped in the same cab: Heidi. But the long silences were even more unbearable than the stilted conversation – silences where Matt desperately wondered if he should take the plunge and tackle Julian head on about Heidi.

Hearing his phone ring was a welcome surprise for Matt. Taking it from his pocket, he presumed it was his mother returning his call. But seeing 'unknown number' instead of 'home' on his screen indicated something more promising. He held his breath and hoped.

"Hello?" His tone held caution, his greeting a warning to his caller that he was not alone. He trained his eyes on the window, watching the blur of New Jersey highways speeding past, keenly aware of the attention Julian was paying his every word.

"Matt? Are you okay?"

Hearing Heidi's voice on the line made his heart sing, caused his cheeks to flush and his stomach to knot. He forgot about the cramped space, concentrating only on the fact Heidi still cared enough to call. A lengthening pause came down the line. Matt imagined her waiting for his response, picturing her chewing on her lower lip or examining her nails with the phone balancing precariously between her ear and shoulder.

"Where are you now?" He kept his tone casual as he waited for detail. He couldn't wait to leave the stuffiness of the cab and breathe in fresh air, itching to ask the driver to detour and bring him to her right then. "I'll meet up with you."

"I can't. Not yet, Matt. I just wanted to check you're okay. I've been de–"

Before she'd finished the word, the line went dead, a loud tone beeping in Matt's ear. And his gut instinct was back with an opinion, screaming that it had been a deliberate disconnection and not one caused by insufficient credit or a weak signal.

He glanced across at Julian, his stomach somersaulting when he met his smug grin. Matt was careful about what he did next, knowing better than to underestimate his travelling companion. Returning his gaze to the blur of passing traffic, he kept the phone to his ear, nodding his head occasionally and pretending to be engrossed in what was being said on the other side. "Sure, I can do that . . . Of course I will . . . Me too . . . Consider it done!" He forced a laugh as he said goodbye to the imaginary caller and ended the call.

"Hooking up with a few mates while I'm here," he said, taking the phone away from his ear and lying to Julian's face. He kept the handset held tightly in his hand, Heidi's voice replaying over and over in his head. What had she been about to say when she'd disconnected? That she'd been *de*-layed? Hardly plausible, he thought, considering it had been two days since she'd left the apartment! What other words began with *de*? Mentally he scrambled through the letters of the alphabet, his face going a greyish shade of pale as he came to the letter *p*. *De-ported*? Is that what she was trying to tell him? Was she being accompanied back home? Is that how these things worked? Matt didn't know the first thing about deportation. It wasn't something he'd ever taken the trouble to find out, preferring to follow the legal access to the countries he'd visited. But Heidi's past wasn't something he'd paid too much attention to, the mysterious glint in her eye or cheeky grin distracting him anytime he'd broached the subject. And that included the number of worldwide destinations she'd already visited. Could she have had an altercation with the American authorities at some point? Surely not. She'd never have been allowed through Immigration if that was the case.

Feeling way in over his head, he exhaled deeply, bringing his gaze up to meet Julian's, their unspoken game of cat and mouse beginning to freak him out. He dropped the phone onto the black leather seat, clenching his fists tightly. The time had come for some straight talking.

"I need to know what's going on here, Julian."

Julian slipped a red band from his wrist and pulled his hair into a ponytail. Then he rubbed the palms of his hands along his thighs in a slow, annoying fashion.

"Not a lot going on that I can see," he drawled. "Two guys sharing a cab from the airport to Manhattan. Nothing strange about that in this town."

Matt leaned his hands on his knees, his body trembling, perspiration sticking his T-shirt to his body, the other man's coyness deeply frustrating. His mouth dried as he formulated the word 'Heidi' on his lips, knowing that once it was out there, it would be impossible to retract.

"I saw you leaving my apartment building on 7th Avenue two days ago," he said finally, biding his time for a short while longer, pursing his lips together, daring Julian to deny all knowledge.

Julian raised an eyebrow and shrugged. "Yeah? Well, 7th Avenue's a mighty long street. I go in and out of a lot of buildings in my line of business so you'll have to be a bit more specific, my friend."

Matt shuddered, recoiling inwardly. You're no friend of mine, he thought, glancing sideways at Julian's guitar case, wondering about his line of business. Serenading tenants? Or helping them disappear? His temple throbbed, the inside of his cheeks stinging where he was biting them in an effort to keep his mouth shut. Eventually, when they were nearing the hub of downtown Manhattan and his time in Julian's company was running out, he couldn't hold back any longer.

"Tell me about Heidi." Her name rolled from his lips, suspended in the air by the force of electricity released with it. There, he thought, I've said it. He wiped his sweaty palms on his jeans and waited for a reaction from his travelling companion.

Julian pulled his guitar case over to him, unclipped the metal clasps and took a twenty-dollar bill from the lining inside. He passed it across to Matt. "That should cover my part of the fare." He secured the clasps of his case once more and called to the driver. "Corner of the next block will do me!"

Matt seethed with rage, turning away from Julian and staring out the window, tilting his head to catch a glimpse of the famous viewing tower at the top of the Rockefeller Center.

"So what's the deal between you and Heidi then?" Julian asked.

Matt jerked his head around, glaring at Julian. "I could ask you the same."

"I think we've got two different girls, you and me," said Julian.

"Don't talk in riddles. Just give it to me straight." Matt turned to look out the window again, watching the pedestrian lights change from red to green and a flurry of people – bunching together like racehorses at the beginning of a steeplechase – charging across the street.

"We go way back."

The lights changed and the cab moved forward, then slowed to a crawl, inching towards the kerb on the next corner as per Julian's instructions.

Matt shrank into the seat and nodded his head. "And now?" His mouth went dry.

Julian leaned towards the driver. "Once more around the block, please."

Julian wasn't in any great hurry to enlighten Matt. And Matt, despite wanting to reach out and grab Julian and shake him until he finally imparted the truth, allowed him control.

As the cab crawled past Sach's on 5th Avenue, already halfway around the block by Matt's estimation, Julian took a credit-card wallet from his breast pocket, flicked through the insert plastic pockets and slid a folded photograph from inside. Wordlessly, he passed it across to Matt.

Matt's eyes narrowed, his hands shaking as he unfolded the tattered photograph. He could feel Julian watching him. Not wanting to give him the satisfaction of seeing him squirm, he tried to remain deadpan as he stared at the image before him. And was he sorry he did . . .

The photo of Heidi was incriminating, not to mention shocking. Matt's knees trembled, his head throbbed and he couldn't decide which he felt more – hurt or humiliated. Her lies and deceit – two things his parents had castigated all his life – stuck in his throat.

And now that he was facing a gigantic deception in the shape of a 6 x 4 photo print, he fully understood his parents' theory that, without truth and honesty, a relationship could only expect ultimate doom.

Grasping onto the matte print with both hands, he stared from the photograph to Julian and back again, his look questioning, his confusion evident. He studied it until his eyes blurred, taking in every detail, storing it in his confused mind, running his finger over the crinkled image as he tried to make sense of it.

A much younger Heidi beamed back at him, the white lace mini she wore clinging to her soft curves, the diamante tiara on her head glistening in the bright sunlight, soft auburn tendrils escaping onto her tanned skin. The boyish groom at her side seemed vaguely familiar. His arm loosely around her shoulders, he posed in a black tuxedo jacket, black trousers complete with purple cummerbund and an open-necked white fly-collared shirt.

"This wasn't taken today or yesterday! How long have you two known each other?" he asked Julian, without shifting his gaze from the snapshot.

"Quite some time as you can see," Julian responded.

"Where did this . . ." he pointed at the photo, jabbing the print with his finger, "where did this take place? And how come you've got Heidi's wedding photo?"

It was Julian's lopsided grin that brought Matt out in a cold sweat, forcing him to stare hard at the print and then study the man sitting opposite him. Comparing the dark-brown eyes, the Roman nose and dark hair colour, he finally recognised what was staring him in the face, or *who* was staring him in the face.

He looked up. "She married you?"

Matt was aghast, Julian amused.

"Yep, Mr and Mrs Ebbs. She didn't tell you, man?" He drew the outline of a heart on the fogged window with crossed Cupid's arrows dissecting it in four.

Matt swallowed his irritation, moving about in the seat, awkward and uncomfortable, gullible and foolish. He offered the photo to Julian.

"I've got a whole bunch of them. You keep it," Julian told him, erasing his artwork with the sleeve of his shirt.

Matt folded the photo back into four. "Are you still married?"

"That's Heidi's story to tell."

"But you do know where she is?"

Julian shrugged non-commitally.

Matt blew out a breath, struggling to remain calm. "Did she actually take the flight to Boston? Why's she playing games? Hurting people?"

Julian snorted loudly. "The only person Heidi's capable of hurting is herself – her own worst enemy."

"Please tell me where she is. Is she safe?" Matt struggled to contain his growing concern. And his growing anger. Is this guy trustworthy, he wondered? Then again, Heidi married him so she obviously thought so.

Matt's mind was on overdrive. If he gave into his frustration and lashed out at Julian, what then? He'd be severing his only link with Heidi, his only hope of finding her. If she chose to be found.

"Heidi's . . . let's just say she's complicated," Julian told him. "She's dealing with some personal issues right now." He tapped the side of his guitar case, beating out a gentle rhythm in time to the music playing on the car radio.

Matt needed fresh air, to be on his own to try and work things out. Though he was still quite a walk from his apartment, he asked the cab driver to stop, the smug way Julian had drip-fed him information firing him up inside, sullying the relationship he'd believed he'd shared with Heidi.

"At least tell me whether she's still in New York?" was his final question before he stepped out of the cab.

Julian stretched his legs into the space Matt left. "What does it matter? She's safe. Trust me."

"Trust you? I don't even know you!"

"She wants space. You know what she's like."

But that was just it – Matt wasn't sure he did know any more. Paying the cab driver his share of the fare, he banged the door as hard as he could, Julian's scornful "Have a nice day now!" ringing in his ears. How he wished his guitar fingers were caught in the jamb.

Chapter 16

"Are you sure you don't want me to come with you, Lucy?" Delia asked as she came to a stop outside Carol's door.

Lucy shook her head. She wanted to collect her car before visiting Sycamore Lodge, a visit she was intent on making without her mother being present.

Delia's hands were tied. Convincing Gloria to wait elsewhere while the sisters surveyed the damage was as likely as getting her mother to keep her opinions to herself. Having very little choice in the matter, she finally relented. But not before offering her final words of caution. "Be careful, Luce," she warned. "It may not be safe inside."

"I'll wear Danny's work boots and hard hat. They're usually in the garage – which is still standing as far as I know."

"And you're sure you'll be able to gain access to the house?" Delia braked gently and brought the car to a stop as near Carol's front door as she possibly could.

"Around the back is my best option. From what Inspector O'Brien told me, that part of the house is still relatively intact."

"Is that the same fellow who wants you to make a statement?" Gloria asked in clipped tones from the back seat. She was still furious that Lucy had forbidden her to go anywhere near the scene of the fire. All this commotion about health and safety, she thought, staring at the back of her daughter's head and willing herself not to give her a good shake!

"Immediately after I've seen the house, I'm going straight to the Garda Station." Lucy's tone was even, despite the resentment intensifying inside. Pulling the lever with more force than necessary, she pushed open the door and stared out at the cobbled driveway.

Gloria was in no mood to placate her daughter. "You can be strolling around looking at the damage when you've all your business attended to. It's about time you got your priorities in order and got the legalities dealt with first."

"Mum, will you give me a break? Please?" Lucy clenched her fists tightly, wincing in pain as her nails dug into the palms of her hands.

"A break? The time for breaks is well and truly over. Has an assessor been out yet? I presume you have reported it?"

Unable to listen to any more of her mother's sarcastic drivel, Delia spun around in her seat and glared at her, her face turning puce, her eyes narrowing. "Leave Lucy alone. She's not a child and knows exactly what she needs to do. I don't suppose it's crossed your mind that she's had more important things on her mind up to now? Like her critically ill husband, for example?" She pressed heavily on the accelerator pedal, drowning Gloria's curt response in the engine's roar. "Go on, Lucy, you've things to do," she said, giving her a gentle push on the arm, encouraging her to step out of the car.

Lucy's stomach convulsed in a tight knot of tension. On the one hand, she cursed her mother but, on the other, she had to admit that for a seventy-five-year-old battle-axe, she had her wits about her and seemed to know a lot more about procedure than Lucy would have given her credit for. Unable for any more advice, she said goodbye and stepped out of the car, breathing a heavy sigh of relief to be escaping the wrath of her mother's tongue.

Gloria sniffed loudly, her annoyance palpable in the close environs of Delia's Honda Civic. She had, however (possibly because of the anger glinting in Delia's green eyes), the grace to keep her mouth shut apart from grunting goodbye to Lucy and refusing Delia's offer to move into the front.

As the car pulled out of sight, Lucy's eyes wandered in the direction of Sycamore Lodge, her view of the house obliterated by mature trees. Her heart raced, every beat pounding in her eardrums, thumping like pins and needles in her fingers and toes as she stared at the only glimpse of her house she could see, the chimneypots. But at least it confirmed the house was still standing. Other than that . . . she'd soon find out.

Dragging her gaze away, she turned and rang the doorbell, hoping as she waited that it would be Carol who answered the door and not her husband, Eric. Something about Eric made her uncomfortable, uncomfortable enough to avoid being in his company. Apart from the fact he was filthy rich and had no problem splashing it about,

Lucy couldn't say she knew much about him. Or wanted to.

He put business Danny's way on occasion and though Danny wasn't one to talk about people – took very little interest in what was going on in any house other than his own – there had been instances down through the years where he'd passed comment about Eric. In Danny's opinion, given the opportunity, Eric would have stepped over his own mother to make a fast buck.

Both neighbours were involved in the property business, Danny at the coalface of construction and Eric – once a stone-mason employing a couple of apprentices – now dressing in designer suits and buying, renovating and selling large-scale developments.

But while Danny's business had expanded at a manageable rate, Eric, in a greedy attempt to surpass his competitors, had taken on enormous projects that turned out to be too large to either manage or complete. Overstretching himself, he cut costs, replaced hard-working Irish workers with non-nationals and took advantage of their gratitude by paying them a rate far below the average wage. Unsurprisingly, he was often without staff on Monday mornings and as a result his contracts ran over time and over budget. His reputation and credibility amongst customers, suppliers and sub-contractors was somewhat suspect and as time passed and his debts mounted, Eric found it increasingly difficult to secure even meagre contracts in the environs.

While the majority of construction firms were enjoying profitable times in Ireland, Eric found himself in increasing financial difficulty. Left with little choice but to expand his business interests to foreign shores in an attempt to try and recoup significant losses, he ignored all the economic warnings, considering himself invincible and powerful enough to withstand the downturn.

Recently, he'd approached Danny to invest in condominiums in St Petersburg, Florida, guaranteed (according to Eric) to make a quick profit. But Danny, already after scaling back to suit the economic air, had no desire to risk what he'd spent years building and turned him down flat. Without elaborating or explaining why, he'd given Eric a polite but firm refusal, declining to discuss the matter any further or give in to his neighbour's whining that he'd live to regret it.

Carol's nerves were tightly wrung, the sound of a car's tyres crunching on the gravel outside her home sending a shiver through her. Could that be the bailiffs now, she wondered, dashing to try and find clothes to put on. She struggled to get into the jeans she'd discarded the night before, then dashing into her walk-in-wardrobe and ignoring the wealth of fabulous designer outfits, she grabbed the first fleece sweater in sight and pulled it over her head. As she dragged a comb through her hair, the doorbell reverberated in the otherwise still house. Carol swallowed her fear, steeling herself for a battle as she clutched the handrail on the staircase and padded soundlessly down on the plush cream carpet. She went to the window and peered through the wooden venetian blinds, vowing she'd have to be pulled kicking and screaming from the house before she'd walk away from her life's dream.

The door still hadn't been answered. Lucy was on the verge of walking away when a movement from inside the window halted her in her tracks. Why is Carol peeping through the venetian blinds, she wondered, unsure whether she should stay or go. But then she heard the distinct sound of a key being turned in the heavy oak door.

"Lucy, thank God it's you!" Carol's eyes darted around the driveway and front lawn before finally giving her neighbour her full attention.

Lucy had never seen her act in such a suspicious fashion before. "Are you expecting somebody? I'm not disturbing something, am I?"

"Far from it." Carol's tone was grave. She gave a cursory glance at her watch, dithering over what she should do. There was still the matter of organising somewhere to store whatever she could move from the house. But what about Lucy? She couldn't turn her away from the doorstep. Not when she must have the weight of the world on her shoulders. And not now when Carol herself didn't want to be alone. "Come inside. You'll get your death out here."

Lucy nodded and followed her in, glancing at the wall of black and white portraits as she walked through the large expanse of marble hallway, Carol's family captured in their most flattering poses. But their smiling faces made Lucy's heart sink even lower. Her family photos, more of the home-grown type than expensive professional, adorned the walls of Sycamore Lodge's hallway. And the lounge. And the bedrooms. And funny ones of the boys were stuck behind magnets on the fridge – were they shrivelled at the corners and scorched through? Had the photos fallen from the walls and shattered, the captured moments lost forever? Either way, she doubted very much they'd survived. Years of memories, a family's entire past, something they could never recapture. Gone. Her chest rose and fell. She bit hard on her bottom lip to stop it trembling, a wave of loneliness flooding over her.

"How's Danny today? Delia hadn't much news last night."

Carol's question snapped Lucy out of her reverie. She turned to face her. "A long road ahead for him. But at least he opened his eyes and spoke to me this morning. Not sure how long a full recovery will take though."

Carol reached out and took Lucy's hands, squeezing them tightly. "You don't deserve this misfortune. Neither of you."

"Carol, thank you from the bottom of my heart for making that call when you did. I dread to think what might have happened if you hadn't spotted the smoke . . ." Lucy's voice broke. She was unable to go on. She gently withdrew her hands from Carol's grip and rooted in her pocket for a tissue to mop her eyes.

"How I wish I could have done more. Watching it blazing like that, I felt utterly helpless." Carol wiped imaginary dust from the back of the chaise longue, knowing she should be dealing with her own problems and not wasting time. But how could she turn her back on Lucy?

"You did everything possible. And I keep telling myself things could be so much worse . . ."

"Have you told Stephen and Matt yet?"

"God no! They'd be on the next flights home. And for what? It's not as if they can rebuild the house or anything, both of them in 'white-collar' jobs as Danny says." Recalling how he'd mercilessly teased the boys about avoiding 'real work' brought a smile to her face.

"Still, it must be hard on you being alone when –" Carol stopped abruptly, holding her breath a moment to listen. She was convinced she'd heard a car pulling up outside and was light-headed with relief when she realised it was nothing but her overactive imagination.

Snapping out of her self-absorbent state, Lucy couldn't any longer ignore the other woman's pallor or how distracted she appeared. Her hair was unkempt, her jeans looked as though she'd slept in them the night before and her fleece like something from the previous decade! Carol Black seldom wore anything from the previous *season*, never mind the previous decade!

"Carol. . . you don't seem yourself. Is there something wrong?"

It was Lucy's turn to reach out, her suspicions confirmed when Carol nodded and accepted her hug.

With a sigh, Carol led the way into the light-filled modern kitchen where purple units adorned one wall and an enormous island unit commanded centre stage in the middle of the floor.

"Coffee?" she enquired, ignoring the pot she'd made earlier and taking a jar of Nescafé instant from one of her pull-out larder units.

Lucy took a seat on a high stool and watched, bemused. In this house, she'd never been offered anything less than rich roast beans from the percolator or frothy cappuccinos. She flinched at the sound of earthenware banging against the granite counter top, watching as Carol dropped one of the mugs she'd been holding (now with a large chip out of the rim) into the dustbin, moving zombie-like to the glass unit to get another.

Lucy got to her feet. "What on earth's happened?"

She took the mugs from her friend and proceeded to make their coffee, surprised when Carol flopped onto a stool and didn't put up any resistance.

Carol rested her hands on her lap and stared into space. The pendulum on the bronze wall-clock swung backward and forward, a droning sound she'd seldom registered in the past.

As Lucy placed a mug of coffee before Carol and sat down across from her, her imagination was running riot. She stabbed guesses at the reasons behind Carol's frightening demeanour. For the briefest interval she put aside the fact that Danny was lying seriously ill in hospital, that their house was a shell of what it used to be, that she had nowhere to live and was being summoned by the gardaí to explain why. Instead, she gave her full attention to her friend.

"I'm terrified, Lucy. I don't know what I'm going to do. We're way worse off than you and Danny now." Carol wrapped both her hands around her coffee mug, savouring the heat.

Lucy's head shot up. Carol's voice was little more than a whisper, her announcement difficult to believe. What on earth could be worse than having your house burn down with your husband inside when you'd forgotten to renew the premium? Could Carol be ill? Had she discovered that Eric was cheating on her? Or worse still, leaving her? Maybe it was one of her daughters? Pregnant? Sick? Involved with drugs? But Lucy kept all these questions tightly locked in her head, the only word escaping her lips being "Oh!"

"The banks are going to take it all. House, cars, jewellery – everything we own." Carol stopped a moment, correcting her previous sentence. "Actually, make that everything we *used* to own."

"How? I don't understand. They can't just throw you out on the streets without warning, can they?" The words tripped from Lucy's mouth. Looking around her at the perfect setting – everything intact, not one item out of place apart from the open jar of Nescafé sitting on the counter where she'd left it – she felt a sense of unreality.

Carol placed the mug on the counter, smearing a dribble of milk with her finger until the white liquid expanded into swirls. "Eric must have known how close to the edge he was playing." She pushed her hair behind her ears and for the first time looked directly at Lucy. "Where on earth will we end up?"

Lucy sprang into action, finding inner strength to help when she recognised that Carol was on the verge of meltdown and too weak to sustain herself. "Where is Eric? Why isn't he here dealing with this?"

"He's at Tampa airport." Carol felt as though she were telling tales out of school.

"When is he due back?" Lucy asked.

"I organised an emergency ticket for him to fly back tomorrow. But I can't get in touch with him." She pulled at a loose thread on her fleece.

Lucy was getting more confused by the second. "I'm not with you. Why on earth did you have to organise his ticket? Didn't he have a return flight booked?"

"I don't know. But he rang in a panic on Saturday evening, telling me to book a flight asap and to pay in cash. He wanted it immediately but I couldn't get an earlier flight. I got all this information in a voicemail."

Jumping from the stool, Carol hurried into the hall to retrieve her mobile phone. The pile of letters she'd dropped on the table seemed to stare up at her. She was tempted to rip them open. Did they hold any answers? Her heart thumped loudly, her fingers sliding over the window of an envelope. What difference would it make now? Grabbing the phone, she walked away.

The two distraught women listened to Eric's plea for help, looking at each other askance, processing the information as best they could. In the space of one weekend, they'd both lost their homes and in a manner of speaking, the support of their husbands. It seemed the responsibility to get through this horrific time lay firmly on their shoulders. It was down to them now. What would it take to get it all back? Or was it gone for good? It was far too soon to speculate.

Before the neighbours could cross the line into each other's affairs, there was an underlying issue hanging in the air between them. Lucy took a sharp intake of breath before broaching the delicate subject. "Danny and Eric . . ." she began, but didn't finish. She didn't have to. Their husbands' mutual dislike for each other was no secret but this was the first time it was acknowledged openly between their wives. Up to now, they'd kept up a pretence.

Carol nodded. "They must never know."

Lucy smiled at her new ally, raised her mug in the air and drained what was left of her tepid coffee to seal the deal, grimacing at its vile taste. "Now, how can I help?"

Carol looked about her house, her eyes travelling slowly around her belongings, mulling over her neighbour's offer. But she didn't want to be too forward, wanted Lucy to offer instead of her having to ask.

Lucy caught her drift and thought quickly. "You pack as many of your valuables as you can while I go across and face my ordeal. Then I'll move what I can of your stuff with Danny's van before making the dreaded statement to the gardaí."

"Have you somewhere I can store it? Somewhere safe?"

"Leave that to me," Lucy said with a lot more conviction than she felt. Although, as the idea took hold in her brain, she decided she might not be taking on the impossible after all. Danny had a number of lock-up containers for work materials, many of them empty since he'd scaled things down.

Carol ran a hand through her hair. "They'll probably take my car too . . ."

Lucy had a solution for that too. "Is it financed?"

The other woman shook her head. "I don't suppose . . . oh never mind, it's stupid."

"What, Carol? Don't be afraid to ask me anything. I owe you, remember?" She reached out and caught the other woman's hand.

"If the ownership was transferred into your name, they wouldn't have any right to take it. Maybe we could backdate the change of ownership . . ." She allowed her voice to trail off, letting her suggestion hang in the air.

Lucy listened with interest. "I don't see why not. At least then you'd be able to get around. And it could be ages before you'd afford another one the way things are now."

Carol appeared uncertain. "I suppose . . . but only if you're sure? Don't feel I'm pressurising you. You've enough to look after without carrying my problems as well."

"Bah, it's always much easier to help others. Your keys, please?" Lucy demanded, anxious not to waste any more time.

Carol shook her head and smiled, letting out a long sigh. "You'll get us both arrested! But hell, I'm willing if you are. We can share a cell if it comes to it."

"I'll lock it in our garage until we've got the paperwork completed and in the post. It'll be out of sight there. Providing it's a fire-free zone, of course," she added quickly.

"I would never have described you as devious, Lucy Ardle." Carol removed the Audi key from a large bunch and tossed it to her.

"Don't think I've had reason before," Lucy shrugged, cupping her hands and catching the key. "Now how much time do you think we have?"

"No idea."

"Get what you can ready to move out of the house. Time may not be on our side. And root out the change of ownership form for the car. We'll get it signed and sent off as quickly as possible."

"Oh, I just remembered, Lucy – your handbag – just one sec and I'll get it for you."

Carol retrieved the bag and, giving her a quick hug, Lucy left the house, the bravado she'd been brandishing on her neighbour's behalf fading like the winter daylight as she crossed the short distance to Sycamore Lodge and came face to face with her own nightmare.

Chapter 17

Lucy had stalled the Audi at the entrance gates, staring in horror and dismay at what had once been her beautiful home. Thinking she was prepared had been a gigantic underestimation on her behalf. Gripping the steering wheel, she tried to fight against the tremors threatening to take hold of her. In the cold light of day, it looked as if guerrilla fighters had attacked from all angles. And not just the house itself. The driveway and garden were equally dishevelled, rubble and debris everywhere, tyre tracks on the lawn she'd taken such pride in maintaining. Becoming increasingly nauseous, she turned the ignition again, inching the car inside the pillars and around the back of the house where it was out of view. In a trancelike state, she stepped out of the vehicle and promptly threw up.

The rain that had begun to fall the previous Saturday evening had continued sporadically through the night and into Sunday. Though it had no doubt assisted the fire brigade as they fought to control the flames, it had also helped extend black soot, smuts and debris in every conceivable direction around the house.

Lucy treaded her way around to the front of the house once more, anxious to get a closer view. Where the footpath ended and the driveway began was impossible to decipher. Pieces of scorched wood from the Tudor framework lay shattered on the ground, black smut covering multiple surfaces. The exterior paintwork was covered in black scorch-marks and smoke discoloration, one particularly ugly mark defacing the whole left-hand side of the house.

Lucy stood gawping, the lingering smell of smoke and dampness clinging to her nostrils. She shuddered as the dank atmosphere enveloped her, her body cold and lifeless, and her heart like stone. The front of the house resembled the set of a haunted house, the glass in the windows shattered. The windows in the lounge had miraculously survived, saved no doubt by the extra durable glass Danny had installed after Matt hurled a *sliotar* through the original panes. Glancing higher still, the slates on the roof appeared intact, but the PVC fascia, soffit and guttering had melted from the intense heat, lying warped and beaten in parts. Instead of running evenly around the house and down the walls as was intended, it hung on for dear life. There was no way it'd survive a flock of birds descending on it as was so often the case!

She moved a little nearer, shaking her feet to rid her shoes of congealed soot. Her bedroom curtains flapped through the smashed windowpane, her heart aching as she watched what had been a beautiful red and gold linen mix. They'd been ripped to shreds, their rich colour no longer decipherable.

She'd dithered for ages before ordering them, guilty because the complete order, including pelmet and tie-backs, was extravagantly priced, pushing her way over budget. But, she'd reasoned with herself as she'd fingered the luxurious material in the shop, they should last for years. Huh! They'd been hanging for little over a month. And now, as she stared at the sorry mess, she noticed that the expensive brass curtain-pole had disengaged on one side, hanging precariously across the window and – like the guttering – was clinging on for dear life.

Side-stepping a large piece of glass, she continued along the driveway toward the back of the house once more, disappointed the gable windows had shattered too, all hopes she'd harboured that the fire had been contained to only one part of the house long since dashed.

She unlocked the garage door and walked back to get Carol's car, parking it in the double garage beside Danny's van. At least the Audi was safe from harm, she thought, pressing the remote control and locking the car doors. Handling her neighbour's problems was easier than managing her own. Finding a hard hat and pushing her feet into a pair of Danny's steel toecap boots, she pressed the button to close the garage door. But nothing happened. There was no electricity. Flicking the switch to manual control, she stretched as far as she could to reach the roller door and pull it to the ground.

As it turned out, she didn't need to use her house keys. The back door was unlocked, even though she'd been certain she'd locked it when she'd left on Saturday afternoon. No doubt the firemen had opened it – or

Danny himself at some point. She gingerly stepped inside, her nostrils assailed by the stench of smoke. She was tempted to turn on her heel, Danny's expected wrath the only thing forcing her to stay. Taking a shrivelled tissue from her pocket, she used it to cover her mouth as best she could. But it would take a lot more than a tissue to mask the disgusting fumes threatening to make her gag.

She stared around the utility room, her eyes following the trail of heat that had wormed its way around the room, silently attacking the surfaces it came in contact with. The plastic air vents were shrivelled, the trim underneath the wall presses melted and warped. The light switches and plug sockets were discoloured and distorted into shapeless lumps of plastic.

Proceeding to the kitchen, her greatest fears were realised. She walked around her table and chairs, tears in her eyes as she remembered years of family meals, thousands of morning coffees and afternoons of supervising homework. Now it was barely recognisable, disguised in a mixture of dust and dirt, with sweeping scorch-marks tarnishing the surface. She ran a hand along the electrical appliances, stooping down to take a closer look, cringing as she took in the smoky yellow shades on the doors. The hob and oven had escaped the worst damage, their heat resistance protecting them. Poor consolation, Lucy thought, dreading to imagine how long it would be before she'd ever pop a casserole dish in the oven again.

She moved to the large wooden dresser, standing and staring fixedly at it, an ache in her heart as she gazed at the collection of trinkets – her heart breaking in two. Their sentimentality proved to be her undoing. The souvenir items perched on top were barely recognisable, her favourite ornaments and silverware a sorry mess. She picked up one of her treasured photographs, heaving rasping sobs when it disintegrated in her hands. Clenching her fists until her knuckles whitened, she turned away from the dresser, rage and hurt fighting for space in her heart. What she'd lost was irreplaceable.

Taking the two steps into the lower-level living area, her feet awkward in Danny's oversized boots, Lucy's jaw dropped as she scanned the room before her. Without a doubt, it was the worst she'd seen so far.

The floor was obliterated under a pile of rubble, the fallout from the large gaping hole in the ceiling. Sheets of blistered plasterwork peeled from the walls like angry burnt skin. The intensity of heat in the room overhead had caused the ceiling to collapse, destroying everything it came in contact with.

She flopped onto the lower step, beyond caring that she was sitting on a blanket of black ash. Owning a home like Sycamore Lodge was something she would never take for granted again. It had never once crossed her mind that it could be taken away from her. Carol's predicament entered her mind. She imagined her over the road, scrambling around the house taking rooms apart, filling suitcases and containers as quickly as she could. Lucy looked around her, picking up a handful of ash and allowing it to fall through her fingers. Not much to gather here, she thought wryly, glancing around her at the filthy mess.

She got to her feet once more, stepping over fallen beams, no longer covering her mouth from the toxic stench of smoke and the stale air hovering in the house.

Cinders and ashes crunched underfoot. She stared at the couch (what was left of it) where Danny had lain fast asleep, his escape miraculous. A small part of her had expected to see her mobile phone melted on the seat. But all that was left of the three-seater were the wire coils, the matching armchairs faring just as badly. In the corner of the room, the television had melted, the wooden table underneath no longer recognisable. The marble fireplace was in one piece. And she was glad her precious oak floor was hidden under the rubble and fallen beams. Her attention was drawn to a hairline crack in the chimney wall. She took a deep breath and ventured into the hallway.

The fuse box, a melted lump of plastic, had fallen to the floor. The wooden handrail on the staircase had disengaged, what was left of it scorched through. She couldn't make out the pattern on the stair carpet as she walked up the steps, the oversized boots on her feet threatening to trip her up. She clung to the wall, terrified of losing her balance in the absence of a handrail. As she stepped on to the top step, a few of the spindles gave way and fell to the floor, her weight on the stairs not helping. She turned and looked down, sorely tempted to retreat.

The landing, as she'd expected, was high-risk, the floor, walls, doors and ceiling black and discoloured. She crossed the landing to her own bedroom, wanting to get the worst over with.

Lucy couldn't hold back the sob in her throat. Their bed – like the sofa downstairs – was unrecognisable, the ornate light-fitting smashed on the floor, the electric cable hanging limply (and no doubt dangerously) from the ceiling. Is there electricity, she wondered, about to flip the light switch but thinking better of it for fear of electrocuting herself, then realising the firemen would have turned it off as a priority.

In the centre of the floor the huge hole gaped and sagged where it had fallen through to the living-room below. Glancing towards her walk-in wardrobe at the far side of the room, she dared to hope. The door was burnt and blistered. But it was firmly shut. Lucy held her breath a moment, daring to hope that what was on the other side of the door had survived. And it wasn't her clothes she was concerned about but the hatbox on the top shelf, her pathetic excuse for a filing system. There was only one way to find out.

She slipped the bulky boots from her feet, leaving them outside the door. Then edging her way along the wall, she kept as far away from the hole in the floor as was physically possible, ignoring the voice of reason in her head that told her the boards under her feet were probably brittle as matchsticks.

Inching her way towards the wardrobe, the flapping curtains in the rising breeze reminded her of a scene from a Betty Davis horror movie. Only a few more steps, she thought, concentrating on the door handle. But then a squawking bird flew through the broken window. Lucy screamed louder than the bird, his untimely entrance making her jump in fright. She lost her footing, the floor creaking underneath her, slithers of wood falling through the hole and into the living area below.

She froze to the spot, afraid to move a muscle in case the slightest movement caused the rest of the floor to give way. She was only a couple of steps away from the wardrobe door. Giving a quick glance behind her, she was horrified to see so much more of the floor had fallen away. Goddamn bird, she thought, convinced the next shudder or vibration would leave the floor impassable.

She leaned against the wall, waiting for her breathing to return to normal. The last thing we need, she thought, is for me to fall through the floor and end up in hospital beside Danny. The hatbox will have to wait.

Her gaze travelled slowly around the room once more, noting that the door to Danny's adjoining office was burnt through. She daren't stretch to get a better glimpse inside. Carefully retracing her steps, she stepped back into her safety boots and went to check the three bedrooms at the back of the house, the stench of smoke overpowering. But at least there was one consolation: there weren't any more holes in the floor!

Gingerly, she went back downstairs, extremely relieved to get her feet (and the blooming boots that were several sizes too big for her) back on solid ground. Peeping into the lounge – the room where Matt had spent hours strumming guitars with his friends – she noticed that like the other rooms on that side of the house, it had escaped the worst of the damage.

Beyond caring about the filthy surfaces, she sat down on the ottoman for a moment, her mind wandering back to Christmas mornings when the boys were up before dawn, echoes of fun and excitement filling the room as they ripped open Santa presents and screamed at the tops of their voices when Santa had yet again worked his annual magic and located everything on their list and more!

Reluctantly ending her trip down memory lane, she

remembered her promise to Carol. It was time she left. She took the keys of Danny's van from the key rack in the utility room, making sure to lock the back door as she left. Leaving the hard hat back in the garage and changing back into her ankle boots, she opened the door of Danny's Ford Transit van and took the keys of the lock-up containers from their hiding-place over the sun visor.

Sneezing and snorting, trying to clear her nostrils of smoke, she walked in the fading light to where the four lock-ups were stored, screened from the acre-sized garden by thick hedging. She hoped there was one vacant so Carol's belongings could be kept together. As it turned out, finding an empty container was easy, as every lock-up was vacant, a hollow echo inside, their floors swept clean. There were no materials and no tools, none of the usual scaffolding poles, wheelbarrows or ladders that normally filled the space. It was as if Ardle Construction had never existed.

Lucy ran back to the garage, yanking open the back doors of the van to check inside, holding her breath as her eyes became accustomed to the dark interior. It hadn't been cleared out as such, not if you included a screwed-up ball of tinfoil and a half empty bottle of Coke: the remnants of Danny's lunch thrown carelessly on the floor.

Reaching inside, she caught the tinfoil and bottle and flung them as far down the lawn as she possibly could, banging the van door shut afterwards. She fought with all her might to push away the idea that Danny could be as deceitful as Eric. But the evidence in front of her was something she couldn't ignore. Empty containers. An empty van. And their main asset burnt sufficiently to quantify a healthy insurance payout.

Waiting for her heartbeat to return to normal, she leaned against the side of the van, the Ardle Construction logo mocking her, the thought of an insurance claim (or non-insurance claim if her suspicions were correct) bringing her out in a cold sweat.

When Danny had parked the van in the garage on Saturday, he'd specifically told her he'd got everything organised for Monday. But what on earth had he organised? What exactly had he meant by that statement? A parking spot for an empty van?

And what about the fire? Oh God, she thought, bending her head, nausea washing over her, bile rising in her throat once more as questions flooded through her mind. Had Danny set fire to the house to pull an insurance scam? Is that what was going on here? He was afraid to tell her the company had folded so he did a job on the house instead? Waiting until the boys were both safely out of the way so it would be less complicated? What kind of men have Carol and I married, she wondered? And what kind of women does it make us that they were unable to confide in their wives?

Lucy sat into the van and reversed around to the front of the house, then accelerated and shot out of the driveway faster than she'd ever done before. She'd keep her promise to her neighbour and after she'd done what she could to help her, she was going straight up to the hospital to question Danny and find out what the hell was going on. There was no way she could give a statement to the gardaí until she knew the extent of her husband's involvement. They'd have to wait a while longer for their pound of flesh.

The shame of being homeless was one thing, but the shame associated with arson was an entirely different matter. They'd be a laughing stock, their good name and reputation ruined forever if evidence suggested Danny's involvement. She parked as near to Carol's conservatory as possible, the level surface and extra-wide French doors making it the ideal exit for her precious belongings.

For the next two hours in the gathering dark, Lucy moved on automatic pilot, lifting and carrying, jumping in and out of the van and driving over and back to Sycamore Lodge with Carol to unload and reload as quickly as they possibly could. She struggled with each item, balancing it in her arms, fighting the urge to give into exhaustion and collapse on the ground and cry.

Out of nowhere, as she struggled with two of Carol's suitcases, she was reminded of the promise she'd made Delia to get on with her life now the boys were moving on with theirs. Little had she known as she'd uttered those vows, that getting on with her life would include reducing Carol's six-bedroom mansion to an empty shell and confronting Danny with the suspicion of arson.

Chapter 18

Carol gulped a pint of water down in one long draught. She was exhausted from lifting and carrying, physical exertion alien to her apart from her weekly Pilates classes and leisurely game of tennis doubles with girlfriends who, like her, spent more time chatting between serves than actually hitting the ball over the net.

Waiting for Lucy to return from Sycamore Lodge, she'd worked robotically to get the most important things packed up, hurrying around the house making split-second decisions on what she could or couldn't live without. Unexpected adrenalin had surged through her body, providing her with the strength to cope with all that was being thrown at her.

Then Lucy's no-nonsense attitude had focused her mind further, the two of them working flat out and not speaking much, until as much of her belongings as they could manage to fit in (or carry between them) were stacked up in Lucy's containers.

But now, as she waited for Lucy who was having a shower upstairs, she was unsure what she should do next.

In dire need of an expert opinion, she picked up the phone and called their solicitor, her heart and hope sinking further when he conveyed a true picture and confirmed her worst fears.

"There are a lot of outstanding documents due back from overseas deals he's negotiated lately, Carol, but nothing to improve the situation unfortunately. If anything, they'll add to an already disastrous portfolio of bad debts."

"And you can't do anything to halt the repossession?" She was willing to beg if she thought it would do any good, although privately relieved that he couldn't see the shame and humiliation on her face. His revelation left her with limited options.

In true legal-speak, Jacob didn't spare her feelings. "Not now, I'm afraid. There's nothing left to salvage. Eric wouldn't listen to my advice. He refused to respond to the warning letters and failed to present himself at court appearances. He stubbornly ploughed ahead despite all caution, putting any good collateral he'd gained against impossible risks and forfeiting anything that had the slightest chance of recovery. Like a gambler, he chased bad debts, frantically raising more capital to invest in the falling stock exchange, trying to recoup his losses."

Carol's anger with Eric drowned in her pool of despair, the only question she could think to ask dying on her lips. What financial institution had released further capital to Eric? Who on earth had made it possible for him to dig the gorge they were sinking in? She didn't need any more detail, concluding from her limited knowledge of these affairs that it could only be a subprime lending institution, the type that charged disgustingly high interest rates. The picture their solicitor had painted was stark, any hope of a period of stay hopeless.

"Thank you, Jacob," she said with as much dignity as she could muster. "I'm sure Eric will be in touch when he returns."

She dropped the phone into its cradle, knowing that if she'd been in the house alone she'd have fired it against the wall, beyond caring about material things that would soon be the property of the bank anyway. By the sound of it, Eric had gambled every item they owned and more. She shook her head, feeling as though she were in the middle of a dream, with every dreadful detail being inflicted on somebody else while she watched the drama unfold from a place where she could never be harmed. It was but another in a lengthy list of disappointments Eric had delivered to her.

However, some years before, she'd acted on her dead mother's advice and stuffed a hidden card up her sleeve, a card Eric knew nothing about. And just as well.

"Lucy!" she called up the stairs. "If I've forgotten to leave any clothes out for you, please help yourself! Don't hold back."

Lucy came down the stairs wearing a knee-length soft tweed dress and black opaque tights, both of them belonging to Carol, with a number of other items folded over her arm. Her clothes – already grubby after wearing them for three days – had been in an even worse state after the furniture removal. Carol had ignored her protestations that Delia would lend her some clothes, insisting she take a hot shower and borrow as many outfits as she needed to tide her over until she got herself back on her feet. And considering Delia was at least four inches shorter – and possibly two inches wider – than Lucy, borrowing from Carol was a much more practical idea.

"Lucky for me, we're around the same size. These are a great fit, thank you," she said. She slipped her feet into her ankle boots, wishing she was a delicate size five like Carol. Then she wouldn't be sinking her feet into mucky black boots that did absolutely nothing to complement the outfit she was wearing.

"I feel like a bum taking all these," she said.

Carol had left a whole wardrobe of clothes behind, mostly garments she hadn't worn in a while, things she was only too happy to pass on to Lucy. "Well, that makes two of us! You've been a lifesaver today, allowing me to practically re-house everything over at yours. I hope you've taken a jacket. It's icy out there now and it's starting to spit rain."

"I took this black mac," she said, pulling on the belt that was hanging from her bundle.

"Good. At least I'm repaying the favour in some small way."

"Helping you took my mind off my own problems to be honest," Lucy admitted, "but unfortunately those problems are still waiting for me. So," she asked, taking her keys from the bottom step of the stairs, the hall table now in one of the lock-ups in Lucy's back garden, "any joy in tracking Eric down at the airport?"

Carol shook her head. "Tampa Airport was a pure waste of a phone call. No response, no matter how many times the telephonist paged him."

"What about trying his mobile again? He might have managed to charge it somehow."

"Dead as a doornail." She leaned her head against the newel post, overcome with exhaustion. "Where will it end, Lucy? What will become of us?"

"No idea, Carol. I wish I could answer you. All we can do is remain a step ahead, deal with every eventuality as best we can. And of course be there to help each other through." Lucy was convinced they'd only seen the tip of the iceberg and there were worse nightmares coming their way, but didn't see the point in upsetting her neighbour any further. She had enough on her plate.

"Speaking of helping one another," Carol said, taking an addressed envelope from her pocket and handing it to Lucy, "can you sign your part of this change-of-ownership form and pop it in the post for me, please?"

Lucy nodded, giving a last look around Carol's home, the open doors allowing her a glimpse inside the dining room and lounge, the absence of ornate sculptures and hanging artwork stripping both rooms of character. They'd made a slight dent in moving the furniture and now – amidst bare walls and partially furnished rooms – what remained looked out of place and forlorn.

"Will you be okay alone?" Lucy asked, before stepping out into the soft rain.

Carol stood in the doorway of her magnificent home, folded her arms tightly across her chest and nodded her head. "Like a skipper and his sinking ship, I'll be the last to leave."

Chapter 19

Heidi sat cross-legged on a threadbare mat on the basement floor, practising the breathing exercises she'd learned at Yoga classes. Mastering the technique of deep inhalation and slow exhalation had taken quite an amount of training but her determined effort had saved her from the worst of her panic attacks, attacks that had cost her a significant portion of her life. For the most part now she managed to control them, but hadn't yet succeeded in extinguishing them entirely.

She leaned her upper body over her knees, stretching her arms as far as she could in front of her. Matt's confused tone floated through her mind, his words reverberating, his hurt a direct consequence of her running out on him in the delicatessen two days before.

The first trace of panic had descended as suddenly as she'd dropped Alex's name into their conversation. Once it had slipped from her lips, she'd known it was a mistake, a mood-changer. She hadn't meant to blurt it out like that, hadn't meant to introduce the past into their new life until she'd created the perfect 'tell-all' moment. Being with Matt made her wish she didn't have history, made her wish there weren't taboo subjects capable of disconcerting him. And now, she thought, wriggling her waist to ease the strain of overstretching, I've jinxed it by panicking and running into hiding, just like I've done so many times before.

Coming to New York should have been a fresh start, a chance to shut the world out – most of it at least – and give their relationship a real chance. Sitting on the Cypriot Airline en route to JFK Airport, she'd spent the entire journey preparing her grand confession to Matt. There was quite an amount to be told, individual incidents in their own right but connected all the same. And there, sitting on the aisle seat with her unread magazine on her lap, she'd been eager to tell Matt everything, eager to begin their new adventure on a brand-new page. And more than anything, she'd hoped he'd be at her side for what the future held in store.

But their excitement at being together, the novelty of being in a new city and the desire to prove her love to him before dropping an enormous bombshell into the mix had delayed her confession, had frozen her prepared speech, making it impossible to deliver. And then, in a most untimely fashion, she had mentioned Alex. The instant change in Matt had made her heart thump, the way their conversation had halted bringing her out in goose-bumps and the blank emotion on his face making her crumble inside. She didn't think he would handle the truth. He'd be the one running and never coming back. So rather than wait, she beat him to it.

As she thought about the incident now, she remembered the speed of his recovery, how he'd tried his best to patch over the moment and pretend Alex was insignificant. And considering his limited knowledge of Alex, apart from a tiny nugget she'd dropped into a conversation one night after they'd made love, she had little faith in how he'd react if he knew the full truth.

The awkwardness between them had tarnished their light mood, Matt's attempt to smooth it over failing to prevent Heidi's body overheating, the shop rotating and rows of spices and shelves of delicacies blurring out of focus. Fear had built inside her, pumping blood faster and faster through her veins, like a dam ready to overflow.

The darkness in his green eyes had been the catalyst to make her turn on her heel and run, the fear of Matt witnessing what was to follow forcing her on to the street and back to their apartment. Her shortness of breath, the tightness in her chest, uncontrollable tears, retching and nausea were not something she was prepared to test on another relationship.

Calling Julian had been a spur-of-the-moment-decision, a cry for support and a scream for help. She couldn't do it alone. Any of it.

Apart from Matt, Julian was the only other person she knew in New York. And he was part of her complicated history. There was a horrifying moment, while she'd rooted through her handbag in blind panic, she'd thought she'd misplaced his number. Or left it back home in Ireland. But after a few panicked minutes of scrabbling through every receipt and piece of paper in sight, she'd found it in the zip compartment at the back of her wallet, folded neatly as though it were hiding from her, as though she'd hidden it from herself.

In the absence of credit in her new SIM card – something she'd discovered when she'd tried to call Julian – she had hurried out of the apartment, unable to find her keys in her haste (and her panic) and leaving the door on the latch instead. If she'd been thinking straight she could have topped up her credit on Matt's laptop. But Heidi was way beyond thinking straight.

Using the nearest public payphone, she dialled his number and waited, moving from one foot to the other, switching the receiver from ear to ear. But luck was with her and Julian was on the next block. He'd finished auditioning for a solo gig in Hooters and, despite his surprise to hear she was in Manhattan, agreed to help her out of a bind. The relief at hearing his voice had unleashed another episode and when she'd turned to leave she'd collapsed in a helpless faint on to the pavement.

Waking up in the safety of Julian's arms, she'd burst into tears – as much from embarrassment as upset – burying her head in his chest to hide from the gathering crowd. Needing to escape probing eyes, she'd pointed out her apartment building and leaned on his welcome support, struggling to concentrate on his voice.

Inside the apartment, it took a while for his soothing reassurance to take effect but she did feel she was making slight progress, her breathing returning to a normal pace. Until the loud buzz of the doorbell filled the apartment, scaring her half to death again and setting her right back to the beginning.

"Matt can't see me like this," she'd said, her breath

rasping, her eyes shining with terror. "You have to get me out of here. Quickly. Please, Julian."

They'd moved outside the apartment door as the buzzer continued to sound at intervals, each time Heidi's panic escalating.

Waiting nervously by the fire-exit door on the first floor, she'd closed her eyes tightly while Julian left the building. Heidi had listened to the exchange of words between him and Matt. The floorboard she was standing on creaked. She yelped in fright, then slapped a hand over her mouth, clinging her body to the sand-coloured wall, afraid to exhale until she'd heard the lift moving in the nearby shaft as it carried her boyfriend to their fourth-floor apartment.

Dashing outside, she'd spotted Julian waiting at the nearest corner. Her auburn hair had bobbed on her shoulders as she'd run to meet him, tears on her cheeks and her heart in her mouth. Anyone could have been forgiven for misreading their relationship as they'd moved hand in hand through the streets of New York.

Chapter 20

Lucy parked her car outside Delia's house, exhausted and confused after a hectic day. And she still had to visit Danny.

Breathing in the fresh sea air, she stood next to the car for a moment and stared at the lighthouse on the opposite peninsula across the mouth of Cork Harbour, willing the lighthouse keeper to flash a signal to her. How she longed for guidance, somebody to tell her how to get out of this fix.

The sound of a door banging inside Delia's house filtered out to her, followed closely by her sister's raised voice. Sighing, Lucy took Delia's frustration as her cue to go inside and help diffuse the situation. She'd got her signal, disappointing as it was.

"Nice dress," Delia commented as she answered the door. "And I don't think I've seen that mac on you before. Were you shopping?"

"As if! They're some of Carol's cast-offs. She was

good enough to let me have a hot shower and give me a few things to wear seeing as everything I own is burnt to a crisp." Lucy lowered her voice. "No need to ask who you were shouting at just now?"

Delia pursed her lips and threw her hands in the air, stepping outside the front door. "I'll swing for her, Luce," she hissed. "She has to be the most annoying, interfering woman I've ever met in my life! How on earth did we turn out sane with a mother like that?"

Lucy ran her hand around the back of her neck, kneading the knots of tension with her fingertips. "I'm not sure I'd describe myself as sane right now, Del." She sighed heavily and linked her sister's arm. "Come on, let's get inside. That wind would skin a cat and the rain is about to start again."

"The blustery weather is why I love living on top of this hill – I can breathe clean air and admire the magnificent cliff-top view. Although if I don't get Mum back to Kinsale soon, the top of a cliff could be a dangerous place for both of us!"

Lucy hadn't the energy to act as go-between. "Would you mind if I made a few calls from here? I'm sure you can guess who's top of my list?"

Delia rested her head on Lucy's shoulder. "Make yourself at home, sis. Why don't you use my workroom? You'll have some hope of privacy there. Although you'd better say hello first or she'll be right in after you."

Lucy nodded and led the way. "Hi, Mum!" she called, making her way towards the kitchen where she expected her mother would be, halting in surprise when she saw her sitting on the living-room couch, her head in her hands, her shoulders heaving. She hurried to her side, their earlier spat instantly forgotten. Dropping to her knees beside her, she took Gloria's hands in hers. "Mum, whatever's the matter? Hush, there now, there's no need to cry, I'm sure."

Gloria sniffled, then the sniffle turned into something between a cough and a sneeze. She took a tissue from the patch pocket of her lavender cardigan and dabbed her eyes. "I feel so helpless and in the way. Your sister doesn't want me staying here. She's made that quite clear. But I can't return to Kinsale with all that's going on. How can I be away from you at this time? I know I'm cantankerous but I love you all dearly. You know that, Lucy, don't you?"

Lucy stroked her mother's hands, her mind racing, the pleading in Gloria's voice cracking her resolve. "I'm sure Delia's only thinking about what's best for you, Mum. The fire has been a shock for all of us. Don't you think it would be more comfortable for you in the tranquillity of the home? Regular mealtimes, afternoon activities?" She posed it as a question, doing her utmost to spare her mother's feelings, noticing additional age lines in her face and hating to think she was partly responsible for their arrival.

Lucy understood her mother's loneliness now more than ever. What it must be like to be without a partner, particularly when unexpected upheaval occurs. Only forty-eight hours before, the fear of being widowed had been a harsh reality for Lucy. How could she dismiss Gloria to the home under the circumstances? Even if renting out her house and settling herself into a retirement complex had been all her own doing, albeit a hasty decision.

Seeing her mum's upset now, however, Lucy began to wonder whether she'd made that decision out of loneliness after her husband's death. Perhaps she'd found living alone a lot more difficult than she'd been willing to admit. We'll have to find a way to muddle along, Lucy decided, and I'll have to find a way to keep my mouth shut or we'll end up at each other's throats. But how will I coax my sister to do likewise?

Delia hovered outside the door, surreptitiously watching her sister and mother embrace. She hung back a moment longer, then entered the room to offer Lucy an excuse to get on with what she needed to do.

"Mum and I will get started on making dinner, Luce. You have phone calls to make. When you're done, you can open a bottle of wine and we can try to wind down a little."

Lucy flashed Delia a grateful smile, refraining from mentioning that she would have to get back to Danny and wouldn't have time for dinner. As for wine, a few sips and she would probably keel over.

Mindful not to pull away from Gloria too quickly, she took one hand from her mum's grasp and fixed a few stray tendrils of hair behind her ears. "There, you look more like your perfect self now," she said with a smile, entwining her fingers in her mum's once more and giving a gentle squeeze.

The radio played in the background, the jingle of advertisements lost on her as she shifted her thoughts to Jenny, Danny's sister. How would she phrase what had happened without sounding guilty? Jenny was sharpness personified. And Lucy was a terrible liar. She'd have to choose her words carefully. Absently fiddling with her mother's diamond solitaire, she decided that limiting what she said would probably be the best way to go when breaking the news. Otherwise, Jenny would make her own assumptions before they'd even finished the call.

Sitting on her sister's floor, holding her mother's hands in hers, the horrid ordeal went around and around Lucy's head. How had their house caught fire? Had it been accidental or was the finger of blame hovering horribly near home?

Relinquishing her mother's hands, she rose to her feet, her knees cramping from kneeling for so long. Without any answers, she refused to entertain the empty thoughts filling her mind, vowing to do everything in her power to protect her family. And their home – what was left of it.

"Everything will be okay, Mum, I'm sure of it," she said, bending to plant a kiss on her cheek and wishing the tiny voice in her head would stop preaching otherwise.

Chapter 21

Danny's mind was racing. He was too far away from the clock on the wall to see the time but the day felt endless. What's keeping Lucy, he fretted, shifting around in the bed to try and get more comfortable. The questions he needed to ask her queued in his head, the answers he hoped to receive making him shiver inside. Reporting the fire to the insurance company as quickly as possible was crucial if they were ever to get back on their feet.

The gardaí were about the place, waiting to speak to him. The nurses hadn't mentioned it yet – probably following doctor's orders not to cause him any exertion – but Danny had spotted Phelim O'Brien hovering around the doorway. He'd shut his eyes and feigned sleep, his heart beating so fast it hurt, the exertion of breathing – even with the help of the oxygen mask – giving him a pain across his chest.

Danny didn't need an introduction to the Carrigaline inspector. O'Brien's bulky frame was impossible to mistake. His presence in the hospital was as ostentatious as it had been the day he'd appeared on an Ardle Construction building site a few years before. His brass buttons and polished boots had shone like beacons amidst the hard hats, high-visibility vests and steel-cap boots.

The five-bedroom detached homes Danny was working on were near completion, the offer Phelim made for one an insult to his integrity.

Danny wasn't swayed by his uniform or the cash deposit he'd brandished.

"I'm a fair man," he'd told him, resting his arm on the steering wheel of the forklift truck he'd been driving when Phelim had pulled the squad car onto the site. "We build good homes, have top-standard work and stand over every square metre."

"Goes without saying. Otherwise I wouldn't be here." Phelim's response was gruff, his determination to get preferential treatment evident. "We're all business people in this town, can't do any harm looking out for one another."

"And I'll do that by selling you a top-notch house."

"At a mark-down price?" Phelim wasn't giving up.

Neither was Danny. He'd leaned back in the seat and eyeballed Phelim. "The price for each phase is set with no special favours, no backhanders and no gazumping. Every prospective neighbour is treated the same."

Phelim's face had contorted. It hadn't been the response he'd been expecting. He'd tapped the front of the forklift with his index finger, jerking his head toward the end of the site. "The wife has her heart set on that large corner site. Does it come with the same price tag?"

Again, Danny had disappointed Phelim. "Number four was sold from the plans, I'm afraid. Number thirteen is the only house remaining – still beats me the amount of superstition out there. The next development I build, I'm going to leave that number out." He'd pointed to the far side of the road, indicating a partially completed house. "West-facing back garden, garage space, not overlooked – it's a great buy. The keys are in the office if you'd like to take a look."

Phelim had put his hands in his trouser pockets, the movement straining the buttons on his jacket until they were in danger of bursting open. "There has to be something you can do on the price, Danny . . . I might be able to squash a few parking tickets for that son of yours."

Danny had turned the key in the forklift, gripping the steering wheel with both hands. "There won't be any need – I'll advise him to park properly," he'd answered, without meeting Phelim's eye.

Phelim's face had flushed bright red. "You do that." He paused. "Maybe I will take a look at that house while I'm here."

"The show house is open this Sunday if number thirteen is still unsold," Danny'd said, seething with anger inside. I'll be damned if I do him any special favours after that outrageous attempt at blackmail. I'd rather sweep roads for community service than get that ignorant oaf to squash a parking ticket. "The first cash deposit secures. Keep an eye on Saturday's *Examiner* if you're still interested and do your business direct with the selling agent."

Phelim gritted his teeth, turned on his heel and left the site.

Now, the memory grizzled in Danny's mind. He fidgeted with the starched white sheet, the large plastic oxygen mask uncomfortable on his cheeks and nose. He remembered Phelim's visit to the site as clearly as if it were yesterday. He hadn't liked Phelim O'Brien and his attitude then and he hadn't had reason to change his mind since.

Lying back against the pillows, Danny put his hands out over the covers. His mouth was arid. The heat of the hospital ward added to his discomfort. The oxygen mask hid his quivering lips. An enormous lump lodged in his throat and for a moment he was terrified he'd cry. He squeezed his eyes shut, emotionally drained and physically exhausted. Where is Lucy, he thought, worrying something had happened to her, his eyes heavy with sleep. He twisted his head from side to side, trying to stay awake, wishing his brain didn't feel so fuzzy.

I need to patch the details together, he told himself, dragging his memory back to the moment when Lucy had stormed out of the house without as much as a goodbye. But it wasn't her hasty departure that concerned him most – it was the events that took place around his kitchen table soon after that.

Chapter 22

Once she'd set her mind on the matter, getting Jenny's number proved to be a lot easier than Lucy had anticipated. How had she forgotten about her sister-in-law's ridiculous obsession with social networking? Facebook had all the details.

Lucy dialled and braced herself as she waited for Jenny to pick up, her insides quivering.

A few moments later, she cringed at the sound of Jenny's curt greeting. Like a lamb to the slaughter, she took a deep breath, exchanged pleasantries and gave her an edited version of events. Pleading exhaustion, which was true – and upset, which was also true – she kept the call as brief as she could, groaning inwardly when Jenny immediately suggested coming to the hospital to support her brother in whatever way she could. And of course she'd be staying in a top-class hotel. She'd have her personal assistant organise it.

Not once did Jenny ask how Lucy was coping. Or

mention her elderly parents or how the devastating news would upset them. But Lucy, fed up to the back teeth of her sister-in-law's selfish ways, tackled the issue head on and landed the responsibility right into her lap.

"I'll leave it to you to break the news to your mum and dad then," she told her. "I'll tell Danny all three of you will visit over the next couple of days. Close family will perk him up a little." After a hurried goodbye, she dropped the phone, anxious to get off the line before Jenny wheedled her way out of telling her parents.

'Helping' in Jenny's eyes would involve a dramatic entrance, followed by an exaggerated fussing over her injured brother. She'd make sure this performance took place in full view of the doctors and nursing staff. And then, feeling as though she'd made an incredible difference, she'd swan back to an imaginary crisis in her busy London life, gracing them with little more than a Christmas card (and not one with a gift voucher inside either) for the remainder of the year.

Noticing the time on the digital display on Delia's computer, Lucy jumped up from her seat. How on earth had the time passed so quickly? Danny would be waiting for her to return. Cursing, she ran back to the kitchen where Delia and Gloria were chopping vegetables while nibbling on cheese, crackers, olives and baby tomatoes. She stuffed a couple of tomatoes in her mouth and stuck a thick slice of cheddar between a couple of crackers to take with her.. "I've got to get back to the hospital. Sorry!"

"Lucy!" said Gloria, outraged. "You must stop and eat! We've enough to deal with without you collapsing on us! "

"Luce, seriously, let me at least make you a sandwich," said Delia, following her sister out the door.

"Thanks, sis, but no – Danny will be getting anxious."

"Any joy with your calls?" Delia asked as Lucy opened the front door.

"Well, I told Jennifer. She's talking about coming to 'support Danny in his hour of need' but she'll be staying in a hotel, thank God. I gave her the job of telling her parents."

"Good for you!"

"I'll have to tackle the insurance problem in the morning. I'll just have to phone around the different companies and check it out with each of them."

"Check what?" Gloria appeared in the hall, her confidence restored, her obstinate pout back in its rightful place.

"Hospital insurance," Lucy improvised. "I'm checking everything is in order to cover Danny's treatment. The membership was in my bedside locker. The hospital registrar was asking loads of questions about what plan we're on."

"What a nightmare," Delia added, the distraught look on her sister's face distressing her.

"Matt was forever on at me to store every little detail on the palm pilot he bought me last Christmas," said Lucy. "Am I sorry now I didn't listen to him!"

Delia's hand flew to her mouth, the mention of her nephew reminding her of his phone call. "Matt rang this morning, Luce. I forgot all about it. I didn't tell him about the fire. He's looking for the long version of his birth certificate and a copy of the reference he got from Rochestown Park Hotel."

"Oh God, what am I going to do?" Lucy said, as much to herself as the others. "Everything is badly smoke damaged, hardly retrievable. Did he sound okay?" She fretted, guilt flooding through her that she hadn't been there for him. His first call home and he couldn't get through to either her or Danny. "Did he ask any questions about why the phones weren't being answered?"

Delia nodded. "I told him the lines were down. Struck by lightning, would you believe?" She rolled her eyes. "You should call him back, Luce. He's probably dying to tell you how he's settling in."

Lucy chewed on the inside of her lip, wondering what to do for the best.

"Don't lie to the boys, Lucy. They deserve better," Gloria pleaded with her daughter.

Lucy's head reeled. Responsibility lay heavily on her shoulders. An image of her youngest son came to mind, his handsome face, green twinkling eyes and happy, carefree nature warming her heart. Her mother's words rang in her ears. Lucy had to admit she had a valid point. Of course he deserved to know his father was lying seriously ill in a hospital bed. It would be good to get it out in the open.

"I'll call him now," she said, retreating to Delia's workroom once more, the rows of completed jewellery pieces and trays of precious stones glistening under the bright light as she walked into the room.

Dialling Matt's mobile number from memory, she waited in anticipation for him to pick up. But as soon as his voice came on the line, she recognised something amiss in his tone.

Her heart sank. Something was very wrong. She

knew her son inside out, had always been able to read his mood from the way he said hello. And the tone of his greeting today made the hairs stand on the back of her neck.

"What's the matter, Matt? Is New York not working out?"

She listened carefully while he muttered something indecipherable. Finding it difficult to comprehend what he was telling her, she begged him to repeat. "Matt, I can't hear a word this end. Start again, from the beginning."

She pushed all thoughts of sharing her horrific news about the fire with him to one side, intent on discovering what was wrong with her son.

Matt sat on the window seat, one leg on the sill, the other on the floor, oblivious to the continuous activity on the street below. Since the call in the taxi, there'd been nothing but silence from Heidi.

He clutched his mobile in his hand, never so pleased to receive a call from his mother. Hearing her voice on the line was helping to ease his distress, reminding him that he wasn't alone. Her timing couldn't have been more perfect. Even before his phone had shrilled, he'd decided his only hope of finding Heidi was to come clean and tell his mother the truth. He was praying she would come to his aid – if she didn't kill him or disown him when she heard what he had to say.

"Mum, will you promise to listen to the whole story before you go off on one." He ran the sole of his foot along the painted sill, his cushioned sock slipping on the high gloss.

"Are you short of money?"

Matt sighed, wishing his problems were so straight-forward. "No, Mum."

"Delia mentioned you needed your birth certificate. Don't tell me you've lost your passport?"

"Mum, please," Matt ignored her question, trying to get her to listen. He eyed the apple pie on the table, promising himself a large slice – he'd heat it in the microwave – after he'd disclosed everything to his mum. "I've been seeing somebody . . ." The words left his lips as though they were in a rush to be heard.

"Already? But you're barely there a few days."

Matt closed his eyes and leaned his head against the rough wallpaper. "We were together before I came to New York. She travelled from Ireland too – sort of."

At last his mother fell silent. She's probably too stunned to speak, he thought. He took a deep breath and launched into his story, afraid that if he didn't get it out in the open that very second, he'd lose his nerve.

"Heidi Black, Mum. We've been seeing each other for a few months."

"Heidi Black?" Lucy was incredulous.

Matt felt his neck and cheeks flush, even the tips of his ears were on fire. Oh damn, he thought, I can't lose my nerve now.

"Heidi Black? You can't mean our Heidi Black? From across the road?"

God, he thought, do I have to spell it out for her? It seems I do. "Doh, Mum! That's who I've been seeing. Heidi from across the road."

Diplomacy had never been one of his mother's strong points and, as he'd expected (after an approximate count of five) she exploded down the long-distance phone line.

"But you can't, Matt. Heidi's years older than you. And she taught you in school. And she used to baby-sit you and Stephen . . ." Her voice trailed off a moment, then came back loud and strong. "But Heidi is practically my age! There has to be a law against an age gap of that size!"

Matt's defences rose. He wasn't going to have his mother speak about Heidi like that. "Give over, Mum! She's eleven years younger than you."

"And twelve years older than you!" Lucy shot back. "Which makes her nearer my age than yours."

"Does it matter?" he asked. "We love each other." At least I love her, he thought, pulling her wedding photo from the side pocket of his combats and staring at it again in disbelief, unable to associate the young voluptuous bride with *his* Heidi.

"Was she after you? Is that what happened? She couldn't get anyone her own age and set her sights on you?"

Matt could hear the disgust in her voice. "Out of order, Mum. You're not being one bit fair."

"Well, it makes me feel sick. She changed your nappies for crying out loud! How perverse is that?"

"I won't have you speaking about Heidi like that, Mum. All I ask is that you listen to what I want to tell you."

He paused, accepting his mother's silence as a green light for him to continue.

"This last year, we took the same bus route morning and evening, got chatting after a while and, well," he paused to find the best way to describe the connection between them, "we just gelled. One morning we went for breakfast – just casual, you understand – and we had a great laugh, so good we both knew there was something between us."

"You're a young man for God's sake, only out of college – you'd feel a connection with any attractive female!"

Matt let that go. "We started seeing each other." He didn't expand on that any further, imagining she could work the developments out for herself. "When I decided to travel, she said she'd come too, then the job offer came for New York and here we are." He left out the part about New York being Heidi's decision, already foreseeing how his mother would go off on one about her dictating his decisions. He heard her gasp.

"She's with you in New York? She's ruining your freedom, the very thing you worked your butt off for in college? New York's supposed to be the opportunity of a lifetime where you explore new things, meet new people, not run away with the girl – sorry, strike that! – the older woman who's been left on the shelf next door!"

"Mum! What are you on about? Heidi's stunning, turning men *away* from the door."

"Pity she didn't turn you away!"

Another comment he let go. "It's not like that. She supports me no matter what. And I want her here. I told you, I'm in love with her." He'd expected it to be an awkward conversation but hadn't expected Lucy's degree of audacity.

"Has she got a job then?"

"Not yet, but you know the Blacks aren't short of a euro or two. She's not that bothered."

"Not that bothered? Going to drain you dry? Who's paying the rent?"

His mother's voice was venomous at this stage. He sensed a strong possibility that she'd hang up on him so hurried to the most crucial point. "Heidi's gone missing, Mum. Our first day here, she disappeared. And there's this guy – he gave me a photograph of her . . ." As Matt uttered the words, he heard how ridiculous they sounded, like something he'd watched on a Monday night drama on ITV.

"What? What do you mean 'disappeared'? What guy?"

Matt recognised a change in his mother's tone, sensing concern – for him more than Heidi, he assumed – and latched on to it. "This guy – Julian Ebbs – he knows where she is but he's refusing to tell me."

"Is he a friend of yours? How come I've never heard of him before?"

Matt placed both his feet on the floor, swivelling around on the sill to lean his back against the window-pane. "He's some guy Heidi knows," he told her, too weary to go into any more detail, certainly not brave enough to challenge his mother's argument on married women. "He said she's complicated and needs space and that he'll let me know when she's ready to talk. But I don't trust him. And I'm worried something's going to happen to her."

"Have you called her phone?"

"She doesn't answer."

"Text her then. Demand that she answers. Tell her you want nothing more to do with her. See how she responds to that."

"No!" Matt dropped his head, etching Heidi's name on the dusty floorboards with his big toe.

"If you're that concerned, there's only one other thing you can do – report her as a missing person to the police. Surely they'll find her."

"I can't. I don't know what type of visa she has. I don't want to get her in trouble. She called me briefly today but hung up without telling me where she is."

"Matt, listen to me. Get on with your own life. Heidi's a mature adult. She'll turn up in her own good time. You don't get to be a singleton in your thirties without carrying plenty of baggage. Who knows what's going on with her?"

But Matt refused to listen, adamant what they had was real. "Heidi came here to be with me, Mum. Don't you get that? I won't be able to get on with anything until I know she's safe. If she tells me she doesn't want to be with me, I'll accept that. But in the meantime, will you please ask Carol if she's been in contact?"

"But Carol never mentioned to me about you two!"

Matt could hear betrayal in his mother's voice. "Carol doesn't know, Mum. She thinks Heidi's in Cyprus."

"But why lie about her location? I can understand she'd be too embarrassed to admit about the relationship but I don't get her pretending to be in another country!"

Matt had wondered about that too and though he'd asked Heidi the same question, she'd stroked his face and distracted him as per usual, assuring him she had her reasons. He sidetracked answering that one. "Mum, will you please help me? Just this once?"

Suddenly ravenous, he went and cut a large piece out of the apple tart and stuck it in the microwave, while

Lucy continued to castigate him. He kept his mouth shut, hoping that when she had let off enough steam she would relent.

"I'll ask Carol on one condition . . ." she said at last

"Anything," he responded, heaving a silent sigh of relief.

"You must promise me you'll end it as soon as you hear she's safe."

"But, Mum –" Matt began, refusing to say yes only to appease, refusing to resort to further lies or promises he wouldn't keep.

"No buts, Matt. Her safety, your freedom."

"If I think she's making a fool of me, then yes. That's the best I can promise, Mum." He was looking at the picture again, admiring the bride's ample bosom, her curvaceous hips and impish smile. It's no wonder I can't remember her looking like that, he thought. I was probably still cycling with stabilisers back then!

"Okay, Matt," Lucy said eventually, "but I'm not looking forward to telling Carol that her eldest daughter is dating my youngest son and that she's currently a missing person in New York! What a position you've put me in – having to tell Carol all that, specially now . . ."

"What do you mean specially now?" The microwave bell dinged. Matt removed the plate and sunk a fork into the hot pastry.

"Ah, leave it, you've enough on your plate to deal with as it is."

I do indeed, he thought, staring at the juice oozing from the tart on the plate in front of him. "Thank you, Mum," he said, sighing with relief that she'd agreed to share the burden.

"In the meantime, Matt, stay out of trouble and stay the hell away from that guy you mentioned. I'll be in touch as soon as I've any news."

"I'll do my best," he said, a smile on his face like a small boy whose mother had just put a cartoon plaster on his cut knee.

"Love you, son."

"Love you, Mum."

The phone call finished, he opened his mouth wide and savoured the taste of hot juicy apple tart.

His mother's words of caution were already forgotten. He was prepared to do whatever it took to get Heidi back in his bed and his life.

Chapter 23

Eric lay on the sand staring at the sky, oblivious to the young couple walking by him until the man issued him a friendly warning.

"You'd want to be careful there, man – the tide comes in fast on this shore."

Eric nodded and smiled, but proceeded to ignore his advice. Instead, he remained lying there, dusk falling quickly, the sky a magnificent blend of orange and pink hues.

He had passed the previous night rambling on the beach, napping briefly now and then. Then he watched as the sun rose, bought coffee and an egg sandwich for breakfast in a little café – he couldn't remember when he'd eaten last – and returned to the beach to sleep in the warmth of the sun. Later he spent the last of his coins on a large bottle of water and a hot dog and went down to the sea again.

The exaggerated euphoria of the previous day had

passed, a surreal calm spreading over him this evening as he watched the water flood toward him, still a good distance away but every foaming wave bringing it nearer and nearer the shore, nearer and nearer the soles of his feet.

How tempting to lie here and let God decide my fate, he thought, nestling his body into the sand, his elbows folded behind his head. He smiled again, the sight of the water flapping gently on the shore a soothing stress remedy. In his mind's eye, his debit balances and overdue payment slips floated in the soft warm water, the ink dripping from the pages into the Gulf of Mexico, the tightening sensation that had choked and controlled him for weeks ebbing away. He closed his eyes, contented within and happy to wait.

A strong male voice penetrated Eric's subconscious and disturbed his dream, forcing him to open his eyes and wake up to reality.

"Hey, sir! What's up! You're half-covered by the sea!" A lifeguard was standing over him.

God damn it, Eric thought, rising to his feet, his wet jeans sticking to his legs, the evening chill causing him to shiver from head to toe. Or had the shivering been caused by the fact he'd been lying motionless for the last while waiting for the ocean to cover his head and bring an end to his misery? He hadn't been brave enough to walk into the ocean and step through the foaming waves until finally he was lost in oblivion. Instead he had waited for the tide to come to him.

As he'd lain on the sand, the water had come as far as his waist. Only another short while and he'd have been fully immersed. But now, standing before the concerned lifeguard, he felt embarrassed and foolish. How could he have imagined he could have drowned himself in shallow water like that? That he wouldn't struggle for breath and simply get up! It had just been a pleasant fantasy.

Dropping his eyes to his feet to avoid the lifeguard's sharp gaze, he stooped to pick up his sopping shoes and socks, along with the cardigan and overnight bag he'd discarded earlier.

"Are you okay, sir? What happened there? Did you black out? Should I call an ambulance?" The lifeguard continued to ask probing questions, all the while leading him away from the water's edge.

Overcome by a sudden moment of mirth, Eric wanted to laugh as hard as he could. What would his buddies in the Royal Cork Yacht Club – or the RCYC as it was famously known, being the oldest yacht club in the world – think if they were watching him being escorted from a public beach with nothing more than wet clothes to his name? Or if they had seen him trying to drown himself in the surf?

"Have you got somewhere to spend the night?" asked the lifeguard. "Or are you passing through?"

Eric shrugged and stopped walking. "I'm not sure yet," he responded honestly. "I've found myself in a strange town without a dime in my pocket. I'm open to any suggestions you might have." As soon as the words were out, he regretted them. *Am I offering myself to this guy on a plate,* he wondered, hearing the vulnerability of his statement.

"Come on – keep moving – you can talk and walk at

the same time." The lifeguard caught him by the arm and led him off the deserted beach, the white sand blowing in dusty clouds around them, the ocean's waves lapping goodbye to him.

Eric shuddered when he looked back, the water losing its appeal under the darkening sky. Following the lifeguard's path toward the beach house, he banished his lack of trust in the man. It wasn't as if he had any choice except to follow him. He barely even knew what part of Florida he was in, never mind how to get out of it. He stumbled along behind the lifeguard, happy to have someone to lead the way, the light stones underfoot pinching his feet. He strained to hear what his companion was saying, hardly in the mood for some local knowledge but too polite (and grateful) to appear rude.

The lifeguard turned and waited for Eric to catch up with him. "We've got fine accommodation here at Sarasota Beach House – once you've got no objection to sharing a room with a few half-crazed lifeguards?"

"Anywhere I can lay my head for the night is good with me. I'm exhausted. Hopefully tomorrow . . ." But he trailed off. Tomorrow wasn't something he wanted to dwell on yet. It was something he'd struck off his calendar when he'd sunk his body into the soft sand earlier.

"Tomorrow will figure itself out. The bunks are through there on the other side of the room. Anyone asks, say Pete sent you." With a wave, the lifeguard departed, leaving Eric to his own devices as he returned to his viewing point on the beach.

Eric stepped into the noisy beach house, the uproar of

a table-tennis game monopolising the room. He slipped quietly by the players, following the lifeguard's directions and entering a room resembling the dormitory he'd shared in boarding school.

Who knows what brought me to this magnificent setting, he thought, gazing through the window, awestruck by the huge expanse of sand dunes surrounding miles of long golden beach. The view transported him to Church Bay in Crosshaven and the carefree summers he'd enjoyed there – first as a child and later as a parent. Bizarrely, this memory evoked more emotion than the bundles of red repossession letters and court injunctions he'd stuffed into an old briefcase at home.

But those carefree days in Church Bay were long gone as were so many other happy memories and pipe dreams. Lying down on the hard bunk, unexpected tears flowed down his sunburnt cheeks, tears of regret for what he'd thrown away. Stupidly, he'd gambled his most valuable possessions of all: happiness and the security of his family who'd placed their trust in him. Thanks to a serious case of negligence, he'd lost miserably. It was too late for recrimination, too late to cancel the risk wrapped up in that bet.

Within seconds of closing his eyes, the strain and worry left his face and he'd returned to the dream he'd been having earlier. For Eric, his day had ended. He was spent.

But in direct contrast to his comforting dreams, his name was on the lips of many, particularly the authorities who were combing Tampa Airport in response to an SOS call reporting him wanted for felony.

Chapter 24

Immediately after breakfast on Tuesday morning, Lucy flopped into the chair beside Delia's desk, pulling the *Golden Pages* from the shelf overhead and checking the index for insurance companies. She owed it to herself – and Danny – to at least investigate the possibility that she had renewed the policy. Grasping hold of that notion, she blotted out all doubts, refusing to entertain any idea other than the one she wanted to be true.

Scanning pages and pages of insurance companies, she focused on the larger block ads to begin with, running a finger down through the list, trying to latch onto anything remotely familiar. Hell, she thought, I could be with any of these companies. I'm sick of hearing them advertised on radio and television every day of the week.

Needing to start somewhere, she picked up the phone, bemoaning the fact there wasn't a central insurance register that could pinpoint her home address and check whether they were insured or not. Dialling each number in turn, she repeated the same mantra over and over, giving her details, asking if their home was on their database. In record time, she'd made her way through the majority of major companies, Aviva being one of the few companies who'd traced Danny's name on the register. As one of the major underwriters in Irish insurance, she'd pinned high hopes on them being able to help her. She had approached that particular call with more thought than the others, trying a different approach.

"Can you tell me what my renewal date is, please?" She let out the breath she'd been holding when the girl on the phone just asked for her name and address.

"Hold the line and I'll retrieve your details."

"Sure, no problem." Lucy dared to hope.

"Can you bear with me? Our network has been acting up all morning."

Lucy leaned back in the chair and crossed her fingers. "I'll hold for as long as you like if you tell me I'm insured," she muttered under her breath when she was put on hold.

Glancing through the *Golden Pages* again, the remaining companies failed to jog her memory and she felt she'd come to a dead end. Or she could be there all day ringing every miniscule brokerage and agency that was listed in the book.

"Sorry for holding you, Mrs Ardle," the girl returned on the line. "Are you sure you're on to the right company? From our records, the renewal notice was sent out, followed by a reminder a few weeks later, but the remittance was never received. Naturally, seeing as so much time has elapsed, your insurance cover has ceased. A letter to that effect was sent out to you."

"And the mistake couldn't be at your end?" Lucy clung to her last shred of hope. "Unlikely," came the response. "Not unless you renewed through a broker? That would be the only other possibility. I can check our brokerage system for you if you like?"

"Please do," Lucy agreed, racking her brain to see if she could remember anything about insuring through a broker. It would be, no doubt, another futile exercise. She rearranged the contents of Delia's pen-holder, dreading meeting another dead end.

As expected, the girl brought disappointing news. "Your details aren't listed as one of our properties on that list either."

The girl launched into a sales pitch and Lucy took a paperclip from the desk, absentmindedly uncurling it out of shape and bending it into a circle. She ran her finger around the light piece of metal, the girl's patter beyond her interest.

"Thank you," she said, when the girl at last paused. "I'll get back to you."

"Is there anything else I can help you with? Perhaps information on one of our savings or pensions schemes?"

Lucy refused politely and ended the call. Her gaze was drawn to the black permanent marker on Delia's desk. Needing to channel her frustration, she pulled off the top and drew a large black X across the centre of the open pages, banging the *Golden Pages* book closed and scribbling all over the cover. Childish, she knew, but she felt the better for it.

As she sat there, defeated, unable to figure out her next move, her thoughts flew back to Matt and his revelations the night before which had left her reeling in disbelief. What on earth had possessed him? Or *her*? Heidi was twelve when Matt was born. How could somebody who appeared so sweet take advantage of a young man, a neighbour's son? From the dreamy way he spoke about her, he was being carried along by the romance of it all.

At twenty-one years of age, he'd assured her he was mature enough to handle travelling to another continent alone, proving his maturity by securing a well-paying job in his field of expertise. But from what he'd announced on the phone the previous evening, that's where his maturity had ended. After that, he had been on freefall back to the immaturity he'd shown in nursery school! And he'd lied to her and Danny into the bargain. Knowing he'd deceived her cut deep, very deep.

Any intention she'd had of confronting Danny with allegations about empty containers had disintegrated after that telephone conversation. Matt's request ran around and around in her head, leaving her unable to concentrate on anything or anyone other than the person he'd cited as holding the key to his happiness.

Her next-door neighbour – the woman whose faded denims and red silk shirt Lucy was wearing right now, the woman who'd had the wits to call the emergency services and save Danny from further harm – would be equally distraught, if not more so, when she imparted the news. What a weave being intertwined, she mused, with Carol's car and belongings hidden on our property, our son seeing their daughter, their money and home at risk, our money and home gone in a puff of smoke. She put her head in her hands and groaned.

187

Too shocked to talk to Delia about Matt the night before, she'd left the house and driven straight to the hospital. Her visit to Danny had been uneventful. He'd slept for the most part and she'd sat at his bedside, staring without seeing, terrified the extra sedation would wear off and he'd bombard her with unanswerable insurance questions again. But she needn't have worried. The nurses' decision to induce rest was something Danny had no control over, leaving the way clear for Lucy to slip away quite soon from the high-dependency ward, knowing her husband was in safe hands.

Evading any more discussion with her mother or Delia on her return, Lucy had lain on the flat of her back in Delia's guest bed for most of the night, too dumbstruck to toss and turn, too alert to grab a wink of sleep. She'd left the curtains slightly apart, her eyes following the moonlit shapes dancing on the wall, her thoughts jumping from one crisis to the next. Her son, while owning up to the bizarreness of the situation he was in, needed her help. So caught up in his own worries, he hadn't asked anything about home, much to her relief. Although keeping the worry from his young shoulders had lost its emphasis now that he was already in such an agitated state. Never, in the twenty-four years she'd been a mum, had Lucy refused either of her sons' cries for help. And she wasn't about to start now, even if it did put her in an extremely awkward position with Carol and force them into a situation where there could only be one winner and one loser. The situation couldn't continue; somebody would ultimately get hurt.

She'd continued to stare at the shadows dancing on the bedroom wall until finally daylight filtered through and erased her shadows. If only daylight could have worked the same magic on the darkness inside her head!

Carol woke early on Tuesday morning, unable to believe she had actually slept. Or that the banks (or whoever would repossess their worldly goods) had not arrived to order her out of her home. She ran a hand over the maroon satin sheet, noticing how smooth it was on Eric's unslept-in side of the bed, wondering if he would be back sleeping beside her that night. And whether they would have a house or a bed to sleep in.

She always made an effort after he'd been away, enjoyed sprucing up the bedroom and her appearance to welcome him home properly, play her part as it were. Thinking about that now brought bile to her throat. All the nights he'd lain beside her without saying a word. That's what hurt most. If he'd opened up to her, let her know what they were dealing with, they could have worked something out together. Checking the time, she realised it was still the middle of the night in Florida, far too early to expect any contact from him. That was if he had any intention of getting in touch again. What was he playing at? Presumably lying low until he landed back in Ireland.

Without Lucy's help yesterday, she'd never have found the strength to clear the house. But opening her eyes to the stark nakedness of her bedroom walls this morning had still been shocking. Her wardrobe door swung open to reveal bare rails. The non-faded parts of the soft beige carpet were a testament to the smaller pieces of furniture she and Lucy had shifted between them. Gazing around the remainder of the room, her eyes fell on the door to Eric's wardrobe. Apportioning blame by ignoring his personal belongings, she'd left his wardrobe intact. But now the intensity of her anger had dissipated – and for the sake of staying busy and keeping her mind occupied – she jumped out of bed and pulled open the large oak doors, reaching for his large suitcase on the top shelf.

As she did, it dawned on her that she hadn't packed a bag for her husband in a very long time. His meticulous nature – bordering on obsessive in Carol's opinion – made him one of the fussiest people on earth. After a few disastrous attempts at packing for him had led to heated (and unnecessary) arguments, she'd vowed never to fold as much as a pair of socks for him again! And apart from sorting his laundry on the days their cleaning lady didn't come in, she'd kept her word.

Quickly unzipping the case, she spread it open on the floor, immediately turning her attention to his collection of ties hanging inside the wardrobe doors. Dropping them into the case, her face paled when she noticed a pink lace trim peeping out from an insert pocket in the case.

Pulling roughly at the lace to reveal a silk negligee, her anger returned full force, her intention to kill him with her bare hands stronger than anything she'd ever felt in her life. "Cheating bastard!" she screamed at the top of her voice.

Is this what he's been up to when he's supposed to be away on business trips, she thought? Wining and dining some floozy while I'm sitting here at home waiting for his instruction to go and get my hair done and look my best on his return so he can strut about our local town and act like the man who has it all? He has it all indeed, the wife, the kids, the mistress. He's got a lot more than he's been letting on. A whole lot more.

She swivelled around to get a scissors, forgetting that her dressing table was one of the items they'd shifted to Danny's containers. And the scissors she usually kept in the top drawer was over there too. Her fingers itched to shred every last item of his clothing: his flashy ties, the pristine shirts he'd insisted should only be dry-cleaned, the trousers and jackets he left out for steam pressing, the designer jumpers, golf shirts, Tommy Hilfiger and other designer items and the rest that filled his wardrobe to capacity.

To hell with him, she thought, yanking as many hangers as she could from the rails, pulling jumpers and tops from the shelving and dropping them in a heap on the floor. He could dress half the men in Crosshaven from this lot! In her bare feet, she jumped up and down on the bundle of mixed fabrics, tears of humiliation stinging her eyes as she caught sight of her reflection in the mirrored door leading into their en-suite bathroom.

She stopped and stared, taking in the unkempt hair – she'd cancelled her hair appointment – lines on her face that hadn't yet been masked by the anti-wrinkle potions she carefully applied daily, and the faded grey nightshirt she'd pulled from the remaining clothes in her walk-in-wardrobe. The image wasn't a pretty one, her ghastly complexion emphasising dark circles under her eyes, reflecting the fifty-something woman she actually was rather than the mid-forties version she liked to present to the world. She pushed the door open to make her reflection disappear, wishing it was as easy to remove it from her mind. Is it any wonder Eric's straying, she thought, walking away from the abandoned heap of clothes and stepping into her wardrobe.

Carol took a shoehorn from a hook overhead and, carefully measuring two footsteps to the right and three hand-widths along the wall, she ran her finger along the join of the floorboards until she found the little groove she was looking for. Then with expert and familiar precision, she slipped the shoehorn in and levered up the false-fitting floorboard to reveal a safety-deposit box. Eric wasn't the only one with secrets.

Punching the four-digit unlocking code into the tiny keypad, she opened the box and took out a folded document, replacing the floorboard afterwards exactly as she'd found it and going to telephone Isobel.

Lucy sat on the end of the bed, lingering in the bedroom longer than she knew she should, time ticking loudly in her head, an impending explosion inevitable, the only question being which problem would come knocking first.

The explosion arrived in the form of the sharp intonation of a squeal from her mother. Lucy groaned inwardly, wondering what on earth was fuelling the promise of another emergency in her mother's yelling.

"Hurry up, Lucy!"

Lucy struggled to stay calm, thanking God for the barrier the stairs provided. Gloria's aching knees prevented her from climbing the steps, giving in only in cases of what she reckoned was sheer emergency. But judging from the high pitch of her squeal this time, Lucy suspected her mother would make a rare exception and climb the stairs if she didn't get herself down to the hall as quickly as possible.

With reluctance, she left the seclusion of the guest bedroom.

"What now, Mum?"

"Stephen's on the phone from Australia. He's in an awful state. He knows nothing about the fire. And he's had the cheek to ask me if I'm getting Alzheimer's!"

Lucy's blood ran cold. Four sentences without a breath, the run-on style of chat Gloria used to hide her guilt.

"You told him, didn't you?"

Gloria blushed, mumbling an indecipherable excuse.

Lucy tuned out, waving away her glib excuses. She'd kill her mother. How many times had she begged her not to tell the boys? Why couldn't she respect her wishes just this once? Was it too much to ask? She was finding it difficult enough to cope with everything without landing the burden onto Stephen's shoulders and then having to worry about him coping with it. At the rate her life was falling apart, she'd be found buried under her growing heap of problems!

She stormed past Gloria, flashing a menacing look in her direction. Dealing with her mother would have to wait, her immediate obligation being to Stephen. If he was to hear the truth, he needed to hear it from her, not the garbled version Gloria would deliver. Grabbing the hands-free phone in the kitchen, she took herself into the back garden and banged the door shut behind her, depending on the double-glazing to allow her a bit of privacy.

"Stephen, how are you, love?" Lucy struggled to keep her voice steady.

"Mum, what's going on over there?"

Hearing his voice brought a torrent of emotion flooding to the surface, emotion she wasn't strong enough to deal with right now. He'd been gone over two years, two long years since she'd held him in her arms and told him she loved him. Her lip trembled, tears threatened to fall. Inhaling deeply, she got her emotions in check.

"Mum? Are you there?"

"Yes, love." She moved to the end of the garden and sat on the swing seat.

"Nana tells me the phones are dead because the house has burnt down. Is that true?"

"Oh, Stephen, you're so far away. I don't want you concerned unnecessarily but –"

"Let me be the judge of that," he interrupted. "I'm not a baby any longer. Oh cripes!"

"What, Stephen? What is it?"

Lucy clutched the phone tightly, his silence deafening.

"Dear God, Mum, how did you think you could keep this under wraps?"

"Stephen?" He was confusing her now. What on earth did he mean?

"I'm staring at our house on the bloody internet. Is it as bad as it looks? Is this some kind of horrible joke?"

"No joke." Lucy leaned her head against the frame of the swing.

She didn't know where to begin but knew that unless she managed to ease Stephen's concerns, he'd be buying his ticket home before she could do anything to stop him.

"Oh my God . . . it says the owner suffered burns and was hospitalised! Christ, Mum, is that true? Was Dad badly burnt?"

"No, no, no – he's just suffering from smoke inhalation – he collapsed on the landing and the firemen brought him out. I was at Delia's at the time. He did get some slight scorching on his lower arms and the backs of his hands but it's not serious. But thank God it's nothing more serious than that and he's making good progress."

She imagined him running his hands through his cropped blonde hair, visualised the intensity of his dark-brown eyes as he pieced the story together. Her head was spinning in confusion as she tried to formulate reasonable responses to his questions. She pulled her knees to her chest, resting her slippers on the edge of the wooden seat, her uneven weight swaying the seat backward and forward.

"I'm coming home as soon as I can get a flight out of here. There's no way you'll cope with all this if Dad's in hospital!"

Lucy sighed. "No, love. You mustn't put yourself to that expense or trouble. You can't risk losing your job."

In truth, she'd have loved nothing more than to see him walking in the door but she refused to let him know that.

"But, Mum, there has to be so much to organise: the company, the rebuild, insurance assessors and engineers . . ."

Lucy paled, too ashamed to admit the truth that all those issues were in jeopardy. "You've got your own life to worry about. Dad will be home in a few days. Maybe when he's well enough, we can take a trip to visit you. It would take him out of himself, give him something to plan and look forward to after all this." She waited while he digested her suggestion – and for the pause on the line to pass – willing him to listen and see sense.

"I don't know, Mum. I'm not happy about this. If Matt was with you same but . . . hey, have you even told him?"

"No, I haven't but –"

"You must, Mum. And I'm sure he'd be able to take a quick trip over to help you out – he's not starting work for another while."

Lucy didn't want to go into the details of Matt's sordid relationship. Afraid she'd let her guard down and blurt everything out if she spoke about Matt, she hurried on to say, "I'm sure I can manage to complete a few forms or whatever else needs doing to get things up and running once more. And I can always get your advice over the phone or by email if I'm in difficulty."

Stephen was reluctant to let go, however. "Mum, I can't be over here while you and Dad are going through all this. How can I believe you're telling me the truth? Are you sure it's not worse than you're letting on? What started the fire? Have you got the results of the investigation yet? I'm sure Matt will –"

At the mention of Matt's name again, Lucy cut in immediately, halting him before he could even finish what he was about to say. "Stephen, Matt has hardly unpacked in New York and he's starting work in the college." No way was she lumping this on top of Matt. If he's to survive his own mess, she thought, he's probably better off sticking it out in Manhattan until the dust settles. Better for him to keep his distance. Better for us too perhaps. "The last thing I'm going to do is ruin it for him by dragging him back to a trail of destruction. Anyway, being very realistic, what can either of ye do to help us? It's blooming builders with jackhammers and sheets of timber and plywood we need, not a gym instructor in the latest leisure gear or a marketing manager in a sharp suit carrying a briefcase!"

But Stephen's determination matched hers. "He'll want to know, Mum, and he deserves to be kept in the picture even if he doesn't return. Same as me. We can't keep something like this from him. And why would you do that anyway? He's not a baby any more . . ."

Lucy shook her head. If only you knew, she thought. She tuned back in to Stephen.

"I'll give him a call later," he was saying, "and then like myself he can make up his own mind whether he wants to come home or not."

Lucy put her feet back on the grass, picking up a recognisable defiance in Stephen's voice. He wasn't going to be easily swayed. He never had been.

She stood up from the seat and walked around the garden as he argued on, struggling to instil a bit of warmth in her bones on that chilly November morning. Feeling the dampness through the light soles of her slippers, she moved onto the footpath instead.

"The house can be repaired, Stephen," she said when she got a chance to get a word in. "After all," she forced a little laugh, feeling slightly nauseous at the falsity of it in her ears, "Dad has his own construction company so it's not as if we won't know what builders to employ to get us straightened out!"

"Yeah, Mum, but if Dad's lads are working on our house, there won't be any wages coming in. Have you thought of that? And without Dad there to supervise, you know only too well productivity will be lower than normal."

His concern came as no surprise, his practical, business-like approach exactly what she'd have expected. Being the eldest, he'd always been responsible and sensitive to the needs of others, first in line to do anybody a good turn. She supposed, though she wouldn't be admitting it to her mother any time soon, Gloria had probably done her a favour by blurting it out as she had. Such a pity things weren't as Stephen believed though, she thought privately, imagining his disbelief if she blurted out her suspicion that Ardle Construction had folded.

"Dad's already giving orders from the bed, Stephen, surely that tells you enough. And," she paused a moment, a shudder running through her, "Jenny is arriving home from London in the next few days."

"Oh God, Mum, will it be safe to have the two of you at the same bedside? Poor Dad, he'll have his work cut out for him with bossy Aunty Jen around the place telling everybody what to do." Stephen's laughter lightened the mood and finally he seemed to accept her wishes. "Promise you'll call me day or night if you or Dad need anything, Mum," he warned one last time.

Lucy let out a sigh of relief, leaning against the back wall of Delia's house. "Apart from anything else, love, we'd have nowhere for you to sleep. At this rate, poor Delia will have to build on an extension to give us all a roof over our heads! Dad and I will stay with her while the repairs are being done. Delia's insisting and I suppose it makes sense. Of course when your nana heard what had happened, she hotfooted up here and has moved in as well."

"Using it as a golden opportunity to get back to Crosshaven without admitting she rushed into the nursing home too soon after Granda died."

He could read his scheming grandmother a lot better than Lucy had realised. "Good point, Stephen. Although I wouldn't let her hear you say that!"

"Watching you all under one roof would almost be worth the cost of the ticket home. You, Nana and Delia bickering at the same table every Christmas Day was torture in itself, never mind what it'll be like on a full-time basis!"

Lucy was filled with dread. Stephen was right. What on earth was she letting herself in for? But it wasn't as if she had any choice in the matter. "This call must be costing you a fortune, pet."

"Not at all, I've got special rates."

"Even so, never mind my ramblings. I'll keep you updated on Dad's progress and, Stephen, promise you won't say anything to Matt for now."

"Okay, but only for a few days more. He should know, Mum."

"Alright. Bye for now, love –"

"Eh, Mum, there's something else before you go. It's the main reason I was trying to get you in the first place. I hate dumping this on you now on top of everything else but I need you to post me over a copy of my long birth certificate."

"You too? They've been sitting in the hatbox for years and now you're both looking for them the same week!"

"Eh, Mum," he seemed to trip over his words, "aren't you going to ask why?"

Lucy was instantly uneasy, moving to the far end of the garden again, standing against the shed and staring at the expanse of hills once more. "You're not doing anything dangerous, are you?" Her heart pounded in her chest. It wasn't like Stephen to play guessing games.

"More risky than dangerous, I guess," he said, the laugh that followed forced and out of place.

"Spit it out, Stephen. What's going on?"

"Mum, I hate telling you this over the phone. But seeing as you're not allowing me come home . . ."

"Stephen!" And then regretting her outburst, she added, "You're not sick, are you?"

With the luck they'd been having, nothing would surprise Lucy. Yet his tone implied something mysterious rather than life-threatening. "Stephen, please tell me." She returned to the swing seat and sat down once more, her inner voice telling her she might need to be sitting on a solid (as solid as the swing seat could be) surface.

"I'm getting married, Mum."

Stephen's voice came quietly across thousands of miles of telephone signal. He paused as he waited for his mother's reaction, his silence speaking multitudes. He was unsure of her response. To Lucy, that was clearly evident. As with Matt the previous night, she could read his mind. And there was a large red beacon flashing a danger alert.

She closed her eyes, a well of pent-up emotion building inside her, a torrent of expletives sitting on her lips, threatening to leave her mouth and ruin the relationship she had with her son, leaving her daughter-in-law-to-be (whoever she might be) to gloat from afar and tell him he didn't need family. He'd have all he'd need with her.

"Tell me you're joking, Stephen?"

"No joke, Mum, just a quiet Christmas wedding here

in Oz. I was hoping you and Dad could visit then and bring
Nana and Delia too – but now I don't know – doesn't look
like Dad will be fit to travel? But if you can . . . And I'll
organise flights for Matt if he can't afford them."

He'd lost Lucy at the part about a quiet Christmas
wedding. Hell, she thought, that's little more than six
weeks away.

"Mum?"

"Christmas?" Lucy's brain had frozen. She stood up
from the swing too quickly, almost toppling on to the
damp grass.

"Aren't you happy for me, Mum?"

She avoided his question. She had so many of her
own to ask. "But who are you marrying? It's all so sudden.
You've never mentioned having someone special in your
life and now you're announcing a wedding?" Now it
was Lucy's turn to fire questions. There were so many
gaps to fill. The tables had turned, putting Stephen in the
hot seat. His hurry to the altar rails (or registry office)
bothered Lucy more than anything, the most important
question of all burning on her lips.

"She's the one, Mum."

Lucy wanted to throw up. *The one*? He's far too
young, a voice she found unable to silence screamed
loudly in her head. His life is only beginning. What
about his career? And the years he spent in college?
Australia was only supposed to be a short-term solution,
somewhere to gain experience. If he's getting married
over there, does that mean . . .? Her heart ached. She
couldn't imagine him settling so many miles from home,
where they'd only see him on annual visits and special
occasions.

"Mum? Please say something?"

"Where did you meet?" she asked eventually. Impulsiveness wasn't part of Stephen's make-up. In her heart, Lucy knew there was more to his announcement than met the eye.

"At a friend's barbecue. Ellie's Australian. You and Dad will love her once you get to know her."

I hate her already, Lucy thought, gritting her teeth to stop from opening her mouth, finding it impossible to listen to his expression of undying love without gagging.

"She's the best thing that's ever happened to me," Stephen continued.

Lucy was consumed by jealousy, her fingernails digging into the palms of her hands, her knuckles so tense she thought they'd burst through her skin.

"It's what we both want, Mum," Stephen said, his tone even but without its earlier exuberance and excitement.

"But what's the rush, Stephen? Move in together by all means but don't rush into marriage."

"There's something else you should know . . ."

Lucy braced herself for what was coming, though in her heart she could guess. She remained silent, waiting with bated breath for his next announcement.

"We're having a baby, Mum. Around Easter time, you'll be a grandma. And Dad will be a granddad and a father-in-law and Matt an –"

"Stop!" Lucy gasped loudly. She didn't need him to go through every relation to his forthcoming child. She could work that out for herself. What she was unable to comprehend, however, was that her darling Stephen was going to have a family of his own very shortly. Some scheming conniving Aussie had obviously recognised him as a good catch and had tricked him into marriage. Her mind raced ahead, blurred moments passing before she became aware of Stephen's silence on the other end.

"I can't deal with this right now," she said slowly. "It's been one shock after the other . . ."

"Your son's marriage is hardly in the same league as your house burning down! Surely this is a good shock? Can't you be happy for us?"

'Us'! She hated the protective way he used the word, jealousy spiking inside her again. She lost control of her tongue, cruel words spilling from her mouth, tact in short supply.

"What about your career, Stephen? And why did you get a girl you hardly know pregnant? There's no shortage of contraception nowadays. She's not even Irish! Does this mean you'll never live in your own country again? What the hell were you thinking?"

His gasp of disgust and disappointment was audible. Instantly, she shut up, aware she'd messed up badly, wishing she could roll up her tongue and suck the words back in.

"I get what you're saying, Mum, loud and clear," Stephen deadpanned. "I'm older than you were when you had me. I'll leave you to get on with it now you've got both of us out of your hair."

The line went dead.

Lucy dropped to her knees on the damp grass, curled into a tight ball and cried her heart out.

Lucy's tears had dried but her heart was still heavy with remorse. Will I ever learn, she wondered, getting to her feet and slowly making her way back inside.

Delia and Gloria eyed her warily, glancing at each other before silently moving toward her and wrapping their arms around her.

"Did Stephen take the news of the fire badly?" Delia asked, her voice little more than a murmur in Lucy's ear.

Lucy nodded her head but didn't speak, slipping her arms around the other two women, relieved to lean her weary body on theirs and accept their support.

Gloria rubbed her daughter's back in slow, circular movements, meeting Delia's eye and raising her shoulders as if to say 'What now?'

"Why don't you go back to bed for a rest, love?" she said. "It's been an exhausting few days."

Lucy shook her head, easing out of their arms once more and covering her face with her hands. "My life is falling apart." She dropped her hands to her side, looking from Delia to Gloria and back to Delia again. "Everything is disintegrating. Why, Mum? Delia? Why is everything happening at once?"

Gloria frowned but remained silent, not wanting to sabotage their unexpected closeness by opening her big mouth and saying something to upset everybody.

Meanwhile, Delia filled the kettle and placed three mugs on the table, along with a bronze ashtray she'd made out of a neck-piece design that went a bit askew. Taking an unopened packet of cigarettes and a box of matches from the little drawer in the dresser, she put them beside the ashtray and left it up to Lucy to decide whether she needed to open them or not.

Lucy sat at the table, playing with the cigarette box, eyeing the matchbox warily. The thought of lighting a match and watching a flame burn held no appeal, the memory of her house amass with flames still too raw. Feeling her mother's hand covering hers, she caught her eye and gave a weak smile.

"If you want to talk . . ." Gloria offered.

Lucy chewed on the inside of her cheek, wanting to open up but afraid she'd live to regret it when Gloria changed from the docile protector mode she was in now to that of nagging tyrant that was no doubt lurking a short distance from the surface.

"I need to call Stephen back," she said eventually. "Is that okay, Del? I promise to fix up with you for all these calls."

Delia waved away her offer, bringing the teapot to the table and filling their mugs. "Don't be silly! Whatever you need to do, just do it. What's mine is yours, sis, particularly now."

Taking Stephen's number from the caller ID, Lucy put a call through to her son. She knew she should get up and go somewhere private to make the call but she just hadn't the energy. Gloria and Delia chatted quietly and Lucy completely tuned out, the only sound she could hear – and feel – being the beat of her heart while she waited. Part of her was terrified he wouldn't answer and the other part dreaded his reaction if he did. She regretted her outburst now, wishing she'd kept her opinions to herself until she'd at least taken the time to digest what he'd said. He was twenty-four after all, not twelve! A consenting adult who was entitled to fall in love and marry whoever he wanted. But her approval must have mattered to him. Otherwise he wouldn't have reacted so strongly. All he'd wanted was her consent and what had she offered him instead? Insults and accusations.

He wasn't answering but she hung on. Thinking of the disgusting bile she'd spouted at him, she regretted every word. Stephen had a kind, generous nature, and had seldom given either her or Danny cause for worry or concern. She remembered the excitement in his voice, the unique warmth in the way he mentioned his fiancée, the anticipation in his voice about becoming a father. He didn't deserve her scorn or nastiness and if only he'd answer his goddamn phone, she'd apologise for her rudeness and tell him that. And she'd also tell him how excited she was about becoming a grandmother – even if it was more than a little unexpected. She'd say whatever she needed to ensure her son knew how much he was loved.

Being such a long way from home must be difficult. He'd called for support, not rejection. But his phone rang and rang in Lucy's ear, the longer it went unanswered, the more distance Lucy believed was between her and her son. His partner – what had he called her? Ellie, wasn't it? She had her family and no doubt a large circle of friends to share the news with. But Stephen, though he'd made a lot of good friends in the two years he'd been living in Australia, had nobody that close – apart from his new fiancée of course!

The phone continued to ring. Lucy hung up, then after a few moments dialled again, picturing Stephen sitting staring into space, too obstinate to answer it. Damn, damn, damn, she thought, shrugging her shoulders to indicate to Delia and Gloria that she was still waiting.

"Leave him a message and try him again later," her mother suggested.

Trying to think of something to say, Lucy waited for

the beep to leave a message on his answer phone. "Stephen, I'm sorry for flying off the handle earlier, love. Can we please talk? I'll call you again later – after I've been to see Dad." Crossing her fingers, she hoped Ellie was out of earshot and prayed Stephen hadn't shared the contents of their earlier conversation with her. A whingeing mother-in-law was not the first impression she wanted to give.

Lucy ripped the plastic off the cigarette box, removed the foil and placed a cigarette between her lips. If she'd ever needed a drag of nicotine to soothe her nerves, she needed it now. She leaned in for a light as Delia struck a match, feeling Gloria's eyes boring into her from across the table. In all the years she'd been on this earth, it was the first time she had ever smoked in front of her mother, proving to herself how close to rock bottom she truly was.

Chapter 25

Eric woke with a start, stretching in the narrow bunk, his clothes wrinkled and grubby after sleeping in them. Air-conditioning hummed overhead, a distant buzz of conversation coming from a nearby room. Rolling over onto his side and facing the wall, Eric put his hand under his head and delayed getting up.

Is there any way out of this mess, he wondered, staring at the white wall and jumping with fright (banging his head against the iron bed-frame) when he heard his name being called. He hadn't given his name to anybody. Damn, he thought, what's going on?

Getting out of bed immediately, he reached underneath and dragged out his bag, searching in the pocket for his passport. It was still there. He sighed with relief. There must be another Eric in the vicinity, he thought, on the verge of rolling back into bed when he was called again, this time by his surname as well as his forename.

Cautiously, he made his way to the public office, his

knees turning to jelly when he came face to face with two uniformed policemen, a snarling dog standing between them.

"Eric Black?"

"Yes, sir," he stuttered, glancing toward the door which was thrown wide open. But there wasn't a hope he could make a break for it.

"You showed up here a couple of days back and yesterday attempted . . . let's say, you ignored the beach regulations, staying there long after the designated times."

Eric nodded, his cheeks flushing. He didn't offer an explanation.

"Do you have business in Sarasota?"

"Eh, not really," Eric answered truthfully. The very mention of business made him shiver. He'd certainly made a mess of his recent business affairs.

The lifeguard who'd helped him the previous evening arrived on to the scene at that moment, breezing in through the entrance doors armed with volleyball nets.

"Feeling better today?" he enquired.

Eric nodded. "Yes, thanks. I'd best be moving on."

"Maybe not so fast," one of the policemen said. "We've a few more questions for you."

Eric raised an eyebrow, moving towards the wall and leaning against it. His legs were still like jelly, a dull ache beginning in his temples.

"We got a call from Tampa Bay. There's a bit of a commotion going on over there with you at the centre of it."

The wall felt cold against Eric's sweaty hands. Had Zebedee Holdings reported him? Was he liable for the balance of the money he owed them? Or could he renege on the contract he'd signed? His chest tightened. He rubbed it with the heel of his hand, swallowing down the acid taste in his mouth.

"Your wife's pretty anxious to speak to you. Any reason why you left Tampa without calling her? Or using the flight ticket she organised?"

Eric faked a smile, struggled to conceal his fear. His mind raced. How did they know all this? How did they connect with him so quickly? Florida was a large state, filled with many, many people. How on earth had they tracked him so easily? He struggled to find a reasonable response. "I knew she was organising my flight but my phone, it . . ."

The stern-looking policeman wasn't interested in Eric's games and didn't pull any punches. "Your phone was found discarded. Its credentials checked out as being registered to you. Disappearing without trace is more difficult than people realise," he said, arching an eyebrow.

The smirk on his lips irritated Eric, made him edgy, made him feel as though he was falling into a trap. "The battery was dead. Getting rid of it made sense."

"So it has nothing to do with avoiding calls from Zebedee Holdings?"

Eric opened his mouth to defend himself, then shut it again, completely at a loss for words, the imaginary bars of a cell sliding closed in his mind.

Eric clutched the handles of his holdall as he sat in the back of the police car on his way to the nearest police station. His stomach growled with hunger, a stale taste in his mouth in the want of a refreshing drink. A lick of toothpaste would have made a difference, even a capful of mouthwash to gargle. But hunger pains and a parched throat were the least of his worries. Wrangling his way out of a property deal with Zebedee Holdings was a much larger concern, the menacing threats he'd received at his business meeting in the hotel bar fresh in his mind. And probably even more distinct in his bank accounts!

He looked out the window at the magnificent stretch of golden sand on the Mexico coast, storing the view in his memory and saving it to help him through darker days. And unless he found a legitimate way out of the financial mess he'd got himself into, the next long stretch he'd have to look forward to would more than likely be in a Florida prison.

Chapter 26

Danny lifted the stainless-steel lid from his plate, grimacing as he looked at the miserable portion of roast chicken, accompanied by lumpy mashed potato and shrivelled peas. With the lid still in his hand, he was tempted to replace it without putting a morsel beyond his lips. But he was hungry. He took off his oxygen mask and speared a pea with his fork.

For the first time since he'd been admitted to hospital, his body felt something resembling normality. His breathing – though still assisted by oxygen – was a lot less laboured. The nurse checking his blood pressure and temperature had given him good news earlier that morning.

"Your readings have stabilised today, Danny. If your blood oxygen levels are acceptable, I think we'll get you up on your feet later. And perhaps a shower, if we're careful not to get your bandages wet – the chance to freshen up might help you feel better. What do you think?"

Though the nurses had treated him to the embarrassment of a bed bath and had removed the worst of the soot from his skin, he couldn't wait to scrub his body properly with hot sudsy water. "I'm game if you are," he'd replied, winking at the ginger-haired nurse.

"Cheeky! You're definitely on the mend," she'd said, her normally pale cheeks flushing a deep crimson. "Think you're about ready to be moved out of high-dependency at this stage."

"But I feel safe under your watchful eye," he protested.

"I'll bet," she said, sticking a needle into the vein in his wrist and drawing blood. "Nurse O'Donnell is on shower-duty later," she told him, her expression serious as she labelled the little bottle of blood. "If you ask her nicely, I'm sure she'll scrub your back. And I hear she's a pro at reaching all those awkward little bits!"

Danny had collapsed on to the pillows, the thought of Nurse O'Donnell – who epitomised the old-fashioned stern matron – coming anywhere near him with a shower-hose a daunting prospect. "Think my levels have suddenly dropped," he'd said, fixing the oxygen mask over his nose and closing his eyes.

The nurse had laughed and gathered her belongings, shaking her head when she caught him looking out from underneath long lashes.

Now, as he chewed mindlessly on the dry chicken, Danny fantasised about sinking his teeth into a juicy steak, cooked medium-rare just as he liked it and accompanied with fried onions, mushrooms and pepper sauce. His stomach growled, the chicken in his mouth tasting more like cardboard than white meat. But, with every bite of food and drop of water he swallowed being recorded, he deduced that eating his dinner was in his own best interest if it ultimately led to an early discharge.

Glancing around at the other patients in his ward, he was grateful that he – despite the misfortune he'd endured – looked to be in better shape than a lot of them. Mesmerised by the efforts of one elderly gentleman struggling to drink pink liquid from a beaker, Danny stared at his quivering lips, willing the old man to get them to work so that at least he could be spared the indignity of tube-feeding.

"Mr Ardle? It's been quite a while."

At the sound of his name, Danny glanced up to find Inspector Phelim O'Brien standing beside his bed. He took a shuddering breath, halted for a moment by the inspector's sullen expression and the thickness of the file he held under his arm. No longer interested in eating – even if it was only for the sake of it – Danny pushed the tray away. Then another man appeared at the end of the bed – another detective by the looks of him. Things were serious if O'Brien had brought back-up. He felt his knees buckle, never so glad to be lying in bed so his legs didn't collapse from under him.

"Have a seat – it's not easy staring up at you," Danny said to O'Brien, indicating the armchair at the side of the bed. "I have a feeling you're not here for a pleasant chat?"

Phelim O'Brien remained standing, as did the skinny, freckled officer staring down on him.

Was it Danny's imagination or had something flashed in Phelim's eyes when he'd heard those words? As quickly as it might have happened, it was gone. Danny watched as Phelim shifted his glance toward the other officer. And then to the file.

"Your doctors have only agreed to giving us a few moments with you," Phelim began.

"For now at least," the other officer added.

Danny looked from one to the other and waited. The screen of the television glowed over the second officer's head. He saw the RTÉ logo and the familiar ticker-tape of breaking news along the bottom as the news reader delivered the latest lunchtime headlines. A thought suddenly occurred to him. Had their house fire been televised? And if so, how many had recognised it as the business address of Ardle Construction? What effect would it have on trade? Without dwelling on the consequences, he turned to Phelim.

"Aren't you going to introduce your colleague, Inspector?"

"Sergeant Richard Collins, Garda Forensics," the sergeant introduced himself, pushing his rimless glasses back on his nose.

"Nice to meet you," Danny said, putting the oxygen mask in place, relieved to hide behind it.

Phelim opened the file, flicking through several pages before pulling one out and scanning through it. "We've received some preliminary findings from Forensics," he told Danny. "Sergeant Collins will go into more detail with you later but first I'd like to create a sketch of events based on your memory of Saturday evening last."

Being questioned came as no surprise to Danny, expecting it would be routine under the circumstances. "My memory's a bit hazy as you can imagine," he said, indicating his bandaged arms and singed hair, "but I'll retrace my steps as best I can."

"In as much detail as you can." Phelim dropped the

file on the bed, folding his arms across his chest. "You want to move up closer, Richard, so you can hear better?"

"I'm fine from where I am, Inspector," came Richard's reply.

Danny eyed them warily, sensing the animosity between them, his regard for Officer Collins increasing a little. "My wife left for the afternoon, leaving me with the Premiership for company – any man's idea of perfection on a Saturday –"

"Stick with the fire, Danny. We're trying to piece a case together, not the lowdown on the soccer league."

The way Phelim said it made Danny shudder, making it sound like anything but a straightforward, accidental event. He cleared his throat and coughed, then pulled himself up in the bed, the effort putting his breathing under intense pressure. As he'd intended. Let that saucy inspector wait, he thought, exaggeratedly catching his breath until he was ready to continue. And I'll do what I can to throw him off the trail, he decided, make him earn his crust as he gathers his evidence and pieces it together.

"I watched the match and then another . . . I can't remember . . . I think I dozed off before the end . . . When I woke again I felt terrible – as if I were drugged. It was a real effort to open my eyes, to sit up. I was so disorientated that it took me a while to register the smell, the stinging in my eyes, the smoky room . . ." He paused to take a sip of water. "I staggered to the door into the hall . . ."

"Why didn't you call the fire brigade at that stage?" Phelim interrupted.

Danny stared at him, aghast at his accusing tone. Why didn't I call the fire brigade instead of running to fix things? He'd been asking himself that ever since he'd woken up. It was why he'd been off-hand with Lucy, his self-loathing along with the weight of blame filling him with anger and hostility, not to mention the other crucial piece of news he was keeping from Lucy.

"If you've got something to say, why not spit it out instead of playing games, Inspector?"

"Danny," Phelim said evenly, "you need to understand the Garda position on this. To us, everyone connected to this case is a suspect until proven otherwise. Are we clear on that?"

Danny gritted his teeth, keeping his simmering anger under wraps. "Crystal."

"You went to investigate? How would you describe what happened next?" Richard joined in at this stage, prompting Danny to continue, his intervention diffusing the tension slightly.

Danny folded his arms across his chest and glanced from Richard's lemon shirt to his gaudy tie. There was the finest line between unique and odd, between what made a grown man look fashionable or downright stupid, like Richard. I must have inhaled more smoke in my brain than they've discovered, he thought, the voice in his head analysing the colour of ties sounding too damn like Lucy's. Or worse still, Gloria's!

He gave some thought to Richard's question. "Catastrophic is the first word that comes to mind to describe what happened next." He gave the first heartfelt response he'd given since they'd arrived at his bedside. "When I opened the door into the hallway, I walked into my worst nightmare, the whole place filled with thick black smoke, unbearable heat . . ." Danny found himself at a loss for words. How do you describe the horror of failure? Failure to save and protect your home? Failure to fight raging flames? Failure, failure, failure, piling high and smacking you in the face. "I dropped to my knees and crawled along the hall, creeping up the stairs, trying to keep my head underneath the heaviest of smoke . . . I knew there was a fire extinguisher in the office . . . the noise was shocking . . . I knew that the flames were mangling and destroying everything that came their way upstairs but I hoped the fire wasn't in the main bedroom and adjoining office . . . I remember being halfway up the stairs, struggling to push ahead . . ."

"Hold it right there." Phelim took a notebook from his pocket and jotted a few notes on the page. "Why did you keep a fire extinguisher in such an out-of-the-way place? Why not on the landing? The hallway downstairs? In fact, most people have them in their kitchens – but why not somewhere with ease of access at least?"

How dare he blame me? Danny fumbled with the oxygen mask, which felt cumbersome all of a sudden. His pulse pounded so hard that his whole body trembled. He looked Phelim O'Brien in the eye, staring him down until the other man dropped his gaze to his notebook.

"I've been living in Sycamore Lodge for the past twenty-five years. That fire extinguisher has been moved from room to room over the years, out of harm's way from the boys when they were kids and out of Lucy's sight when she had to move it each time she wanted to vacuum the floors. Never once have we had as much as a chip-pan catching fire. Why would we have been obsessed with the location of the fire extinguisher? Or does carelessness on our part put us in a line-up of chief suspects? Would you be quite so arrogant if you'd experienced a loss like this yourself?" He stopped talking, his face red with exertion. Then he continued, blowing air through his mouth with each word. "But oh, I almost forgot, you've already had a taste of losing everything. Except in your case, you threw it away. Isn't that right, Inspector?"

Richard glanced from one to the other, excusing himself to take a phone call.

Phelim almost snarled. "The location of the fire extinguisher mightn't put you in a line-up but your attitude sure as hell will!" His voice was menacing, his face white with rage. He broke off when the ginger-haired nurse arrived, a scowl on her face. She had obviously heard the distress in her patient's voice.

"I said you could see him for a few minutes, Inspector," she reminded him, fixing Danny's mask more securely, ensuring he was getting maximum benefit from the oxygen, because judging by his facial colour (the blue-purple hue showing through the tiny thread-veins), he was in serious need of it. Strapping a blood-pressure machine on his upper arm, she turned around to address Phelim again. "And I also instructed he wasn't to be upset!"

"We're almost done," Phelim grunted.

"You *are* done," the nurse instructed, refusing to have her patient-comes-first rule ignored. She stood – one hand on her hip and the other pumping the blood-pressure apparatus – and stared at him, waiting for him to leave, leaving him in no doubt but that the interview was well and truly over.

Danny ran a hand through his hair and gave the nurse a grateful smile. "I'll take you up on that hot shower now."

Phelim O'Brien was standing at the door of the ward, disgusted he hadn't got the opportunity to probe Danny further. He spotted Richard at the end of the corridor and strode towards him.

"Richard – those mobile phones you found in the ashes – have you had a chance to get them analysed yet? Or retrieve the last calls made?"

"Expecting preliminary results this afternoon as a matter of fact," Richard responded. "Pity our little chat was cut short." He jerked a thumb toward Danny's ward. "I wanted to quiz him about the three mugs we took from the kitchen table, dredges of coffee in all of them. I took them for fingerprinting to be on the safe side . . ."

Phelim stopped walking and looked directly at Richard. "You're in line for promotion, aren't you?"

Richard's cheeks went bright red. "There or thereabouts but with the moratorium in place now, it'll probably never happen."

Phelim patted him on the arm. "Wait for me outside. Just remembered something."

He doubled back to the ward.

"Won't take a minute," he said quickly, when the nurse (or Ginger as he'd come to think of her) gave him an evil stare.

"I'll give you thirty seconds," she said and went out.

Danny's eyes had shot open at the sound of his voice. "Back again?"

"You did say you were alone in the house after your wife left?"

Danny's eyes narrowed. "That's right."

"But your phone was beside you on the chair. And you still didn't think of calling the emergency services before leaving the room?"

"I thought we'd covered that already. I'd only woken up and was completely disorientated – probably already suffering from smoke inhalation. Okay, so it was stupid to go upstairs but that's what I did."

"Okay, point taken," Phelim said, nodding his head and pondering a moment. He scratched his belly through his white nylon shirt. "What was the final score of that second game as a matter of interest?"

"Arsenal won by a goal."

Phelim squared his shoulders and smiled at Danny for the first time. Then he turned and left the ward.

Danny stared after him, feeling his head start to swim, his mind replaying their exchange over and over like a compact disc on repeat mode. He pushed a finger against the nurse's bell, needing permission to make an urgent phone call.

Chapter 27

Waiting in line to speak to a cashier in the Permanent TSB bank in Carrigaline, Lucy couldn't stand still, her mind fleeting from one problem to the next. With her bank-account access-passwords burnt to a crisp in her bedside locker, she had no way of checking online statements.

"Excuse me! Next, please?"

"I'm so sorry," Lucy apologised to the young brunette cashier when she got to the counter. Unzipping her handbag, she took out her chequebook and bankcard, sliding them into the chute. "Can you print me off a detailed statement from our personal and business accounts please?" she enquired. "And I'll take a Visa statement as well if you don't mind."

The brunette punched the numbers from Lucy's card into her computer. "Names and addresses on the accounts, please?"

Lucy verified her details, stumbling over Danny's date of birth but getting it right in the end.

The assistant drummed her fingers on the counter as she waited for the account details to appear in front of her. "Is it only one month's details you need?" she asked, a frown creasing her forehead as she scanned the variety of accounts linked to Lucy and Danny's names.

"Twelve months, please."

"There's a standing charge for statements that go back further than one month. The fee will be deducted from your account and you'll receive the statements in the post within five working days." She explained all this to Lucy, her eyes fixed on the computer screen, her fingers flying across the keyboard, making no eye contact with her customer.

"But surely you can print them now? It's an emergency," Lucy delivered the last sentence through gritted teeth, pressing her face close to the glass, mortified that she had to succumb to begging this rude assistant for help.

The bank assistant's head shot up, her hazel eyes finally meeting Lucy's. "The online banking facility is available 24-7. Simple to use and available in your own home."

Lucy didn't mean to cry, but the cashier's words penetrated deep, bringing her helplessness (and hopelessness) to the fore and fresh tears to her eyes. She wiped them away and cleared her throat before she spoke, inhaling deeply to make sure there wasn't a wobble in her voice.

She clutched the edge of the counter, biting on each word that left her lips. "Let me explain my predicament. My house has burnt down. Our documents have been destroyed." She paused a moment, waiting for a reaction from the other girl, intent on making her squirm! "Put it down to shock or lunacy. Either way, I can't remember what home-insurance company we renewed with or the exact date the premium was paid. But it has to have been at some point during the past twelve months. Does that explain my urgency?"

The cashier pushed her long black hair behind both ears, glaring at Lucy through the glass. "I'll give a quick scan at your personal accounts. What about a standing order or direct debit? Had you one set up for this policy?"

Lucy stared at her, setting her dislike aside and allowing her hopes to lift slightly. Could the girl have hit on something she hadn't thought of herself? "That's a strong possibility, I guess. Go ahead and check, please." She waited and hoped, taking a withdrawal slip from the counter and tearing it into shreds, her heart skipping a beat when the cashier looked up from her screen.

"There's a monthly payment to Allianz Insurance from the Ardle Construction business account. Could that be what you're look for, do you think? Part of the reference number is here on the screen." She picked up a pen and began to write it down.

But alas, it didn't solve Lucy's dilemma. She shook her head and asked the girl to continue checking.

"There's also a monthly transfer of thirty-four euro to New Ireland Assurance . . ." she glanced at Lucy expectantly.

But again, Lucy shook her head. "That's our life assurance. It's paid from the company account, something to do with a discounted business rate or something."

A short while later she was standing outside the bank, no more enlightened than when she'd entered in the first place. Moving systematically to the ATM machine, she withdrew a large amount of cash and stuffed it into her purse.

Crossing the street to Dunnes Stores, she went to the men's department and picked up two lambswool jumpers, a tracksuit, denim jeans, socks, underwear for Danny. Other than the pyjamas and slippers Delia had bought for him, he hadn't as much as a pair of socks to call his own. Laden down by the time she approached the cash desk, the saleswoman took them from her, rang them through the till, folded them neatly and asked if she wanted the hangers too.

Lucy couldn't help but smile. Clothes hangers, she thought, grimacing slightly. How long before she'd have a wardrobe to hang them in? But she had to cling to the belief that one day things would get back to normal. "Yes, please," she said, smiling at the saleswoman, "I'll take them. And one of these silk ties as well, please." Hell, she thought, if nothing else it will do him for Stephen's wedding. She grabbed the brown paper bags of purchases and left the store, her purposeful stride belying her internal fear as she made her way to the car.

Calling to the Garda Station was her next stop. Recognising the garda behind the counter as the same guy she'd shouted abuse at, the evening of the fire, she lowered her eyes as she approached him.

"Mrs Ardle, isn't it?" he said, his gentle welcome easing her embarrassment. "My name is Jack Bowe. What can I do for you?"

"I have to make a statement about the fire. I'm sorry it's taken so long but this is my first opportunity," Lucy explained, giving a nervous smile – a smile that wasn't

225

really a smile – glancing around the Garda Station, finding it difficult to meet his eye.

"How's your husband doing?"

She let her fingers trace the letters on the large print notice on the desk, unable to stop fidgeting. "Danny's still very ill but he is making progress." For the first time, she looked directly at him, but turned away quickly when she recognised sympathy staring back at her.

"I'll go and get your file. Back in a tick," he told her, disappearing into another room.

Lucy thumbed through the bundle of passport-application forms on the nearby information stand, biting her lip and wishing she could be anywhere else.

Coming back empty-handed a few moments later, he shrugged his shoulders. "Your file's not there. I'll give the inspector in charge a quick call to see what amount of detail he wants." He disappeared again, leaving her unattended but arriving back a few minutes later with a page of notes in his hand. "If you wouldn't mind accompanying me to the interview room."

The Garda interview room was furnished in typical sterile, bureaucratic fashion: a desk, a table, six chairs and two filing cabinets. Lucy moved around the table and took a seat, watching the garda's every move until he was seated opposite her. She studied his handsome face, guessing he wasn't much older than Stephen and found herself wondering how somebody with so little life experience could possibly solve a case. "I'll need your fingerprints for the file," he said, keeping his tone casual despite how obvious his reasons for the request were.

"Oh right," she said, pressing her index finger into the pad he provided.

"The fire seems to have started in the front upstairs bedroom. Any thoughts on how it may have ignited?"

Lucy slumped in the chair. She could picture her bedroom, the gaping hole in the floor, smashed window and shredded curtains foremost in her mind. What on earth could have triggered that? Looking across at the garda, she shook her head. "Nothing at all. I can't believe it has even happened, to be honest."

"What about electrical appliances? Anything old or faulty that you'd be concerned about?"

"Other than reading lamps, there's nothing else plugged in during the day."

"We're waiting for the results of a technical exam, so in the meantime we're gathering whatever information we can."

"Technical exam? That's normal procedure, I presume?"

He nodded, turning the page in his notebook. "If the cause isn't obvious. Now getting back to the questions, what form would you say Danny was in when you left?"

Lucy felt she was centre stage as she fumbled around in her brain for a non-incriminating response. What could she tell him? That they'd had an argument, had shouted at one another and she'd stormed out without even saying goodbye. She speared her fingers through her hair and then smoothed it down again. She'd never felt more in need of a cigarette.

"Danny's a creature of habit," she said eventually, avoiding the truth, self-preservation top of her list of priorities. "This time of year, his Saturday afternoons amount to monopolising the remote control and having the living room to himself so he can watch the footie without me – or anybody else – annoying him. And if he's allowed those two luxuries, he's quite content."

The garda took a deep breath and nodded, making an indecipherable scrawl on the page before placing the pen down and looking across at her. "So he was watching television when you left?"

"Yes."

"Did you leave through the front or back door?"

"Back."

Without warning, he changed the direction of his questioning. "One of your sons left home recently. Would he have left any flammable objects in his room? Anything likely to ignite?"

"No. Nothing out of the ordinary." What? Were they going to blame Matt now?

He began to doodle on the page, lifting his eyes to hers after an obvious pause. "We're in the midst of a big case, Mrs Ardle. Everything is questionable until it's solved."

Lucy suddenly realising the young garda sitting opposite her was more astute than she'd originally believed. She must be careful to keep her fear and guilt under wraps, terrified he'd twist her responses, paranoid about every nuance and hand-movement she was making now in case she was being analysed as a nervous wreck with something serious to hide.

"When will the full forensic report be back?" she enquired as evenly as she could, her throat and mouth dry.

"The length of time for results varies, depending on the amount of material being scrutinised, but hopefully another day or two will bring an end to your waiting. And ours."

Lucy stared out of the window, the bars inside limiting her view of the outside world, stress expanding inside her, limiting her hopes of surviving this horrific ordeal.

"As a matter of interest," he said, "would you consider yourself house-proud?"

Lucy stared incredulously at him. The interview was bordering on the ridiculous. What connection could he possibly make between her housework habits and their house going on fire? Ignoring his question, she got to her feet. "Am I done here?"

He shook his head, gesturing for her to sit. "We're nearly there," he promised.

She sat again.

"Mrs Ardle, I need to know whether you'd normally go out for the afternoon and leave dirty dishes on the table?"

Lucy stared at him, bewildered. "Why it matters is beyond me but, for what it's worth, I prefer to come home to a nice tidy house to be honest. So I would wash and tidy away everything before I left."

"Which you did on the Saturday afternoon in question?"

"Yes."

He nodded as though it had been the response he'd been expecting. "And the back door, seeing as Danny was sleeping, did you lock that on your way out?"

That question threw her. Remembering her surprise at finding it open when she'd called to inspect the house, she tried to recall Saturday once more. But she honestly couldn't be certain that she'd locked it, particularly as she'd walked out the door in a huff and had almost taken it off the hinges when she'd banged it hard. "Honestly, I can't be sure," she told him without blinking once.

"And your insurance company, Lucy? We haven't had a call from them yet. It's surprising they haven't been on to check out the details of the fire with us."

"But why would they be calling the gardaí?" Lucy's heart missed a beat. She pretended to study her nails, feeling the weight of the garda's gaze falling on her. "I'm not familiar with procedure."

"It's how these situations work. It's policy. They have to ensure that we've been notified and that the ESB and gas connections have been disconnected for safety reasons. As you can imagine, there's a lengthy safety statement following house fires. Nothing's left to chance after a claim has been reported and . . ."

Lucy couldn't carry the burden alone any longer. She had no control over the next words that came out of her mouth. "I didn't renew the policy." Her voice was barely audible, her head bowed, her face red with humiliation. As soon as the words were out, she wanted to take them back, knowing full well that Danny had a right to this privileged information before anybody else, including the gardaí.

He put his pen on the table, taking a moment to respond. "But how on earth will you afford the cost of rebuilding, Mrs Ardle? And why didn't you renew the premium?"

Lucy fiddled with the belt buckle on her jacket, hating every moment of the hell she was going through. "I don't know. I forgot."

Jack Bowe was thinking hard as he processed her revelation. Her admission wasn't equating with Inspector

O'Brien's suspicions or the way he was leading the case. As far as Jack knew, O'Brien was homing in predominantly on an insurance scam. Not much point if there wasn't any insurance in place, Jack thought, his sympathy lying with Mrs Ardle. Imagine the horror of forgetting to renew a premium? How easy it must be to let it happen though? And what bad luck for your house to go on fire the very year the premium has lapsed!

"Does your husband know this?"

"I haven't told him. Yet. I've been holding on and holding on, praying I'd find out I was wrong."

"There's no chance he could have paid it?"

Lucy lowered her voice – pointless as they were the only two in the room but her shame making it the natural thing to do. It wasn't information she felt like shouting from the rooftops. "I remember I was supposed to do it. I started to – compared prices and all that – but for some reason I didn't follow through."

And then, as Jack stared at the vulnerability of the woman across from him, he swallowed hard, piecing together the nuggets of information she had imparted. She'd admitted that *she* had forgotten to renew the premium but she'd also announced that Danny was ignorant of this fact. Perhaps O'Brien is right after all, he thought, disgusted that the most arrogant member of the force he'd ever met would be proved to be correct. Again. Regardless of his lack of popularity or his lack of regard and respect for his peers and the general public, Inspector O'Brien's reputation for successful case-solving was something that couldn't be argued with.

"Are you worried about the effect it will have on his health?"

Lucy paled. "I'm worried about the effect it will have on *my* health! He'll kill me."

"I'm sure he'll understand, particularly as he's had such a lucky escape with his life," the garda attempted to appease her.

Lucy raised an eyebrow in disbelief. "I can't dump it on him while he's still in hospital. He's barely coping as it is. I'll tell him when he gets out. At least then we'll have privacy." I hope, she added silently, privacy being in short demand in Delia's house at the moment.

The garda turned his attention to his notes, seeing no point in breaking the news that only a short while before Danny had been interrogated at his hospital bedside. Or that it hadn't gone very well. "That should do for now," he told her. "I'll read the statement back to you and ask you to sign it."

Lucy nodded in relief, sneaking a peek at her watch to check the time. It was mid-afternoon already. Yet again, Danny would be irritated she'd left it so late to visit. And then there was Carol and the uncomfortable subject she had to approach with her. Another ordeal she wasn't looking forward to.

Happy the statement was a fair reflection of their conversation. Lucy accepted Jack's pen and scrawled her name at the bottom of the page.

"You'll hear from us as soon as the forensic report is back," he promised. "And, Mrs Ardle?"

She held her breath. "It's Lucy," she told him, standing up to leave.

"Lucy," he repeated after her, "this thing with the insurance – I hope it works out for you and your husband."

Not half as much as I do, she thought, leaving the

Garda Station with her head bowed, the interview swimming around in her head.

Pushing open the main door, she walked right into Inspector Phelim O'Brien. He stopped to allow her past, his eyes small and beady in his bloated face, the way they scanned her body making her skin crawl. She stepped around him.

"Danny's got those nurses running around him up there. You wouldn't want to leave him alone for too long." The smile on his face hardened, twisting into a sneer.

Lucy frowned in confusion. What on earth had he meant by that comment? "No fear of that," she told him, his sly sarcasm infuriating her. She was damned if she was going to let him goad her. His old feud with Danny had obviously reared its ugly head once more. As he'd promised them it would. She was damned if she was going to let him see how much his words and insinuations had rattled her. "In fact, I'm on my way to the hospital now," she added.

The buttons on Phelim's jacket were close to bursting, yet he had pulled it tight around him.

"Surprising all the same. You'd think an accident like that could never happen to a competent builder like Danny Ardle."

Lucy shivered, his words ringing horribly familiar. She had no answer to that.

"The question is," he leaned in closer, "why?"

"I thought finding that out was your job."

Phelim's cold steel-grey eyes narrowed. "After what Danny's told us, I'm sure you two have a lot of detail to catch up on. Don't stray too far from Crosshaven. We'll talk again once the forensic results are back."

Half an hour later, she was walking along the hospital corridor, her heart set on having an open and honest conversation with her husband. Entering his ward, however, she spotted his sister, Jenny, performing something resembling amateur dramatics at his bedside. Lucy's heart sank as she watched the size-zero blonde fluffing his pillows and forcing him to sit upright in the bed. A curious mixture of annoyance and jealousy flashed inside her. She watched Danny's arm creep around Jenny's waist as she helped him into a comfortable position. Why hadn't he embraced her like that when she'd remained vigilant at his bedside for hours on end? Lucy pursed her lips and scowled. How dare Danny clutch his sister's arm lovingly as she held a glass of water to his lips! How dare he treat her with anything less than the disdain she deserved for the appalling way she ignored him and their parents the majority of the time! With Jenny dancing attention on Danny and Lucy in danger of hitting Jenny with his oxygen mask, she knew there was little point in joining the brother and sister team. Let Jenny have her hour of glory, Lucy thought, because that's as long as it will last before she legs it back to her perfect, commitment-free London lifestyle.

Unable to watch any more of Jenny's ridiculous attention-seeking antics, Lucy turned on her heel and marched towards the elevator, desperate to get out of the hospital as quickly as possible. Once outside in the fresh air, she broke into a run, gasping for breath by the time she reached the car. The conversation she needed to have with her husband would have to wait but she wasn't about to let the afternoon go to waste.

Chapter 28

Heidi pulled Julian's dressing gown around her as she left the poky bathroom of his basement apartment, a towel wrapped turban-style around her head. "Tell me again how you ended up sharing a cab with Matt yesterday? And what was he doing at Newark Airport?" She flopped onto a beanbag and stared up at him, waiting for an explanation that actually made sense. So far the snippets he'd given her were vague and uninformative but she'd been so distracted and absorbed in reliving her own wonderful experience at the airport that she'd accepted his blasé explanations. Now she was beginning to be concerned about Matt again.

Julian opened the refrigerator and took out a can of coke, flicking open the ring-pull and taking a long swig before responding. "Choking when I saw him! I saved his life, don't forget!"

"Give over, Julian. Matt doesn't deserve to be made a fool of. None of this mess is down to him."

He narrowed his dark eyes and brought the can to his lips once more, gulping back some more of the sweet, cold liquid, smacking his lips together and belching loudly. "And I'm supposed to believe his choking wasn't part of a ploy to speak to me?"

Heidi dropped her head to conceal her flushed cheeks.

"I think, Heidi," Julian continued, "you're the one responsible for making a fool out of him. You should have seen his face when I handed him that photograph of us! Priceless!"

"There wasn't any need for that," she retorted. "I was planning on telling him in my own time. But everything together was too much for me to cope with." She pouted a little, annoyed that Julian had taken the decision out of her hands, yet partly relieved that it was one less secret lying between her and Matt. "And why the hell are you carrying that photo around after all these years?"

"Never mind that," Julian said, sidetracking her question in case his answer caused her mood to either spiral or spike. There was no reason in particular, just nostalgia he supposed, but the way Heidi interpreted everything as a personal slight on her, he wasn't taking any chances. "Why haven't you been honest with Matt if he's as great as you say he is? And if you stay together – like you've told me you're going to – he'll find the truth out sooner or later. Don't you think the remainder of the story would be best coming from you?"

Heidi nodded, tapping her foot nervously at the same time, her lower lip trembling, her fingers fidgeting with the belt of the dark-green fleece dressing gown.

Julian noticed the change in her, recognising the familiar signs of panic, knowing she was a long way from being able to appreciate either his humour or his advice. He moved across the room and sank onto the floor beside her, folding his arms over her knees to steady her shaking body.

"Deep breaths, Heidi. Take them right into your airways . . ." He watched as she inhaled, her lips moving as she silently counted to ten. "And exhale now, Heidi . . . that's it."

Her face was pinched, her eyes filled with terror, her voice quivering when she spoke. "I can't seem to get the panic under control, Julian. Just when I think I'm getting a grip on it, it sweeps up and chokes me all over again. And I need to get back to Matt. I want him to be part of this new beginning, I want to include him every step of the way. But how can I? How can I impose this –" she gestured at herself, "this affliction on him? I've been so unfair and selfish following him here . . . if it weren't for . . ."

Julian reached for the box of tissues and handed them to Heidi. "Give yourself time. Don't rush it. Matt will wait. What are another few days out of the rest of your life?" He got to his feet, making to put on the television, then stopped and turned back to face her. "If he loves you like you say he does, he'll understand . . ."

The air conditioning suddenly choked to life, the dull thudding noise drowning the end of Julian's pronouncement.

But Heidi had heard enough to know she disagreed entirely. "He's twenty-one years old, Julian. Don't you remember? Love is the equivalent of perfection at that age . . ."

Julian relented. "I certainly remember what it was

like at eighteen when you and I exchanged marriage vows with a gang-load of college friends looking on and laughing at us, a few slabs of beer and bottles of the cheapest wine they could find tucked beneath the trees in Stephen's Green!"

Heidi's mouth turned up at the corners, the faded memory lightening her mood. "Shortest marriage in history," she commented dryly. "I think the hangover lasted longer!"

"Maybe," Julian said, "but it served its purpose."

She sighed and nodded in agreement. "So what was Matt really doing in Newark?"

"Looking for you. Had got it into his head you were taking a flight to Boston. Had you mentioned anything to him? Or left some info lying around?"

Heidi wrinkled her brow in concentration, thinking back over things. She'd been so careful about keeping her arrangements quiet, preferring to handle it alone until she could be sure there was something to tell. And look how that turned out, she thought wryly, embarrassed as she remembered begging Julian to stay with her, pleading with him that she wouldn't be able to go through with things if he didn't.

Julian got to his feet and moved away from her again, leaning against the fireplace in the corner of the room. He too was remembering the scene at the airport, recalling the effort it had taken on his part to push her forward and make her take that important step alone. Her dependency had scared him, demonstrated how her fear could evolve into something bigger and scarier if he allowed it. She'd tried tears, sulks and tantrums to get him to acquiesce to her wish, apologising later that she'd acted unfairly by expecting him to attach himself to her dreams and desires.

But for Julian, that scene was an eye-opener, a snippet of how things would be if he stuck around. He knew Heidi of old and, despite her slighter figure and the intensity she'd acquired with the passing of years, she hadn't changed that much. She was still demanding, using that disarming pity of hers to wear a person down until finally she got her own way. And that was exactly why he was planning to move on for a while and gather his thoughts, work out what was going on in his head, how all this affected him.

Oblivious to Julian's dilemma, Heidi's face flushed as she remembered jotting the Newark to Boston detail in her diary, the arrangement so surreal she'd been afraid she'd mess it up. Why had she taken the risk of Matt seeing it? She could never have confused or forgotten something so important to her, so why write it down? And then she remembered her upended handbag and her diary. Oh God, she thought, imagining Matt's horror if he'd read her diary and found that particular entry. As he must have.

Part of her wished now that she hadn't insisted on leaving Newark Airport alone after her meeting with Alex. He was catching a flight to Boston, travelling for a basketball game, and she'd jumped at the opportunity of meeting him before his flight. Despite the success of the meeting, her head had spun afterwards and she'd wanted to be alone. She needed time to relive every moment. Now she regretted that decision because if she'd remained with Julian, she too would have met Matt and things would be out in the open.

Deep in thought and full of angst about Matt, she missed the pitying looks Julian was bestowing upon her. Soon he'd be cutting loose and escaping the lasso she was using to trap him and there wouldn't be a thing she could do about it.

Chapter 29

Eric blinked as the camera flashed, following instructions and turning his left profile to the policeman.

"Look forward, please."

Eric stared ahead.

"Got it. Okay, come with me." He led him down a long poorly lit corridor and into an office where an older policeman was sitting behind a massive desk, studying some paperwork. He didn't look up.

Eric's escort gestured to him to sit down facing this more intimidating senior officer.

Eric sat. "What's this about?" he blurted out. He still hadn't a clue whether he was under arrest or being held for questioning. He didn't understand enough about Florida law or its criminal offences to know if he'd actually committed fraud. And so far nobody had thought to enlighten him.

The officer looked up and fixed him with a stare he could not read. "Precaution for now," he said, "but who knows how far Zebedee's want to take this? It's their call. They're out there looking for evidence right now. But as it stands, we're looking at a minimum of sixty days imprisonment for misdemeanour."

Eric risked quizzing the policeman a little more, while 'everything he said was *not* about to be taken down or used against him'. "So you're just holding me to see if they'll want to press charges?"

"As I said, they're checking clearance for the finance you put up for that apartment complex. They don't take too kindly to being double-crossed. Based on the information we've received from them so far, we'll be holding you until confirmation comes through."

Eric stifled a laugh. What a joke! There wasn't a hope in hell that finance would clear, not when he hadn't succeeded in bagging a speedy deposit for its resale. He sighed resignedly.

Sixty days behind bars was far from appealing, particularly in an unknown court system in a country far away from home. Being deported to Ireland suddenly felt like the most attractive choice in the world. It wouldn't bother him if he was returned on a slow boat via the longest route. The Irish legal system would be easier for him to deal with and at the very least he could get Jacob to manage his representation.

"I didn't . . ." he stopped abruptly. He'd been about to say he hadn't double-crossed them because they'd copped on to him first. But thankfully, he realised just in time how incriminating that admission would have been. He ran a hand through his damp hair, his shirt clinging to his skin, the stale smell from his clothes and body making him nauseous. How long before this nightmare ended in some fashion or other, he wondered?

Cutting loose from reality was turning out to be next to impossible. Returning home, on the other hand, would be like walking into a minefield. No money, no home, no status and probably no family into the bargain. Heidi? He didn't dare imagine her wrath or how she was managing in the absence of credit. He'd have a lot of grovelling to do but he would make it up to her.

Isobel, on the other hand, had inherited his aloof characteristics, but he knew his latest mistakes would shake her to the core. And she wouldn't hold back in telling him so.

As for his wife, Carol – she was another matter. Without question, she'd have his head on a platter, was probably already gunning for him. Their home was her pride and joy, the creation of her making, the sculpture she'd moulded from tidy beginnings. Wrapping new builds around their original modest four-bedroom detached, she'd planned and designed every extension, supervised every ornate detail, watched her dreams come true and gave Eric the status home he desired.

"Mr Black, are you listening to me?"

Eric jolted back to the present. "Yes, sir."

"Perhaps we'll allow you that telephone call you were enquiring about before we do a quick search of your person and take you to a holding cell. Do you have a number at hand?"

Eric leaned against the wall, put his head in his hands and felt the rough stubble on his chin. He was determined to make the best use of this opportunity. One call. Most people in his situation would know instantly who they should contact. But Eric had difficulty deciding. Calling

Carol was the obvious choice but at what cost? Hearing her humiliation and anger over the phone? Wasting the one opportunity he was being given to help himself out of this mess? He wasn't in any rush to hear her incessant nagging. Contacting Heidi was out of the question, considering her difficulty dealing with her own problems. She wasn't exactly reliable in a crisis, not even when the crisis was of *her* making.

Relying on her was a definite non-runner and something to be avoided at all costs. As for Isobel – while she was the steadier of his two daughters – he didn't feel she could help him this time. Getting a solicitor probably made most sense, providing Jacob was still interested in representing him, knowing this time payment was becoming increasingly doubtful. And taking Jacob out of the loop only left the American lawyer he'd hired in St Petersburg. But what allegiance would he have for Eric – a bankrupt Irishman? Why would he represent him against a reputable realtor in Florida? He wouldn't, Eric guessed, striking him off his list of possibilities and racking his brains. This was his one chance, his final '*get out of jail*' card and he had to play it right.

"We can't wait forever, Mr Black," the policeman warned.

Eric took his hands away from his face and nodded, biting his lip as he made up his mind. He was taking a gamble, one that could easily blow up in his face.

"I can write down the number for you. It's in Ireland."

The policeman took a paper and pen from his pocket. "And who is this person?"

"An acquaintance of mine," he answered, his legs shaking under the table. He put his hands behind his back and crossed his fingers. "Inspector Phelim O'Brien, Carrigaline Garda Station, County Cork."

Chapter 30

Matt banged the door as he left the apartment. The walls and ceiling had started to close in on him, the silence from his mobile phone haunting. His mother hadn't called him though she'd promised. There was still no trace of Heidi and as for trusting Julian that she'd be back when she'd sorted her 'personal issues', well, that was a joke. Going such a long time without fresh air was unusual for Matt, going out of his mind with worry being something he'd never experienced before in his life.

NYC College had called him early that morning, inviting him to meet the other tutors (he'd have to get used to calling them tutors and not lecturers) as well as offering a guided tour of the sports complex where he'd be conducting most of his lessons. He'd accepted their invitation, setting up a time for the following day. But his heart wasn't in it, the excitement of being in New York destroyed by Heidi's disappearance as well as the eye-opening subject of Julian's photograph.

Matt had marched the last few blocks to the apartment after storming out of the cab the day before, leaving Julian and his smug attitude behind. Tempted by the delicious aromas coming from Roy's deli, he'd stockpiled several of his favourite dishes and cocooned himself in the apartment since, watching mindless television, eating and waiting. Speaking to his Mum on the phone had been his only contact with the outside world. After that conversation, Matt had felt less alone. And exceptionally glad to be a safe distance away from his mother. He knew once the news he'd imparted had sunk in, she'd bombard him with questions and strong words of advice.

But enough is enough, he thought, sick of the apartment and sick of waiting. If they want me, they have my number. I'm not holing myself up indoors. I've got to get out of here. Grabbing a quick shower, he pulled on a striped sweater and pair of soft, comfortable baggy denims with dark brown hiking boots.

Banging the door on the 7th Avenue apartment building, he stepped onto the pavement, and shivered in the biting wind, zipping up his tracksuit top. The weather had turned wintry at last. Turning on his heel, he ran back inside to get a few padded layers to keep out the cold. He felt around the top shelf of the wardrobe for the black thermal hat and gloves his mother had insisted on packing. In a fit of playing house, Heidi had unpacked most of his luggage, tidying everything away in neat piles. Now all he needed was a road map to help him find anything!

Tired of searching blindly, he dragged a kitchen chair to the wardrobe, grateful for the high ceiling so he didn't bang his head. Seeing Heidi's neat piles brought a smile to his face. Her vibrant and unique style, the kaleidoscope of colour she managed to make work where others would look utterly ridiculous, added to her pixie-like appearance and contributed to her youthfulness, which was probably why the twelve-year age gap that existed between them didn't seem important. One thing he could never feel around Heidi was boredom and there was something consoling about the careful way she'd arranged their clothes. Looking at the his 'n' her piles side by side filled him with a renewed sense of hope that he hadn't imagined her love for him, that it matched the love he felt for her.

But what had Julian meant when he'd accused her of being complicated? How many hidden layers were there to Heidi, he wondered, stepping from the chair onto the floor and wrapping up warm before leaving the apartment. He didn't bang the door this time and the thump in his chest was no longer fuelled by anger.

His hands pushed deep in the pockets of his parka jacket, he moved swiftly through Manhattan, walking more than twenty blocks to 34th Street, crossing the street at Macy's Department store and making a beeline for Madison Square Gardens arena. Ignoring the array of hotdog stands lined up near the entrance and resisting the delicious aroma of mustard and sizzling frankfurters, he stepped away from the noisy streets and inside the enormous arena. Gaping around in awe at the larger than life-size murals of the greatest American basketball players ever known, Matt's jaw dropped open when Stefan Maybury, one of his favourite players of all time, walked right past him, so close he could smell his aftershave. Letting out a long sigh of satisfaction, Matt unzipped his coat and stuffed his hat and gloves into his pockets, leaving his problems at the door and allowing himself a well-deserved break from worrying about Heidi.

Chapter 31

Heidi shook her head, refusing to contemplate leaving Julian's apartment. "No, no, no, Julian. You can't put me under pressure like this. I'm still not ready."

"That's too bad, Heidi, because I've got plans that don't include you. Come on, you've been here for several days."

His words stung. His eyes glared. She knew he would not back down.

Heidi threw down the magazine she'd been flicking through and marched into the smaller of the two bedrooms, closing the door with a loud bang. God damn him, she thought. He owes me. Sitting cross-legged on the bed, her mind spinning, she found it impossible to meditate. But her thoughts were less jumbled and surprisingly his announcement hadn't brought on an attack. She was ready to venture outside alone but not to move away entirely.

A short while later, she got up, grabbed her jacket and strode through the living room.

"I need a few more days, Julian," she told him from the doorway as she left, then opened her mouth to say something more, but stopped short. This isn't the time, she thought.

She'd shut the door behind her when she realised she didn't have any money. She was too proud to go back and ask Julian. Slipping her hand into the back pocket of her jeans, her fingers slid against her plastic credit card and she breathed a sigh of relief. Bracing herself against the biting cold, thinking longingly of her collection of winter woollies packed neatly in the wardrobe in Matt's apartment, she realised she'd made a huge mistake. She should never have run out on Matt.

Chapter 32

Eric put his hands behind his head and stretched out on the narrow bunk, his back aching from the lumpy mattress. He'd spent his night in Sarasota prison in a two-by-four-metre cell. The furnishings were basic, but he had fallen asleep within minutes of the key being turned in the lock. There was nothing else to do in the tiny prison cell, nothing to do but wait.

The odds were stacked against him. After they'd allowed him his one telephone call, the police had showed him to a cell and went to check out his story. Phelim O'Brien's reaction hadn't exactly bowled him over with enthusiasm. Eric's heart had missed a beat at his coldness, terrified he'd made a huge mistake, wasting his only phone call.

"I wouldn't ask only . . ." he let the sentence hang, keenly aware of the lack of privacy.

"Only there's no other schmuk you can call," Phelim had finished.

Eric had thought for a moment, conscious of the two policemen standing close. He'd chosen his words very carefully. "There's the matter of correspondence, Phelim, and if I don't get home to . . . eh . . . deal with it . . ." Again, his sentence trailed off.

After a thoughtful pause, Phelim had given a grunted response. "What state is prosecuting you, Eric? And what exact jurisdiction are you being held in?"

Eric had relayed the question to the policeman, repeating the response to Phelim, giving him as much detail as he could.

"Right, hold tight and I'll see if I can get the financial institutions to issue prosecutions here. Florida authorities should be very happy to hand you over to your mother country once they hear about the trouble you're in at home. Will you ever learn, Eric?"

Eric had been tormenting himself with that exact question for many days now, along with many more. "I suppose there's no way you can get me off back home now?"

"Don't push it," Phelim had barked down the phone before disconnecting.

Eric, on the other hand, had replaced the receiver gently on his side, seeing every advantage in staying on the right side of the two bullish policemen waiting to interrogate him further about his investment disasters. His dodgy dealings.

After intense questioning, he'd followed the policeman down a narrow corridor, shuddering at the sight of the caged door. The clunk of the key securing him in the cell had pierced through his soul. I'm nothing better than a common criminal, he thought now, staring around him at the bleak cell, grimacing at the absence of '*get out of jail free*' cards. The deck had run out and Eric knew he had already folded his hand.

Chapter 33

Carol added the final touches to her make-up, smearing a dab of bronze shadow on her eyelids, pleased with the blend of dark-green eyeliner and chocolate-coloured mascara, noticing the exaggerated depth it gave her eyes. And it helped shift the emphasis from her ageing skin.

Reasonably happy with her appearance, she went to the wardrobe to fetch her olive-green maxi dress. Today of all days, she needed something she felt her best in. "Damn it," she said, after checking through the few items left on the rail, disgusted to realise her dress must have been packed in one of the cases she'd brought to Lucy's. Damn, damn, damn, she thought, pulling a soft beige cashmere wrap-over from the rail instead and slipping it on. It fitted snugly over her hips, falling just above her slim ankles. But her make-up seemed too pale against the beige neckline, her dark eye-shadow over-dramatic with the softer colour. But there's nothing I can do about it now, she thought, the empty wardrobe-rail beseeching her for more clothes but its importance miniscule in comparison to the bigger issues requiring attention.

"Looking somewhat respectable as I go cap in hand can't do any harm," she muttered aloud, kicking Eric's pile of clothes out of her way as she left the room and made her way down the sweeping staircase where she sat on the bottom step and waited for her invited guest to arrive.

"Jacob, thanks for seeing me at such short notice," she greeted her solicitor when he stepped inside a short while later, his face red from the biting cold.

"I see you've made a start on the clear-out," he commented, nodding at the partially furnished sitting room to his left and the dining room to his right.

"If only I could lift the house and move that too," she replied drily. "Coffee?"

But he declined. "I've fitted this visit in between two clients so I'd prefer to get on with it if you don't mind."

His curt response startled her, making her shudder inside. She'd met Jacob on a few black-tie occasions where they'd all drunk too much wine and had very little problem keeping the conversation going. But conversing with him in the stillness and intimacy of her home was a lot more awkward and uncomfortable. For her at least. He, on the other hand, oozed austere professionalism, her urgent request for help clearly an inconvenience, and he was doing very little to hide this fact.

Broad daylight and a slate-grey single-breasted suit did his pale skin and fair hair a lot less justice than the Mediterranean tan and smart tuxedo he'd been sporting the night he'd flirted outrageously with her. During the auction at a charity fundraiser, he'd left her in no doubt about the prize he was interested in securing that night. His eyes had wandered brazenly over her cleavage, lingering on her pouting lips, meeting her gaze with a cheeky grin, his knee touching hers, rubbing seductively.

Flattered by his attention, Carol had blushed at his compliments, responding eagerly to his humour until she'd caught Eric's warning glance from across the table. And though she had no intention of misbehaving or taking Jacob's drunken attention seriously, she couldn't deny a private thrill to be singled out from the other women in their group or the low ping in her stomach screaming 'Chemistry!'.

When she'd invited him over for advice today, she'd assumed a pretty dress might distract his attention, loosen his professional etiquette (when he was sober at least) and soften him up enough to advise her on the plan she was hatching. But judging by his sour expression and the frequency of his time-checking, Carol felt she could be wearing her oldest tracksuit or a tatty dressing gown for all the attention he was paying her. For the briefest moment, she wondered about introducing a bottle of wine into their conversation, shoving the ridiculous idea away almost as soon as it entered her head. She'd already lost everything. Would her self-respect be worth casting aside in favour of a risqué meeting with their family solicitor? Would it get her over one of her remaining survival hurdles?

"What's this about, Carol?" Jacob came straight to the point, turning to face her.

Her breath caught, the moment of decision upon her. Am I crazy, she wondered, remembering his smiles and joking at the charity dinner, the memory giving her the confidence to go on.

"An inheritance I never disclosed to Eric. I want to know whether I can use it to get my family out of the mess we're in. If I remember correctly, Jacob, you're very partial to a nice glass of wine – one of the few things I've got left to offer you?" She ran her tongue slowly along her upper lip, holding his gaze until finally the scowl left his face, his lips shaped into a smile and he undid the buttons of his jacket.

Chapter 34

Lucy shivered on Carol's doorstep, her curiosity piqued by the strange car in the driveway. She rang the doorbell for the second time, keeping her finger on the buzzer for a longer spell this time.

If she hadn't needed to speak to Carol so badly she wouldn't have waited any longer. But she'd promised Matt she'd make enquiries about Heidi and had herself mentally prepared for that confrontation now. Peeping through the glass by the hall door, she caught a movement from the kitchen. They mustn't have heard the bell, she thought, the biting wind cutting through her. Damn it, she thought, I'll go around the back and see if I can get their attention.

Shouting "Hello!" as she neared the kitchen window, she was relieved to hear movement inside.

"Lucy!" Carol stuck her head around the back door. "I'm so sorry – I must have missed the bell. Come on in."

Lucy was glad to step in out of the cold, rubbing her

hands together as she entered her neighbour's warm kitchen. Obviously the gas hasn't been cut off yet, she thought, peering around, surprised to see no trace of a visitor. She turned to Carol who was fussing at the sink, cleaning down what seemed to be a sparkling draining board and counter.

"Everything okay, Carol? You seem a bit flustered. Nice dress by the way."

The other woman paused for breath, sweeping her hair away from her face. She turned to face Lucy. "Are you surprised I'm flustered? This sodding mess is too much to get my head around. Eric hasn't even tried to make contact since. I have no idea whether he will be on that flight or not but I'm damned if I'm going to meet it either way! I'm clutching at straws here trying to hold it together. And now . . ." She turned towards the sink again, her sentence trailing off. She looked out at the garden, hiding her face until the blush had passed.

Lucy leaned against the counter. "Yeah? You were going to say?"

"It doesn't matter," Carol sighed, drying her hands on the towel and beckoning her to sit at the island unit.

"Has Heidi been in touch?" Lucy asked tentatively, taking a red leather coaster from the pile and standing it on its edge.

"Not a word from her. And Isobel's still in Dublin and probably won't be back till Thursday at the earliest – she's up to her eyes in work, anchoring for another promotion. Let's hope she earns enough to support the rest of us!" She gave a hollow laugh.

"Hmm," Lucy attempted a smile at Carol's dry humour, trying to get her timing right to introduce her reason for calling into the conversation. "Are you concerned not to have heard from Heidi?"

Carol shook her head. "Not at all. She's probably sunning herself to a crisp." She gave a shrug.

The wind hissed through the vents on the windows, drops of rain splattering against the panes.

Lucy tapped her fingers on the granite. There wasn't any way of working up to this. She took a deep breath. "Heidi's not in Cyprus, Carol."

Carol frowned, visibly taken aback. "Excuse me?" She held Lucy's gaze.

Lucy returned her stare. "She's not in Cyprus."

"What do you mean? What do you know about where she is?" Carol sat up straight, leaning against the back of the stool, arms folded across her chest.

This was hard for Lucy to add to Carol's confusion and upset, but nevertheless she had promised her son she'd do whatever she could to help. "She's in New York. With Matt. At least she was a few days ago."

"What are you on about? She's in Cyprus. Has been all week."

After a moment of agonising internal debate, Lucy sighed. "She's been seeing Matt for the past few months. She followed him to New York, Carol, flew into the States last week from Cyprus."

Carol screwed up her face in confusion. "Matt? *Your Matt?*"

Lucy laid a hand on her arm. "Yes. My son, Matt."

"What do you mean she's 'seeing him'? You can't mean . . ."

Lucy nodded reluctantly. "Yes, 'seeing him' as in 'having a relationship'."

"But she can't be! She's old enough to be . . ."

"His mother," Lucy finished for her, relieved they were on the same wavelength and hopeful that Carol would support her in getting them to put an end to their so-called relationship. "It's beyond ridiculous, Carol. But that's not all. There's more . . ."

"She is okay, isn't she?" Carol, suddenly overcome by a sense of dread, brought a hand to her chest.

"Well, apparently, something's happened and she's not –"

"She's not what, Lucy?" Carol gasped. The room began to swim around her. "Tell me! Has he hurt her? What's going on?"

Lucy drew back, her eyes narrowing at her neighbour's insinuation. "Matt hasn't *done* anything to her. She's gone missing. He doesn't know where she is."

"Missing?" Carol screamed, her voice echoing around the house. She looked at Lucy with scary, burning eyes. Breathlessly, she asked, "How can you sit in my kitchen and calmly tell me my daughter's missing? In New York City?" She half-rose, her face bright red, her lips trembling.

Lucy waved her hands, trying to get her to sit back down and listen. "Carol! She's not 'missing' like in a missing person – it's just that Matt can't find out where she is. She's staying with some guy called Julian, but Matt's genuinely worried about her and he was hoping you might help him figure out whatever the hell's going on."

Carol flopped back into the seat, letting out a deep sigh that seemed to come from her toes, her thoughts miles away as she muttered almost to herself, "So she's met up with Julian? After all this time. Why, I wonder?"

Lucy watched her closely, wondering who Julian was and what significance he had in Heidi's life. And Matt's, now he'd got involved. "Matt's very hurt, Carol," she prompted her neighbour. "And confused."

Carol nodded very slowly as though she was processing everything in her mind. "I'm confused myself. I can't visualise them together, can you?"

Lucy sighed. "Visualise it, Carol, because that's how it is . . ."

"But if she's with Julian now then maybe Matt should back off. They shouldn't be seeing each other. Matt's young, he'll get over it quickly." Carol's demeanour slipped from concern to nonchalance.

Lucy struggled to conceal her anger. How dare Carol dismiss Matt's feelings so casually? Was she insinuating that her son wasn't good enough for Heidi? "Is that all you can say?" she burst out, gripping the leather coaster so tightly her fingers hurt. "Heidi taught him in school for crying out loud, baby-sat him when he was younger. *She* shouldn't have involved him in this mess! And all you can say is he's not suitable for your precious daughter!" Lucy got up and made to leave, her lips pursed in annoyance. She didn't trust what she'd say next. Nobody had the right to speak about her son with anything less than respect. And what was more, he deserved that respect.

"Lucy, please, you don't understand . . ."

"Well, tell me then, help me understand."

"Okay. Heidi is thirty-three years old, big enough to make her own decisions. Or so you'd expect," Carol's gaze strayed to the remaining photo on the windowsill, Heidi's troubled eyes peering from beneath layers of expertly applied copper eye-shadow.

"Exactly!"

"But she's had it tougher than most over the years, tougher than people realise."

"No excuse to treat Matt like something she scraped from the sole of her shoe!"

Carol flinched. "From what you're telling me, he's serious about her, already involved?"

That's what worries me, Lucy thought, fighting back the retort on her lips that she wished he'd never laid eyes on her. "He's concerned about her, wants to know she's okay. Matt's considerate, wouldn't hurt a fly," she added, swallowing her animosity. She'd keep the lines of communication open with Carol in case she did hear something from Heidi, anything that would ease Matt's concern.

"Hopefully it's infatuation, a storm in a teacup, nothing he won't get over in time," Carol commented, her forehead creasing into a deeply etched frown. "But why has she contacted Julian after all this time? I thought their history was buried a long time ago."

"History?"

"Didn't Matt tell you?"

Lucy raised her eyebrows, shaking her head.

"Julian is Heidi's husband, well, ex-husband to be precise."

Lucy's mouth dropped open. "How come I never knew she was . . ." The rest of the sentence died on her lips.

Carol's lips shaped into a grim line. "It wasn't something we were shouting from the rooftops. Anyway, by the time we found out about it, the relationship had already fizzled out."

263

"But they're still in touch?"

"So it seems," Carol replied dryly. "Still, she's got over him once before, I'm sure she can again." She went to fill the kettle. "Coffee?"

"No, thanks," Lucy said. "Are they still married?"

"Divorced."

"Can I tell Matt not to worry then? Her old flame Julian will look after her?"

Carol nodded reflectively. "Yes, tell him that."

"And your advice? Knowing your daughter's history as you do?" Lucy's tone was icy, steel in her expression.

"That's not fair, Lucy," Carol shot back. "She's still my daughter no matter what." Inside, Carol's stomach churned. This isn't good, she thought. Why had Heidi set her sights on Matt? Why now? Damn it. Everything's spiralling out of control, one problem entangling itself with the next.

"And *he's* my son." Miffed at her neighbour's lack of concern for Matt, Lucy couldn't wait to get away. "I'll be off."

Carol nodded, stumbling awkwardly over her next request. "Eh, Lucy, those documents for my car? Have you put them through yet?"

Lucy nodded mindlessly, not trusting herself to speak.

"Thanks," Carol responded sheepishly. "It's okay for me to insure it in your name then?" She pushed her hair back from her face to reveal dark circles under her eyes despite the heavy layer of make-up she was wearing.

Lucy raised her eyes to meet Carol's when she spoke again. "If that's what you want, Carol, but there is one condition . . ."

Carol nodded. "Anything."

Lucy noticed immediately that her expression had

changed. Her eyes hollow, no trace of the nonchalance she'd displayed earlier. "You have to stop Heidi from messing with Matt's head."

"If I can find a way without destroying Heidi into the bargain. She's fragile. More than I can explain since . . ." Carol stopped abruptly, retracing her steps after a moment's pause. "No point regurgitating the past, but let's just say she's fragile, Lucy."

Not too fragile to wreck my son's chance of adventure, Lucy was thinking, but held her counsel and kept her opinion to herself. For Matt's sake.

"I don't suppose I could cadge a lift from you and collect my car from your garage. Would that be okay, Lucy?"

And though it was the last place she wanted to visit, Lucy acquiesced and drove through the entrance gates of Sycamore Lawn once more, averting her eyes as best she could to avoid staring at the intense damage.

Barely a word was spoken between her and Carol in the car and she pretended not to notice her neighbour's salute as she drove the Audi away. Heidi's mysterious and complicated past rolled around her mind, the amicable friendship she'd once enjoyed with her neighbour already under threat in Lucy's mind.

Returning to Delia's house with a heavy heart, Lucy stepped inside the front door with the intention of treating her aching bones to a long hot soak. But the welcome awaiting her soon shattered that idea.

Jenny, who was only short of donning a nurse's uniform as she fussed around Danny and ordered Gloria and Delia about, marched right up to her and stared her in the eye, spit flying from her lips as she set upon her.

"Here she is now," Jenny sneered, glancing around at her befuddled audience – Danny, Gloria and Delia. "The lady decides to grace us with her presence! Couldn't even make the time to visit you. It's as well I arrived when I did, Dan, or you'd be stuck in that hospital for weeks. God knows what infection you'd have picked up! The grime in that place . . . don't get me started!"

Ignoring Jenny, Lucy turned her attention to Danny, trying to hide her shock at the sight of him in a wheelchair, focusing on his face and not the chair. "How come I wasn't told you were being discharged? Was it sudden?"

Danny's voice was gravelly, his eyes downcast. "Jenny happened to be there when it was suggested," he said. "There was no way of contacting you when you didn't show up this afternoon as promised."

Lucy's eyes darkened. He's hiding something, she thought, glaring at Jenny, wishing she could wave a wand and make her fly off on her broomstick. He's twisting everything to make me guilty. There was no point explaining she had visited but hadn't gone in, not with Jenny hovering. She's got something to do with this, she thought, hurrying to Danny and hugging him awkwardly.

"It's great to have you home, Dan," she whispered into his ear, "but are you sure it's not too soon?" Her mind was spinning.

Danny grunted something inaudible but didn't hug her back.

Lucy pulled away, dejected. "I'd best organise our bedroom," she said, looking to Delia for help. If she didn't get away from Jenny, she couldn't be held responsible for what she'd do to her. "I'll leave you chatting to your sister.

I'm sure she'll be leaving shortly for Clonakilty to visit your parents."

"This way, Luce," Delia said, grabbing her by the arm and leading her up the stairs before anything else came out of her mouth. She'd had enough drama in her living room for one afternoon.

"What a bitch!" Lucy said as soon as she'd closed the bedroom door. "She's done this. She's caused uproar in the hospital and insisted he come home. Typical of her, breezing in and upsetting everybody. Didn't she even call you first to see if it was okay? To check the house was warm, that there was somebody here to let him in?"

"Look, I don't know what happened and you'd better wait till you've got the full story before you get carried away," Delia responded simply.

Lucy chewed on her nails. "But, Del, have you seen him? How can I take care of him? He's barely breathing, his arms are singed. He's in a wheelchair for God's sake! He was getting intense nursing care up to a few hours ago."

Delia forced her to sit on the edge of the bed, sitting beside her and holding her hand. "Perhaps you should give the hospital a call? Ask the nurses about his medication – you might find more out that way. Did you get any of the nurses' names?"

Lucy closed her eyes and tried to remember, Jenny's squeaking tone audible through the ceiling, making it impossible for her to think straight. "You've got to get her to leave, Del," she begged her sister. "If you invite her to stay or offer her tea, I'll never speak to you again."

"I've a better idea," Delia answered, her eyes twinkling as the idea came to her. "I'll set Mum on her."

Lucy picked up the phone to call the hospital, Nurse O'Donnell's name coming to mind. She bestowed a grateful smile on her sister, once again a stalwart in her eyes. Jenny and Gloria, she thought, a match made in Heaven.

The girls lurked in the hall a short while later, the door open a crack so they could hear Gloria's exchange with Jenny. And it wasn't pleasant. Lucy couldn't help going to peep through the crack in the door.

"Danny's tired now, Jenny. And your parents will be waiting to find out how he is," Gloria was saying.

"I'm not going anywhere . . ." Jenny spluttered, cowering slightly under Gloria's menacing expression. "My brother's in trouble and I'm here to help him, in the same way he'd –"

"Jenny, don't!" Danny warned, but didn't seem to have anything else to say.

Through the crack in the door, Lucy noticed the look he'd shot at Jenny, a look that had made her blush bright red.

Lucy rejoined Delia, frowning in confusion. "What's all that about?" she whispered.

But Delia put a finger to her lips and listened with interest to Gloria once more, taking her turn to creep up to the door so she could hear better.

"Nonsense. Taking care of Danny is my daughter's job. And in a few days, after he's got some proper rest, you can bring your parents up from Clonakilty to visit. But call first. You wouldn't like to upset your mum and dad by letting them see him in a wheelchair. Or hadn't you thought of that, you selfish girl?"

Lucy and Delia held their breath as Danny spoke.

"Gloria's right," he said. "You should leave now."

Lucy and Delia rejoined the others in the room in time to see Danny's sister depart. Her face was a picture, her cheeks bright red and her thin lips pursed together tightly as she grabbed her sable coat. Without another word, she planted a peck on her brother's forehead and left the house, the glass vase rattling on the windowsill from the force of the banging door.

Chapter 35

Delia ran around tidying and organising the house as quickly and quietly as she could. It was half past five on Wednesday morning and pitch dark outside. She'd delayed her morning shower, not wanting the humming sound to wake Lucy or Danny. And she certainly didn't want to wake Gloria! She skipped breakfast too and by quarter past six was immersed in sketching some new jewellery designs.

At ten minutes to seven she heard a gentle knock on the door and took it as her cue to take a break, whether she wanted one or not.

"Do you ever sleep?" Lucy asked, handing her a steaming mug of coffee and placing a plate of warm buttered toast on the desk. She yawned widely and ran a hand through her unkempt hair.

Delia shrugged, switching on the radio but setting it at a barely audible level. "And how about you? Why are you awake?"

"It's impossible to sleep with the buzz of that oxygen tank in our room," Lucy said, rubbing the sleep from the corners of her eyes, not bothering to mention all the other problems keeping her awake at night.

Delia devoured her toast, savouring every mouthful. "Is his form any better, Luce?"

Lucy shook her head, pulling her dressing gown tight around her. "He takes the head off me for the slightest thing." Her eyes glazed over, aware that the distance between her and Danny was intensifying by the day. She focused on a knot on the wooden floor.

"How did he take the news about Stephen's wedding?"

"A lot better than I did," Lucy replied honestly, fidgeting with a button on her dressing gown. That much was true. Although Danny's reaction hadn't been negative, neither was it filled with enthusiasm. He'd grunted something about Stephen being in charge of his own life now.

"At least it's one less secret you have to keep, Luce." Delia fiddled with the sketches she'd been working on, wishing she could get back to finishing them but Lucy's desire for a chat, particularly one that wasn't interrupted by Gloria, far outweighed anything else at that moment.

Lucy picked at crumbs and moved them around the plate. "Does the postman come at the same time every morning?" She'd arranged for her letters to be redirected to Delia's house and was waiting impatiently for the bank statements to arrive.

"You could set your watch by him. The dog across the road barks his head off around half nine every single morning and two seconds later my letter-box is flapping."

Both of them turned around at the sound of the door opening, surprised to see their mother coming into the room but not very surprised that she was wearing a disgruntled expression on her face.

"Delia, this house is freezing! Would you ever time the heating to come on in the mornings? My hands and feet are like blocks of ice."

"Morning, Mum!" Delia and Lucy chorused simultaneously.

Gloria fixed the collar of her candlewick dressing gown to fit snugly around her neck, rubbing the palms of her hands together to try and instil some heat into them. "Well?" She looked expectantly at her youngest daughter.

"Well, what?" Delia snapped.

"Are you going to turn on the heating or at least show me how to do it myself? Or will I have to stand here all day freezing?"

"What are you doing up at this hour of the morning?" Delia asked between gritted teeth. She had no intention of giving her mother a demonstration on how to use the heating controls. She knew what would happen if she did. The house would be like a sauna from morning till night and the cost of running it would shoot through the roof.

"When I'm cold, I can't sleep." She turned on her heel and left the study, muttering something about a hot cup of tea.

Delia looked at Lucy and threw her eyes to heaven, on the verge of commenting on Gloria's antagonism when she heard Crosshaven being mentioned on the news bulletin. She turned up the volume, both girls silent as they listened attentively to the broadcaster.

". . . *Sycamore Lodge, a detached residence on the outskirts of Crosshaven. Based on findings from Garda forensics, the case is now being upgraded to arson. Carrigaline gardaí are following a number of lines of enquiry. Anyone with any information, please call in strictest confidence. . .*"

Delia turned off the radio.

Lucy's body shook, her face ashen, her voice little more than a whisper. "How have the media got hold of something like that before we've been told anything?"

Danny's poor state of health had made it impossible for her to quiz him about the empty van and containers. The evening before she'd held a mirror for him while he'd shaved, tensing as his shaking hands brought the blade close to his earlobe, the questions she wanted to ask dying on her lips.

"The gardaí won't be too far behind breaking news, Luce," Delia warned. "You have to come clean about the insurance as soon as he wakes this morning. What if Phelim O'Brien or Jack Bowe turns up and starts questioning him? You can't humiliate Danny like that."

Lucy felt trapped, seeing no escape. Arson, the news broadcaster had said. Arson! What evidence made them issue a statement like that? She swallowed hard, her mind in a tailspin.

"What if Danny's responsible, Del? Do you think it's possible? If the company was in trouble, would he resort to doing something like this? Use compensation to get him out of a bind?" She voiced her suspicion, her eyes fixed on her sister, willing her to disprove the gardaí's suspicions.

Delia was horrified, unable to believe for a moment

her brother-in-law was capable of such fraud. She couldn't think of a single response, filling the breach with an offer of help instead. "I'll take Mum to town. I can pick up the birth certs and organise the hotel to email the reference to Matt. It'll leave you and Danny some time to yourselves to talk. And I mean really talk, Luce, not skirt around the serious issues and use Danny's health as a reason to avoid any unpleasantness."

Chapter 36

Carol took a bottle of perfumed gel from the shower rack, squirted it on to the loofah and scrubbed every inch of her skin until it tingled. Her insides still crawled at the memory of her encounter with Jacob the day before. It didn't matter how many times she scrubbed and exfoliated under scalding water, her skin raging red from the intensity, her self-loathing remained.

"How could I have degraded myself and my family by throwing myself at him," she muttered through gritted teeth, a brand-new feeling of disgust filling every pore as though his fingers were still trailing her thigh.

She lathered once more, massaging until she could no longer feel her fingers, wishing she could believe she'd had no choice. But in hindsight she realised with regret that there's always a choice. If Jacob hadn't provided her with the information she'd needed to prevent the holding in Barna, County Galway, being part of Danny's debt portfolio, she could have tried elsewhere. But in her panic she hadn't thought of that, had tapped into the drunken interest he'd previously shown her instead. And now she'd have to live with the mortification and shame, which if she were honest lowered her exactly to the same disgusting level as her cheating husband. How pathetic, she thought, running the sudsy loofah over her thighs once more to try and eliminate the memory.

The more she scrubbed, the more the memory came to life. Jacob hadn't refused the cabernet sauvignon she'd offered to loosen his tongue. She'd allowed his bony fingers trail along her sheer stockings, right to the point where they'd found her suspender belt. She swallowed down the bile rising in her throat, remembering his repugnant touch. But all the time his fingers were making circles on her thighs (without – thankfully – straying any higher), she was quizzing him for information and he – his senses clouded by testosterone – was falling right into her trap by handing her the means to orchestrate a legal loophole.

He'd drained the first glass and indicated he'd like more. She'd eased away from his touch, conscious of his eyes transfixed on her shapely figure as he'd followed her to the kitchen where she'd slipped another bottle of wine from the rack. Like an eager puppy, he'd panted in anticipation, his face flushed, his trousers bulging.

Carol's heart had raced, the flirtation getting out of control. She'd stood at the sink and punctured the wooden cork with the tip of the corkscrew, stalling for time, freezing in disgust when he'd circled her from behind, his body pressing tightly against hers. She hadn't prepared for this level of persistence, had only intended to tease until she'd extracted the information she required. Trapped in the circle of his embrace, at a loss for words, she was unable to believe her good fortune when the bell chimed loudly in the hallway.

"Ignore it," he'd ordered huskily, nuzzling against her earlobe, his sharp teeth biting her soft skin.

His breath was hot on her neck, his hips writhing in slow circular movements. I asked for this, she'd thought, her body convulsing at every touch, her heart continuing to race.

The doorbell had echoed loudly through the empty house, a long persistent ring, somebody who wasn't leaving quietly. Carol sincerely hoped they wouldn't.

"I won't be a moment," she'd whispered huskily to Jacob, swivelling around to face him, still trapped in the circle of his arms.

"Leave it. Whoever it is will come back. You and I aren't finished yet." His grip tightened, the circle decreasing, his lips descending slowly on hers.

Carol recognised a warning threat in his eyes, a threat advising her against playing him for a fool. Her head had lightened, the sense she was losing control swilling over her. Focusing her attention away from his flushed face, she willed the person at the door to stay, ready to welcome anybody – friend or foe, even the bailiffs – to save her from her own mistakes. Anything to help her out of the fix she was in.

The memory brought a bout of angry tears to Carol's eyes. She leaned her head against the tiled wall, the loofah falling from her hands, yelping when the shampoo bottle fell from the overhead shelf and dropped on her toe. Grimacing in pain, she knew full well that a thousand hot showers wouldn't be enough to purge the feeling of Jacob's touch from her skin. Or her conscience. She thanked God Eric was out of the country. And she also thanked God for sending her a means of escape from Jacob's clutches.

She turned her face to the cascading water once more, letting it flow on her tearstained cheeks. Only that Lucy had knocked on the kitchen window, God only knows where it would have ended. Or how far he would have taken her ridiculous teasing encouragement. Where it could have led had been sending shivers through her ever since, the dangerous line she'd crossed disturbing her sleep at night. Too late, she'd realised the risk she'd taken. But the sight of Lucy outside the kitchen window – timely for Carol as it turned out – had made him drop his arms and rethink his actions. He valued his reputation too much to be caught fraternising with clients. A harsh laugh, a look of scorn and he'd disappeared, the sound of the front door clicking closed behind him making Carol's knees buckle.

Letting out a long sigh she pushed away the nightmare memory and turned off the shower, her cheeks burning, shame still eating her up inside. Her kitchen window blinds had at least prevented Lucy noticing anything untoward, sparing Carol the embarrassment of explaining Jacob's close proximity.

Still shaken from the solicitor's persistence, she'd found it next to impossible to concentrate on Lucy's lengthy lecture as she relayed her concerns about Matt's relationship with Heidi. Carol hadn't been fooled by her forced nonchalance. It hurt deep when she'd laid the blame entirely at Heidi's door. And though she'd responded as best she could, she couldn't ignore her daughter's chequered past or the distress and upheaval she'd suffered down the years. She doubted, knowing Heidi's fickle nature (a bit like her father on that score, enjoying the chase much more than the procurement), her obsession with Matt would last longer than the return date on her airline ticket. Ex-boyfriends rarely kept contact, happy to walk away from her eccentricities without as much as a backward glance. Apart from Julian of course. But her connection with Julian was many years old, a deep-rooted bond held together with a spider-webbed history, a butterfly effect of a brief episode from the past lingering between them for eternity. Everything is disposable except the past.

Carol lathered body lotion on to her damp skin, wishing Heidi and Matt's relationship hadn't occurred, wishing Eric hadn't been so damn irresponsible, wishing more than anything that things between her and Lucy could be salvaged. She hadn't laid eyes on her since and was too apprehensive to get in touch.

Dressing quickly in jeans, white T-shirt and plaid shirt, Carol pulled on her brown leather boots, combed her damp hair and ran downstairs. Void of make-up or perfectly groomed hair, she looked a lot less sophisticated than normal. Her appearance matched her mood and more importantly, it portrayed a waiflike image, the impression she wanted to give when calling to Jacob's office.

About to take her car keys and leave, she did a turnabout and went upstairs once more, lifting the floorboard in her wardrobe and removing the deeds of her deceased aunt's holding. They were the only thing separating her from devastation and she wasn't going to risk losing them. If only she could prevent the bank from claiming them as payment against Eric's accrued debts.

Her mobile rang as she drove off in the Audi. Hearing Isobel's voice, the dread of confronting Jacob vanished temporarily. The biting agitation in her daughter's voice sent a shiver through her. Isobel normally had a calming effect, fitting the description of cool, collected and practical.

Pressing the button on her phone, she switched the call to speaker-phone. Carol felt a clunk in her stomach as her daughter's despondency reverberated around the interior of the car. She forced a brightness she didn't feel. "Sweetheart, how are you?"

A deep sigh came down the line, followed by a throaty cough. "Okay."

"Did your throat hold up for the presentations?"

"It held up better than my concentration which is shot. Have you heard from Dad?"

"No," Carol admitted, her eyes sparking with anger. Eric, despite the sorry mess he'd landed them in, hadn't even the decency or courage to come home and face the music.

"Nothing at all?" Isobel's gravelly tone distracted Carol's thoughts.

"Afraid not, pet."

"And the banks? Have they started proceedings . . .?"

Carol's heart ached for Isobel. "Still waiting, love."

"Waiting's the worst part, Mum. It's God-awful. How the hell –"

"Sweetheart, human beings make mistakes. All we can do now is move on whatever way we can."

"Move on?"

Carol sought to change the subject, wanting to calm her eldest daughter a little, divert her attention from losing their home and so much more. "You won't believe where Heidi is, Isobel."

Her daughter's intake of breath came through the speaker. "What's she done now?"

Carol couldn't help a smile. Her daughters were polar opposites, neither understanding the other, yet caring about each other in their own unique way. "She's in New York . . ." She changed into a lower gear, slowing the car as she rounded a dangerous bend, wondering whether Isobel had enough on her plate without dragging her into Heidi's troubles too.

"New York? What, shopping on Dad's Visa? Oh shit, have you told her? Does she know her credit's cut off?"

"I've tried but she's not answering."

"But . . ."

Carol wasn't sure her daughter could handle the upset of her sister's disappearance, her reunion with Julian or disclosing the identity of her latest boyfriend. Best tell her that face to face, she thought. It wasn't as if another day would make much of a difference.

"Why don't you stay in Dublin for a few extra days?" Carol suggested on impulse. "At least until we've more certainty about everything."

"I can't, Mum. I'm on the red-eye flight in the morning and then it's straight to the office for a hot-shot meeting."

"And you're sure you're up to this exploding in front of our faces? It's only a matter of time before the papers get their hands on the fact your dad's gone belly-up. Imagine the uproar when his creditors hear the good news?"

"To hell with them! What about our family? I'm scared, Mum."

Carol tapped her fingers on the steering wheel, chewing on the inside of her lip, her heart aching for Isobel who felt so obviously let down. She'd stepped in so many times to offer her wayward father nuggets of wisdom, her sober intelligence and clear thinking, something Eric lacked in abundance. And though he'd listened in theory, in practice he'd seldom adhered to her advice, pushing ahead with his car-crash business methods, leading them to where they were now.

"What time's your flight landing, love?" Carol kept her tone light, trying to disguise her fear, protectiveness her only remaining weapon.

"Shortly before eight in the morning."

"I'll be waiting in the Arrivals hall. Can't wait to see you, pet."

"Oh, Mum. Why has this happened?"

"Hush, love, none of it is of your making." Carol's heart quickened.

"But I should have made Dad listen."

"Nobody can make your father listen," Carol responded flatly.

She could hear Isobel's sigh before the line went dead.

Carol seethed with anger as she veered the car too quickly around the roundabout on the approach to Carrigaline, turning her head sharply when she noticed one of the Crosshaven Yacht set out walking. Eric had made a lifelong career of image creation. It became an obsession, an illusion. Meeting the striking brunette's gaze as she slowed the car at the red traffic lights, Carol dared her to register disgust at her appearance. Calm. Stay calm, she repeated silently. If you're calm, you're in control.

She pressed the button to open the window. "Rosemary, hi!" she shouted.

Rosemary gave a hurried wave but dashed off in the other direction, turning her leisurely stroll into a power walk, unable to get away fast enough.

The rumour mill is alive, Carol smiled wryly, closing the window once more. Rosemary's haste to avoid her was all the confirmation she needed. Do they think I'm stupid? Out of nowhere, the lingerie in Eric's suitcase flashed into her mind. How many knew of his infidelity? Is it Rosemary, she wondered, taking off in a blur of exhaust fumes when the car behind her honked his horn. The lights had been green a while now, Carol's racing brain failing to register. Shame, humiliation and fear stripped her of confidence and every shred of trust she'd ever possessed.

Aching to hold her daughters and keep them close – and safe – she kept a close eye on the shop-fronts along Main Street, her head spinning when she pulled the Audi into a parking spot outside Jacob's office. She struggled to control the fear that trickled like electricity down her spine, her legs threatening to give way as she stumbled through the entrance door.

Through clenched jaws, she asked the receptionist for a quick moment with Jacob, her voice cracking. "It's really important I speak to him."

The assistant shook her head. "Unfortunately he's not available at this time but I can make an appointment for you and relay your urgency."

Carol heard a muffled conversation through the closed office door. Angry with herself for begging, she could see no other option and scurried past the assistant into Jacob's office.

His face like thunder, the person he was in discussion

with turning around to see who'd barged uninvited into a private meeting, Jacob rose from his chair.

"Five minutes," he apologised to his client. He got up and steered Carol back into the reception area. "I'll be in the conference room," he told his assistant.

Pasting a nervous smile on her face, Carol did her best to shut out her rising terror, experiencing a shocking taste of the panic attacks Heidi had been experiencing for years. In that moment she agonised for her youngest daughter more than ever before, understanding first-hand the incredible force of panic exploding through her body, obliterating everything apart from a nuance of white light calling to her through the descending blackness.

Chapter 37

Phelim O'Brien undid the top button of his shirt and loosened his tie. He stared at the forensic report on his desk, scanning through the detail for the umpteenth time. The findings weren't one-hundred-per-cent conclusive, exactly as he'd hoped. He bit into a jam doughnut, licking the sugar from his lips, convinced he had enough evidence to nail that bastard, Danny Ardle. By the time I'm finished with him, he thought, he'll regret the day he refused me that corner site. Because if we hadn't bought Number 13 overlooking the valley, Anne wouldn't have . . .

Phelim shoved the rest of the doughnut into his mouth, blocking out the memories, sealing them into a closed compartment of his brain where they'd been trapped since he'd moved into a one-bedroom apartment in the village. Renting a two-bedroom had been tempting, particularly as the large balconies boasted a sea view. But separation was difficult enough without the emptiness of a guest bedroom reminding him of his son and daughter who would have absolutely nothing to do with him.

He scrolled through the dialled numbers on his mobile phone, removing the number he'd called to leak information to the press. His media contact had ensured it wouldn't be traced but it didn't do any harm to cover his tracks. The detail he'd imparted had drummed up a bit of curiosity, transmitting a cryptic message to some of Danny's public in particular, the customers who relied on him, the suppliers who valued his credit rating. And the news bulletin he'd just tuned into ticked all those boxes, casting quite an amount of doubt on Danny Ardle, the trusty entrepreneur and model family man.

Phelim sat back in the chair and stared around the office where he'd worked for the past twelve years, his eyes falling on the framed certificates hanging on the wall, all from an era in his career where he'd actually given a damn and taken immense satisfaction in bringing perpetrators to justice and giving victims the exoneration they deserved. He closed his eyes, letting his defences fall temporarily. Things hadn't always been like they were now. His heart hadn't been shrivelled with bitterness, making him ready to lash out at anyone who got in his way. Shutting away emotions isn't a crime, he thought, but it can lead to serious freefall. And freefall is a very mild description of how I'm feeling right now.

He left his office and made the journey he'd been dreading, stopping at a florist on his way to pick up an arrangement of the yellow tulips that had always been his wife's favourites.

Chapter 38

Shortly after Delia and Gloria had left the house to refill the depleting grocery supplies (as well as giving Lucy a welcome break from Gloria's incessant nagging), Lucy ripped open her post. Moments later, pages and pages of banking transactions slipped from her fingers onto the tiled kitchen floor. She rocked gently in the chair, staring unseeingly through the window. Days of hoping and waiting ending in tears, the moment of truth dropping through the letterbox in the shape of an A4-sized white windowed envelope.

"I didn't pay the damn premium," she muttered under her breath, voicing her worst reality in the empty room, her fingers nervously pulling the zip of her black velour leisure top up and down, up and down. So disgusted with Carol's attitude about Heidi and Matt, Lucy couldn't stomach wearing her cast-offs into the bargain, and she'd asked Delia to pick her up a few casual items she could wear around the house and it had felt good getting into something that actually belonged to her that morning.

She held the pages up to her face, muttering aloud and inhaling the smell from the paper. "What on earth are we going to do? Is there any way to survive this damage?"

"Lucy! Where are you?"

Startled when she heard Danny calling her, she looked around for something to clean her tear-stained face, not wanting him to see her upset (again). Guessing he'd be in the kitchen in less than a minute, she bundled up the bank statements and shoved them back in the envelope as best she could, looking around frantically as she tried to think of somewhere to hide them. She stuck them behind Delia's microwave, took a deep breath and painted a smile on her face.

"Hi there," she said brightly, pulling the drawstring on her velour pants, tying it in a neat bow. "I thought you'd take a rest until at least lunch-time after such a broken night's sleep."

His colour was ashen, his eyes lifeless and the jeans she'd bought him hung from his hips. Jenny's interference had cost him a few more days of hospital care, slowing down his recovery as far as Lucy was concerned. But she hadn't raised that particular subject or argument with Danny, biting back her retort every time he mentioned his sister's name, hoping her 'emergency' trip home would come to a swift end. Ferrying her parents from Clonakilty to Crosshaven to visit Danny would probably happen once and once only if Jenny's track record was anything to go by and Lucy was praying she'd disappear on the next London flight and keep her opinions and interference to herself.

Danny put a hand on the back of the couch to steady himself. "I can't stay in bed. If I'm cooped up much longer, I'll go off my head. Not being able to work is depressing enough but staying indoors finishes me. You of all people should know that by now."

"Dan," she pleaded, "please take it easy for another few days. Give your body a chance to recover. I told you what the nurse said when I called. Lots of rest, oxygen for up to eighteen hours a day and avoid putting yourself at risk of infection."

He shot her a dark look.

Oh God, she thought. What have I said now? Why am I his scapegoat? "I'll make you some breakfast. Why don't you sit down?" She daren't suggest he use the wheelchair. The hospital had told him to use if for another few days. But she stopped short of reminding him.

"Stop fussing over me! I can put two Weetabix in a bowl and pour milk from a container."

Lucy watched him move, his shoulders stooped, his slow step making him look a lot older than his forty-five years. It broke her heart seeing him like that. Her eye twitched as she stared after him.

"I don't suppose you thought to grab the key of the van from the utility room when you called to the house," he said. "Or was that room destroyed too?"

Lucy stared at his back. He hadn't even had the manners to turn around to face her when he was speaking to her. Or should she say insulting her? He was making it sound like it was her fault! Oh blast and damn him, she thought. I can't play these games any longer. He's not the only one with questions. I've a few questions of my own to ask him.

"Yeah, Danny," she shouted, "the utility room survived. And luckily, so did you. But ever since you've come around after the fire, all you've done is shut me out, snipe at me, make me feel like I struck the match. And to be perfectly honest, I've had enough. Life hasn't exactly been a bed of roses for me either, you know. And while we're on the subject of your van . . ."

Danny kept his back turned as though he hadn't heard a word out of her mouth.

Lucy marched across the kitchen. "God damn you. Tell me what I'm supposed to have done!" she shouted, grabbing his shoulder and forcing him to turn and look at her.

But he shrugged her off, reaching into the press for a cereal bowl, freezing her out with a look that screamed disgust.

Unable to be in the same room as him, she pushed open the French doors and hurried into the back garden. Bending down on her hunkers, she pulled at stray weeds, a few that had obviously escaped Delia's careful eye. Fiddling with the short green stems between shaking fingers, she swallowed hard, choking back hot tears, refusing to shed any more on Danny's behalf. His behaviour and attitude towards her was appalling. And without justification. If she'd already told him about the insurance, he'd have reason to treat her with such disdain. But God damn him, no amount of illness or shock excused the way he was treating her or speaking to her right now. God damn his insolence.

She'd left the door swinging open, was able to hear him fiddling about in the kitchen, opening and closing drawers, hearing a chair scraping as he pulled it to sit down. She shivered a little, the cold cutting through her light clothing. But she refused to go inside and face him, anger and stubbornness partly holding her back, fear making her want to escape over the garden wall and run like hell. Still on her hunkers, she stared at the twelve-foot wall, counting the cavity blocks, knowing in her heart the notion was ridiculous, not to mention unmanageable. It would take a lot more than a Twelve-foot concrete wall to help her escape the mess she was in. Nothing short of a miracle could get her out of the mess she was sinking in right now.

She stood up, wrapped her arms around her body, moved back to the open door and made a decision. She'd already been running for far too long. It was time to get off the merry-go-round and face reality.

"Danny," she said from the threshold, keeping her eyes downcast but speaking loud enough for her husband to hear, "there's something you need to know . . ."

Pausing for breath, she raised her eyes and looked inside, a shriek leaving her mouth as she saw Danny slumped over on the table.

She dashed inside. "Danny, Danny, wake up! You're scaring me. Please. God damn you, will you wake up!" She shook him and shook him, getting little response apart from a grunt and groan. She hurried to the phone and called the emergency services, rushing back to Danny's side as soon as she'd dropped the phone. Her heart raced in her chest. She tried to lift his head but failed. Massaging between his shoulder-blades, she slapped his back hard, doing anything she could think of to try and revive him.

"Danny, wake up! Danny, wake up! Don't you dare die on me!" She spoke loudly as she'd seen the nurses doing, repeating his name, trying everything in her power to make him come around. For the first time since she'd run inside, she looked at his face properly, noticing the purple hue on his skin and realising his oxygen levels were depleted. The nurse had told her to watch out for this. Instantly she remembered what to do, hoping it wasn't too late.

"I'll be right back, Danny."

She ran to their bedroom, dragging the cumbersome oxygen unit to the bedroom door and attaching the oxygen mask on to the tubing. She pulled the extended plastic tubing down the stairs and along the hallway, hurrying as fast as she could, then strapped the mask over his head and fixed it tightly onto his face to ensure he got full benefit. Taking a tea towel, she soaked it in cold water and pressed it to his forehead.

He struggled slightly and groaned. Lucy wasn't sure if she'd imagined it. Then he did it again, pushing against her arm, trying to lift his head from the table, shoving against the icy towel.

She kept the towel to his forehead. "Come on, Danny, that's it. Try to put your head up."

He's coming around, she thought, hope leaping in her heart.

His forehead creased into a frown, his eyes flickering open for a moment.

Lucy held her breath, watching him closely. She pressed the wet cloth against his skin again, reaching behind her and tearing some kitchen roll, wiping away droplets of water running along the side of his cheek. "Come on, Danny. You're going to be fine. The ambulance is on its way. They'll help you."

But instead of reassuring him, this information had the opposite effect. "No!" he said, shaking his head from side to side. "No hospital!"

"Okay, relax," she said, rubbing his cheek again as a drop of water ran behind his earlobe and down his back.

He brought a hand to the mask, his body heaving up and down in fast rhythmic movements. Then he opened his eyes and looked up at her with a bleary expression.

"You're doing much better, Dan. Keep inhaling through the mask. I'll hold the towel to your forehead for a while longer. Remember the nurses did this as well?" She was terrified that if she took it away, he'd pass out again. Her head was in crisis, more guilt mounting on top of the large mound that was already there.

What kind of person screams at somebody who's been through what he has?

Husband and wife remained silent for a while, Lucy holding a damp towel to his head and Danny inhaling oxygen, his eyes closed. As though moving in slow motion, he lifted his head from the table, continuing to breathe heavily, his chest rising up and down.

By the time the doorbell rang, he was sitting up properly in the chair, the purple colour in his face a lot less prevalent.

"I've got to open the door, Dan. I'll be right back."

He nodded his head, but remained silent, his eyes following her as she dashed from the kitchen.

Surprised not to hear an ambulance siren whirring outside, she pulled open the door, her mouth dropping open when she saw who was standing there.

Bursting into tears, she rushed into his arms and sobbed into his jacket, not caring that she was snivelling all over him, not caring about anything other than the fact her son was home.

"Stephen!" Lucy pulled back and stared at her eldest son, giving herself a few precious seconds to take in his familiar features: dark-brown eyes, tightly cropped blonde hair and a warm smile that made her heart melt. Despite the horrible things she'd said to him, he had got on a plane and travelled halfway across the world to be with them.

She found her voice at last. "I'm so sorry for all those hateful things I said, love. But, Stephen, your dad . . ." She dragged him towards the kitchen to let him see for himself the state his father was in rather than trying to explain.

But before they'd reached Danny, Stephen stopped her in her tracks, putting his hands on her shoulders and looking her in the eye. "It's okay, Mum. I shouldn't have shocked you with my news the way I did but when I heard about Dad and everything, I wanted you to know everything, especially about the baby. Ellie is a keeper, Mum, and us having a baby together has made me the happiest man in the world."

Lucy nodded but couldn't speak, choked with emotion and refusing to let go of him. She was torn between clinging to her son and rushing to her husband's side. Then she heard the ambulance siren come screaming up the road.

"It's for your dad, Stephen – he collapsed just now – he's in there. Go to him and I'll show the emergency crew inside."

She ran to the front of the house, opening the door wide to let the ambulance driver and his colleague through with the stretcher.

"He collapsed over the table, but revived when I gave him oxygen," Lucy said, leading them to Danny. "His colour's improving and at least he's sitting up again."

"What's the patient's name?" the ambulance man enquired.

"Danny Ardle. He only got out of hospital a few days ago suffering from smoke inhalation after our house went on fire."

Stephen was sitting beside his father, his hand around his shoulders, holding a glass to his lips. "That's it, Dad, little sips."

Lucy let the tension slide from her shoulders, relieved to let her son take control, feeling for the first time since the fire that she wasn't alone.

Danny pushed away the glass after one or two sips and turned to Lucy. "Did you make Stephen come home?"

"Of course not!" she replied, her face reddening with embarrassment at Danny's rudeness. She felt like slapping her husband's sour face, venom rising inside her. *How dare he,* she thought, turning to the ambulance men. "Can I get you anything?"

But they waved away her offer, attending to the patient instead. "Now, Danny, we'll get you to the hospital for x-rays, find out what's going on with those lungs of yours."

Danny shook his head defiantly, holding out his arm to have his blood pressure checked. "I'm not going back. This was my own fault. Didn't do what I was told."

Stephen's heart went out to his father, imagining how difficult it must be for him struggling to cope with what happened, hating the confinement of hospital where he probably wasn't allowed to even visit the bathroom on his own. "Look, sir," he said to the paramedic, "he genuinely seems okay. Can't you check him over or something? Wait a while to see if he takes another turn?"

The paramedic frowned, unwrapping the blood-pressure

apparatus from Danny's arm. "I'm not sure if keeping him at home is the safest thing to do. He could have an infection."

"Come on – please!" Stephen tried harder this time, his brown eyes appealing to the crew. "Put it down to the shock of seeing me walk through the door from Australia. He hasn't seen me in over two years."

Danny nodded his head in agreement. "It's true," he said, patting Stephen's arm awkwardly. "And if you cart me off to a ward, I'll spend a few days on a trolley and barely get to talk to my son."

Glancing from one to the other, the driver conceded, but not without caution. "If his vitals are good, I'll make a call but if his situation changes, he'll have to be admitted."

All three Ardles nodded their heads in unison, with Stephen clasping both his parents' hands, filling a noticeable void where Lucy and Danny remained firmly apart.

"Come on, Mum," Stephen said after a moment, "let's leave these guys to get on with their job. Dad, we'll be in the other room. Talk to you in a while." He gripped his father's shoulder tightly for a moment, letting him know he was rooting for him.

Lucy left the room with Stephen without looking back. She didn't think she could take another one of Danny's furious glances. Tears came to her eyes but she wiped them away. That snide remark he'd made about her calling Stephen home hurt. Didn't he realise she was doing her level best to keep things together under the circumstances? If she were alone, she'd have sobbed her heart out but she'd upset Stephen enough recently without dumping all her woes on him now too.

"Mum," Stephen said eagerly, once they were out of

earshot, "there's someone waiting in the car that travelled halfway around the world to meet you."

Lucy groaned inside, raising an eyebrow in feigned interest when in reality she didn't want to share this precious time with Stephen, particularly not with an absolute stranger, a person who was on the verge of slotting into the position of number-one woman in Stephen's world.

Sensing her hesitation, he added, "I thought it best to come in alone first." He waited for his mother's approval, his searching eyes betraying uncertainty about the welcome his fiancée would receive.

Lucy fiddled with her hair, understanding only too well why he would feel that way and realising that this was a very important moment, her opportunity to salvage the damage already done and pretend – if that's what was necessary – that as far as she was concerned anyone important to Stephen was also important to her and Danny. She pulled her son into her arms, too uneasy to let him see her expression as she uttered words of reassurance.

"I'm so sorry again for being such a bitch over this. It was a shock, on top of so many other shocks this week. But now, I'm looking forward to meeting her, Stephen."

Stephen planted a kiss on his mother's cheek, extricating himself from her tight hug. "Sure you're ready for this? Ready to meet your future daughter-in-law?"

Lucy nodded (a bit too enthusiastically), forcing a happiness that was nothing like the emptiness she felt inside. "We'll have to take care of her if she's carrying my first grandchild. Although if you must know," she added, tears brimming in her eyes, "I'm a bit miffed you're making me a granny so young!"

"And there's me thinking it was exactly what you

need now Matt's gone," he teased. "Wait there and I'll be back in a mo." He ran out the door and down the path.

Lucy didn't dare look out the front. In her heart, she was far from ready to face what Stephen was imposing on her. Oh God, she thought, staring at her tired eyes and pale complexion, please don't let her be a manipulative bitch like I first thought and, most of all, please let her love and respect Stephen for the true gentleman that he is. Glancing quickly in the mirror at her dishevelled appearance, she pinched her cheeks to give her pale face some colour and then made a half-hearted attempt to fix her hair. She inhaled deeply, tremors running through her body as she waited to meet the girl who'd stolen her son's heart.

Stephen returned a moment later, a broad grin on his face as he swept into the room with a tall, thin blonde following closely behind.

Lucy had a smile fixed on her face, cringing inside as she took in Ellie's sleek elegance, her doll-like face and lean figure. Her silky hair fell to her waist. 'Barbie' was the only word coming to Lucy's mind.

"Ellie," Stephen said, a protective arm around her tiny waist, his index finger slipping inside the loop holding her black-patent belt, "this is my mum – Lucy."

"How lovely to meet you," Ellie said, her smile reaching azure eyes, her naturally tanned face breaking into a big smile, displaying a mouthful of even white teeth. Her warm presence filled the room, Stephen's adoring eyes glued to her face.

No wonder he's in love with her, Lucy thought, finding it difficult not to stare at the model-like vision standing in front of her, already falling under her spell. She picked up on the easy warmth between them. Despite her reservations, a picture of the most magnificent baby came to mind – a mixture of Ellie's Australian beauty and Stephen's kindness and reliability. Unable to deny Stephen the support he deserved, she pressed an imaginary pause on her worries and concerns and allowed this isolated moment of perfection shine through.

"It's really nice to meet you too, Ellie. I can't believe you've made this journey with Stephen at such short notice." She extended her hand to Ellie.

"It's so good to meet you at last. Stephen never stops talking about his family."

"I'm not sure that's a good thing," Lucy laughed, sharing an understanding smile with her son.

"It's all good," Ellie assured her, covering her mouth with her hand as she yawned widely. "You've got to excuse my manners but this baby," she patted her stomach, "is taking it out of me."

"Do you want to have a lie-down?" Stephen asked quickly, his concern evident.

"Later perhaps, but first I want to get to know your mum a little."

"You've got to take care of yourself, El," he insisted.

"Was he always this fussy?" Ellie asked, addressing Lucy. "He doesn't realise how tough women can be."

"Just a bit," Lucy replied. "But you'll have to excuse the upheaval. Our lives are upside down right now."

Ellie nodded gravely, pushing her long fringe back from her face. "How dreadful for you! Is the investigation going well? Did they find out how the fire started yet?"

Both Stephen and Ellie looked to Lucy for an answer.

"Not that we've been told," she explained. But they have declared an upgrade to arson on national airwaves, she thought privately, deciding against sharing that news for now, in case she scared Ellie away from the family before she'd even had time to take off her coat! Now Stephen was home, she wasn't going to compromise their relationship again. "Why don't you bring in your luggage, Stephen," she suggested in a quick change of subject.

"Plenty time for unpacking later, Mum," he said, as the ambulance men came through to the living area, carrying the stretcher between them once more.

They stopped to talk to Lucy, plunging her right into the seriousness of the present reality once more. "His blood pressure is a bit on the high side but, other than that, he's remarkably well considering. Keep a close eye on him and make sure he keeps that mask on him for the rest of today."

"Of course," Lucy responded, walking them to the front door. "You're happy he's safe to stay here?"

"Once he behaves."

Lucy pulled opened the door, concentrating so hard on what the ambulance driver was telling her that she didn't notice Phelim O'Brien parking outside Delia's garden wall. It was only when the ambulance crew walked away that she noticed the inspector coming through the gate. Oh no, she thought, despair flooding through her. This is all I need. He's going to come in now and throw his weight – and his information – around. He'll humiliate us in front of Ellie and send Danny into relapse. Her hands shook as she pulled the zipper of her top tightly closed, pulling the hood up around her neck.

Phelim's presence unnerved her, his large frame overpowering as he stepped past her and entered the room without being invited.

"Mrs Ardle," he said, a sardonic grin on his face. He gave a cursory nod to Stephen who'd come to stand protectively by Lucy's side. She never appreciated having support as much as that moment. "Some new information's come our way that needs to be discussed."

'Discussed' – his choice of words made Lucy smile. From what she knew *of* him and *about* him, the majority of Phelim O'Brien's discussions were one-dimensional. And the studied look he was giving them convinced her that this particular discussion would not lead to anything good. Feeling Stephen's hand grasping hers, she clutched it tightly as though her life depended on it.

Chapter 39

Lucy hovered nervously in Delia's living room, wondering if she could get Danny to the bedroom without Phelim seeing him. Danny would never forgive her if O'Brien (as he referred to him) saw him thrown on the kitchen chair like a defenceless invalid with a wet towel stuck to his forehead.

"I'd like to speak to you both at the same time," Phelim pointed out, as though reading her mind.

"Stephen, will you let Dad know the inspector is here."

Picking up on his mother's anxiety, Stephen took Ellie's arm and both of them went to Danny, leaving Lucy to deal with a man intent on getting what he'd arrived for.

"It's not a very good time for Danny today. He's not feeling very well and . . ."

"He'll be feeling a lot worse after he's heard my news," Phelim interjected, the hard set of his face displaying zero sympathy. "And there are a few holes – or maybe they're just deliberate oversights – in his story from the other day so I'll be going over the detail with him until I'm satisfied he's giving an accurate account."

"As I said, it'll have to wait. Danny's really not up to it today, Inspector," Lucy insisted, with as much conviction as she could muster. "Surely you can understand. You've met the ambulance men carrying a stretcher out, isn't that proof enough?"

Lucy applied great effort to keep her tone civil. More than anything, she wanted to avoid antagonising Phelim further, knowing very well they would suffer the consequences of such action. What a boor, she thought, wondering whether he treated everyone with as much disdain or if he kept it solely for them. His bullying behaviour had to be in breach of the Garda code of conduct. But she didn't dare consider reporting him, confident it would be a grave mistake on her part. She rued the day Danny had ever come in contact with him, wishing for the umpteenth time Phelim had given Ardle Construction a wide berth. Any other developer would have been welcome to him as far as Lucy was concerned. They might even have gone as far as courting his dishonest proposals.

In the kitchen, Danny was acquainting himself with Ellie and judging by the twinkle in his eye, Stephen wasn't the only one carried away by her good looks and striking figure.

"Your first time in Ireland, I presume," he asked, his voice muffled behind the mask.

"Yes, indeed," Ellie responded. "We've only got a

week this time but once the baby's born, Stephen guarantees we'll be over and back a lot more."

"Stephen, make the girl tea or coffee like a good lad. She must be shattered after that endless flight!" He glanced at Stephen, his eyes twinkling. "Though, come to think of it, you could probably do with a cuppa too after being in the air for the best part of twenty-four hours!"

Stephen went to fill the kettle. "I've been dreaming about a proper cup of Barry's tea since I used the last of the teabags Mum sent over!"

"Hey," Ellie teased, pushing a stray blonde strand out of her eyes and behind her ear, before pinching Stephen on the arm, "are you saying our Australian tea isn't living up to your Irish standards? Bah! We have every flavour imaginable down under. You're just afraid to experiment, mate."

"Nothing will ever compare with my mother's cooking or Barry's tea! You should know that seeing as you've agreed to marry me!" But to reassure his girlfriend that he wasn't choosing his mother over her, he put his arm around her shoulders and pulled her to him in an affectionate squeeze.

"Who's this Barry guy anyway?" Ellie's question was innocent enough and she looked on in confusion as Danny and Stephen burst out laughing, dispelling the sense of formality prevailing in the room. The ice was well and truly broken.

But Danny, though he was enjoying their surprise visit, had other ideas and was looking upon Stephen's timely arrival as an opportunity to get his own way and get out of the house.

"I've a better idea, Stephen, once you've had that cup of tea. I want you to drive me somewhere. I haven't seen the house since the fire and need to put arrangements in place. Sooner repairs get under way, sooner we can move back in and put all this behind us. You'll drive me over, won't you? I'm sure Ellie needs to have a nap. It's not just herself she has to take care of now, is it?" He smiled broadly on the young couple, his first reference to their unborn baby since Ellie had entered the room. "Will you do it, son? I could do with your support to be honest."

Stephen shrugged, realising the time had come to tell his dad about the other visitor waiting to speak to him. Or more to the point, interrogate him. "Great idea, Dad, but I'm afraid it's going to have to wait a while. There's an inspector in the other room wanting to speak to you. And he doesn't look like a man who takes too kindly to being kept waiting."

Danny's face flushed right up to his forehead. He pulled the mask off. "What the hell does he want now? I've told him everything I know. God damn him. He's got it in for us, that's his main problem! I don't trust him, Stephen. Will you make sure you stay and listen to whatever he's got to say now?"

Stephen abandoned his tea-making, reached out and placed a hand on his father's shoulder. "Take it easy, Dad. Nobody's accusing you of anything. Calm down for a moment. Get your breath back."

But Danny's agitation increased. He got up from the chair and made to walk to the living room, dropping the mask on the floor.

Ellie picked it up and handed it to Stephen. But other than that, she didn't interfere.

Stephen wasn't about to let his father do anything silly, however. "Dad! Do you want to end up back in hospital?"

Danny turned to face his son. "You know I don't."

"Well, calm down, top up your oxygen and listen to me for a moment."

Seeing sense, he did as he was bid – apart from the calming-down bit.

Stephen and Ellie sat down as well, all three deep in thought for a few moments.

"Has your engineer sent in his report yet, Dad?" Stephen asked then. He wanted to have as much information as possible before facing the inspector. "The insurance company won't touch the house until there's an engineer's report. Usually the assessor deals directly with the engineer, agreeing estimates and such."

"I presume he's been out already. They don't usually mess around. How are you so well up on the subject?" Danny's colour had returned to normal.

Stephen was happy to distract his father with something other than their own disaster. "One of the software companies I worked for had a fire in a production room. The company had to close for days while the red tape was being sorted. Thankfully they were well insured for loss of earnings and productivity, not to mention our salaries, but even so it took ages to catch up afterwards. One or two weeks out of circulation in the world of business and you're all but forgotten!"

"Thanks for that, Stephen," Danny said dryly, his thoughts instantly turning to Ardle Construction. There were urgent overdue calls to be made. But first he needed names and numbers from his van. Thank God for

Stephen, he thought, he'll understand things a lot better than Lucy. And he won't ask as many questions!

Stephen was deep in thought, his hand gently stroking Ellie's fingertips.

Ellie, on the other hand, had been staring around her, admiring the unique handmade pieces hanging on Delia's walls, imagining how well similar pieces would look back home. Stephen had briefly mentioned his aunt's talent but not for a moment had she expected such a unique style. She had tuned out of the conversation, visualising sample designs she'd ask his aunt to create for their home. Warmth filled her. She touched her stomach, an automatic gesture. We're on the edge of something amazing, she thought, the intensifying love she felt for her fiancée deepening another notch.

"You'll have to get an estimate of the repairs," Stephen was saying to Danny, rubbing his chin thoughtfully. "I suppose they'll hardly let your own company do it. They'll want an independent assessment."

"Why can't I do it myself? I'm a registered contractor. Who the hell else would I trust with that now?" He pushed back the chair and got to his feet.

"Dad, will you calm down," Stephen pleaded, deciding it wasn't such a good idea to be discussing these matters with him just yet. "They're independent estimates, that's all. And at least cost won't be a concern for once. That's what you're paying insurance for!"

Danny muttered something indecipherable, stopping when the door opened.

Lucy's face dropped as she entered the kitchen, Stephen's words ringing in the air.

"Are we summoned?" Danny asked gruffly.

Lucy stood gawping, stuck in a frozen moment between deception and open admission. She nodded her head slowly.

"Let's get it over with, Dad," Stephen said, getting to his feet. "Ellie, it's up to you, love, whether you want to sit through a boring interview or not."

"I'm cool here. There are some magazines I can take a look at."

Lucy looked from Ellie to Stephen and then Danny. She had to tell them the truth. This would be her last opportunity. Phelim O'Brien had reduced her to tears just now, spitting accusation after accusation in her direction, cross-questioning the statement she'd given Jack Bowe. As bad as things were, she couldn't allow another member of her family to walk into the same trap without warning.

But the words wouldn't come, no matter how hard she tried. And then, as though she were watching her son reach out to put his hand in the fire, she watched Stephen turn the door handle. In the nick of time, Lucy made a lunge forward and caught a hold of his arm.

"Don't go in there yet. Please wait. There's something you need to know."

Stephen looked at her askance.

Lucy trembled inside. She turned to meet her husband's confused look, then dropped her eyes to the floor. She was thinking of the past, their contented family life, normality she'd taken for granted. And now it had been snatched away.

"What is it now?" Danny snarled. He was anxious to get this over with and didn't need Lucy playing silly games at this crucial time.

308

Jolted back to the urgency of the moment, she remembered their guest and turned to face Ellie. "I'm so sorry you've had to deal with this upheaval . . ."

"Will you tell me what's on your mind, for crying out loud?" Danny all but shouted.

There was a knock on the door and Phelim O'Brien's thunderous face peered around. "I can't wait much longer."

Stephen pushed through to the living room, leaving his parents in the kitchen with Ellie.

Two seconds later he was back. "Right, Mum, spit it out because delaying tactics are not helping your case with your man in there." He jerked his thumb towards the inspector.

She had to take the plunge.

"It's the insurance. I didn't . . . I don't know . . ."

Danny's patience had run out. "Lucy!"

"I'm trying, Danny."

"Are we underinsured? Is that it?" He glared at his wife, unable to believe she could be stupid enough to try and save a few euros in renewal costs. Hadn't she listened to any of the stories he'd told her about owners falling into the category of underinsurance. Their settlement had only been a percentage of the actual cost of rebuilding, leaving them far worse off in the aftermath of the claim, a minority unable to pay his refurbishment costs.

Clutching at the unexpected life raft, Lucy was tempted to defer the truth again to save further outrage. She was caught in a living nightmare but resisted temptation, the truth blurting from her lips while she still had a modicum of strength left inside.

"The problem isn't underinsurance, Danny, it's no insurance."

She saw she had stunned everybody into silence. Danny looked at her, astonishment, shock, indignation and disbelief registering on his flushed face in quick succession. Stephen and Ellie's eyes widened, both speechless. But the only emotion Lucy felt was relief. It was too late to turn back now. And even if she could, she didn't want to. The burden wasn't one she could carry alone any longer. Fear itself pressed her ahead, forcing words from her mouth and getting the deathly truth out in the open.

"Danny, it's been hell on earth for me over the last few days. I was terrified to tell you, scared I'd upset you even more, slow down your recovery. I can't get near any of our documents to check for confirmation. I've been to the bank requesting statements." She reached behind the microwave and pulled out the white envelope, waving it in the air as proof.

Still no reaction from anybody in the room. And no response.

"Nothing materialised, there's no record of any payment being made, I've rung insurance companies, nearly every single one in the phone book but every avenue I've tried has come to a big fat nothing. I'm so, so sorry. Our house isn't insured and now ..."

She paused for breath, turning to look at Danny. His eyes were closed. Her gaze moved to Stephen and Ellie who were rooted to the floor, clutching each other's hands for support.

Who'll support me? The question flashed in Lucy's mind, no answer following.

"Will one of you please speak?" She looked from one

to the other, noticing the embarrassment on Ellie's face, instantly ashamed. "What are we going to do?" she asked aloud. *How will we rebuild our home? Our lives?* The last two questions she screamed silently.

She swallowed hard, her eyes wide in anticipation, her breath held in her chest as she waited for Danny in particular to digest her horrific announcement. She wanted him to tell her what they could do. She wanted his forgiveness and understanding. Most of all, she wanted him to take her in his arms and hug her, tell her everything would be okay.

A dog barked in the distance, the sound a welcome reprieve from the deathly silence.

But Danny merely stood there, his mouth hanging open, gawping in disbelief.

Remaining very still in the middle of the floor, clenching and unclenching her fists as she continued to wait, Lucy stole a glance in Stephen's direction, a piece of her dying inside as she took in his horrified expression, a perfect match for Danny's.

She couldn't bear it. "Don't look at me like that!" she burst out. "I know what I've done! Everything we've spent years building has been ruined. This mistake has blown away any chance of retiring comfortably!"

Phelim O'Brien was sick of pandering to these imbeciles, first Eric Black thinking he was going to jump through hoops to get him home from Florida – damn idiot, how he regretted the day he'd got him to testify on his behalf! – and now the Ardles thinking he had nothing better to do apart from hang around admiring the view while they plotted and got their story straight behind his back.

Well, he'd had enough and was going to take matters into his own hands and move it up a notch. Then he'd happily hand in his badge and leave it all behind.

He had been standing with his ear pressed to the kitchen door for some minutes, fury rising inside him. To his immense frustration he could catch only the odd word when the voices inside rose occasionally. But he caught Lucy's last words clearly – "any chance of retiring comfortably".

Bursting into the kitchen, he interrupted Danny who had just begun to speak. "Right, Ardle. I've heard enough. Retiring early, what an excellent motive for arson! Come on, you're busted, there's a cell waiting with your name on it."

"But that's insane!" Danny spluttered, his fists clenched, his eyes opening wide in shock. "Lucy, tell him I had nothing to do with this. *Tell* him! How could I –"

Phelim cut him off mid-sentence. "Anything else you have to say will be said at the station. You, too, Mrs Ardle. Let's go."

Chapter 40

The house was empty when Delia and her mother returned from the city. Delia escaped to her work-room. Her latest jewellery orders were ready for creation, her newest launch collection inspired by a selection of seashells and stones collected on a recent trip to Alvor. Her fingers itched to get stuck in.

But Gloria was into the room before Delia's bum had touched the chair. "Let me give you a hand with what you're doing." She picked a handful of metallic beads from the table.

"Mum, please leave them."

Gloria let the stones roll from her fingers as though they were hot coals. "Where are Lucy and Danny?"

"How do I know? I arrived back the same time as you and the house was empty. Remember?" As quickly as the sharp words left her mouth, Delia wished she could suck them back in. But too late, her barb hung in the air between them.

Gloria let out a snort.

"Okay, Mum, if you want to give me a hand, please do. It'll help take our minds off Lucy."

Gloria was caught off guard. She hadn't been expecting an olive branch.

"Polishing, you're a dab hand at that if I remember rightly?" said Delia. "I've got some new brass sections – they're not even cut yet."

"Well, I suppose if it's important, I could do that," Gloria offered begrudgingly, masking her enthusiasm behind a concentrated frown.

Delia steered her mother out of the workroom and into the conservatory. "You make yourself comfortable, Mum, and I'll get you my brass and silver cloths and an apron to protect your good cardigan."

Gloria's face was animated, the twinkle in her eye making Delia nervous. What's she up to now, she wondered?

"I have an idea, a way to let Danny and Lucy have the space they deserve," she announced, her voice filled with pride as though she were some form of wizard waving a magic wand.

"Yeah?" Delia waited for her mother to elaborate, praying furiously – for sanity's sake – that she was about to vacate the guest room.

"Yes, indeed, I'm hatching a plan on how to get Danny and Lucy from under your feet," Gloria told her coyly, buffing the brass disc vigorously.

The doorbell rang. Delia left the conservatory before she said something else she'd regret. It's not *them* I have a problem living with, she screamed inside, it's *you*!

"Can I help you?" she asked the ruggedly handsome

314

man standing at her door, wondering where she'd seen him before.

"You're Lucy Ardle's sister, aren't you?"

"That's right," Delia responded slowly.

"I'm looking for Danny. I went up to visit him in hospital but they said he'd been released."

"That's right. Are you a friend of his?"

"Eh no, I mean yes. I work for him and I needed a quick word."

Of course, Delia thought, he's the roofer who came to fix the tiles on my shed, a vivid image of his tanned muscular torso coming to mind. The weather had been unusually hot those couple of days he'd worked in her back garden, his presence a sexy distraction. For once she was glad she delayed buying garden furniture, happy to share the narrow wrought-iron seat with him as they sipped iced tea in the hot afternoon sun.

"Is he here?"

Delia snapped back to the present. "He is, I mean, he's staying here but he's out with Lucy right now. Can I take a message or get him to call you?"

He thought about it. "Get him to call me I suppose is best. Don't want to bore you with work stuff – materials and the like." He started to walk down the path.

"Your name and number?" Delia called after him.

He swivelled around again, cocking his head to the side, his face breaking into a teasing grin.

She noticed the stubble on his chin, his even white teeth.

"How's your shed roof holding up?"

His question took her by surprise. "Grand. No problems at all."

"If you ever want me to take a look, ask Danny for Tony's number. Be seeing you so," he said, raising an arm over his head and waving.

Tony, Delia jotted down on the notebook beside the phone, childishly encircling it with an inky heart-shaped boundary.

Chapter 41

Matt was preparing for his meeting at NYC College. Unsure what to wear on this occasion, he'd gambled on formal attire, wishing Heidi was there to advise on the right tie and the colour of his socks. For the umpteenth time, he undid his tie knot and struggled to fix it again.

The tour of Madison Square Gardens had been breathtaking. He'd literally stepped in the shoes of some of the greatest basketball players of all times, watched a real live rodeo demonstration and sat on the very same stage where Frank Sinatra had once played for a New Year's Eve ball. But the hustle and bustle of New York City was waiting for him outside the arena, people running and racing, barely taking the time to look at each other, amplifying how much he missed Heidi. And since then, he'd waited faithfully in the apartment for her to return.

Trying to find her in this crazy city is a long shot, he thought, the collar of his shirt tight around his neck. His hope that she'd return to him was fading fast, the lengthening silence from his family chilling and out of the ordinary.

Telling his mum about his relationship with Heidi had been difficult, but a conversation easy to predict. He'd anticipated shock, fury and disappointment. His dad, on the other hand, was a level-headed man who cared little for outside judgements, preferring to let his sons form their own opinions. Matt felt it really wouldn't be too much of a problem for him, apart from the fact he despised Heidi's dad.

As for Stephen, he had a situation of his own to worry about. Speaking to him before he'd left for New York, Matt had detected a strain in the conversation, as if his brother had something to say but wasn't spitting it out.

"Stephen, if you think I'm making a mistake going to New York, will you just say so? I know there's something bugging you." The brothers, despite the vast differences in their personalities, were loyal friends. "Stephen? Do you think I should cancel my trip?"

"Jeez, no, Matt. Go for it, bro. It's not you that has problems, it's me . . ."

"It's not you, it's me!" Matt had hollered down the phone at his corny coin of phrase. "Pathetic or what, Steve? This is your brother you're talking to, not some ex you're trying to break up with." He waited for Stephen's retort, but instead he let out a heavy sigh.

"Seriously, Matt," he said, "I'm a bit distracted at the moment."

Matt had stopped folding clothes and putting them in his ruck-sack. It was alien territory to hear Stephen

318

admitting anything close to a problem. He'd always managed to figure things out for himself. But now that he had, Matt was going to at least pay him the courtesy of listening carefully to what he had to say. Taking his mobile off speakerphone, he flopped onto the bed, lying on his side with one arm under his head and listening to what his brother told him.

"Surely if you're into her, it's pretty cool though, isn't it?" he'd said, wincing a little when Stephen told him about Ellie's pregnancy. Personally he felt nowhere near ready to be tied down with a young baby but Stephen was three years older and a hell of a lot more settled in his ways – he always had been. Matt could tell by the warmth in his voice that Ellie – as far as Stephen was concerned – was a keeper. "Don't worry about Mum and Dad. They'll get used to the idea after a while. And so will you, Stephen."

Happy with his tie knot at last, he stared into the mirror and spat on his fingertips, running them through his hair to try and fix it into place. Stephen has a lot more on his mind than calling his little brother, he thought, slipping on the jacket of his suit and grabbing his keys to leave, concentrating on what lay ahead. As he pulled the door behind him, doubt lingered in his mind. There was something he was forgetting, he just knew it. Something nagged, yet he couldn't figure out what it was. He was halfway down the hallway when he realised.

The reference, he thought, stopping in his tracks and turning back. He dashed to the laptop to check if by some miracle his mother had actually emailed it through. Scrolling through his inbox, however, his hopes were dashed. Nothing at all from his parents, but to his surprise there was one from Stephen with an unusual title in the subject box: *no smoke without fire bro*.

I'll read it later, he thought, no time now. Stephen is finally getting a sense of humour. This Ellie person is good for him. He grinned as he imagined his brother pushing a buggy, changing nappies or, God forbid, kicking a football around with his little toddler. He still had plenty of time to get to NYC but he wanted to stop to eat a proper breakfast – and there was a deli filled with scrumptious pancakes waiting down the street. Without bothering to turn his laptop off, he hurried to the door, his mouth watering in anticipation as he tried to decide on the pancake filling to choose, his appetite healthy as ever despite the distress in his life.

But his longing for an egg, tomato and mushroom pancake was replaced with acidic indigestion when Julian pushed his way in the door of the apartment.

"What the hell?"

"Heidi," Julian began, his face black as thunder, his dark eyes boring into Matt's. "She needs you, Matt."

Matt's heart lifted, hope pushing through his long days and nights of despair. "What do you mean? Where is she?"

"Listen," Julian ordered, beginning to pace the small floor space in the apartment.

Matt kicked the door closed, his craving for pancake a distant memory as he listened to the unabridged life story of someone who bore no resemblance to the person he knew as Heidi Black. Keeping a close eye on his watch so he wouldn't miss his appointment in NYC College, he gave his full attention to Julian, rapidly realising that locking himself away in the New York Gym could be his only hiding place from what was coming to life in his living room.

Heidi browsed through the magazine rack on Canal Street in Chinatown, slightly intimidated by the traders approaching her in turn to see if she wanted handbags or belts, perfumes or jewellery. "Let me offer you the genuine Juicy Couture," she'd heard at least ten times in as many minutes.

Memorising the route she was taking so she'd be able to find her way back, she continued walking, mulling over the events of the last few days, one event in particular. She wrapped her arms around her body, embracing the unexpected warmth flooding through her veins. Wrinkling her nose at the smell of fish from the row of seafood stalls, she hurried by as quickly as she could, relieved to reach the welcoming aroma of hot baking from a storefront bakery some fifty metres further along. The smell of fresh bread reminded her of Matt. He'd be in his element here, she thought, imagining his green eyes lighting up at the array of luscious pies and dough-breads. Her heart picked up speed as she thought of him, the depth of her love taking her breath away.

Julian had made it quite clear he'd had enough of her, the temporary haven he'd provided coming to a very abrupt end. In fact, she thought bitterly, standing at a pedestrian walkway, waiting to cross the Avenue of the Americas, she hadn't liked his tone when he'd told her to move on. God damn him, she thought, quickening her step to keep time with her rising anger. She'd helped him out when he'd needed it and in return had asked for very little. Even when . . . well, that's best forgotten now, she thought, spotting a diner up ahead.

The diner wasn't nearly as inviting as the delicatessens in Midtown Manhattan. Her mouth watered as she thought of the brownies she'd seen that first day. It seemed so long ago now. But the diner she was standing near accepted all major credit cards according to the tatty sign hanging outside, so that was enough to swing it for Heidi. Under normal circumstances, she wouldn't dream of entering such a shabby establishment, but hunger pinched and her mouth watered as the smell of sizzling bacon greeted her. Oh God, she thought, this must be what Eve felt in the Garden of Eden.

Putting her eye on a free seat that faced out onto the street, she fought the temptation of something fried and greasy, ordering a Manhattan bagel and skinny latte instead. Waiting at the counter, she hoped the seat would be still unoccupied by the time she got her food. It gave a bird's eye view of Canal Street, a colourful mirage of stalls, the hustle and bustle of trading bringing the street to life. Scanning the other tables, she was glad she wasn't carrying a handbag, judging the clientele to be far from savoury.

"Can I get you a salad on the side, Madam?" the assistant interrupted her musing.

"No, thanks. Just the bagel, that'll be all," Heidi replied, impressed by the customer service as she handed over her credit card, finger at the ready to enter the PIN code.

"Will you eat your food here or do you want it wrapped to go?"

"Here, please," she said and watched him take her

order from the hot plate, place it on a tray and slide it across the counter towards her.

Her bagel smelt good. Unusually, she was looking forward to sinking her teeth in the layers of chicken, cheese and onion. Sipping her latte, she waited patiently, willing the assistant to hurry. She wanted to enjoy her food before her calorie-laden guilt set in.

"Your credit card has been refused, Madam. Do you have any other form of payment?" The waiter removed the card from the machine and handed it back to her.

Heidi clutched her tray tightly. How on earth had her credit card been refused? Dad took care of it, committed to ensuring she had unlimited funds and Heidi made very good use of the privilege. "Try the card again," she said to the assistant, clinging to the belief he was mistaken. Cash was something she used very little of, barely carrying enough for an emergency. And judging by the waiter's expression, she was in the middle of an emergency without a cent to call her own, either Irish or American currency. "Let me try entering that PIN again."

"It ain't the pin, Madam. The card isn't clearing. Your bank's refusing the transaction. You got cash? There's a line building behind you." His tone spoke multitudes. Her denied transaction wasn't a first in his diner and to him she was another idiot thinking she'd get food for free.

"No, I don't have cash," she said, letting go of the tray, tempted to offer to wash dishes for the afternoon if he'd just allow her eat the bagel. In support of this theory, her stomach growled loudly.

The waiter pushed the tray aside. "I'll leave it at the side if you want to go and get some. Next please?" And shifting his gaze to the lengthening queue, he dismissed her as yet another fraudster trying to pass off a dodgy credit card.

Heidi fixed her auburn hair behind her ears, pushed her shoulders back and left the café, conscious of several pairs of eyes following her, mortified that they had witnessed her embarrassment and were probably having a snigger at her expense. To think she'd looked down her nose at them! *God damn it, what the hell is going on?* She needed to contact the credit-card company. *Or perhaps I should really call Dad,* she mused. As it happened, neither was an option as she hadn't the price of calling anyone.

Moving away from the diner window, she was unsure whether to continue along Chinatown district or retrace her steps to Julian's basement apartment. She glanced around the street as she tried to make her mind up, her heart leaping when she spotted a bank-link point at the far end. The diner's machine must have been faulty, she thought, clutching her card in her hand, renewed confidence building inside. *I'll withdraw a decent amount of cash to be on the safe side,* she decided, slipping the card into the designated slot and punching in her PIN code.

Your transaction cannot be processed. Please contact your bank.

Heidi stared at the screen, her mouth dry, her knees shaking. The waiter was right then. Her access to cash had been severed. *How could Dad do this to me? What the hell is going on? Have they been trying to contact me? Is that it?* She yanked the card from the machine, banging the side of her fist against the rough wall. *What the hell is he playing at?* Her mind went into overdrive. She'd never had to survive without money before. She broke into a run, the harsh wind blowing through her hair, forcing her breath to catch. Rounding the bend, she crashed right into a teenage girl, almost knocking her to the ground and stopping to ensure she was okay. "I'm ever so sorry," she gasped.

"You should really watch where you're going," the teen responded, flicking long dark hair over her shoulder and moving away from Heidi.

She probably thinks I'm a crazed lunatic, Heidi worried, tears stinging her eyes. And what if she's right, what if I'm never going to control these attacks? She leaned over, resting the palms of her hands on her knees, unsure what way she should turn. What choices had she? Return to Julian's basement where he'd made it obvious she wasn't wanted? Or follow her heart and crawl back to Matt, unburden herself and complicate his life even further? She was suddenly aware of how desperately she wanted Matt by her side.

Matt had had enough of Julian ordering him about in his own apartment. And he was itching to tell him so. But this was perhaps his last chance to get to the bottom of the mystery about Heidi's past.

Just enough time, he thought, to probe a bit further. I'll still make my appointment at NYC College.

"Julian, you say she married you to give you residency status in Ireland after you'd dropped out of Trinity? Not exactly a crime in my book, no. And not something that should cause any ripples in our relationship seeing as it's a lifetime ago." While he had to admit his pride was dented, he wasn't naïve enough to think she'd got this far in life without history. "But the marriage isn't the only problem, is it?"

Matt was not the walkover Julian had expected. He hadn't jumped to Heidi's defence or insisted on Julian bringing her back to him as he had hoped.

Because Julian had had enough. As far as he was concerned, his debt to her was paid in full. And how she handled that was her problem, not his. He'd had enough of her dependency and boundary issues. Managing it from afar had been easy, nothing more than the willingness to sit on the floor for hours taking the occasional lengthy phone call, listening to her woes and concerns like an unpaid counsellor. But now she was in his city and sleeping under his roof, he felt trapped and claustrophobic, found her self-doubt and the pursuit of her latest project suffocating.

"No, not the only problem," he admitted.

Matt hesitated for a moment. Grimacing, he continued probing for information.

"When did your wedding take place exactly?"

Matt had already done the mental arithmetic but he wanted clarification. Julian was up to something. He hadn't come here out of the goodness of his heart. Nor was Heidi his priority. The only person he was looking out for was himself.

"Fifteen years ago." Julian didn't have to stop and think.

His fidgeting, the way his eyes roved around the apartment, settling anywhere but meeting Matt's gaze told its own story. There was more.

Matt tried some reverse psychology. "I've heard enough, Julian. I think you should leave. I've an appointment to keep." Would that produce results?

Julian fixed his pony-tail, then stepped back toward the wall and leaned against it, the floral wallpaper clashing with his garish shirt. He needed to make a stronger appeal. He fixed a stern gaze on Matt. "You Irish guys, you're so good at sticking your head in the sand, ignoring what's under your nose. You think you'll be able to forget her. You won't. You love her. And she loves you, Matt. What's more, she needs you. You were making a whole person of her again. You were her salvation. Are you going to abandon her now? Had your fun and that's it? Throw in the towel at the first appearance of reality into your dream?"

Matt flushed, Julian's remarks hitting too close to home. "Look – *she* abandoned me, not the other way round – remember?"

"She didn't abandon you. She was trying to protect you."

"Protect me? From what? Spit it out, Julian. I'm sick of your riddles."

Julian's expression darkened. "From what? From her emotional issues, her brush with anorexia, alopecia and panic disorder to mention but a few – and all before she'd reached her twenty-first birthday – some of which she is still struggling with."

Matt's head was spinning. The anorexia he could believe: her obsession with calories, the change in her body over the years, the clever way she avoided large meals, it all made sense now. He looked up to find Julian staring at him.

"That's in the past. She's a stable person now, a qualified schoolteacher," he protested, struggling to equate the person Julian was describing with the fun-loving woman he'd fallen for, without giving him the satisfaction of seeing shock registering on his face.

"A qualified schoolteacher who has only ever held temporary positions," Julian clarified, "health issues getting in the way of any real opportunity."

Matt pushed up his sleeve and checked the time on his watch. Shit, he thought. I'll have to catch a cab right away if I'm to make the college on time. I've got to get him out of here.

"Julian, we've nothing left to discuss. I can't deal with all this right now. I have an urgent appointment."

He tapped the face of his watch and hurried Julian out of the apartment and down the stairs, worried that by running Julian out he might be severing any chance he had of seeing Heidi again but too agitated to think the problem through.

A very dissatisfied Julian parted from him on the street. He had his mind set. He wasn't interested in responsibility. He'd made up his mind on that right from the outset. Heidi's choice to cling to buried history was hers alone. He'd done his best for her down through the years and right now he thought perhaps the only choice he had was to disappear for a while without a forwarding address.

As Matt was charging down 7th Avenue at an alarming pace, waving furiously to stop the first available cab, Heidi climbed the front steps to their apartment building, her legs aching after walking over thirty blocks. She pressed her fingers on several bells at once, determined to get inside the building no matter what.

Chapter 42

Phelim O'Brien barged through the double doors of Carrigaline Garda Station, ordering Danny to take a seat in the waiting area.

"My office!" he roared at Jack Bowe. "I want a full update on all priority cases, starting with the Ardle fire. Whoever's behind this won't get away with it!" He gave a sideways glance at Danny who was still within earshot, sneering at his pallor, taking immense satisfaction in seeing he was making him sweat. Look how pathetic he is, dragging a canister of oxygen along behind him like a wayward puppy, Phelim thought. Not the tough businessman now, is he? Not the guy who lorded it over me and dictated where my future went.

Making his way through the open-plan office, the inspector growled under his breath when he noticed the coffee machine was switched off. God damn it, he thought, kicking the door to his office closed behind him, is a fresh cup of coffee too much to expect on a cold

November morning? If the on-duty unit can't remember that much, how on earth will they ever solve a crime? Although on second thoughts, he decided, their pathetic lack of attention to detail might have its uses. Looking at his wristwatch he smiled and picked up the phone, dialling Sergeant Richard Collins' number to check on the status of the forensic results.

"Richard," he bellowed down the line, tapping a pen impatiently on the table, "that promotion we discussed? Have you mulled it over? You'd want to have your mind made up before I retire in three weeks' time or it'll be too late for me to submit a recommendation. And with the way things are now, it could be a very long time before the opportunity comes along again."

He listened to the sergeant's long-winded response, tempted to interrupt him at several intervals but allowing him to have his say. What difference could a few more minutes make at this stage, apart from adding to Danny's discomfiture? And Phelim wasn't concerned about Danny, apart from making him pay for past history. Leaning his feet on the footrest underneath his desk, he closed his eyes, Richard's self-justification on why he merited the position of inspector a long boring monologue in his ear. But eventually, as Phelim had guessed he would, Richard acted in his own best interests by acquiescing and accepting his offer to talk him up to the superintendent.

"Perfect, wise decision," Phelim said to him. "But before I submit the paperwork to the Super, there's one more thing . . ." He's not really in a position to refuse me now, he thought, launching into his less than honest request.

By the time a flustered Jack Bowe entered his office with an armful of bulging files, Phelim O'Brien was grinning broadly and very pleased with how his day was turning out.

Stephen had driven behind the Garda car taking Danny to the station. "Care to tell me what the hell is going on here, Mum?"

He had insisted on driving. And Lucy had insisted Ellie take the front seat.

"There's more to this than meets the eye," he went on. "I know you're holding something back. What is it? I can't help unless you tell me the truth. And God knows but you need all the help you can get."

Lucy looked away from the mirror, focusing instead on her bitten nails. Giving his words some thought, she spoke eventually. "Stephen, you're making me feel as though I'm the guilty one!"

"Touché, Mum! I'm not accusing you of anything but this mess has to be dealt with. How bad is the house exactly? I only got to pull up outside so I couldn't really judge. Will it have to be gutted? Is the roof still intact?"

"It's certainly not good," she admitted, bringing her hand to her mouth and chewing nervously on one of her nails, a picture of the hole in the bedroom floor coming to mind. "To say I was shocked is putting it mildly."

Stephen sighed and thought for a moment. "Are you sure the insurance isn't paid? How long since the policy lapsed?" Perhaps, he thought, there's a period of good-will cover if they've been with the same company for years.

Lucy's head throbbed. "The renewal had increased a

lot from the previous year but when I rang the company they wouldn't reduce it." She paused for breath.

"So you decided to try elsewhere?" Stephen wanted to hurry his mother up. They'd already taken his father inside the station. At this stage it didn't matter why she hadn't renewed, but he wanted the full story in case there was something she'd forgotten about.

"Yes," Lucy frowned, meeting his eye in the mirror. "I definitely called a few places and remember going on line to see if I could do any better. But then I must have got distracted and forgot to follow it through!"

"And you have tried to check with them?" Stephen reached across and gave Ellie's knee a gentle squeeze. He felt guilty for dragging her into this mess but there was nothing he could do to change it.

"Believe me, Stephen, I've rung nearly every insurance company in the phone book."

Stephen remained silent for a moment, his business head kicking in as he mulled things over in his head.

There was one last hope – one thing that would be worth following up – but he wasn't even going to suggest it to his mum until he'd checked it out with his father first. Now, he decided, wasn't the time to go confusing her more and raising possibly false hopes. He checked the mirror again, recognising the anguish and despair on his mother's face.

"Look, Mum, it's not the end of the world. Things would be so much worse if we had a funeral on our hands." And then he let it go.

Lucy, on the other hand, was only warming up. "Stephen," she began, leaning forward and clutching on to the headrest, speaking into his right ear in the hope that Ellie wouldn't catch what she was saying, "I'm worried about your father's business. You don't think he'd . . ."

Stephen kept his eyes firmly on the road but leaned his ear closer to his mother. "Don't think he'd what, Mum?" He didn't like where this was going, a cold feeling spreading through him.

"You don't think he's capable of arson, do you?" Lucy whispered. She proceeded to tell him about the empty containers and van, hating herself more with every word that left her lips.

Stephen jammed on the brakes and pulled the car onto the hard margin. He could feel the blood rush to his head. Damn and blast, he thought, fighting to conceal his panic from his mother who was weeping in the back seat, to say nothing of a frightened Ellie.

"We've got to get to Dad before O'Brien does." He weaved the car into the traffic once more, breaking every speed limit until he'd pulled up right outside the station.

"Stay in the car," he ordered the two women.

"What are you going to do?" Lucy croaked.

"I don't know but I have to get to Dad," he replied, jumping out of the car. "In the meantime, call your solicitor and get him to sit in on this interview. I've a feeling you might need him."

Chapter 43

Matt shook the college dean's hand when he stood up to leave his office. "Thanks for the tour. I'm looking forward to working here."

"Awesome!" The dean – an energetic thirty-something – pronounced in a strong Brooklyn accent. "Your students will be looking forward to meeting you."

"I'll see you first thing Monday then."

Matt's stomach turned somersaults. *My students*, he thought, the realisation that he'd be putting his college degree to proper use finally sinking in – a scary prospect as he still felt like a student himself. And this realisation was closely followed by a tinge of fear coursing its way through him. Will I be able to control a class of confident American students, he wondered. And what about that enormous gym? It's twice the size of any I've worked in back home. Jeez, I need to get fitter. And though he'd run summer camps as part of his work experience, he was daunted by the responsibility facing him.

The college dean had given him a broad overview of the campus, explaining there were two other new tutors starting on the same day. He'd share a week's intensive introduction with them, its purpose being to help them adjust to their new surroundings and bond with their fellow tutors. At least that's how the dean had portrayed it.

But his enthusiasm was encouraging and contagious, if a little frightening. The college's standards – and expectations – were high, a challenge for Matt as an inexperienced tutor. But spurred on by the positive attitude he'd sensed around campus, he was determined they wouldn't regret making him an offer.

As he crossed onto 5th Avenue, Matt checked his watch, surprised to notice that three hours had passed, three hours when he hadn't given Heidi as much as a fleeting thought. He let out a long sigh and strode up the street, the predicament he'd found himself in nudging its way into his mind once more. *What if she's in love with Julian? What if Heidi's baggage is more than I can carry? What then? Perhaps we're not meant to be together. Maybe that's why she's run off?* And the recurring thought: *I still haven't found out about her relationship to Alex.*

Heidi's striking face and twinkling eyes flashed into his mind as he strode past Roy's deli, their last moments together ingrained in his memory. Spotting the proprietor inside the window, he raised his arm and gave a friendly wave. His stomach growled. He couldn't ignore the delicious aromas wafting through the open door, vowing to return to savour the renowned pancakes once he'd changed into something more comfortable.

Dashing up the front steps of his apartment building,

he hopped into the waiting lift and pressed the button to get out on the fourth floor. He was outside his door when he was grabbed from behind.

"What the . . .?" He flipped around.

"Surprise!" Heidi said, as though the previous few days had never happened. "Pleased to see me?"

A rush of anger flooded through him. "That's it? You turn up and ask if I'm pleased to see you?"

Heidi's smile faded, her eyes searching his. She had the grace to look apologetic. "I can explain."

Matt froze, staring at her askance. "I think you should," he snapped, the euphoria he'd expected on her return non-existent.

Seconds passed. She opened and closed her mouth a few times but didn't volunteer the promised explanation, pulling away from him instead and tugging at her sleeves like a small child being reprimanded by a scolding teacher.

Matt took his keys from his jacket pocket and averted his eyes from her piercing gaze. "I think you should collect your stuff and leave, Heidi."

"Why? I'm back now. And I can explain, truly I can. But . . ."

"I want you to leave," he repeated, his face set. "I can't do this any more."

His obstinacy was new to Heidi, the finality in his tone forcing her to try harder. "Perhaps if you listen to what I've got to say, you'll reconsider any hasty decisions?"

"We're not suited, Heidi," he said, holding the key in his hand but waiting before inserting it into the lock. It was on the tip of his tongue to tell her about Julian's visit but he thought better of it. That was something he wanted to put to the test. Would she at least show him the respect of telling him the truth? "Waiting around for you to decide you're coming back wasn't exactly how I'd envisaged my trip to New York. You even took your passport with you! Where did you go?"

Heidi's lower lip trembled. "My passport's hidden in my luggage, Matt. If you let me in, I'll show you."

He pushed the door open, standing aside to let her past.

She stepped inside and stood there, struggled to breathe evenly, fighting with all her strength to keep panic at bay – and make things right. She'd hurt Matt. Who could blame him if he walked away from her? Her mind whirled, her thoughts spun, the months of fun she'd spent with her young lover catapulting away from her. The least she owed herself was one final attempt to fight for a man she was falling in love with. If her honesty – albeit a bit late – didn't change how he felt, then Matt was right, she should leave.

She stared hard at him, taking in how handsome he was in his black suit and maroon tie. She made to reach up and undo his tie-knot properly, dropping her hand again when he visibly flinched. He looked older, wiser, different. Seconds passed. Silence lingered. She didn't know how to start, blurting the most important fact out first.

"I have a son. He's fourteen years old and he's here in New York."

Matt gawped at her. *A son. Fourteen.* Her words went around his head. *He could be my younger brother!* Questions multiplied, his mother's warning screaming loudly in his head, the promise he'd made her to walk away suddenly a consideration. He pulled his jacket off, ripped his shirt open, forgetting to undo his tie. "Shit," he said, pulling at the knot that threatened to choke him.

The upbeat atmosphere at the college, the freedom of the gym, even the hustle and bustle of Manhattan had all seemed incredibly normal. But now – he glanced around at Heidi, noticing her left eye twitching, her fingers fidgeting, her tongue running over her dry lips, traits of panic obvious as she struggled to get words out – now he was out of his depth. If I stay and listen, what am I signing up for, he wondered? Undoing the button and zip on his trousers, he dropped them on the floor, unnerved by a side of Heidi he'd never witnessed before. Julian hadn't been lying. Her sanity *was* questionable. Wouldn't it be easier to end things now instead of prolonging the agony? It was obvious there wasn't room in her life for both him *and* her son. And it was more obvious where her priorities lay. His expression darkened, something else coming to mind.

"Your diary – you were meeting Alex?"

Heidi blushed a deep red. "Yes."

Matt's intake of breath was audible. "Is he your son's father? Or is Julian? No – don't bother to answer that. Just go now, Heidi."

She shook her head, hurrying to his side, grabbing his face in her hands and forcing him to look at her. "Alex is my *son*, Matt." Her voice was barely more than a whisper. "And, yes, Julian is his father. But Julian wants nothing to do with him. Alex was adopted as a baby."

The quivering in his stomach surprised him. It took effort to squash the relief building inside. Alex was her son. Not a lover she'd been holding dear in her heart.

Confusion got in the way then. She'd painted it

differently, had masked the truth. Male ego refused to let her away with that. Wary of causing further histrionics and distress, he kept his voice even.

"Pack your stuff, Heidi. Go to your son. Go to Alex. I understand. It's what you must do."

He pulled away, turning around to get dressed, missing the change that came over her.

Heidi was having trouble breathing, the room beginning to close in around her. Tears pricked her eyes but she refused to let them fall, dignity already in short enough supply. The next few minutes were crucial. She had to maintain a semblance of control, prove – to herself as well as Matt – that she wasn't an entire basket case. If nothing else, the growing distance between them assured her of one thing, she loved this man. Despite the age difference and their parents' undoubted disapproval, she wanted to be with him. Having Matt at her side gave her renewed strength and hope. Things were fun with him around. Problems faded, difficulties seemed manageable. She recognised that now. And with the truth about Alex out in the open, their relationship could only improve.

But falling in love had consequences. It made her realise how much work she had to do. On herself. On her coping mechanisms. How could she expect him to believe in her when she didn't believe in herself? How could she expect Alex's adoptive parents allow her time with him otherwise? She had to learn to trust. She had good reason now – two great reasons in fact – to push her fears and inadequacies aside and focus on regaining emotional control. *The power of survival lies within.* Her counsellor's advice had never been more pertinent.

She watched Matt stretch his arms over his head,

stalling for time, ignoring her presence. Calmed by his gentle movements, she counted her breaths, holding for a count of five before exhaling deeply, inhaling air into her lungs again, repeating the process until her heart rate slowed right down. She found her voice.

"Matt? Please listen. If you still want me to leave afterwards, I will."

He swung around, raising a cynical eyebrow when their eyes met. Truth, lies, would any of it change where they were now, he wondered? Running a hand over his tightly cut blond hair, he sighed heavily. The weeks of taunting and flirting before they'd got together had been elating, every day bringing them a step nearer the inevitable. The chemistry, the chase, all the components that had made him burst with anticipation when she was near. Secrecy, near misses, planning – all adding to the attraction, the way their fingers brushed unknown to prying eyes. And boy, had their explosive lovemaking been worth it! But that precious layer of dangerous excitement was stripped away now, leaving two confused individuals with a difficult choice to make.

Heidi crumbled under his piercing gaze. She began to pace the small apartment, stopping by the window ledge, turning her back to Matt and staring onto 7th Avenue.

The last time he'd watched her stare onto that same street, she'd been fizzing with excitement, drinking in the New York atmosphere. There was no excitement now.

Then she turned and faced him, calm and resolute.

"No, Matt – you must understand – I didn't abandon you to go to Alex – I left that day because I got a severe panic attack and it frightened me – I didn't want you to see me like that – I lost faith in my power to overcome my problems and thought I should leave you for your own good. I would have told you about my meeting with Alex – I had intended to – but, in fact, I wasn't even sure at that stage that it would happen. You see, I had to push hard for that short meeting with him as his adoptive parents weren't ready to meet me – kept talking about their busy schedule. But when they let slip he was flying out of Newark that morning, I told them I'd be there. I was still waiting for their response when I had the panic attack and walked out on you that day. I never intended to deceive you."

Her words swayed him but yet he felt he had been abused. "But you *did* deceive me. You've deceived me every day since we met."

He made his way toward the kitchen area to get a cold drink of water, and as he did, the flickering laptop caught his attention, reminding him of the unopened email from Stephen: *no smoke without fire, bro*. He noticed another from Rochestown Park Hotel – Mum must have contacted them – he'd email it directly to the college dean later. And there was a brief message from Delia, telling him she'd put his birth certificate in express post.

Not ready to continue his discussion with Heidi yet, he opened the email from Stephen and quickly scanned the first line. Then re-reading it very slowly, he digested every horrific word. His disagreement with Heidi faded into the background, Stephen's written description jumping to life on the screen. A cold feeling penetrating him, he clicked on the newspaper link, stepping away from the screen as though it'd reduce the impact of what he was about to see. An enormous change came over him, a switch had been flicked and the channel inside his head had changed. What had concerned him two minutes before was suddenly insignificant. So what if Heidi had kept a few secrets? Even the son she'd forgotten to mention no longer posed a threat. How could anything else matter with a true disaster staring him in the face? He clicked back to Stephen's email. Reading and re-reading his brother's plans to fly home, Matt ached to join him.

"Matt, what is it?" Heidi was at his side, his agonised expression alarming her. "What's happened?"

His eyes never left the screen. "There's been a terrible accident."

She moved closer. "Is somebody hurt?"

Wordlessly, he pushed the screen around to let her read the text for herself. Then he opened the newspaper article, her gasp mirroring the terror he felt inside.

Putting his needs before her own, Heidi wrapped her arms around him and held him in a warm embrace, pulling him tighter still when she heard his quiet weeping.

"I have to go home," he told her in a muffled voice.

She nodded, the tears she'd been holding in check slipping on to her cheeks. Their differences had moved aside, she had never felt as close to him. For real this time, nothing to do with dangerous excitement or mind-blowing sex. But why did it have to come down to a choice? Matt or Alex? Ireland or New York? And then it dawned on her that he hadn't actually invited her to join him. He'd told her *he* was leaving.

Chapter 44

Stephen sat close to his father in the waiting area of the Garda Station. "Dad, tell me. Why are the containers empty? Where are the supplies you normally store there? Not even a tool in sight. What the hell's that about?"

Danny rested his hands on his knees, turning to face his eldest son, his green eyes lifeless.

"Dad?"

"How come you've waited till now to take an interest? None of you bothered before."

"You know that inspector is going to interrogate you, Dad? Are you ready for cross-questioning? Wouldn't you rather come clean with me now if there *is* something you're holding back?"

"Stephen –" he began, stopping abruptly at the sound of O'Brien's bellowing voice.

"What the hell are you doing here?" Phelim glared at Stephen. "And where's your mother? It's her I wanted to interview, not you. Get her in here now."

Stephen gave his father a discreet pat on the back, a silent offer of support. "Just going to get her now, Inspector," he said, standing to leave.

Danny's complexion matched Inspector O'Brien's white shirt as he was led into the interview room, his son staring after him until the inspector closed the door behind them.

Stephen pushed through the double doors on to the street, his thoughts a million miles away as he descended the concrete steps, taking very little notice of the other people moving in and out of the station.

"Stephen!"

He lifted his head at the sound of his name, the face staring back at him jolting him back to his college years. He struggled to remember his name. "Jack Bowe," he recalled eventually.

The other guy grinned, extending his hand to shake Stephen's.

"Look at you in brass buttons, talk about a sight for sore eyes. A far cry from the combats and check shirts you lived in when we were in UCC."

Jack brushed imaginary dust from his uniform jacket and laughed. "The shabbiest first-year debating team in history, I'd say!"

"So this is what you did instead of returning in second year?" Stephen had got on well with Jack in first year but they'd lost touch during the summer months, with everybody doing their own thing. He hadn't laid eyes on him since.

"Yep," Jack explained. "I got the offer to join the force and decided to take it. The rest, as they say, is history."

"How long have you been stationed here?" Stephen asked.

"Only a few months. And you? Are you living around?"

Stephen shrugged. "The parents live in Crosshaven. I've been in Oz for the last couple of years . . ."

"So what brings you into the station, Stephen? Home for holidays and need a passport form signed?"

Stephen pulled him aside where it was a little more private. "My parents' home went on fire and there's some sort of enquiry going on. My dad's in there now being questioned. And I've been instructed by the inspector to get Mum in as well." He looked at Jack before adding, "A very pleasant guy, isn't he?"

Jack remained noncommittal but his face said it all.

Stephen got the distinct feeling that Jack loved his job. And hated his boss.

"Any help or advice you can give will be gratefully received," he tried.

"Your father was a lucky man to get out. I was there that night, at the scene." Jack rubbed his chin thoughtfully, wondering if there was anything he could do to help but feeling very much – under the watchful eye of Inspector O'Brien – that his hands were tied. Still, Stephen had been a good friend in that first year in UCC. The least he could offer was his support. Taking his notebook and pen from his pocket, he jotted down his mobile number, ripped out the page and handed it to Stephen. "Just in case there's anything you need. Write yours down as well," he said, passing him the notebook and pen.

"Thanks, Jack. It's real good to see you again, but I'd better get Mum or your man in there will have steam coming out of his ears," Stephen said, shoving the folded-up piece of paper into his pocket.

Jack laid a warning hand on his arm. "The inspector . . ." He paused, unsure about continuing.

"Jack? Anything at all that can help us?"

"He has the reputation of being a very vindictive man."

After they'd spent a few hours working on Delia's jewellery collection – Delia creating and Gloria polishing – mother and daughter travelled to the village in silence, both lost in their own thoughts, both pleasantly surprised at how successful their time together had been.

Driving by Moore's Jeweller's on Main Street, a young couple walking along caught Delia's attention. Slowing the car right down, she shared her suspicions with her mother. "Isn't that guy the image of Lucy's Stephen? He's as close as you'll get to his double!"

"I think it *is* Stephen!" Gloria shrieked, knocking on the window trying to catch his attention. "Where has he sprung out of and who is that girl with him? What's he doing back here? Stephen!" she yelled at the top of her voice, having eventually found the button to let down her window, attracting several glances in their direction. "Stephen!"

Delia pulled the car into the first parking spot she could find on Main Street, grinning broadly when Stephen came running up and opened the passenger door for his grandmother. Oh, Delia thought fondly, he hasn't changed one iota! Thank God, he's the same old Stephen. No matter how old he is, he never forgets his manners. He's exactly who Lucy needs around at the moment.

"What on earth are you doing here, you rascal?" Gloria's voice softened, her eyes filling with tears as she took Stephen's arm and eased herself out of the car. "Let me have a look at you. My God, you've turned into a fine young man. Although I can't say I like those highlights in your hair!"

"It's the sun, Nana," Stephen explained, planting a kiss on his grandmother's cheek, taking in the stoop in her shoulders and deep-etched lines on her face. She's aged, he thought with a pang, relieved in a way that her sharp tongue had stayed the same.

"Stephen! I can't believe you're here," Delia gushed, rushing around the car to hug her nephew, tears glistening in her eyes as she got caught up in the emotion of the moment. "When did you arrive? I only posted your birth certificate to Oz a few hours ago. Have you met your mum and dad yet?"

"Slow down, Del," Stephen laughed, deciding against mentioning the fact that they were being interviewed in the nearby Garda Station at that very moment. No point worrying Delia or his grandmother right now, at least not until he knew a little more. "Cool haircut," he said, running a finger over the short gelled spikes, liking his aunt's modern funky look. "Punk's making a comeback, I see?"

Delia could only laugh. "Less of your cheek, young man! Don't think for a moment you're too old for a good scolding! Aren't you going to introduce us to your friend?" She smiled at the beautiful girl at his side.

Stephen instantly remembered his manners, a little embarrassed by the street show their exciting reunion was providing for passers-by.

"This is Ellie, my fiancée," he said, putting a protective arm around her shoulders and pulling her closer to him.

"Ellie," he added, "my aunt, Delia, and my wicked grandmother, Gloria." His eyes twinkled as he introduced one loved-one to another.

"Fiancée?" Gloria's mouth dropped open. She looked accusingly from Delia to Stephen before smiling at Ellie and shaking her hand in a tight grip. "When did this happen? Yet again, I'm the last to know."

Stephen, catching the look of dismay on Delia's face, made an attempt to remedy things. He didn't want their announcement to cause any further upset. It was a happy occasion – one of the only good things going on in his family right now – and he didn't want it ruined by his grandmother's huffiness.

"It's a surprise, Nana," he explained sincerely, flashing her one of his best smiles. "A surprise for all of you!"

Delia let out the breath she'd been holding, stepping sideways to allow pedestrians to get by them on the narrow pavement. "Come on, we're causing an obstruction here. Let's go for a coffee where we can catch up without an audience." She took her handbag from behind the driver's seat and locked the car.

"But I just want to find out how . . ." Gloria began, already preparing a list of questions for her grandson.

"All will be revealed," Stephen promised, leading the way to a nearby café.

Finding a seat in a nice quiet corner, Stephen insisted on treating his aunt, grandmother and fiancée to a hot drink. Finally, he thought as he made his way to the counter, poor Ellie will get that cup of tea we've been promising since she arrived. Yawning widely, he stood at the service counter, unable to resist a stolen glance at the table where he'd parked the three women, leaving his grandmother to get on with her probing questions. No doubt poor Ellie was being interrogated but what could he do? He had prepared his fiancée as best he could for the women in his life, explaining they'd only be satisfied to accept her into the bosom of their small family once they'd found out as much as they possibly could about her. And Ellie, being the fabulous broad-minded creature she was (and Stephen felt he wasn't being biased with that opinion), had laughed and said she'd no secrets to hide and didn't mind what they asked. Once they could cope with her honest answers. She was straight-talking and carefree and wasn't in the habit of dressing up the truth just to keep people happy, as she had correctly deduced was often the practice in Ireland. Stephen found it really difficult to give a direct response if it meant he might hurt somebody's feelings but he knew Ellie understood him now. His kindness and sincerity were part of the attraction, she'd told him on more than one occasion, that and his fantastic physique and intelligent mind of course! As he put a hand in his pocket to pay for the tea, he suddenly realised he only had Australian dollars. It hadn't even crossed his mind to get Irish currency from the cash dispenser at the Airport, using his credit card instead to pay for car hire. So much for acting like the generous tourist returning home!

"Just a moment," he said to the apologetic waitress when she explained they didn't accept VISA for any amounts less than twenty euro, "I'll get some cash for you now."

Red-faced, he brought the laden tray to the table where the three women chatted amicably. "Eh, I never thought to get any Euro and they won't take a credit card for this amount," he explained, looking beseechingly from his aunt to his grandmother, hoping at least one of them had their purse with them.

"Well, Ellie," Gloria laughed, putting a hand on Delia's arm when she went to take her purse from her pocket, indicating the occasion was to be her treat, "it seems our little Stephen isn't as grown up as he's letting on. He's still looking for money from his nana!"

Lucy and Danny weren't quite so amused or contented. Sitting together in a small interview room, their solicitor beside them, they both felt they'd woken up in the middle of the same nightmare.

There had been a long delay before the solicitor had arrived but now at last Phelim O'Brien was taking charge of proceedings, his manner abrupt, his tolerance for any dithering on their part non-existent. A tape recorder whirred on the desk beside him recording every sound in the room.

"I want you both to think long and hard about Saturday afternoon. And this time when you're giving your account of events, perhaps you could tell the truth." He leaned both elbows on the table, his chair pushed back to make room for his rotund stomach. "Without leaving anything out."

Lucy and Danny glanced at each other, Lucy overwhelmed and unsure, Danny infuriated.

She felt a lump in her throat when Danny's hand clutched hers tightly underneath the table, his first and only display of affection since the fire. Not knowing or caring what had brought about this change, she covered his hand with her other one, feeling instantly stronger, her husband's support meaning the world to her.

Danny was struggling to make amends, realising he'd

have to own up about the visitors he'd entertained that fateful evening.

Phelim leaned towards Danny and fixed him with a glare.

"Now maybe you'd like to start by explaining the three coffee mugs we found on your kitchen table," he said. "Your wife didn't mention visitors. When we went back and checked your statement, Danny, you conveniently forgot to mention it too. Care to enlighten us and give a true picture of what went on in your house that Saturday?"

Danny heard Lucy gasp in surprise. He closed his eyes. *Visitors*. The word alone conjured up images of laughter and chat. Everything that afternoon had lacked . . .

He had just woken up from a snooze and was settling down to watch the remainder of the match when the doorbell rang. He'd thought he was still dreaming when he'd answered the door to find Jenny and his parents on the doorstep. He hadn't even known his sister was home from London. And his parents seldom visited without calling first. Bleary-eyed after a long nap, he'd welcomed them into the kitchen and put on the kettle for coffee, his own thirst leaving him when he'd listened to Jenny brazenly outlining outrageous demands.

Danny had listened agog, announcing in no uncertain terms that she had a cheek arriving home expecting handouts. She'd lost her job, apparently through her own negligence, and was in need of urgent assistance to get her out of serious financial ruin. Dramatised no doubt, Danny thought, knowing his sister as he did.

But Jenny had a simple solution in mind, unabashed to say it aloud as though it were her basic right.

The hurt and trepidation in his parents' eyes had been too much to bear as they offered time after time in the course of the conversation to sell their home in Clonakilty and move into somewhere smaller, wanting the ordeal over and their daughter safe as soon as possible. But, and that was their primary reason for landing unannounced on Danny's doorstep, they wouldn't hear tell of selling their home without their son's approval. Approval he wasn't about to give.

Danny had paced the kitchen, refusing to tolerate any mention of his parents leaving their treasured home or the community they'd been part of for many years. Glaring at his sister, he beckoned her to follow him outside to discuss the issue privately. But Jenny refused to budge, adamant she was only asking for what would be hers eventually and knowing that her only hope of securing it would involve her parents' presence. Challenging Danny without them was an argument she wouldn't win.

He'd been appalled that she could sit at his kitchen table, in front of their concerned parents, and discuss their death as casually as she would an upcoming movie release. Eventually, out of love and respect for his parents, he'd brought an end to the problem by promising to help her repay the gigantic debts she'd accrued in London, thereby saving his parents from having to sell their home and hand her (which was the solution she'd desired) a premature inheritance.

After they'd left for Clonakilty once more – his parents relieved and Jenny smug as a bold child who'd got her own way again – he'd poured himself a stiff brandy and pondered on following through on his promise. A year or two earlier, when profits were rolling in, he'd have swallowed his anger and cleared his sister's debt. Refilling his brandy glass, he imagined his parents' distress if they knew the damage Jenny's exorbitant loans could do to his business. But he couldn't put that truth on his parents' shoulders, feeling a responsibility to his family as their only son.

"Are you refusing to answer the question, Ardle?" Phelim snarled. "What about the three coffee cups?"

Danny heard the anger and gloating in the inspector's voice but, eyes still closed, he ignored the bullying voice and continued piecing the events of the past few days together.

Coming to in the hospital after the fire, his emotions had snowballed, pushing him onto a runaway train of fear, depression, self-pity and lack of control. Seeing Lucy sitting at his bedside, her eyes filled with terror, his reaction – unfair as it might seem – was to shout orders at her and push her away from him. As the breadwinner, he had a duty to protect. In his mind he'd let her down. On top of everything, he couldn't bear to announce the substantial bail-out he'd promised his sister. Now Jenny would have to get off her spoilt backside and earn a salary to pay for the spoils of her lavish lifestyle. He'd called her from the hospital (she was staying with their parents for the first time in years, usually preferring to book into a luxury hotel while she was in West Cork) and summoned her to visit him. He'd demanded her word that she wouldn't mention their agreement to anyone, threatening to withdraw his offer if she did.

Danny opened his eyes and met O'Brien's sour face glaring at him from across the table, demanding impossible explanations. He wasn't sorry he hadn't told him about his family paying a visit. Or why. As far as Danny was concerned, his family's financial predicament wasn't any of O'Brien's business. It had little if any relevance to the case. But O'Brien would use it, twist it, Danny knew, his expression darkening. Gritting his teeth, he returned O'Brien's glare, ready to match his arrogance.

"What grounds are you holding us on?" Danny asked. "You've got no proof . . ."

"We can hold you for thirty-six hours, and if it takes that long to get the truth, that's what I'm going to do. And I'll extend if I have to. Now are you finally going to give me an explanation for the three coffee mugs?"

Lucy looked sharply at him, her reaction instantly noted by the inspector. Underneath the table, she eased her hand from Danny's grasp, her heart thumping as she waited intently for his explanation. Who were these ominous visitors?

"My client has responded satisfactorily to all your questions," their solicitor intervened at last.

Lucy had already come to the conclusion that he was the biggest waste of time and money ever. Their family solicitor was tied up in court all day and they'd been forced to accept the junior partner. They'd do just as well without him. 'My client this' and 'my client that' was as much as he had to say for himself.

Phelim O'Brien sneered. "Not from where I'm sitting. I'll spell it out to you, shall I? The forensic results prove the fire was ignited by a particular substance, an inflammable substance frequently associated with deliberate arson. And your *clients'* account of their movements that afternoon has several holes in it so I'm perfectly within my rights to continue questioning them. And holding them."

He watched their faces, studying them in turn for a reaction.

Danny cleared his throat, gripping Lucy's hand again, refusing to let go when she tried to wrench it away. He concentrated on keeping his breathing even. He'd been managing without the oxygen so far, an important factor. "What exactly are you implying? That we set fire to our own house? For what gain?"

Phelim scoffed. "Give over with the innocence malarkey. You're in the building trade, Danny. You've been up close and personal with cases like yours. Business in trouble, a bit of an accident involving a box of matches and hey presto there's a massive payout. Get a company right back on its feet. Easy if you can get away with it. And then of course you'll hire the most expensive developer for estimates and naturally do the rebuild below cost price."

In the stifling room, Danny exploded. "You honestly think I'm stupid enough to lock myself in, collapse and be carted off in an ambulance?" He banged his fist on the table.

The inspector shrugged, his indifference deliberate. "A bit extreme but you got out of it alive, didn't you? Maybe," he said, turning to look at Lucy at this point, "maybe you were both in on it and your wife here came along at just the right time, screaming and shouting that you were trapped inside." He clapped his hands slowly . . . *clap . . . clap . . . clap.*

Lucy finally got her hand out of Danny's grasp and snapped her head around to glare at their solicitor. "Are you just going to sit there and allow him abuse us like this?"

Danny was breathing slowly and deeply, fighting against the overwhelming sensation of suffocation. He glanced at

Lucy, taking in her white face, the disbelief in her eyes as she tried to comprehend the ferocity of the accusation. He wondered, and not for the first time that day, how their normal life had tilted on its axis so suddenly. He wiped his sweaty palms on the knees of his jeans, wondering whether his wife had already condemned him as a guilty man.

"And what about you, Mrs Ardle, my sources tell me you've taken ownership of a flashy Audi A6. Is this true?"

It was Danny's turn to look shocked by this announcement. "Luce? What's this about?"

Phelim's smile was menacing, the way he tapped the side of his nose disconcerting.

"That Audi isn't mine," she blurted, looking from her husband to the inspector, her face reddening. "I can explain."

Phelim leaned back in the chair, enjoying watching her squirm. "Please do."

Danny coughed and coughed, grasping the edge of the table as he struggled to get his breath.

"Can you please get my husband a drink of water?" Lucy sat forward in her chair, her heart racing as she demanded to be heard. She and Carol were the only ones who'd known about the arrangement with the car. The paperwork hadn't even been processed yet. How the hell had O'Brien got wind of it?

Phelim took his time standing up. "Interview interrupted," he muttered into the tape recorder playing on the desk.

Conversation was minimal when he left the room, the solicitor and Lucy too concerned about Danny's distressed state to snatch a few words.

"Please put on the oxygen, Danny. It'll take a lot of pressure off your lungs." She went to the corner of the room to drag the portable tank towards him. His harsh breathing was the only sound in the room.

"No," Danny barked, clinging to his remaining dignity and waving away the oxygen. "An Audi? What's that about?"

Lucy was spared answering his question when the inspector returned and banged a glass of water on the table in front of Danny, some of it spilling over the top and splashing onto Danny's lap.

"Are we ready now?" Phelim asked after the briefest interlude.

"Get on with it," Danny said gruffly.

"Interview resumed," the inspector began, turning the tiny machine back on to play again. "Now, Mrs Ardle, would you care to explain about your new car. From what my team have told me, your building containers are no longer filled with construction materials but an attractive supply of furnishings. Stockpiling for when you move back in by any chance? Seems to me you managed to hoard quite a bit in the lead-up to a house fire."

Again, Danny looked at his wife, then back to Phelim. "What on earth are you talking about?"

Lucy put her head in her hands, refusing to reply to Danny or meet his eye. "My neighbour, Carol Black, she needed temporary storage. And the Audi is hers too . . . she, we . . ." Her voice trailed off, heat spreading through her body. *How on earth can I admit we were hiding goods from repossession companies?*

"Have you anything to say about this little arrangement, Danny?" Phelim leaned back on the chair and rested his left ankle on his right knee, his lack of respect for the distressed couple obvious.

Danny glanced sideways at their solicitor, disgusted at the blank look on his face. "I haven't the faintest idea what you're on about."

The solicitor sat up a little straighter after Danny's withering look. "Can I have a few moments with my clients please?" he requested.

Phelim shrugged. "Five minutes while I go and get myself a coffee. But that's it. No phone calls. And nobody's to leave the room. There's a camera looking down on you in case you're wondering." He pointed to a tiny red light flashing in the furthest corner of the ceiling.

Chapter 45

Matt stared at the phone, unsure what to do next. Delia's landline and mobile were ringing out. Who else could he call? He picked up the phone and dialled his brother's mobile number, his pulse racing as he waited for him to answer, hoping against hope that his Australian number worked in Ireland.

"Matt?"

"Stephen, what on earth's going on over there? Mum and Dad? Are they okay?"

He listened attentively to his brother's account of the fire, gasping when Stephen told him their parents were being questioned for arson.

"But that's ridiculous. Mum and Dad would never . . . I'm getting a flight . . ."

Stephen interrupted him, asking about his starting date with the college.

"Next week, but that's not important now. I have to go home. Hell, I want to go home."

Stephen's next words shook him. "We don't have a home right now, mate. And Delia's is already packed out. Wait a while. I'll keep you posted. Don't throw up your job."

"I won't be able to concentrate!"

"You will," his brother insisted. "Mum'll go mad if you come rushing back. Throwing away the opportunity of your dream job will give her something else to fret over. And no disrespect intended but there's nothing you can do until all this red tape's sorted."

"But you're there," Matt returned. "I feel I should be too."

"And I'm pretty useless if you want to know the truth but one good thing is they've met Ellie now. I'll call you every day, keep you updated."

Unwillingly, Matt relented, overcome by a need to share his relationship problems with his older brother. "I'll hold on here for a while but . . ."

"I've to go, Matt, but hold tough for now and I'll be back in touch."

Matt kept the phone to his ear though Stephen had hung up on the other end, his thoughts with his parents, imagining how terrified they must be right now.

Heidi appeared from the bathroom, a soft cream bath towel wrapped around her lightly tanned body.

"Are you okay?" She mouthed as she glided across the floor to the couch, sinking into it and tucking her feet underneath her.

Matt shrugged, concealing his yearning to be close to her. More than anything he wanted to sink onto the couch too, take her soft hand in his larger one, entwine his fingers in hers.

He pocketed his mobile and was about to join her on the

couch when her phone rang. He watched her closely, noticing her eyes light up. She was all fingers and thumbs, her voice unusually high-pitched as she answered. "Alex . . ."

Matt slipped a fleeced sweatshirt over his head. Three was a crowd. He was surplus to requirements.

As for Heidi, the thump of her heart drowned out the sound of the apartment door closing in his wake.

Chapter 46

"On your feet, Eric," the policeman ordered as he entered his cell. "Zebedee Holdings are pushing for compensation. I've spoken to their lawyer. He's issued confirmation."

Eric stood up, careful not to bang his head on the upper bunk. "And this compensation involves what exactly?" The floor felt unsteady beneath him.

"Repaying the deposit cheque that . . . but I don't have to tell you what happened to your down-payment cheque, do I?"

Eric shook his head slowly. "Am I legally bound to this deal?" He'd given up reading small print a long time before.

A vision of his monopoly board and 'Chance' cards returned. That cheque had 'Chance' written all over it, the banker refusing to bail him out. He'd chanced his luck and lost.

"Yes," the policeman responded firmly, "the realtor is prosecuting for contract default."

"And he won't change his mind?" He was sure he'd caught a glimmer of sympathy in the policeman's eye.

"The grid system has been changed in that area, the complex you bought on the wrong side. It'll take forever to resell, if ever. I doubt they're going to let you off the hook."

Eric's pulse pounded in his ears, the imaginary dice hot in the cup of his hand. Even the highest score, a double six, wouldn't save him in the game now. "What's the punishment? A stretch inside?"

The policeman sighed, finding these deal-breakers a waste of state funding. "I guess . . ."

"Phone call, Officer," came a voice from the opposite end of the corridor.

"I'll be right back."

Eric's insides quivered, any hopes of returning home crashing like a surfer fighting the strongest current. Calling Phelim was a waste of time, he thought, looking through the window at the clear blue sky.

He regretted the day he'd thrown himself into chasing property deals in the hopes of building a legacy to be proud of. All the legacies in the world wouldn't compensate for destroying his family. Ridiculous dreams – they had fizzled into nothing and destroyed all they came in contact with. Regrets were all he had left.

Suddenly feeling cold and a lot older than his fifty-five years, he pulled the thin blanket around his shoulders and sat there waiting for the policeman to return. His conscience nagging, he dug deep into his soul and confronted the decisions he'd made in life, no longer shying away from his shame at the dishonest man he'd become. His justification for greed, his reasons to continue wanting more and more? Who was he kidding? Every step he'd taken, every dodgy deal he'd entered had been more about massaging his massive ego than anything else. But that dream had faded, that ship had firmly passed, the vibrant orange prison overalls the only brightness left to look forward to.

When the policeman returned to the cell, he found Eric curled into the foetal position, weeping like a baby. Seeing no urgency in explaining the extradition laws between Ireland and the United States, he turned the key in the lock and left him there to cry his heart out for lost dreams.

Chapter 47

"I can't believe you stuck your neck on the line for *them*," Danny fumed.

"And I'm still waiting to find out who you had in the house after I left on Saturday!"

"Never mind that. I want to know why you're making a fool of yourself for the likes of Eric Black."

"I did it for Carol – but that was before –" the words were out of her mouth when she realised Danny knew nothing about Matt and Heidi.

"Before? Before what?"

She lifted the glass from the table, draining the remaining water in one gulp. Her clothes stuck to her skin, her hair damp on her forehead as she dug herself deeper and deeper into trouble. And that was with Danny, never mind the authorities.

"Matt and Heidi."

"What about Matt? He's okay, isn't he?"

The solicitor intervened at this point. "We're getting

nowhere. Stick to what's relevant. Were the containers empty or not?"

"Yes," Lucy said.

"No," Danny snapped, banging his fist on the table, though he really wanted to direct it at the solicitor's nose.

Phelim re-entered the room, a sarcastic smirk on his lips. "We're no further on, I see." He pressed the play button on his machine once more. "Interview resuming."

A knock on the door. He got to his feet, opening the door a fraction.

Lucy's eyes narrowed, hoping for a miracle. She focused on O'Brien, watched as he nodded his head, pointed a finger and refused the unwelcome visitor access. The door banged shut. His expression was murderous when he faced them. Lucy shrank into her chair, afraid.

"Your mobile phone records are back," he paused, watching his suspects grimace, noticing how unsure each was about the other. Neither spoke. The disjointed facts irritated him. He wanted to wrap this up, make an arrest. "The accelerant used to start the fire. Perhaps one of you would care to explain why it was upstairs?"

Lucy leapt to his bait. "There was nothing upstairs. What accelerant? Danny, tell him." She willed him to agree.

Danny barely heard. He was still fuming over the containers. What filthy scheme was Eric involved in now? Lucy's heart was too big, her generosity boundless. The Blacks had taken full advantage. Nothing new there.

"Danny! Will you keep up?" Lucy cried. "We're being accused of having some form of fire accelerant upstairs."

Phelim folded his arms across his bulky chest. Watching them bicker pleased him.

"He's bluffing," Danny insisted eventually, glaring at

his wife. Would she calm down? Being hysterical wasn't helping.

"Want that accusation in your statement?"

Silence from Danny.

"Sure you wouldn't like to own up now and save us all a headache," Phelim prompted, staring fixedly at the printed forensics document in front of him. "We have your fingerprints for comparison."

"You can use fingerprints, footprints or any prints you like because I'm innocent," Lucy couldn't hold back any longer. "The only thing we're guilty of is having the misfortune that this ever happened to us." Her stomach did somersaults. It took all her will not to vomit.

Phelim clapped his hands again . . . *clap* . . . *clap* . . . *clap*. "Excellent performance, Mrs Ardle. You should be on stage! You had me going there for a moment. I honestly thought your husband had kept you in the dark but now my jury's out again."

Danny scraped the chair on the tiled floor as he got to his feet, his face burning, his frustration evident. "That's enough, Inspector. You will not speak to my wife –"

"Take it easy." The solicitor placed a warning hand on his client's arm, his only comment since the inspector returned to the room.

To hell with you, Danny thought, pushing him away from him, imagining the enormous rate he'd charge for sitting there like a ventriloquist's dummy. "You can leave now if you've nothing constructive to say."

The solicitor's face went bright red and without another word (in short supply with him by all accounts) he gathered his papers and left the room.

Husband and wife looked at one another and shrugged,

both in agreement on one thing at least – that man hadn't been worth having in the room.

Lucy exhaled deeply, getting back to the argument with Phelim. "I already told you we don't have any insurance cover. So how does that fit in with your arson assessment?"

Phelim's eyes narrowed. "Not renewing private home insurance doesn't necessarily mean your property wasn't insured. As I'm sure, Danny, you know only too well. In fact, it was probably a pre-meditated ploy to remove suspicion from your door while all along you'd included your home in your business policy. An easy thing to do when your office and equipment are all housed in Sycamore Lodge. And the rest, as they say, is a walk in the park!"

Danny lurched to his feet. "How dare you! What do you know about my intentions?" Lucy's head was reeling. Their exchange had gone over her head after the inspector's suggestion that their home may have been covered by the business policy after all. Could she dare hope? "Danny? Is this true? Are we covered?"

"Sit down, Mr Ardle!" shouted Phelim.

Not even registering Lucy's question, Danny flopped into the chair, eyeing the oxygen tank in the corner of the room.

"Danny?"

"Be *quiet*, Mrs Ardle!" Phelim roared. "I am asking the questions here! This is a police interview not a family chat!"

Lucy subsided, hoping Danny would too. She would put nothing past O'Brien, confident he'd throw them in a cell for harassment if nothing else.

"Right. The accelerant," said Phelim.

"Petrol?" Lucy dared to ask. She rubbed her hands over her face, pushing away the images forcing their way in.

Danny cast her a sideways look.

"White spirits," Phelim revealed, shifting the enquiry up a notch. "Your prints are all over it. Both of you."

"I did use some when I was painting the bedroom last week" Lucy interjected, protesting her innocence, "but the bottle was well out of harm's way. And it couldn't have spilt. I wrapped it in newspaper and tidied it away." She still had the radiators to paint, the only reason she hadn't returned the white spirits to the garage.

"Couldn't have spilt without a bit of help," Phelim said, picking up his pen and tapping it on the table.

Lucy and Danny didn't look in each other's direction. The truth was being bent out of shape, the inspector's probing intimidating, yet neither had a handle on what the other was thinking. At this point they were doubting themselves and each other.

"Perhaps the sunlight caught it?" said Danny.

Lucy was sure she heard a tremble in his voice.

"You excel yourself, Danny," Phelim laughed, shaking his head. "The five minutes of sun we got that afternoon barely cast a shadow never mind cause something to ignite. Before you make any other ridiculous suggestion, bear in mind the liquid had been splashed around."

"How can you be sure?" Lucy shivered.

"The speed and direction of the fire tells its own story," the inspector joined his hands.

"Forensics." Lucy's mutterings were more to herself than to the others in the room.

"You didn't do your research very well, did you?" Phelim sneered. "The substance was identified at the fire scene. The Fire Brigade don't just sprinkle water on every fire. They're selective about what retardants they use, depending on the substance base."

Lucy clutched Danny's hand. She refrained from asking any more questions, terrified of enraging O'Brien again. Besides, his responses were making her feel stupid and about two inches tall.

"Well then, you want me to believe that neither of you are responsible even though every conceivable reason points a finger in your direction?" Phelim laughed. "Okay. Either of you have any enemies capable of stealing into your house on Saturday afternoon last, creeping upstairs while you were sleeping, pouring white spirits all over your bed, striking a match and leaving quietly in the same way they'd entered?"

Danny stared straight ahead, the inspector's question ringing loudly in his ears, his eyes firmly fixed on Phelim's.

Lucy shut her eyes, opening them quickly when he spoke directly to her.

"Mrs Ardle, we'll leave the matter there for now," he announced, tidying his notes and picking up the recorder.

Lucy stood up so fast she was dizzy, almost fainting with relief. "Let's go, Dan," she said, remembering the oxygen tank and going to the corner of the room.

"Your husband might need that, best leave it." Phelim was standing now too.

"What do you mean?" Danny was also on his feet.

"Your wife's free to go, but you on the other hand will be staying another while. There's a cell with your name on it down the corridor so unless you can come up with concrete proof to clear your name, that's where you will spend the night."

"You can't do that!" cried Lucy. "He's a sick man!"

"Just watch me!"

"You won't get away with this," said Danny, his voice hard. "You can't pin it on me."

"But you're caught, Danny. Own up and quit wasting time. Even your own wife is doubtful of your innocence, aren't you, Lucy?"

Lucy shook her head. She would stand by her husband, no matter what. "That's not true, Inspector."

"Your loyalty's commendable but won't convince a jury." The inspector strode to the door and held it open for her, snorting a laugh when she bent to kiss her husband's cheek.

Chapter 48

Phelim stirred two spoons of sugar in his coffee. Needing a break from questioning Danny, he'd left him to stew over his options, retiring to his office to gather his thoughts. He stared at the calendar on the wall, two adorable black Labrador puppies staring from the glossy print. Everywhere he looked that day he was reminded of his wife, Anne, her passion for animals as he stared at the doe-eyed puppies, her habitual excitement during the long build-up to Christmas when he heard a festive ad on the radio. But excitement and memories were lost to her now, a pained blank expression her only welcome for Phelim.

He visited every day, sitting with her and reading to her. On the brighter, warmer days of the summer months he'd pushed her wheelchair around the grounds, talking incessantly for both of them, her contact with other patients non-existent.

The care home was expensive, her treatment mostly

covered by the Garda Síochána medical insurance plan but a sizeable chunk left for him to meet every month, which would prove difficult when his pension kicked in.

Phelim let out a long slow breath. His visit to Anne had been no different this lunchtime, the faint flicker in her eyes at the sight of yellow tulips for her birthday almost breaking him, the glimpse of his son and daughter taking an alternate route to their mother's room as soon as he'd left gnawing a jagged wound. He'd half-raised a hand to salute his children, the long corridor separating them akin to the widening gap in their relationship. Overcome by his fight for justice, Phelim had become obsessed with making someone pay the price for causing his wife's condition. He forgave nothing.

Anne's accident had occurred three years before, their family details splashed all over the newspaper at the time, giving a very detailed account of the electrics in their home – they'd barely moved in when it happened. Anne had been in the house alone, Phelim working and their son and daughter in college. Her physical injuries improved with time. And though Phelim travelled and researched extensively to find a doctor who could regain his wife's brain functionality, he had never succeeded. How the accident happened had never been fully disclosed but the fact that Anne was electrocuted by a wiring problem in a faulty product was proven beyond doubt. The case against the manufacturers was still unresolved, due for hearing the following year but Ardle Construction – despite Phelim's numerous objections and appeal requests – had been cleared of negligence.

Anne's release from the rehabilitation clinic had been a day of hell for her family, the weeks that followed leaving them screaming at the authorities for help and unable to cope when adequate services weren't available. His son and daughter had neither understood nor forgiven Phelim's decision to commit their mother to full-time care, the empty home he returned to that evening a poignant measure of what his life was now.

Draining the last of his coffee, a residue of sugar crystals remaining at the bottom, he rose to his feet, his creaking body a weary reminder of what his family were suffering. And right or wrong, if he were to ever get a full night's sleep again, somebody had to be brought to justice.

On his return to the interview room, Phelim wasn't perturbed by the visible layer of sweat on Danny Ardle's brow, the sight of it a promise that his endless years of troubled sleep were coming to a gratifying end.

Chapter 49

Carol and Isobel hugged tightly in Cork Airport Arrivals hall, mother and daughter holding each other for a few moments longer than necessary. Carol pulled away first, stroking her daughter's cheek and noticing black circles under her eyes.

"You haven't been sleeping, have you?"

Isobel shrugged and clutched the handle of her travel case. "How can I, Mum? Every time I shut my eyes . . ." she gave a shudder.

"Are you sure you want to go straight to work?" her mother cut in. "You could come home and hop into bed for a few hours, go in later?"

"While I still have a bed," Isobel pointed out wryly, her eyes tinged with sadness. But she refused her mother's suggestion. "I wouldn't relax, Mum, waiting for the doorbell to ring, waiting for . . ."

Carol nodded, understanding only too well. She could count on the fingers of one hand the number of hours' sleep she'd had over the last few days and nights, her exaggerated imagination going into overdrive in the still hours of the early morning. But lack of sleep was way down the pecking order of her problems.

Now that Isobel was home, she didn't think she should delay telling her about Heidi any longer – just in case she ran into Lucy. Without doubt, the news would be better coming from her. Not a conversation she was looking forward to but she gently broached the subject. "I don't suppose Heidi's been in touch?" She noticed the intensity in her daughter's blue eyes, the strain of recent days showing in her chalk-white face.

Isobel shook her head, pulling her suitcase along behind her and linking her mother's arm as they walked the short distance to the car park. "Not a word. She's coping okay, isn't she? You did warn her against using her credit card?"

Her mother straightened her shoulders. "I didn't get to speak to her yet. She's not answering her phone."

There was something in her mother's tone that made Isobel stop walking. She flipped her head around to face her mother, ignoring the glares of passers-by when she halted abruptly in the middle of the busy terminal. "Mum? What exactly are you saying?"

The airport was busy at that hour of the morning, business people hurrying to catch taxis, holidaymakers excited to be leaving the drab Irish weather behind and airport personnel getting on with their daily routine. But Carol and Isobel were locked in the heightening tension of their own dramatic lives, oblivious to the activity around them.

"You're not going to like this . . ."

"Spit it out, Mum," Isobel hissed.

"Lucy's been great, Iz, storing loads of our furniture in Danny's lockups, even agreed to sign a change of ownership so we don't lose the car."

Isobel groaned, deeply humbled by their neighbour's generosity. "You allowed her do all that for you?"

"She insisted," Carol explained.

"But what has that to do with Heidi? I thought you were going to explain." Weariness swept over her. Standing in front of groups of eager managers and delivering presentations on a complicated IT system had taken it out of her. Relying on slides more than normal, she'd stumbled through each section, grateful to the enthusiasts who'd volunteered to demonstrate their knowledge and make her job easier. But the whole time, even as she'd corrected their assignments at the end, her mind had focused on one thing: home.

Carol glanced warily at Isobel, wondering if this shadow of her daughter was able for the truth right now. "Lucy told me Heidi was in New York."

Isobel ran a hand through her hair, pushing it back from her face to display hollow cheeks. "Lucy told you? What the hell's going on, Mum?" Nothing made sense, not any more, not since her father's frantic telephone message the previous week.

"It's complicated . . ." Carol began, her voice drowned out by the airport loudspeaker. Putting an arm around Isobel's shoulder, she ushered her out of the terminal building towards the car park. "Let's wait till we're in the car and chat then."

"But is Heidi okay, Mum? At least tell me that much. Please."

"I think so."

Isobel's forehead creased into a frown. She clutched her mother's hand and squeezed tightly. She didn't always see eye to eye with her sister but if anything happened to her . . . she couldn't bear to imagine. She pleaded with her mother for more information. "What do you mean you think so? For God's sake, Mum, I've enough on my plate without you holding back on me."

Carol glanced upward at the Aer Arann plane soaring overhead, wishing for a moment she was on board. The destination wouldn't matter, not once it took her far, far away. She sighed. "According to Lucy, Heidi's been seeing Matt . . ." She paused at that point, watching her daughter for a reaction. And it only took a moment to materialise.

"Matt? Matt Ardle? No way. She can't be. Can she?" Isobel was so intent on their conversation that she failed to notice her work colleague approaching, not until she was right beside her, squealing excitedly in her ear.

"Isobel? Are you catching the next Dublin flight? We can sit together if we hurry." She raised an expectant eyebrow.

A startled Isobel shook her head. "I've just got back, Liz. Heading into the office now to be honest."

"Go home to bed, girl," Liz laughed, shaking her head at Carol and jerking a thumb towards Isobel. "This one's a glutton for punishment. First in every morning, last to leave at night, disgracing the rest of us mere mortals!"

"Tell me about it," Carol feigned lightness. "Don't know where we got her from."

"Liz, this is my mum," Isobel remembered her manners and introduced the two women.

"You're her mum? Could have sworn you were sisters," Liz laughed, shouting over her shoulder as she hurried away. "Better run! Ryanair is waiting for me!"

Isobel's head spun, the other girl's energy overpowering. Without another word, she grabbed hold of her suitcase and walked on, Carol trailing behind her.

Isobel waited until they'd driven onto the dual carriageway before enquiring about her sister again and this time Carol told her everything she knew, Isobel's immediate reaction being to call her sister's mobile number.

"Mobile customer not available right now," she repeated to her mother. "I'm not sure which is worse, Mum. Heidi with Matt or with Julian?"

Keeping her eyes trained on the traffic, Carol reached a hand across and squeezed Isobel's closed fist. "There's not a lot we can do about either but the worst part is, Lucy's furious, blaming Heidi for leading her son astray."

"We've turned into the local pariahs! Everybody's going to hate us soon."

This statement sent Carol into fight or flight mode, forcing a decision she'd been contemplating for a few days. "Isobel, what are your chances of getting a transfer to a Revenue office in Galway?"

Isobel's screech made Carol jump. "Galway? Are you out of your mind? Who do we know there?"

"We don't know anybody there – it'd be a proper fresh start. No disappointed or pitying eyes following us, nobody crossing the street to avoid chatting to us. We could just get on with our own lives, do the best we could. Don't you see – that's what makes it perfect?"

Carol veered into the inside lane to allow an impatient driver overtake her.

Isobel screwed up her face. "But where would we live? You're broke. And my chances of getting a mortgage if . . ." she trailed off, shrugging her shoulders.

"A few years back, I inherited a tiny holding in Barna," Carol came clean.

"You did? Does Dad know this? How come you never said?"

Carol shrugged but didn't explain her reasons for keeping it to herself, the doubts she was having at that time about Eric's greedy behaviour, the fear of him gambling this acquisition or trading it for another non-profit making white elephant. So she'd kept quiet, hadn't breathed it to a soul. Until now. "I've started proceedings to transfer it into your name."

"My name? Why? What if. . ." Isobel began, leaning her head against the headrest.

"Because I'm tied up in some of your dad's accounts, Iz," said her mother, "and there's no guarantee it wouldn't be taken from us. But I've spoken to Jacob, figured out a way to avoid losing it, give us a chance of building some kind of future . . ." Heat rushed through her body as his name left her lips but, stealing a glance at Isobel, she breathed a sigh of relief that she hadn't noticed.

A bewildered Isobel was too stunned to notice anything amiss. Staring through the window at the group of cyclists up ahead, she envied their freedom. "Will you invite Dad to Galway?"

Her question was loaded but Carol chose that moment to berate the slow driver up ahead, conveniently ignoring Isobel's tentative enquiry. There were some things a daughter didn't need to hear, sexy underwear in her father's suitcase being one of them.

Isobel sat in her office on the top floor of Revenue House, scrolling through a multitude of emails, deleting at random and barely checking their content for importance. She'd avoided joining the girls for tea break, had cancelled her meeting and excused herself from pilot-testing a new computer system for possible rollout in the Audit area. Yawning widely, she removed her glasses and placed them on the light oak desk, wincing at the dart of pain pinching the base of her throat. She was tired, probably dangerously so. All that emotion and forceful smiling, giving presentations for three days and no sleep, had taken it out of her.

She gargled a mouthful of water, worrying about her father and what was happening to him, her dark waves tickling the back of her neck as the liquid eased her stinging throat. Where are you, Dad? she asked silently, her annoyance with him fading to concern. She opened her Internet browser, scanning the latest news headlines, half-expecting to read about a wayward Irishman being jailed in the US. Or worse.

Her diary lay open, her heavy workload for the week staring her in the face. Banging it shut, she shoved it away from her and hesitated for about a tenth of a second. Then typing hurriedly into the search engine, she waited for the selected page to open, scanning through the details appearing in front of her. She noted the logistics. It was a smaller office, not near as many staff, but enough of her current grade to make it worth her while enquiring about a transfer. Her family's mess was her mess too. Mum was right – a fresh start was their best option, probably their only option. Procrastination behind her, her mind made up, she dialled the number for Human Resources.

"Isobel Black here," she said politely. "I wonder if I could make an appointment to discuss a transfer."

"You're joking?"

She smiled at the note of surprise in the other woman's voice, a woman around the same age as herself. They'd started in the Civil Service the same year, Isobel's endless promotions pushing her way up the ladder in a short space of time. But they still got on. Isobel was nothing if amenable, her hard work and well-earned rewards recognised throughout the busy department. Her success wasn't begrudged, her female colleagues seeing her as a breakthrough in the male-female divide at the highest level. But their open admiration made it all the more difficult to stay. Seeing their pity and hearing their shocked whispers when her family's scandal became public knowledge wasn't an experience she was going to wait around for.

"I'm restless here – feel it's time for a change. Can you slot me in asap?" The words came out in a rush.

"I'll get right back to you," she was told.

Isobel replaced the phone and swivelled around in her chair, staring mindlessly at the multicoloured rooftops in her line of vision, dreading the prospect of leaving an office she loved. If only her heart were stone.

Chapter 50

Stephen locked the back door of Sycamore Lodge, sick to his stomach after going through every inch (what he could walk on at least) of his home. He sheltered in the garage doorway, watching the rain bounce against the ground. The weather matched his mood. He'd gone through everything in his old room – clothes, music collections, World War II books, even his Action Man figures. The smell of stale smoke lingered, poisoning every item, destroying its past and future. He'd bought refuse sacks on the way over, had planned on sorting the good from the bad, but when the time came he couldn't stomach keeping any of it. He'd filled refuse sack after refuse sack, pulled the grimy covers off the bed, covering his mouth when a cloud of dust and smut filled the air around him. With every heavy-duty bag filled to capacity, he stood them in the centre of the room and turned around and left.

Taking a quick glance in the containers out back, he

could understand the gardaí's suspicion. What was stored would easily furnish an entire house.

Quizzing his mother on their return journey from the Garda Station the day before, she'd given a garbled account through her tears but never properly explained why the Blacks had used their containers for storage in the first place. Instead she was intent on listing every shred of evidence being used against Danny, most of it questionable even to her.

Danny had been returned home quite soon after that, ghastly and exhausted, and had taken to his bed, sleeping solidly through the night and well into the morning. But Phelim O'Brien had turned up again just after lunch and taken him back to the station. This time Danny had stubbornly insisted that Lucy and Stephen stay at home. In the face of his father's obstinacy, Stephen had no choice but to give in. Then, when he'd told Danny that he would inform the solicitor and get him to meet him at the station, Danny had hurriedly said he would deal with that himself. Stephen had felt powerless and hugely frustrated.

Now, with his father detained and his mother too upset to discuss anything apart from getting him released, Stephen decided a visit to Carol was in order. A statement from her couldn't hurt the case.

Putting his hand in his pocket for a tissue, his fingers touched the piece of paper with Jack Bowe's number. The ink was smudged, the numbers barely recognisable. Quickly, before the paper disintegrated entirely, he saved the details on his phone, very much fearing he'd be calling his old friend in the not-too-distant future. But not yet.

Kicking debris out of his path, he memorised as much exterior damage as he could, anticipating his father's questions as he walked around the perimeter of the house, frowning at the crack stealing its way up the front wall. Assessing the full extent was beyond his untrained eye, the amount of materials, labour or compensation required to restore it to its original form a job for the professionals, but it didn't take a genius to realise it would be a sizeable refurbishment project.

Leaving his hired car outside Sycamore Lodge, he strolled across the narrow country road. It was a little over two years since he'd last walked there, yet nothing much had changed – once he didn't look over his shoulder at the sorry state of his home. He shoved his hands in his pockets as he turned into the Blacks' driveway, a memory of the times he'd been sent to ask if one or other of Carol's daughters would baby-sit creeping unexpectedly into his mind. He found himself comparing the familiarity of home with the Australian neighbourhood where he and Ellie lived. He knew very little about even his closest neighbours, could never imagine trusting them with a spare key to his home, never mind baby-sitting his child. The thought caused a tug in his heart, the road ahead suddenly lonely without family close by. But for now he didn't dwell on it, hoping things would work out in their own sweet time.

Pressing Carol's doorbell for a third time, he was about to leave when the door was pulled open and a dishevelled Isobel stood in front of him. He did his best to hide his shock at her appearance.

"Yes? Can I help you?"

"Isobel?"

He smiled as he watched her scrutinise his features. *Who'd have thought my neighbour wouldn't recognise me?*

"Stephen Ardle?" Her face was drawn and pinched. She clutched the sides of her open cardigan and pulled it tightly around her, the action accentuating her gauntness. "When did you get back? What brings you here?"

The smile left Stephen's face, her rudeness too blatant to excuse. "I was hoping to have a word with Carol actually."

Instantly, she retracted her sharpness. "I'm sorry. You must think I'm a right bitch. I've got a blinding headache and honestly didn't recognise you at the door. If it's about Heidi . . ."

Stephen frowned in confusion, surprised to be kept on the doorstep when he'd always been welcomed in the past. Things *had* changed around here after all. "Heidi? Why would I be here about her?"

"With her and Matt being in New York together, I presumed he'd sent you here."

Stephen was convinced he must be dreaming. "Together? That can't be right."

Isobel bit down hard on her inside lip, wishing he'd leave. "But I presumed you knew. It was Lucy who told Mum. Why don't you ask her about it?"

Bloody hell, Stephen thought, what other revelations am I going to hear about my family? "Is Carol due back soon?"

"Hard to say." She picked a scab on the inside of her wrist, a droplet of red blood appearing when she broke through the crisp surface. "There's a lot going on right now as you've probably heard."

Stephen didn't react, allowing her to presume he knew more than he did.

"I don't suppose you'd give Carol a call and find out when she'll be back?"

"She left her phone behind when she went out. What's so urgent?" She dabbed at the blood with the cuff of her cardigan. It was flowing heavier now.

"Just something the Gardaí mentioned. I'm hoping she'll give a statement to help clear up a few details." He gave nothing away, wasn't about to castigate his father on their neighbour's doorstep, despite his growing concern.

Isobel backed away from him. "I'll tell her you called."

"Here's my number," he began, but she'd already slammed the door.

Carol and Isobel chatted quietly at the kitchen island-unit, both looking around them and drinking in as many details as possible.

"I still can't believe this house is no longer ours, Mum." Isobel stepped down from the stool and walked around the room, sliding kitchen presses open and closed before moving to stand at the glass doors and stare into the darkness.

"I know, Iz." Carol stood behind her daughter, slipping her arms around her waist and resting her head on her shoulder. "But we have to salvage what we can, no matter how small by comparison."

"I'm worried about Heidi, Mum. She still hasn't called."

"I suppose we could ask Lucy for Matt's number and contact her that way?"

Isobel pulled away from her mother and took her soft leather handbag from the counter, swinging it over her shoulder. "Mum, no way. She has our mobiles. She will call eventually."

Carol watched her daughter move around the kitchen, the strong glare from the sunken spotlights accentuating the black rings under her eyes. "Perhaps. But what if she arrives home suddenly and finds the place locked up? Or worse, what if the bank has a *For Sale* sign in the garden?"

Isobel let her mother's questions unanswered. "I'll go up and pack. Is my large suitcase still in Dad's wardrobe? He's got so much more space than me. I've been leaving it there for the last while." Her mother's expression changed, Isobel immediately assuming the suitcase had been deposited across the road. "You've dumped it along with the furniture and stuff, I bet?"

Carol yawned widely, camouflaging the sense of giddy relief flooding through her. Isobel's suitcase had been the one she'd dragged from Eric's wardrobe, the pink negligée obviously hers too.

She smiled at her daughter. "No. It's still there. It's thrown on the floor."

Eric wasn't playing away. He wasn't cheating. Her heart soared. Being so angry with him had sapped her energy but now his infidelity had turned out to be a figment of her imagination, she found empathy in her heart. Though it's unlikely he'll be sharing my bed for quite some time, she decided firmly, his monetary deception one of the many issues remaining to be dealt with.

"Mum?"

"Yes?"

"Can we leave tonight, Mum? Please?"

Isobel's heartfelt request sobered Carol once more. "Are you sure about your transfer? You'll miss the crew."

Isobel shrugged. "No choice, have I, Mum? I'll contact

the office tomorrow, tell them about Dad and apply for extended leave. . ."

Her phone rang. She rummaged in her bag, pulled out the slim mobile and answered the call.

"Iz, hi, you okay?"

"Oh Heidi, thank God!" she cried, never so glad to hear from her younger sister.

"Guess you and Mum have been wondering about me?" Heidi pulled her knees up to her chest, sensing something amiss in her sister's tone. She cradled her phone between her ear and shoulder, pulling at her split ends, separating strands of hair as she listened to Isobel's string of questions and concerns about Matt, New York, their distress at her disappearance . . . "Iz, can I get a word in please? And yes, I did have trouble with my credit card." She listened closely, her mouth dropping open when Isobel went into the harrowing detail of *why* her credit card had been refused.

The consequential effects snowballed in her head. No credit card, no financial support. How could she survive in New York without it? Would she have to return home? Sever her contact with Alex after only just finding him?

"But how will I survive?" she burst down the phone, her sister's sharp intake of breath audible on the other end.

"My God! Can't you ever think of anyone but yourself?"

"That's uncalled for, Isobel. I'm not being selfish. I'm sitting in a tiny apartment in Manhattan not knowing how I'll pay next month's rent, so of course I'm bloody thinking of myself. You've got your job —"

Isobel interrupted, her speedy explanation and accusatory intonation making Heidi's head thump.

I'll have lost my nerve, won't be able to tell her about Alex if she doesn't let me get a word in soon, she thought, jumping to her feet at her sister's next proclamation.

"What do you mean you're moving to Galway? Crosshaven's our home, always has been!"

She blinked back angry, hot tears, her grasp on normality slipping away from her. What Isobel was telling her was too much to take in.

"I want to speak to Mum. Please, Isobel."

She listened to her sister's attempt at apology, relief coursing through her to hear her mother's muffled voice in the background as she took the phone.

"Mum, Isobel's not making any sense . . . I know I should have called but for once I was trying to sort things myself . . . and Dad, is he okay?"

Carol hushed her, promising that nobody was apportioning blame. Her explanation was gentler than Isobel's but the context unfortunately was exactly the same. Although despite her private concerns, she did assure her daughter that her father would survive this ordeal.

Heidi couldn't hold back a moment longer, desperate to explain why she couldn't obey her mother's instructions that she fly to Galway and meet them there.

"I've found Alex, Mum, I'm not walking out on him again."

She spoke quietly into the phone, feeling the distance between them extend until eventually her mother retaliated strongly, demanding to know how she could be sure it was Alex.

"Of course it's really him, Mum. I know his adoptive parents are Irish. But by all accounts they moved to New York shortly after the final papers were signed. Who could blame them?" she added, as much to herself as her mother as she recalled the dreadful pain she'd caused them before relinquishing the final document.

Adoption had made perfect sense, was even recommended by her counsellor at the time, but Heidi's troubled mind made it impossible to let go. She'd done everything in her power to call the adoption procedure to a halt, caught unawares on the cusp of a lengthy panic episode when she signed away her legal rights. Was it any wonder they'd hightailed it to the other side of the world as soon as they got the baby into their hands?

Her mother's confusion was evident, her interest in her grandson welcome, but far, far too late.

"I'm not sure when I'll return, Mum, but probably not for quite some time," she answered eventually. "If I can find some work and earn enough to live, I'll stay here indefinitely. Being with Alex is important to me, something I'm going to prioritise if he'll allow me . . ." Her phone beeped. "My battery's dying, Mum. Write this down." She called out her phone number, the line going dead as she delivered the last digit.

For the first time in her thirty-three years, Heidi was without support – financial or otherwise. She was in charge of her own survival. Freedom settled inside her. Moving to the window, she sat on the deep ledge, savouring the unfamiliar, but extremely welcome, feeling of peace.

Chapter 51

"Thanks for nothing!" Lucy said, slamming down the phone and storming into the living room where the others were waiting patiently.

"Well?" Stephen asked, moving closer to Ellie to make room for his mother on the sofa.

"Nothing whatsoever. He's still being questioned apparently." She pushed her hands through her hair, shaking her head. "They're treating your father like a common criminal."

"They can't do that," Gloria piped up. "I hope you told them that?"

"Mum! I'm not the one *telling* them anything. They had *me* in there too. Remember?"

Gloria tossed her head. "Stephen, surely there's something that can be done?"

Delia came into the room. "Leave him alone, Mum. Lucy, I've run you a nice hot bath. You could do with it, up you go."

Stephen followed his mother upstairs, taking the first opportunity to speak to her alone. There were questions he needed to ask – without his grandmother's prying ears.

"Do you want to use the bathroom, love?" Lucy stepped aside to let him in.

"No, Mum. Look, what's the story with Matt and Heidi Black?"

Lucy took two fresh towels from the hot press. "I'm sorry love, with everything else I didn't get to tell you. He's been seeing her for a while and she's followed him to New York apparently."

"But she's years older than me, never mind him!" Stephen stated the obvious.

"Did Delia mention it?" she asked.

"Isobel."

Lucy had been staring longingly at her bubble bath but swivelled around to face Stephen. "Isobel? Were you over there?"

"Briefly. I got a fairly cold reception."

"That's odd. You've done nothing wrong."

"Mum, you never did explain why their stuff is in Dad's containers."

"They're broke, waiting for the bailiffs to repossess everything."

"No way! No wonder Isobel looked awful. All Eric's hotshot deals?"

"Landed him in serious hot water apparently. And speaking of which, do you mind if I have a soak before mine goes cold? I promise we'll chat properly after. And Stephen, will you see if you can get an update on your father? His medication's long overdue. I'm worried about him. He's on his own there now . . ."

"Alone?" Stephen frowned. "But he has his solicitor with him."

"Useless. Well, the junior partner we got yesterday was. We sent him home. Dismissed him effectively, I guess."

Stephen clutched the banister tightly, speaking through gritted teeth. "Whatever hope he has in there, Mum, he *has* to have a solicitor!"

"But he was a pure waste of money!"

"Leave it with me," Stephen insisted, his foot on the top step of the stairs when he turned to his mother again. "You don't suspect Dad, do you?"

"Of course not."

"Okay, I'll organise a brief and see if there's anything else I can do." He made no mention about meeting Jack Bowe, seeing no point in raising her hopes unnecessarily. "Try to relax and enjoy your bath."

Lucy dipped the soft pink sponge in and out of the bubbled water, letting it fill with water, then squeezing it out again. She hadn't been entirely honest with Stephen, had found it difficult to explain the way Danny had sidestepped the inspector's questions about who'd been in the house the afternoon of the fire. Water splashed over the edge of the bath when she slid under, Lucy's eyes shut tight as she forced away the unwanted images in her head. *What* the hell was he hiding? And *who* was he protecting? Was it his family or his mysterious visitors?

Stephen arranged to meet Jack Bowe near the soccer pitch on the Ballea Road outside Carrigaline town.

"I wasn't expecting to hear from you so soon, Stephen. All a bit undercover, isn't it?" Jack joked, easing himself out of the low sports seat of his black Golf GTI.

Stephen gave a weak smile. "I'm afraid you're nearer the truth than you probably realise."

Jack leaned on the bonnet of Stephen's hired car, watching a juvenile team running laps of the pitch, urged on by a militant coach. "So what's so important you dragged me away from the final episode of *Shameless*?"

"My father's being framed for arson . . ." He looked at his old college friend, the yellow street-lighting reflecting on his skin.

"Go easy, Stephen, that's a serious accusation you're throwing around," Jack warned, looking at his old friend questioningly. "I know how tough it can be for families when something like –"

"Jack, stop right there. Dad's being used here, plain and simple." Stephen instilled confidence in his voice, belying any trace of doubt lingering underneath. No matter how things may look, in his heart he clung to the belief that his father was an honest man who wouldn't do wrong to anyone, least of all his family. And with that firmly at the forefront of his mind, he'd arranged this meeting to press his friend for an honest and fair investigation.

"What makes you think that? And if he is innocent, who do you think started the fire? And why?" Jack rose to his full height, taller by a margin than his friend.

Stephen inhaled deeply. That puzzle he couldn't solve but it didn't alter the facts that his father was an honest man in the frame for something he hadn't done.

"O'Brien's an experienced professional – he's good at what he does. To the best of my knowledge, his record's exemplary." Jack was resolute.

"Are you sure about that?" Stephen threw the question as more of a test than anything, eyeing Jack carefully, watching for a reaction. He paused a moment. "Not a man you can be sure of, is he? At least be honest with me."

"You sound as though you have good reason for thinking that," Jack sidestepped the question, watching as the juvenile team changed direction on the floodlit pitch and following instruction from their coach ran backwards towards the nearest goalpost.

Stephen launched into an account of Anne's accident, Phelim's vicious accusations against his father's workmanship, the findings and outcome of the case, every detail vivid in his mind. "He's had it in for Dad ever since and made no secret of it. At least not to my family."

Jack pulled at the zipper of his brown-leather jacket, hating the position he was put in yet belligerent against any member of the Garda Síochána using their position for personal gain. "What are you asking from me?"

Stephen sighed. "Nothing dishonest, I guarantee that much. But surely there's procedure in these instances? Where a member of the force has an unbiased interest in a case? Where their judgement is being coloured?"

Jack kicked at the loose earth by the wheel of his car, disentangling stones from their safe position and watching them roll over the embankment. The simple action made him wonder about Phelim O'Brien's theory in the Ardle case. How well would it hold up to a little digging? "I'll see if I can have a look at the technical report or at the very least have a discreet word with our Forensics guy. Without putting my neck on the line, you understand?"

Stephen nodded, blowing out a long sigh of relief. "Thanks, mate." He wanted to tell him hurry, to order him straight to the station to check out the technical procedure this instant. Time was of the essence. But they weren't on the debating team now. He wasn't the one in charge. There was nothing he could do but sit tight and wait.

The sound of a referee's whistle drifted towards them, the team bursting into a sprint for the last few metres of the pitch.

"Don't expect miracles, Stephen. I'm not here long enough to throw my weight around."

"If you can assure me that the case is being handled without prejudice and evidence isn't being covered up, I promise I won't bother you again."

"By the way, I hope your dad has a good brief?"

"That's another problem. Can you believe he told his solicitor – well, the junior partner – where to go?"

Jack shook his head. "I'll check into it back at the station," he promised, narrowing his eyes a moment as he met his friend's grateful gaze. "Strictly off the record – and you didn't hear this from me, Stephen – O'Brien's permanently in foul humour. He's got it in for everybody. A time bomb with the pin already pulled is the best way to describe him. The station's on tenterhooks waiting for him to retire in a few weeks."

The floodlights went out, the exhausted players descending into darkness, their voices carrying in the distance as they made their way to the dressing rooms.

"A few weeks could be too late for Dad," Stephen replied, shaking his friend's outstretched hand before sitting into his car and driving away.

It was after seven and Danny had been at the station for hours, subjected to repetitive questioning.

Danny's back ached. He'd had little choice but to succumb to using oxygen when Phelim left the room for a brief interlude before returning for further interrogation.

"Jenny's your only sister, that right?"

Danny sighed and nodded, conserving as much of his energy as he possibly could.

"And little sisters aren't normally impressed by older brothers throwing their weight around? Stopping them from getting what they want?"

Danny seethed internally. Despite his grievance with Jenny, she was still his sister. "What are you implying, Inspector?"

"Seeing as you're not inclined to confess your guilt and I want to wrap this up, perhaps it's time I brought your sister in. And maybe your parents too. They were your last visitors, isn't that correct?"

"Leave my family out of this." His voice was gravelly. "They have nothing to do with it."

"Your sister the glamorous type?"

Danny refused to respond. He might not have a solicitor beside him but he knew better than utter anything that could later be found incriminating.

"Long nails, long legs too, I bet."

"What . . .?"

Phelim glanced at the file in front of him, running his index finger underneath an important paragraph. "A fingernail was identified at the scene. Don't think it's yours, Danny." He eyed Danny's bitten nails.

"Your evidence won't hold up, so now you're trying to pin it on my sister?" He fought against the explosion of anger rising inside him.

He looked the inspector in the eye, then repeated

exactly what had happened when his sister and parents called over. The only thing he left out was his sister's venomous look, the whispered threats she'd uttered once their parents were out of earshot. He kept that to himself, believing O'Brien was doing his utmost to bamboozle him into admission. *Innocent until proven guilty*, he repeated the mantra over and over.

"So you don't think your sister would have the balls to get her own back on you? To give you a taste of her worthlessness?"

"That's unthinkable."

"But not improbable."

Danny was glad Lucy hadn't been privy to every miniscule detail of this interrogation. Or his verbal assault on O'Brien when he'd insinuated that Jenny's trip to the upstairs bathroom had been a well-devised plan on his behalf to put her in the frame and divert attention from himself, push her higher on the list of suspects.

"Go on, hit me!" the inspector goaded. "Prove how worthless you are. It'd give me pleasure to add assault of a police officer to your accusations."

Danny's knuckles whitened. Keeping his hands off the other man was becoming increasingly difficult. "I'm an innocent man," he hissed at O'Brien, repeating it a few times until the man opposite pushed back his chair.

"Not for long more," he said, rising to his feet, listing what sounded like closing arguments on the fingers of his left hand. "Insurance scam to save a dying business or urgent compensation to bail out a destitute sister? I need a moment to decide which is most likely. Interview interrupted," he said, silencing the whirr of the recorder and banging the door when he left.

In the space of time he was alone in the room, Danny braced himself for O'Brien's return, startled when the door opened a few minutes later and Jack Bowe walked in, looking a lot younger in his civilian clothing of faded denim jeans, indigo polo shirt and brown-leather jacket.

"Has *he* sent you?" Danny clutched the small table with both hands, intense anger accentuating his breathlessness.

"Not exactly," Jack responded, pushing the door closed behind him. He'd taken a chance sneaking into the room, seizing his opportunity when the inspector had retreated to his office with an enormous pizza box in his arms.

"Oh?" Danny raised an eyebrow, his surprise evident.

"I bumped into Stephen earlier. We were on the same college debating team. I promised him I'd check on you. Where's your solicitor?" He protected Stephen's confidence, not wanting to undermine the proud man sitting before him.

"Sent him home," Danny said immediately. "A useless waste of space, better off without him."

"Are you insane? You need to organise representation straight away. Who're you using?"

Danny gave him the name of his company solicitor, frowning at Jack's obvious disapproval.

"Experts in property law," said Jack, "but wouldn't have the first clue about keeping clients out of prison."

"Oh?" Danny's gaze flickered over and back to the door, O'Brien's imminent return making him uneasy. If Jack was advising him to engage one of Cork's most reputable defence lawyers, it didn't say much for his chances of being released without charge.

As though on cue the young garda's phone rang. He

pulled it out of his pocket and checked the caller ID. "One moment," he said into the phone, then covered the mouthpiece with the palm of his hand to utter his parting statement to Danny. "I'll get a legal rep here asap," he promised, "and we'll get you out of here pronto. You're a sick man, Mr Ardle – they daren't detain you overnight without some serious evidence."

He turned to go.

"Thanks for getting back to me," Danny heard him say as he left, the remainder of his conversation lost when the heavy door clunked behind him, the scent of his new leather jacket lingering in his wake.

After Jack left the Garda Station, he waited five minutes before dialling the number of the Garda Forensic Unit. Richard's input had been minimal, Jack seeing no other option except to get a look at the Forensic report for himself. How was he to justify his request for duplicate results? Wherever the original set were, they had not been updated on the Garda network as was customary. And if he did manage to secure a report, then what? His call was answered and he asked to be put through to the relevant section, planning a strategy while he waited. But what self-respecting superintendent would take the word of a relatively new recruit against the skilled investigation of an experienced inspector?

A female voice on the line brought an end to his speculating, his attention required on the phone instead.

"Carrigaline Station in Cork here." Jack used the most official tone he could muster. "I'm enquiring about File ref CCAA4670."

"Your Garda ID?"

Jack inhaled deeply. Was he mad identifying himself? Probably, he decided, but what was the alternative? Ignore his gut instinct, ignore his friend's request? At the very least Stephen deserved a second opinion. He parted with his ID detail, thanking the official on the other end when he asked him to wait while he went to check the records.

"Your station already received the originals, are you aware of that?"

"Of course," Jack said quickly, "but they're nowhere to be found and muggins here has been given the job of requesting duplicates." He ran a finger over the VW badge on his steering wheel, pushing his luck a little further. "We've a suspect in and there's only a short time left before he has to be released. As you can imagine, the missing report is causing uproar. The powers that be will do anything rather than let our chief suspect walk out the door. Any chance you could fax a copy through, please?"

He heard a loud yawn on the other end, guessing the young female he was speaking to would rather be at home in a warm bed. "I know how you feel," he continued, looking forward to calling it a night himself after a long, hectic day on duty. "I'm out of here once I get this wrapped up."

"Do you have the fax number handy? It'll save me checking for it on our files."

He happily rhymed off the number of the fax machine furthest away from the interview room where Danny Ardle was being held, doubling back to the Station as quickly as he could to ensure the documentation fell into his hands and nobody else's.

Chapter 52

Jack worked at the kitchen table in his Monkstown apartment until the small hours. He sat bent over the faxed copy of the forensic report, so engrossed that he jumped out of his skin when his girlfriend left the warmth of their bed and joined him, peering over his shoulder to get a peek at what was distracting her handsome boyfriend. To date in his career, he hadn't had to cope with anything more than traffic accidents or unpaid fines. But he'd worked alongside more senior officers and understood some of the principles involved in analysing forensics or at least trying to. The intricate technical jargon went over his head but the trace evidence found at the scene, that had so far gone unchecked to Jack's knowledge, was listed in simple English. He paused a moment, yielding to his girlfriend's attempt to lure him to bed, her soft caress making him turn his head to meet her lips. He was tempted – oh, so very tempted – to walk away from the table and take her in his arms.

"Want to help me with this?" He offered, knowing if he walked away from it now, it'd be morning before he'd return. And he felt so close to making a connection, the findings on the document in front of him like the outer edges of a jigsaw, the pieces required to frame the picture.

"I'll be waiting," his girlfriend said, declining his offer to play cops and robbers and scuttling out of the chilly kitchen, leaving him to concentrate.

He underlined the word *blood*, an obvious finding that required further analysis, but not the only one. He wondered whether he should return to the station, the filter of light streaming from the bedroom making it difficult to decide. As he stared at the pages spread out on the table, he wondered why Danny Ardle was being held as chief suspect when the forensic results were screaming female? Whoever had sprinkled white spirits in the bedroom and adjoining office couldn't possibly have escaped without some form of bodily contact or injury. At least now he had a lead to follow and one task he could accomplish independently in the morning. Setting his alarm for 5.00 a.m., he padded into the bedroom and stared at his girlfriend who lay naked under a single sheet on their bed. According to the green numerals on the digital clock, they had three hours before his alarm would burst into life and his promise to help the Ardle family would begin for sure. Putting his hand into his trousers pocket, his fingers found his Garda badge and he prayed he wasn't about to jeopardise his most treasured possession – his career. Slipping between fresh cotton sheets, Jack pulled his girlfriend's warm body against him, shoving away all concerns and inhaling her fresh floral scent as his fingers trailed along her soft skin until finally she turned to face him.

Carol's eyes adjusted to the dark country roads as she took a lesser-known route out of Crosshaven. Leaving before dawn had made more sense than making the unfamiliar journey in the dark of night. Another hour and they'd be travelling in daylight.

Isobel sat rigid in the passenger seat, her handbag and laptop at her feet, a heavy wool coat covering her body from her neck to her ankles. And still, though she'd turned the heating on full power, she couldn't get warm. Her meeting with Human Resources had been surprisingly positive, their reaction to her transfer application thought-provoking in the main. Instead of urging her to wait a while and follow through on some of the unfinished projects she was involved in, they'd listened to her plight and suggested utilising this unexpected move as an opportunity – premature though it was – to develop the Galway office and improve its status in the department overall. Isobel walked away from the meeting feeling she'd been handed a lateral promotion and carte blanche to progress the IT division as she saw fit.

Without delay or preamble, the Human Resources Manager had drafted and signed Isobel's contract and pushed it across the desk. "Good luck," she'd said, smiling.

"I wish I didn't have to go," Isobel had replied, the loaded statement of truth her parting words.

Carol branched onto a more familiar road, pressing on the throttle as the dual carriageway spread open before her. A few hours of effortless driving and they'd be there. After that, she had no plans but at least they'd been saved the humiliation of watching the bailiffs at work. Breaking the silence, she snapped on the radio, the song being played bringing a smile to her lips.

"Remember, Iz?" she asked, humming under her breath and wiggling her bum on the seat to Cher's 'Shoop Shoop Song' from the memorable movie *Mermaids*.

Isobel gave a weak smile, the catchy tune instantly conjuring a picture of her and Heidi dancing on their mother's bed with Carol twirling around the bedroom floor with a black polo-neck on her head pretending to be Cher. She slipped a hand out from underneath her heavy coat and increased the volume, the jovial tune filling the car, yet failing to drown out the sounds in her head.

"I remember."

Chapter 53

Jack Bowe turned ice-cold. He'd just got off the phone from Sergeant Richard Collins and was convinced he'd walked into a minefield by asking for his assistance. Only time would tell. They'd made an appointment to meet, the intervening time giving him a short few hours to build a worthy case to convince the sergeant to take him seriously. His instinct hadn't changed from the previous night, his hunch about the perpetrator's gender still with him when he'd opened his eyes that morning. By his reckoning, it could only be one of two females.

Rising before the alarm had the chance to shrill to life and disturb his sleeping girlfriend, he'd crept into the lounge area, grabbing the *Golden Pages* from his untidy coffee table and opening it on the first page of hospital listings. Immediately, he got down to the task of calling Accident and Emergency departments, extending his search beyond County Cork when his enquiries delivered nothing remotely of interest. Exhausting the Munster region, he was about to abandon his exercise when his eyes fell on the extensive Dublin listings. For no other reason apart from the fact the motorway to Dublin was one of the easiest escape routes out of Cork, he dialled a few more hospitals, repeating his questions multiple times, everything running around his head. If he were honest, he hadn't been expecting success, not really. So when a hospital registrar read the scanty details of one of their casualty patients to him, rattling her surname and address down the line, he'd smiled and printed the detail on his page in block capitals, not trusting his usual illegible scrawl not to let him down.

Two hours later, after he'd met and convinced Sergeant Collins he'd uncovered a new lead warranting serious investigating, he pulled up outside the designated address and stepped out of the car. It was a bright morning, the orange sun casting long shadows on the ground. But the weather was immaterial, the results of this visit crucial, not least because he felt he had something to prove to the Forensics sergeant.

Following Richard's lead, Jack kept very close to him, stopping up short when there was no car in the driveway. Damn. He'd hoped the early hour would prevent any delay, convinced their targets would be still asleep in their beds.

"You're sure about this?" Richard asked. "This is the address the hospital gave you?"

Jack nodded, his face darkening when their third ring on the doorbell went unanswered. He glanced at the sergeant, staring at the mass of freckles on his cheeks and imagining his fury if he'd brought him on a wild-goose chase. He had to think fast.

"I'll check out back," he offered, hurrying around the rear of the house and glancing through the windows.

It was as if the family had left without any intention of returning. What the hell was going on this neighbourhood? First the Ardle fire and now the Black family's disappearing act. Is there a connection, he wondered. He took out his phone and dialled Stephen Ardle's number, relieved when he answered on the first ring.

"I thought you should know we're following a new lead."

"Does that mean Dad's off the hook? Mum's beside herself with worry," Stephen shot back instantly.

Jack recognised desperation in his friend's voice. "We've got definite evidence," he explained, "but until we track down the suspect in question . . ."

"Can I be of any help? Anything at all I can do?"

"Unless you know how we can track down Isobel and Carol Black?"

There was silence from Stephen. Jack eyed Richard warily as he approached the front of the house once more.

"My brother's living with the other daughter in New York. I'll see if he knows anything."

Jack was bewildered. And he'd *wondered* about the families being connected! "Find out what you can and get back to me. Every second counts for your father, Stephen." And for me, he added silently.

"Well?" Richard barked. "Any other far-fetched notion you want us to follow?"

Jack was beginning to wonder whether he should have bitten the bullet and gone directly to the superintendent with his plight. What if Richard wasn't trustworthy?

"You want me to question an inspector who happens to be my superior?"

"I want a fair hearing for decent people. Innocent till proven guilty." Jack's heart thumped. Sergeant Richard Collins was glaring at him as though he'd personally accused *him* of some involvement. Was he part of a scam to hide evidence? He was never so relieved as when his mobile rang.

He quickened his step and beckoned Richard to follow him to the car, listening carefully to Stephen as he walked. He reminded himself he was on very thin ice. "They're either *in* Galway or on their way. They're travelling in an Audi A6. We need to set up roadblocks as well as tracking down the registration plate and radioing it out to the various traffic teams."

"Are you actually assigned to this case?"

The sergeant's question stalled Jack in his tracks, his recovery surprising even to himself. He felt uneasy, Richard's negativity a growing concern. But Jack decided he'd plead lack of experience if criticism were raised. He wasn't about to back off now. He'd say he'd assumed an overt interest on account of being present at the scene.

"I took a statement from Mrs Ardle and I had other involvements too. To answer your question, yes, I *am* on the case. Now let's go, we're wasting time. If we can find them, I'll need your expertise to test for forensics."

"Maybe," Richard muttered, his expectation of promotion sliding through his fingers. He sat into the car, banging the door with more force than necessary. Following the inspector's instructions were becoming impossible now this junior whizz kid had taken a sudden interest in the evidence collected. Under different circumstances he'd have admired his initiative. As for himself, he was faced with a choice now: upset someone who'd be a distant memory in the force in a few weeks or work to impress the superiors ready to fill the inspector's shoes. "What prompted you to scrutinise the forensic report?"

Should he lie or tell the truth? Jack dithered a moment, fixing his seat-belt into place and avoiding the other man's eye. "The case was a new scenario to me, an opportunity to put some of my Garda training to use."

"That's it?"

"And I went to college with one of their sons."

"Another officer with personal interest in this case."

Jack noticed a smile on Richard's lips. "Except my interest is a healthy one."

Without further conversation, Richard put a call through to the station and asked to speak to the superintendent. If they were going to follow every possible lead, they might as well do it properly.

Lucy was at home. She felt paralysed and unable to concentrate, a little juice and cereal being as much as she could manage for breakfast. All the time she expected someone to call and tell her that her husband was either hospitalised or in custody, but never released. Through the night she'd caught herself thinking over and over about Danny's strange behaviour since the fire.

When Stephen walked into the kitchen and explained about the call he'd received from Jack, she'd jumped as though someone had fired a shot overhead. Even though his words held promise, promise that somebody other than Danny was responsible for setting fire to their beautiful home, it didn't ease her distress. Carol had been the one to raise the alarm. And what on earth had Isobel to gain by striking a match? None of it made sense.

Phelim O'Brien put Jenny Ardle into the back of his police car. Before he closed the door, his gaze fell on her. Their eyes met. She smiled but looked malicious. Phelim frowned and banged the door, missing her withering look but noticing the horror on her parents' faces peering through the large bay window.

Jenny met her brother at the door of the interview room, he being escorted out along with his new solicitor, she being escorted in. Their exchange was brief and hushed. As things stood now, there was no-one either could protest to. She was alone with her truth and he was too exhausted to fight.

Phelim O'Brien knew the two classic ways to interrogate a suspect. The bad cop and the good cop. The bad cop intimidates, shouts, instils fear where possible. The good cop listens sympathetically, offers coffee and toilet breaks. He'd played bad cop with the brother. He'd have fun playing good cop with the sister.

"I had nothing to do with the fire," Jenny said when Phelim turned on the recorder.

"That's what we're here to find out. Should we take it from the beginning?" He paused and gave an eerie smile. "You've returned unexpectedly from London? Care to explain why?" He took a sip from his coffee, aware that hers was untouched.

Once Jenny began to talk, she couldn't be stopped. The recorder ran out before the interview.

Chapter 54

Lucy and Danny huddled together in the back of Stephen's car. Their ordeal had ended very suddenly when Danny was released without charge and advised to organise transport home. Bumping into his sister as he'd left had been a surprise but not a shock. Inspector O'Brien had apparently collected her in person – or so he'd taken delight in informing Danny. It was no accident how their paths had crossed. He could see it had been perfectly timed.

Assessing his helplessness and vulnerability in the situation, Danny had resisted the temptation to defend his sister, his only attempt of support being his offer to share the legal representative, which she'd categorically refused. She'd irritated him with a passion in that moment, acting as though she were invincible. He'd bit his lip, accepting her fate was out of his hands. Tired, cold and cramped, he'd scurried out of the station without a backward glance, a hot shower followed by a warm bed and a few hours' uninterrupted sleep his only desire. Everything else would have to wait.

Lucy's relief was palpable. If she sat any closer to Danny, she'd be on his lap! Her reaction to the phone call, when it had finally come, held a mixture of relief, gratitude and fury. The ordeal they – Danny in particular – had been put through was inexcusable and not something she'd forget in a hurry. Her concern for Jenny, however, was non-existent. She was morally and legally responsible for her actions. If it turned out she was guilty, then Lucy would happily watch the justice system dole out her punishment.

But for now, reunited with her husband once more, she believed they'd completed Act 1 of the theatre production they'd found themselves in but were nowhere near reaching *The End*.

Chapter 55

The roadblocks had been planned at short notice. Gardaí in the bigger stations along the route had been radioed the case details – the make and colour of the car, the number of people travelling, their revenue identifications and dates of births.

Richard and Jack sat before the duty superintendent and brought him up to speed on the case.

"Inspector O'Brien has a great many opinions but a worrying shortage of evidence," stated Richard. "He *claims* he has a theory but is offering nothing to back it up, basing his assumption on the myth of an insurance scam. If you scrutinise the trace results, you'll arrive at the same conclusion we have – the evidence suggests a female – a painted fingernail, long hairs and small prints. What's puzzling is why he's ignored these facts . . ."

Pause.

Jack's mouth went dry.

Richard sipped from the bottle of water he'd brought

with him, taking a moment to bask in the look of admiration on the younger officer's face.

The superintendent leaned his elbows on the arms of his swivel-chair and joined his hands, nodding at Richard as if he'd enjoyed his speech.

"So what you're saying is you think he's guilty of a set-up? A deception? A conspiracy theory? That *is* what you're insinuating? It's why you're both here? Am I right?" He looked from the senior officer to the junior.

Both made a funny movement with their heads but neither affirmed their agreement.

The superintendent left the room and came back with a single printed sheet. "The inspector's current suspect, Jennifer Ardle. She's being questioned as we speak. Danny Ardle was released a short while ago, disproving your theory. Jack, get a set of fingerprints from his sister and check for a match . . ." He turned to face Richard, shaking his head. "With your years of experience, I'd have thought you'd check the facts before casting dangerous aspersions around."

Richard's face had turned a deep shade of purple, clashing with his red hair. "I'd like to sit in on the questioning."

The superintendent frowned. "Why? To collect more evidence against O'Brien?"

Richard didn't answer directly. "I've been working with Phelim throughout, I'm anxious to follow through to the end. And let's face it, up to now he's been set on convicting Danny Ardle." Not to mention the fact that I was prepared to overlook plenty myself in return for a glowing recommendation. I'm in deep if Phelim senses I've switched sides.

Jack pushed back his chair and rose to his feet, cursing inwardly. Everything's gone pear-shaped. What would Stephen think if he knew he was testing his aunt's fingerprints?

"When you're done with that, Jack, get confirmation of her blood type," the superintendent added. "I'll organise female officers to examine for any cuts or scars, see if we can match the blood found at the scene."

Richard also got to his feet, the details of the case like dots in his head, a pattern forming and making him remember something. "We'll need to find out what she was wearing the day she visited," he said to Jack. "Send a car to her parents' house. Have them check her things. Find out her movements for the rest of the day. We're looking for a scorched garment, anything that looks like it was in contact with a naked flame. Don't rule anything out."

Jack remembered how hard he'd worked the previous evening and the lead he'd come across that morning. He'd given Stephen his word he'd do what he could. He wasn't about to acquiesce quite so easily. "Can we extend that courtesy to the Black household too?" The fact that their home had been practically cleared out could make it a fool's errand but it'd also make their search easier.

The superintendent sighed heavily, trying to decide which new recruits annoyed him more: the enthusiasts or the slackers.

"Get a warrant, seeing as your mind's set. And this time, try and do something that will make a difference."

Chapter 56

In the third hour of their journey, Isobel dozed off, her restless slumber brought to an abrupt end by Carol's sudden stop.

Through sleepy eyes she watched her mother roll down the window. "Why have the gardaí stopped us? Were you speeding, Mum? You promised . . ."

"Definitely not speeding. I've never been so careful to stay within the limits. I'm sure it's a routine tax and insurance check."

Isobel took her sunglasses from her lap and put them on, not in the mood for small talk with cheery gardaí.

"Told you," Carol mumbled as she watched him glance at the documents on her windscreen.

"Nice day for travelling," he commented when he came to the window.

"Sure is."

"Are you the registered owner of this vehicle?"

"Sure am," Carol answered.

"And your name please?"

"Lucy Ardle," she responded without blinking or changing her expression.

"Where have you travelled . . ." he began, breaking off suddenly when a white Honda Integra came speeding around the bend, accelerating even further when he spotted the Garda checkpoint (if there was any more speed left on the clock). Losing control he veered across the road, just missing Carol's car, exhaust fumes filling the air as he sped away from the scene.

The garda hurried back to his squad car and radioed for back-up. He turned on the siren in the Garda car and sped after the Honda Civic in the hopes of catching the reckless driver who'd recently been causing havoc in the local village, speeding dangerously through at all hours of the day and night.

Isobel sat motionless, the speed that her mother took off at clinging her to the seat. Carol's ringing mobile interrupted their silence, both women looking at each other in open surprise when Carol accepted the call and a familiar voice filled the interior of the car.

"Dad!"

"Eric!"

Chapter 57

Four people sat around the meeting table in the superintendent's office: the superintendent, Richard Collins, Jack Bowe and Phelim O'Brien.

Jack's day was not going well, the accusing glares the forensics sergeant was casting in his direction adding to his discomfort. If only they'd checked the status of the case *before* reporting their suspicion to the super, then things wouldn't be in such a mess now. And O'Brien wouldn't be beaming like a bloody Cheshire cat!

Phelim had welcomed the short-notice meeting, using it as an excuse to get away from Jennifer Ardle's whining. Overhearing the super on the phone to Richard earlier had been a stroke of luck – one of the few he could remember in recent times. He'd had to act fast. The horrified look on Danny's face when he'd marched his sister past him had been memorable. Although, much to his disgust, his questioning wasn't throwing up anything worthwhile. Still he was reluctant to let Jennifer go. Not yet. He hadn't given up his quest for revenge and had every intention of hurting Danny Ardle in any conceivable way.

Richard was growing increasingly agitated, regretting allowing the impetuous young garda to grate on his conscience, even if Jack's theories merely voiced what he'd already known to be true. Phelim O'Brien *wasn't* giving the case a fair hearing – anything but! The inspector was clever and devious. And judging by this morning's quick turnaround of suspects, he had his avenues well covered, leaving Richard in a very awkward position. Grovelling to Phelim had never been on his agenda but it was something he was prepared for if necessary.

The superintendent tapped his pen against his glass of water, demanding quietness. "Can we straighten out the confusion with the Ardle case please? Phelim, will you bring me up to speed, and then, Richard, I'll hear your theory."

Phelim cast a sly look at Richard, cleared his throat and pulled his notebook from his shirt pocket. There were damp patches on the underarms of his shirt. He hadn't bothered changing in a couple of days.

"Danny Ardle's been released without charge. His sister, on the other hand, is still being questioned. I'm waiting on her DNA and fingerprint results. Jack, you were looking after those. Any updates?"

Jack shook his head, his cheeks flushed. "Not yet."

The superintendent frowned. "It sounds to me, Phelim, as though your suspicions are predominantly based on assumptions and circumstantial evidence. I'm not happy you're holding people for so long based on very little tangible evidence. A sick man at that."

Phelim looked the superintendent squarely in the eye. "Both Danny and his sister had strong motive and opportunity and there are still plenty of questions to be answered."

He glanced at Richard, a sly look out of the corner of his eye that didn't go unnoticed by Jack.

"It's a reasonable assumption about Danny, but Jenny?" said Richard. "What could she possibly hope to achieve apart from revenge? Or the Blacks for that matter?"

The superintendent interrupted at this stage. "Any other findings apart from the hospital report?"

"We found a few laundry items in Black's house. I've sent them for analysis," Jack told him. He'd almost missed the white plastic bin when he'd gone with another officer to check the house, gaining access through an open downstairs window when the bell went unanswered. It was the stack of newspapers sitting on top that had actually drawn his attention to the bin. The untidy bundle looked totally out of place in a practically empty house, not something he felt anybody would bother hoarding in the circumstances.

"Anything show up?"

Before his question was answered, there was a knock on the door.

"We've received a call from the Galway traffic corps," a female garda explained when she stepped into the stuffy room. "There was a sighting of a similar car at a roadblock but there's appears to be a bit of confusion."

Jack urged her to explain. "But it's the correct make of car? Did they log the reg? Has it been checked?"

"The description and reg matches but not the driver's name. She gave her name as Lucy Ardle and that checks out."

Jack got to his feet. "Do you have a physical description of the driver? Is she still at the checkpoint?"

"No. The garda in question was interrupted unexpectedly at the scene. By the time he'd returned, she was long gone. They've followed her of course."

Jack's face contorted. "Damn! What a moron! Tell them to keep us updated."

"Yes, of course."

Phelim scratched his head, a nasty smile on his lips. He was enjoying watching them go around in circles. It would have been easy for him to clear up the mix-up with names – after all, spotting the Audi in the Ardle's garage had been a stroke of luck. He'd wanted to laugh out loud when Lucy told him about changing the ownership of the car. But why bother clarifying any of this to the officers around the table. More suspicion on the Ardles. Perfect. The more complicated it got, the better as far as he was concerned. He leaned back in his chair, folded his arms over his rotund stomach and watched the game unfold.

Carol stopped and filled her tank at a small petrol station, the smell of hot food assuaging her nostrils as she entered the shop to pay. Isobel had been eager to get on the road, refusing to allow them time to have any more than half a cup of coffee before setting out. Unable to resist the aroma of crispy bacon and spicy white pudding, Carol ordered oversized portions for both of them, her appetite making a welcome appearance for the first time in quite a while.

It must be the country air, she thought, queuing to pay for her purchases. She caught sight of Isobel in the passenger seat, her hair pulled into a tight ponytail, her side profile emphasising her strong bone structure and her distinct likeness to Eric. Carol inched her way along the queue, thinking about her life with Eric and wondering what he'd say when he found out she'd kept something as big as an inheritance from him. Would he resent her or understand? And then she caught herself up, realising that her indiscretion was nothing compared to what he'd kept secret from her. As she pondered on their pitiful situation, it came to her that she really wasn't angry with him. Not any more, not when it was pointless. When he eventually decided to return to Ireland, he might not be in a position to tell her how to live her life. Carol didn't understand the punishments involved in bankruptcy and unpaid loans so had no idea where this would end. She sighed heavily, raising her eyes to see a motorbike roar into the courtyard, her stomach lurching when she noticed the Garda logo on the back of the motorcyclist's jacket.

Oh shit, she thought, I shouldn't have taken off from that checkpoint without being waved on. Could he be following us? Guilt and panic overcoming her, she discarded the boxes of food on the sweet counter and walked swiftly through the out-door as the garda entered by the in-door.

"Didn't I see you with some takeaway breakfast, Mum?" Isobel glanced up from the magazine she'd been flicking through as Carol slipped the car into first gear and took off as inconspicuously as possible.

"Ah, I left it in the end. The queue was endless and the girl on the till was taking forever. It would have been stone cold by the time we got to eat it." Carol's voice belied any trace of the panic tightening her chest, her eyes scanning the rear-view mirror at every given opportunity, expecting blue flashing lights to appear any moment. She turned off the dual carriageway with a sense of relief, somehow feeling protected by the narrow country roads. She drove for five minutes before she exhaled properly, relief coursing through her that she hadn't been followed. She slackened her grip on the steering wheel and sank her tense body into the leather upholstery. *Running away from home at my age,* she thought, *will I ever have an easy mind again?*

Lucy helped Danny to take the long-awaited hot shower, an awkward business as they had to avoid getting his bandages wet, then left him to dress.

She went to the kitchen to put on water for coffee and then began buttering fresh white bread to make some of Danny's favourite sandwiches. When she was done, she sat down at the kitchen table and was thinking hard when he came back into the room. She studied his face, his eyes sunken with tiredness, his hair sticking out in all directions. He hadn't even bothered to comb it.

"Why don't you get back into bed and rest? I can bring a tray upstairs."

"Why don't you leave the tray here and join me?" He held out his hand.

Lucy allowed him to lead her upstairs but once they'd closed the door of their bedroom she ordered him to lie on his front, ensured he could breathe properly, and spent five minutes massaging his back.

"Turn over, Dan," she whispered in his ear, realising as she did that he was already fast asleep.

Lucy got up from the bed and went to the window.

The sea sparkled in the distance, a soft hue of sunlight flickering on the lighthouse tower. The euphoria of Danny's release had worn off. From what they'd been told, forensics had found more than enough to convict somebody. Unfortunately, they still had to catch that perpetrator. What raced through Lucy's mind was why the fire had been started in the first place. Who could hate us that much and why, she wondered, studying the hedgerow across from Delia's house, envying the wildlife hibernating within and wishing she too had immunity from the world around her.

"What's on that signpost, Isobel?" Carol was weary by now, her sense of direction askew.

This was their third time finding themselves at the same fork in the narrow country road. Their problems had begun ten minutes after they'd left the dual carriageway, every junction since similar to the one before.

"Ring Fort, is all it says, Mum. I told you that last time we drove through this junction."

"We'd better ask for directions."

"Have you seen the size of the dog in that yard? There's no way I'm walking past him!" Isobel took off her sunglasses and pointed toward the nearest bungalow.

"Shouldn't need to," Carol placated her daughter. "Here's a car now." She rolled down her window and flagged the driver down. "Can you point us in the direction of Gortmore by any chance? We've been going around in circles." She threw her hands in the air.

A clean-cut gentleman stepped out of the navy Ford Mondeo, leaning his elbow on the roof of Carol's Audi and peering through the driver's window.

"Not from around here, I take it?"

If we were we wouldn't be lost, Carol thought privately. "Afraid not." She forced herself to keep smiling.

"How far have you travelled?" he enquired.

What is this, she thought, *twenty questions*! "Been on the road a few hours," she answered non-commitally.

"Would you mind stepping out of the car, Madam?"

To say his question came as a surprise would be a serious understatement. "Excuse me?"

He reached into his pocket and produced Garda identification.

The engine of the car was still running, Carol's foot depressing the clutch, her hand on the gear knob pushing it into first gear . . .

"Don't even think about making another run for it."

In the passenger seat, Isobel began to weep, all the time shaking her head in disbelief.

"Shh," Carol whispered out of the side of her mouth before switching off the engine and turning to the plain-clothes officer.

"Are you the owner of this vehicle?"

"Yes, Garda." Her palms were sweaty.

"Name and address please?" Hearing the police radio coming to life, he strained to hear the muffled voice. But there was a lot of interference on airwaves and he failed to catch the gist of the alert message. Giving up, he returned his attention to the task on hand instead.

Carol's face flushed a bright red. "Lucy Ardle, Crosshaven, County Cork."

"And your driver's licence, please. I need to see verification."

His request shook her. The temptation to drive away

was overwhelming. "Let me just get it from my handbag."

"Mum, what's going on?" Isobel's expression was filled with fear, her nails digging into her mother's arm.

"Listen to me," Carol hissed. "Stay here and don't say one word. Leave the garda and the questions to me . . ."

"What if . . ." her daughter argued.

"Everything okay here?" The garda pulled open the driver's door, startling both women.

"Yes, of course. I was sure I'd left my licence in the glove compartment but I can't seem to find it now."

"Are you aware it's an offence *not* to carry your licence when driving, Lucy?"

Carol was fumbling in her handbag, turning her body away from the garda and twisting the nib on her silver pen to scrawl a few words on the outside of a torn envelope.

"Lucy, can you please step out of the car?"

"Mum!" Isobel's squeak was tinged with terror.

"What?" She let the pen fall into the bottom of her bag, slipping a scrunched-up piece of paper on to her daughter's lap.

"He wants you to step out, Mum."

Carol jerked her head up, smiled at the garda and stepped out of the car.

"Bring whatever identification you have with you."

Seeing no other way, she carried her handbag with her as she left the car, the words she whispered to her daughter a hurried decision on her part, the instructions in her note crystal clear.

"Anything with your name and address on it will do for now. Then I'll allow you forty-eight hours to produce your tax and insurance documents at the station." He folded his arms across his chest and exhaled through his nostrils. "Now can you tell me why you left in such a hurry?"

Carol's heart stopped, hung unmoving inside her chest. She found her brain unravelling, like a ball of wool twirling unaided, any attempt she made to reel it back in useless. "Everything is so messed up . . ."

The garda shook his head. "Save the story and tell me, is this your first offence?"

She shuddered at his mention of the word 'offence'. Her voice croaked, her forehead creasing into a deep etched frown. "Offence?"

"Doing a drive-off from a petrol station without paying is considered an offence in my book!"

"Petrol station? Did I drive off without paying?" She was giddy with relief, reaching into her purse and pulling out a fifty-euro note. "This should more than cover it. I'm sorry. I've been very distracted lately. I am *so* embarrassed."

"Give me a moment while I make a call," he instructed, needing to verify more detail with the petrol station in question and decide whether it was worth a long trail of paper work to charge the apologetic woman in front of him.

Carol didn't mind how much time he took. She watched him stroll past her car, her face contorting in dismay when Isobel pushed open the passenger door and called after him.

"No, Isobel." Her first attempt to get her daughter's attention was a whisper, her second a caged lion's roar as she watched the garda's eyes widen in bewilderment. Panic dogged its way through Carol. It took all of her powers to get her legs to move. By the time she reached her daughter's side, she was collapsing in a faint on the side of the road, the crumpled scrap of envelope falling from her grasp.

Chapter 58

"What am I looking for?" Jack Bowe ran his hands through his hair, muttering aloud and staring at the fax report. The prints found at the scene weren't a match for Jennifer Ardle's. Whoever lit the match in that house was still walking – or driving – around thinking they were going to get away with a serious crime.

"Bowe, there's a phone call for you!"

He left the machine room to take the call. "Garda Jack Bowe speaking."

Richard passed by at that moment, his sleeve brushing against Jack's elbow. Jack covered the mouthpiece and called after Richard, noticing his ashen complexion when he turned to face him. "They've found something on the garment we took from Blacks!" He thanked his caller, asked him to fax on a written report, and caught up with Richard. "Should I bring this info straight to the super rather than jumping to assumptions again?"

"A bit of friendly advice," Richard cautioned. "He's

more interested in getting the suspects than their clothing! Follow up with traffic control first, don't rely too heavily on others to do the job for you. It takes your eye off the ball." And with that, he took his long brown gabardine from the coat-stand and made for the exit doors, his expectations of imminent promotion disappearing into the wind as he stepped outside.

Jack took his advice and called the Galway division for a traffic update. His timing, as it turned out, was spot on.

"We've had a call in just now as it happens."

"Yeah?" Jack waited patiently, his eyes opening wide as he listened to the detail. "No way? And it's definitely the same car?" This was the last thing he'd expected. Was Lady Luck shining on him after all? "I don't suppose you could email the video footage to this address?" He called out the email address.

Making a cup of strong coffee, he went to his computer and stared at the screen, getting to work immediately when the email came through. Watching carefully, he held his breath while the image came to life on the screen. He was pleased with the result. Though it didn't link directly to the scene of the fire, it did fill in a part of the gaping hole in his investigative work. At least now he could pinpoint Carol and Isobel's whereabouts *and* he had more than enough reason to bring them both in for questioning. Right on queue his mobile beeped – Stephen texting for an update.

"Soon", Jack replied, returning to the machine room and grabbing a few black and white stills from the printer, his concentration so intently focused on the pages that he walked right into Phelim O'Brien, their collision causing the CCTV footage to fall from his hands.

Both men stooped to retrieve them, Phelim's shovel-like hand grasping them a millisecond before Jack. He glanced at them, screwed the pages in a ball and dropped them silently onto the floor.

"Turning into a proper little detective, aren't you?" Phelim sneered, disdain curling the corners of his mouth.

"Just trying to do my job, Inspector." Jack's face reddened, revealing how intimidated he felt alongside his glowering superior.

Phelim bellowed at the young recruit. "I'm leading this case. Now butt out unless you're asked in future!" He kicked the rolls of paper out of his way and stormed towards his office.

Jack stared after him, intimidation turning to disgust. He hadn't trained in Templemore to be bullied, hadn't pored over a lengthy thesis on the unfairness of the justice system to become a key player in it himself. First and foremost he was a defender of the law and God help me, he thought, I'll do my utmost to find a way around this obnoxious monster. And starting as he meant to continue, he stooped to retrieve his CCTV images, found a quiet corner to study them and decide what he should do next.

Chapter 59

During the entire procedure of transporting Carol and Isobel from the rural crossroads in Gortmore to Carrigaline Garda Station, neither said a word to their escorts. Two uniformed gardaí had come to get them. Mother and daughter had been ordered to travel in the unmarked Garda car while, much to Carol's disgust, an accompanying officer was leading the journey in her precious Audi.

From Carol's perspective, too much had already been said and despite her outward silence, conversations raged inside her head.

Isobel's fainting episode had come right *after* she'd blurted out the first part of her admission. The problem was that Carol couldn't be sure what she'd said. With a garda separating them in the back seat, she hadn't been able to question her daughter to any extent.

It had been decided that the Audi would be delivered to Carol's home and then they'd continue to the Garda Station for questioning.

And right when Carol and Isobel thought their day couldn't possibly get any worse, there was a welcome party waiting in the driveway: the bailiffs had chosen that day to arrive and take ownership of their home and what remained of their belongings.

The sight broke Carol's resolve. She put her head in her hands and wept, anguish and strain leaping to the forefront, her coping mechanisms disintegrating. Seeing her home invaded had been too much.

In contrast, Isobel sat ramrod straight in the back of the car, maintained a stiff upper lip and averted her eyes from the harrowing scene. Succeeding in a male-dominated field had taught her about survival in the most extreme circumstances. Pining for something that was already gone was a waste of time. Concentrating on what was coming next was a lot more important.

Jack stayed out of Phelim's way, at least until he'd received proper confirmation that Carol and Isobel Black were being brought in. Ensuring there were two free interview rooms, he went to the front public area to wait, mulling the case over and over in his head. Which one is guilty, he wondered. Mother or daughter? And the most interesting question of all, what motivated such an act? On impulse, he made his way to the super's office, knocking twice on the door and waiting until he was invited in.

Breathless, he asked to be allowed sit in on the questioning.

The superintendent was a man in his early fifties, grey since his teens, tanned from his hours on the golf course and wise from the experiences he'd gained during his years in the force.

"With two running concurrently, I don't see why not," he answered. "Sit in on the daughter's one, she might be more at ease with somebody her generation."

"Thanks, sir." He made to leave, the super's next comment holding him in the room a moment longer.

"The extra work you've done on this case is noted, Jack. Now tell me, is Inspector O'Brien still around?"

"Yes, I think so."

"Tell him not to leave until I've had a word, please."

Jack nodded and left. The last thing on earth he wanted to do was speak to the inspector but he was not about to ignore the superintendent's request. As he made his way to his office, he couldn't help wondering what the meeting between his superiors would be about and whether there would ultimately be a knock-on consequence for the rest of them working in the station.

Reaching Phelim's door, he paused a moment before knocking, the superintendent's words repeating in his head. '*Extra work*', he'd thanked him for, advised him it had been '*noted*'. What if the inspector wheedles his way out of this? What if he turns the tables and suggests I was interfering just to get the heat away from Danny Ardle? His knuckles connected with the wooden door, the dead thud of his single knock sounding forlorn in the empty corridor.

Chapter 60

Isobel stared after her mother, watching as she was led from the Garda waiting room. When they'd arrived at the station, they'd both given a DNA swab and blood sample. She had been instructed to remain seated, that somebody would be with her in a short few moments while her mother was ordered away. They hadn't been allowed any time alone, still had no opportunity to exchange conversation, apart from the few loaded looks she'd received from her mother. Though the exit door was close, there wasn't a hope of sneaking past the eagle-eyed female garda who'd been placed there. Isobel's memory as to what happened in the moments before her fainting episode was unclear, her mother's scribbled note about what she should do vivid in her mind. Could she go through with her mother's wishes? Would she able to follow through with the consequences? She couldn't be sure. The alternative would undo years of effort, would undermine the mountains she'd climbed where others had failed. Under the circumstances, she thought, crossing one knee over the other and swinging her leg, regardless of what choice I make the outcome will be harrowing.

As Carol waited for her ordeal to begin, she worried incessantly about Isobel. A female officer sat at the table beside her, two males opposite, a large stack of paper between them. Then the door opened and a red-haired man with glasses entered the room, the other officers instantly taking from the stack of papers. Progress, she thought. We're finally going to get this ridiculous ordeal underway.

"Sergeant Richard Collins." He nodded in Carol's direction, pushing his glasses up onto the bridge of his nose.

Carol's face and eyes were impassive. She didn't move a muscle and was surprised by how calm she felt. Is this how condemned prisoners felt when they waited for the gallows, she wondered.

Richard looked at her expectantly before dropping his head to the documents in front of him, scanning an entire page and then turning to face her again. Following a brief silence, he cleared his throat. "Let's proceed directly to the events surrounding the Ardle property in Crosshaven. We shall attempt to bring clarity to how and when you noticed the house was on fire. Can you take us through that again, please?"

A couple of minutes passed. Carol didn't respond.

"Are we to interpret your silence to mean you don't want to answer my questions?"

Carol looked at him. "I would like to speak to my daughter."

"We've already told you. That's not possible right now."

She let out a long sigh. "Why am I here? What am I being accused of?"

"You haven't been accused of anything as yet. As I said we're trying to clarify a few details first."

"Could you please repeat the question?"

"How did you notice that the Ardle house was on fire?"

Carol lapsed into silence again.

"Was it a mere coincidence that you saw it? Were you driving past?"

"I don't believe in coincidence."

"It must be tough losing everything when those around seem to be flourishing?"

Carol thought for a moment. "No. What's tough is some people's attitude to another's misfortune!"

"Do you have anything to say about the vapour traces found on a jacket taken from your house?"

She shrugged. "Only that the jacket's mine."

Richard sat back in his chair. He'd been a member of the forensic team for quite some time. Suspects didn't usually acquiesce with so little fuss. He rose from his chair. "We'll suspend for a moment." He turned to the female garda. "Erin, I'll leave you to take a full statement of admittance from Mrs Black."

In another office further along the corridor, a similar line of questioning was getting underway.

"Did you go to a hospital to be treated for smoke and heat-related injuries you sustained in a fire?"

Isobel opened her mouth to answer, her pallet drying, her throat withholding the words. "Certainly not."

Jack watched with interest. So far he'd been more of a spectator than a participant. He eyed Isobel carefully, watching her eye twitch every few seconds, watching her worry the hard scab inside her wrist.

"This is how it is. We have already gathered more than enough forensic evidence to prove your presence at the scene. Your visit to Beaumont hospital with an inflamed throat was found to be a direct result of fume-inhalation. More than a coincidence surely."

Her voice was clear and ice cold. "It wasn't me. I didn't do it." She dug her fingernails into her wrist, bright red blood spurting from the open scab. She'd reopened her wound for the umpteenth time.

Jack slowly got to his feet, whispered something to his nearest colleague and left the room.

The interrogation continued in his absence.

"We have no interest in hearing your story unless it's confirmation of what you already admitted in Gortmore earlier today. You know who set fire to Sycamore Lodge. But the question we would like an answer to is *why*? What possesses someone to set fire to a house with the owner sleeping inside?"

"I already told you I didn't set fire to anything. But as I said from the outset, I can tell you who did."

For a split second, the room was still.

"Go on then. Tell us."

"My mum, Carol Black."

In the station meeting room, Phelim O'Brien was being questioned at length, the superintendent in charge surprised at his outspoken admittance.

He had entered the superintendent's office with a

brash attitude, the welcome he received from the Southern Region Garda Unit halting him in his tracks. There was no shaking of hands – only shaking of heads.

"We could begin by having coffee," Sergeant Richard Collins suggested. He'd just joined the sombre group, the scorn on Phelim's face making him regret his sympathetic attempt at easing into his interrogation. Fixing the grey-and-peach-coloured tie he'd chosen at random to match his salmon-coloured shirt, he opened the detailed file he'd brought with him and shoved aside any notion he'd had of softening the blow for the inspector he'd once respected. Pushing photocopies around the table, he ensured all present had full data. "Will I recap on the forensic findings?"

"Give Phelim a copy first," the superintendent instructed, wanting to witness first hand how he reacted to the information he'd purposely overlooked. He studied his haggard face, his defeatist demeanour, deciding there was no easy way apart from bulldozing right to the crux of the issue. "Let's start with the history between you and Danny Ardle, Phelim, and the personal grievance that has clouded your professional judgement."

"Don't waste your time going over old ground. I won't make this difficult for you or waste any more of your valuable time," Phelim told them right from the start, his tone laced with scorn. "I'm pleading guilty as charged. *He's* only suffered a bit and he'll get his life back on track. Me, on the other hand, my life is over, has been ever since –"

"So you're admitting that you just wanted to make Danny Ardle's life a living hell for as long as you could get away with it?"

"You could put it like that, I s'pose."

"But why deliberately pervert the course of justice, Phelim? Why jeopardise your future? Your pension?" The superintendent was amazed one of his best inspectors had stooped to this level.

Phelim remained silent.

"Ardle will have to decide for himself whether he wants to make a formal complaint against you for harassment and false interrogation."

The inspector shrugged.

"You were days away from retirement, freedom only a short few weeks away."

Finally the super's words sparked his rage. Phelim banged his fist on the table, glaring at his boss. "Freedom? You don't know the meaning of the word. Try spending day after day visiting a convalescent home, pushing a wife you love but don't know any more around in a wheelchair, talking but getting no answers, not even a smile. A prison sentence if I get one will make a welcome release."

Richard saw no further need for his assistance. As he left the room, he wondered at the ease of guilty pleas in the station that afternoon. Too much of a coincidence, he thought. And it wasn't Phelim's admission he doubted.

Chapter 61

Eric Black leaned his head against the seat, waiting for the Aer Lingus flight to take off. *"Good afternoon, ladies and gentlemen, this is Captain Wilson speaking. I'd like to welcome you on board this flight to Cork Airport . . ."*

Eric glanced sideways at the burly policeman who'd escorted him from Florida to London and sat beside him now on the final leg of his journey home to Cork where he'd be handed over to the Garda Síochána and would receive further instructions from there.

Once again, he'd been offered the privilege of one phone call. And this time, he'd called his wife. Though she'd barged at him for his errant ways and screamed at him about the mess they were in, he detected the tiniest shred of promise that perhaps one day in the future there might be hope for them again. That would be enough to keep him going for now, would see him through his days behind bars should it come to that.

Chapter 62

Matt glanced through the *New York Times*, the black print blurring before his eyes, the millions of words of text failing to register. His eyes stung. He'd lain awake all night on the sofa, Heidi tossing and turning in their double bed.

"Pancakes for an Irishman, lashings of golden syrup," Roy announced, carrying Matt's plate aloft in true New York style.

He folded the newspaper, the long-awaited breakfast pancakes barely bringing a glimmer of a smile to his lips. The fault didn't lie with the aroma of steaming pancakes wafting around him, the sticky syrup sweet on his pallet as he savoured his first mouthful.

Roy arrived with a cup of boiled water and a teabag on the saucer, pausing for a moment when he placed it in front of Matt. The delicatessen was hectic, a place of efficient chaos as it was most midweek mornings, the staff behind Roy's counter working feverishly, smiling and interacting with their customers while filling a record amount of breakfast and takeaway orders in the shortest time.

"What do you intend to do?" Roy tidied the *New York Times*, allowing Matt more room to eat.

"I was hoping you'd have the answer to that." Matt half smiled. He was no further on than he'd been the previous evening when he'd divulged his problems to Roy over a plate of jelly donuts and a several mugs of hot chocolate.

Roy glanced around and checked his staff could manage the waiting clients. He pulled off his hygiene gloves and dropped them into the waste-disposal bin. He felt a sudden tenderness as he often did for customers who shared confidences. If he were to believe every word Matt had told him last night, he'd had enough of his girlfriend's problems and needed to focus on his family's loss instead. To Roy, however, he resembled an injured sparrow nursing a broken wing.

"Pancakes not living up to your expectation?"

Matt turned to him and laughed. "You don't need my confirmation that your pancakes are second to none. It's me, I'm afraid. For the first time that I can remember I've lost my appetite."

"Bah! Nothing should come between a man and his pancakes. You need to wise up and make a decision. There are no guarantees with anything – you've got to take a chance sometimes. And be honest with yourself about that sexy redhead. Don't give up because she's got a bit of mystery about her."

Matt chewed and listened, Roy's jovial nature and straight-talking advice lifting his spirits and reawakening his taste buds to a point where they could appreciate the quality food in his mouth.

"What're you suggesting, Roy?"

"Which side of the bed did you sleep on last night?"

Matt stuffed a forkful of pancake into his mouth so he wouldn't have to answer.

Roy nodded knowingly. "No wonder you were my first customer this morning. You hear any more from your family? What's going on back there? Your dad's name cleared yet?"

Finding it impossible to get comfortable on the couch the previous night, his knees cramping and pins and needles making his toes tingle, Matt had pored over everything Stephen had confessed, his primary concern being for his father and what he must be going through. When he'd done torturing himself about the sorry state of events, he'd mulled over Heidi's bombshell. Expecting an interrogation about their relationship when he'd returned to the apartment, he'd been horrified to find Heidi staring numbly through the window, deep in thought. Jumping with a start when he'd come to stand beside her, she'd spilled out the horrifying news she'd received on ringing Isobel, tears falling on her cheeks when she'd explained about them running away to Galway and begging him to help her find a job so she could stay close to her son. And Matt. But the pause before she'd mentioned Matt had hurt.

"Matt? What about your dad? Has his name been cleared?" Roy repeated.

He snapped back to the present. "Still waiting for my brother to call with the latest update."

"Well, there's nothing you can do about that then. In

the meantime, you have got to follow your heart. Remember what I told you last night? There was only ever one girl who made my heart flutter, made me confuse ingredients, caused my pastry to burn in the oven. And I let her go. And with her went my dreams of owning a chain of high-class restaurants." He waved his arms around the deli, the crowd after thinning out a little now. "See this place? Roy's Deli?"

Matt nodded soberly, following Roy's gaze around the premises, watching as Roy's eyes stopped to scan the menu board, recognising a wistfulness he hadn't seen there before.

"Roy's Deli is nothing to the great plans I'd been hatching. Turning my back on the chemistry in our relationship quenched the fire inside me. I made the biggest mistake of my life."

Matt sighed. "But it wasn't your fault – you said her father denounced you, barred you from his land, insulted Latin Americans . . ."

"Her *father* did but *she* ran after me, begged me to stay and prove to her family our love was real . . ." His voice trailed off, his black eyes seeing a beautiful young woman clutching at his arm, pleading with him to stay.

"And you strode off into the sunset without a backward glance?" There was still some pancake left, a drain of syrup congealing on top. He dropped his cutlery onto the plate and pushed it away from him, waiting for his companion to respond.

"Only after I'd broken her father's nose and he'd punched me in the mouth!"

Matt shuddered at the thoughts of breaking Eric's nose, although landing a fist on Julian's smug grin mightn't be such a bad idea now that he thought about it. "You think I should take a chance on Heidi, despite the added complication of her son, despite her sudden disappearing act?"

Speaking in a grave and serious tone, Roy pointed to his chipped front tooth. "Every morning I have to look at this reminder of *my* stubborn pride." He lifted the plate, eyeing the corner of pancake he'd left at the edge. "A woman who takes your appetite away is a rare commodity. Don't you forget that." He resumed his day's work, leaving his customer to ponder on his advice. Ultimately, the decision could only be Matt's.

Chapter 63

"Your mother set fire to the house, she says," Richard Collins said.

"That's that then," the young woman remained motionless, her face bleached of colour.

"She was too cut up to explain her motivation but told us you'd explain," he went on.

Isobel's forehead creased. "I don't have the explanation. I'm not my mother's keeper."

"I'm not disputing that. Just hoping you can help us piece things together." He removed his glasses and polished the lenses on the sleeve of his shirt, popping the spectacles back on his nose once more.

"Not possible," she said.

"Not even when she was calling the fire brigade. She didn't tell you why. Or was it you who dialled the number? When you knew she was inside the house."

"No. Calling the fire brigade was her idea. Believe me, it was all Mum's idea."

"Why is she relenting now? Why isn't she denying it?"

"Because in her opinion the game is up. She misread a situation, mistook one incident for another."

Richard shook his head. "It's very big of your mother to take the rap for you, very big indeed. But she's overlooked a few slight issues."

"How dare you!" Isobel was indignant.

"We have evidence putting you at the scene too, stronger evidence than the traces found on your mother's tweed jacket."

She shut her mouth. They have their admission, she thought, and they're still wading in for more. Why can't they just stop?

"I'm going to talk to your mother now. Any message? Will I tell her thank you but you're big enough to carry your own mistakes? That you're ready for some admissions of your own?"

Isobel pursed her lips.

"You can't fool science, Miss Black. I'd advise you to drop this charade now while you still can. Traces of your blood," he pointed to the document Jack had left on the table earlier, "match those found at the scene. Catch your wrist on something in your hurry to dispose of evidence?"

"What is wrong with you? I've told you it was me. I was jealous, confused. I wanted to hurt my neighbours, give them a taste of what it was like being down and out."

Erin concentrated on the page in front of her, the biro moving across the page, her neat handwriting transcribing Carol's comments word for word. "But the evidence tells us otherwise. Your call to the emergency services tells a different tale too."

"I panicked. I had set the fire when I woke up to the danger I had put everybody in, including myself. Of course I called the emergency services."

"We have your daughter on CCTV, in a sorry state as she entered the Cork Airport terminal."

"Isobel had to catch a flight. She was upset. She'd just heard her father had lost everything, that when she got back she might not have a home any more."

"Your protectiveness for your daughter is admirable but we can't let you go down for this," Erin insisted. "The perpetrator must be caught and punished. And it's not you, despite the lies you're telling. Taking the rap doesn't excuse the wrongdoer – it just puts you in trouble too. You do realise you are perverting the course of justice? You understand that leading police officers astray is a crime?"

"I started the fire." Carol didn't waver but her eyes misted over when the door opened and her daughter was led into the room.

"Mum . . ."

Jack pulled out a chair for Isobel, placing her next to her mother.

"Isobel . . ." Carol reached out for her hand, squeezed it until her knuckles hurt.

The daughter stared at her mother's weary face, shocked by the degree of vulnerability in her eyes. It was as though a light-bulb went on in the room, waking her from a harrowing nightmare. How can I let her take the blame? How can I continue my life while she withers in an institution? She's not a survivor. I am. Nothing I do will bring back what I had, will wipe the stupid error of judgement from my brain. No sentence can punish me more than I will punish myself. The axe has fallen on me. I might as well have guided the handle.

Over their heads, Jack and Richard exchanged a look, both intrigued by the heightened emotion in the room and prepared to stay all night if that's what it took to find out why the calculating woman in front of them had splashed white spirits on her neighbour's files and bed linen and watched them go up in flames.

As it happened, neither officer had to burn the midnight oil. Isobel had come to a decision, dropped her gaze to the floor and began to speak, barely taking time to draw breath until she'd finished.

"I could have lost my job."

"Speak up, Isobel," Jack encouraged, pressing the play button on the recorder.

"Oh Isobel, please don't do this to yourself!" Carol's voice quivered.

But her daughter was beyond reason. The weight she'd carried in her chest for the past week was in danger of choking her. "I used my position in Revenue to help Dad out of several tight scrapes."

Jack and Richard exchanged a glance. "Go on," they said simultaneously.

"Dad sub-contracted work to Danny Ardle but when it came to paying his portion of VAT, he didn't submit his return. Danny never trusted Dad, demanded proof of payment so that his company would never be dragged into anything dishonest."

The jigsaw was piecing together for Jack now. "You organised as much proof as he required, I take it. Used your status in Revenue to document the evidence and send it to Ardle Construction."

Her eyes were like stone. "The amounts were sizeable, phenomenal loss to Revenue. I organised the reports. I made sure to delete the electronic trail from the server. But in my job, I know there's no such thing as completely getting rid of anything. Everything is traceable." She paused at this point and lifted her eyes, looking from one to the other, demanding their attention before continuing.

Carol kept shaking her head, the venom in her daughter's tone shocking.

Jack was writing furiously, Richard listening attentively and waiting for Isobel to continue.

"When Dad called to say he'd lost everything, I knew instantly there'd be an investigation. I had no choice . . ." She looked directly at her mother. "I'd worked too hard to allow anyone ruin what I'd become." Her mouth twisted into something between a smile and a sneer. "I'm in Revenue long enough to know what happens in situations like ours. Every deal, every document is scrutinised. Ardle Construction's dealings with Dad were numerous. I wanted to protect myself. I slipped out of our house – my mother thought I was upstairs – I just ran and ran to Sycamore Lodge and slipped in the back door. The house was quiet, the television the only sound –"

"Isobel!" Carol was shocked into speech. "You told me there was no-one in the house!"

Isobel ignored her mother's outburst. "I'd baby-sat Stephen and Matt. I knew Danny's office was off the bedroom. The computer was switched on. I hacked into his email account, distorted the settings and deactivated the account. I changed his user permissions, encrypting his files, making them impossible to open or read. The filing cabinet was unlocked. I pulled open drawer after drawer, fumbling with files. There was no order to follow. It was impossible to find the docs I was looking for . . ."

"Isobel!" Carol's exclamation interrupted her but only for a moment.

"Mum, you know how important my career is. I've earned my position, damn it! I couldn't let it slip away from me. Not for anybody."

"Can you tell us what happened next?" Richard intervened, anxious to get her to finish her account before she had a change of heart.

"His filing cabinet was a mess. I hadn't a clue where to start, couldn't remember how many statements and reports I'd sent out. Time was against me. The smell of fresh paint was overwhelming and I noticed a bottle wrapped in newspaper in the corner of the room – it was white spirits – obviously the bottle had been left behind after a painting job – it was as though it had been sent to me . . ."

Her eyes glazed over. To the others in the room, her calculating assessment of the situation that evening was without question. Her voice held no trace of remorse.

"And did you just happen to have a cigarette lighter in your pocket?"

Isobel shook her head. "Lucy was forever telling Mum she didn't think she could survive without the sneaky cigarettes she kept in the bathroom. Her hiding place was pathetic. Once the lighter was in my hands, I knew what I must do. I spilled the files on to the floor, kicked them around, set them alight . . ."

"But why didn't you leave then? Get out before doing more damage? Why set fire to the bedroom too?"

"To divert attention from the files, confuse the motivation." She was staring at the floor now, as though she was talking to herself about somebody else, as though she were a third party looking on. "In my defence, it was self protection . . ."

Richard had the confession he required. "Isobel Black," he began, "I'm arresting you on a multiple charge of arson and endangering a life . . ."

Jack heaved a sigh of relief, his softer side unable to ignore the weeping mother in the room. But he refrained from any further involvement. Now that Phelim O'Brien's theories had been disproved, he could rest easy and wear his badge with pride and confidence. Times like these, he loved his job.

Chapter 64

Lucy and Danny had just turned out the bedside light when the muffled doorbell chime filtered up to the first floor. They were exhausted and not in the mood for entertaining. Stephen shouted from the bottom of the stairs and, hearing who was at the door, Lucy was off the bed and standing in the living area in the space of time it took him to finish the sentence.

"Well? Has there been an arrest?" She looked expectantly at Garda Jack Bowe, hoping he'd brought her good news. She wouldn't rest until everything was finalised, not putting it past the Blacks to worm their way out of this unscathed.

"You've nothing more to worry about. Forensic evidence put Isobel at the scene. She's admitted everything."

A sob caught in Lucy's throat, tears misting her eyes, betrayal slicing through her. "I still can't believe she set fire to our house. And Carol in on it . . ."

"Mrs Black was just an accessory after the fact – the fire had been set before she knew what her daughter was up to. Nor did she know there was anyone in the house, it appears."

Danny appeared at her side. "Jenny's been released, I presume?"

Lucy glanced sideways at her husband, ashamed she hadn't given her sister-in-law a second thought. But feeling his arm slip around her shoulder, she knew he understood.

Jack removed his Garda hat and placed it on the side table beside an ornate bronze lamp. "On her way home to Clonakilty in a squad car. Can you believe she demanded transport?"

Stephen, Danny and Lucy exchanged a knowing look, all three nodding their heads. "Yes," Danny replied for all of them. "Dare I ask about O'Brien?"

Jack threw a glance in Stephen's direction, remembering his comradeship when he'd felt lost in UCC, deciding he could trust his old friend with the truth despite the inspector's official entitlement to confidentiality – even if he didn't deserve it in Jack's opinion. "I'll tell you in confidence. He resigned early, took the super's advice apparently and left on medical grounds. He only had two weeks to go anyway. By all accounts, there's a disciplinary action pending. He left without a fight."

"I'm just so relieved we can finally get on with our lives," Lucy announced, bursting into tears and collapsing on to the sofa.

Danny felt a sudden chill as he pondered on 'what if'. What if Stephen hadn't gone to college with Jack? What if Jack hadn't been a decent enough guy to go the extra mile on their behalf? The answers didn't bear thinking about. "He's a bad egg, that O'Brien, has been for years.

Is he going to walk away with a full state pension? Will it be overlooked that he covered up evidence and tried to frame me, for no other reason than revenge?"

"There'll be an enquiry," Jack answered honestly, "but you know how long these things take. He could be pushing up daisies before it comes to trial – if ever." Phelim O'Brien's story had been spreading through Carrigaline Garda Station, rumours rampant about where it would end and the shocking example his behaviour had given to the younger members of the force.

Lucy clutched Danny's arm, her eyes pleading when he turned to face her. "Let the authorities do their job, Danny. The important thing is we're free to do whatever we please."

For the sake of peace, Danny held out a hand to Jack. "I don't know what we would have done without you. Or how this would have turned out."

"Not at all. Stephen did all the work, just used me as a catalyst to speed up the formalities."

Stephen shook his head, reaching out to pat him on the back. "Your modesty is admirable, Jack, but seriously you deserve all the credit, and I'll be telling them that down the station."

Jack's blush started at the base of his neck, running all the way to his forehead. "I'd best be off," he said. "Nice catching up with you again, Stephen. We'll meet for a pint before you go back."

"Lose the uniform though," Stephen laughed, already looking forward to a proper catch-up.

"One more thing," Danny asked earnestly. "How long before I can get my men into the house to make a start on the repairs? My sister-in-law needs her house back."

"Another few days at most," Jack replied. "I'll be in

touch as soon as possible." He paused. "Oh, Mr Ardle, there's one more box I'd like to tick if only for my own satisfaction . . ."

"Yes?"

"The insurance? You did have cover after all for the house?"

Danny looked shamefaced. "Yes, the business insurance covered it but unfortunately my poor wife was unaware of the fact and I didn't have the wits to tell her."

"I'll never forgive him," said Lucy, looking like she half-meant it. "Nor my son either as he suspected that was the case but he never told me!"

As soon as he'd left, Gloria joined her daughter, son-in-law and grandson in the room, her face ashen. She'd heard every word. "Did I hear him right? That Carol Black's daughter started the fire?"

Lucy and Danny looked at each other, silently agreeing not to lie to her.

"Yes, Mum, that's how it's looking." Lucy sank into the couch, hugging her knees to her chest.

"What is the world coming to? When you can't trust a young woman?" She shook her head in disbelief, moving towards the couch to sit beside her daughter. "If women stayed at home like they did long ago, there'd be none of this competitive business. They'd be content to put a good meal on the table every evening."

"Brave statement, Gloria," Danny responded. "Even I wouldn't chance slandering women like that."

Gloria tutted loudly, holding back her retort and changing the subject. "Where's Ellie, Stephen?"

"Having a rest, Nan. Jet lag has finally caught up with her and we've only got a few more days before we go back. She'd really like to see a little of the area – other than the inside of this house – before we do go back so she wants to be on form for it."

"You won't stay on then?" She daren't look in Lucy's direction in case she bit her head off for interfering.

"Not this time. Who knows in the future though?" Stephen answered truthfully, succeeding in reassuring his grandmother (and his parents) that a day might come when he'd be back on home ground.

Danny was still on edge, anxious to cut all ties with the Blacks as quickly as possible. "Get those lock-ups emptied for me tomorrow, Stephen, please. Dump *their* furniture anywhere you like but get it off my property. And first thing in the morning, call the office in Shannon and cancel that change-of-ownership arrangement for the Audi. What they've done to us makes my skin crawl. After that you might come with me to the construction site – I need an update."

Gloria also had a request for her grandson. "Will you do me one favour before you go please, Stephen?"

"Anything, Nan?"

"Shift those tenants out of my house so your mum and dad can move in until their own place is ready. Otherwise I can see Danny camping out in the garage!"

"Ah, Gloria, there's no need for that," Danny insisted, although if he were honest there was nothing he'd like better than a bit of peace and quiet. "Lucy and I can rent somewhere."

"You'll do no such thing," Gloria said firmly. "Stephen is the smart one in the family. He's good with contracts and the likes and will understand the lease and how we can get the tenants to move out as soon as possible. Then we'll give the place a good clean and you and Lucy can keep it aired for me."

"And what about you, Mum?" Lucy dared ask. Poor Delia would need her space too.

Gloria stole a look at Delia. "If I'm getting under your sister's feet, there's nothing stopping me going back to Kinsale. We'll see how it goes. Don't look so worried, Lucy," she giggled. "It's not forever. As soon as Sycamore Lodge is ready and you're reinstated again, I'm moving back home. I've decided I can do it alone and I'm actually looking forward to living in my own home again, as well as keeping up to date with all the goings-on in Crosshaven."

"You can keep me posted, Nan," Stephen laughed, planting a kiss on her cheek.

"And don't think I haven't noticed that girl of his is expecting," his grandmother scolded.

All this without drawing breath! Lucy smothered a smile, blushing instead that her mother had guessed correctly. "You're right, Mum. Ellie is pregnant with your great-grandchild."

Stephen was remorseful. "I'll set you up on a computer with Skype. Then you'll be able to see me and the baby when we're talking on the phone."

Gloria looked confused but refused to admit her ignorance. "Nonsense. You'll have to do better than that. You'll have to bring that baby home at least once a year. Great grandparents have their entitlements, you know!"

The ringing doorbell interrupted Gloria's flow.

"Tony," Delia exclaimed, her cheeks flushing a dark shade of red, her hand flying to her mouth. With the excitement of Danny's release, she'd forgotten to pass on his message. She hurried to the door. Unable to meet his gaze, his crooked grin unsettling her, she invited him to step inside. "I'll get Danny for you."

"No need, I can see you've a houseful. Just tell him the materials and tools are locked away on the site where we're working. The lads weren't too happy traipsing in and out of Sycamore Lodge the way things were so we moved everything for handiness."

Danny moved faster than he had in days, hurrying to greet Tony and ensure he'd heard him correctly. "You've no idea how good it is to clear that mystery up," he said with a grin, bemused at the simple explanation that was available in the end. "You've probably saved my marriage! My wife was suspecting me of arson!"

Tony grinned, copping on at once to what Danny meant. "Well, you can tell her I'm responsible for the missing materials!"

"Come in and tell her yourself! Let's have a drink. God knows I could do with one!"

The days that followed were business as usual in Delia's house, with Gloria storming around sticking her nose into everybody's business and all others holding their tongues so they wouldn't upset her.

"Now, we need to organise Stephen's wedding? Shouldn't we be pricing our plane tickets? And Danny? Will he be able to travel or should you talk to Stephen about moving back home and getting married here? Now that Danny's out of work, he'll need someone he can trust to run the business. Would you not have a word with Stephen, Lucy? Surely he wants to bring his children up near his family? You could mind the baby while they go out to work."

Lucy would have loved nothing better but didn't dare interfere. "I'd be first to roll out the red carpet and welcome him with open arms but he has Ellie to consider now so we'll just have to wait and see."

Gloria nodded resignedly, not one bit happy about any great grandchild of hers being reared on the other side of the world! And she'd be telling Stephen that too. Once his mother was out of earshot.

Lucy cleared the table and loaded the dishwasher, her thoughts miles away. Being accused of arson and the fear of losing their home had occupied her thoughts for such a large part of the previous week that everything else seemed trivial. Listening to Gloria listing things off now, however, reminded her that life would indeed go on, the magnificent power of nature defying all other forces.

But before she could attend to anything else, there was something very important she needed to do. Getting the kitchen tidied in record time, she told Gloria she was nipping into the village to stock up on vegetables for the dinner. "I won't be long, Mum," she called over her shoulder, thankful that her mother hadn't suggested accompanying her. "And, Mum, please don't disturb Danny and his folks. Let him have some quality time with his parents. She is their daughter after all. Go easy on them."

"Quality time," she heard Gloria mutter under her breath. "What a made-up load of claptrap."

Getting out of the house while they were discussing Jenny is probably safest for both of us, she thought, still getting her head around the fact her sister-in-law was still demanding a bailout. But she pushed Jenny to one side, confident that Danny wouldn't squander the insurance money paying his sister's debts.

Knowing the Ardle Construction business insurance policy covered all their losses had her floating on air, taking her so high that there was very little she believed she couldn't accomplish. Confronting Carol Black was the first of those missions. In the privacy of the car, she sent her a text message.

Coffee? Waterfront? 15 mins?

Five minutes later she was still waiting for a reply. She was just about to give up when her phone beeped loudly. She started the engine of the car after reading Carol's response, anxious to be sitting in the café before her neighbour arrived.

Taking a seat by the window gave her a vantage view and the upper hand. She hadn't planned what she was going to say but knew it wouldn't take too many words. Staring through the window, she noticed a woman in a shabby green coat, jolting in surprise to realise it was Carol.

When she entered the café and sat opposite Lucy, the two women looked at each other. Lucy's flesh crawled. Carol remained motionless.

"I don't know what to say, Lucy." Tears were streaming down her face. She wiped them away with the grubby sleeve of her gabardine.

Lucy was trying hard to control her anger. "How could Isobel do it?"

Carol's face contorted. "Fear of losing her job."

"I know *why* she did it, Carol. I asked you *how* she could do it."

"You have to believe she never intended –"

"Never intended what? To burn our house down or leave Danny for dead? How can you justify what she's done, whether she had intent or not?"

Lucy nodded, studying her a moment, saying without preamble. "And she was happy to let Danny go down for a crime he didn't commit. As you were."

Carol was growing more desperate. Her neighbour's face was filled with hatred, her eyes boring through her. "I'm going to be sick," she mumbled, covering her mouth with the palm of her hand and hurrying to the rest room at the back of the café.

Lucy took her purse and car keys from the table. Confronting Carol had been a mistake. Any explanation she offered wouldn't change how she felt, wouldn't alter what had happened.

By the time Carol had returned, Lucy had disappeared.

Chapter 65

Nine Months Later

The terrible nightmare was gradually fading away. Sycamore Lodge was a safe haven for the Ardle family once more and Lucy'd had enough adventure to last a lifetime. Normality was more than enough to fill her days.

"Feet off the new couch, Danny," Lucy implored, scurrying around with a duster, ensuring every surface was squeaky clean. "Everyone will be here shortly. Can you please go and change? I don't want Ellie's family seeing you in overalls when they visit our home for the first time."

"Will you stop fussing, Luce?" Danny said in desperation, trying to see around his wife to catch the last few minutes of the game. She'd been nagging him since she'd opened her eyes this morning and now she was rushing him upstairs to their newly refurbished bedroom to change into the navy chinos and Ralph Lauren shirt she'd left out for him. "They'll have to take me as they find me! Wasn't Ellie's Dad wearing shorts when we visited them? Hell, we spent most of our time sitting in their back garden."

Lucy turned around and glared at him. "Danny, just do it! Our little grandson will be here any minute and you're fighting with me over a change of clothes." She changed to using her most persuasive tone. "Please!"

Danny laughed then, the desperation in his wife's plea pitiful. He couldn't understand why she got into a flap over these things. But rather than upset her and cause a fuss, it was easier to do as he was told. Anything for a quiet life was his new motto. "Okay, Grandma. So much for having time to ourselves after the boys grew up. We're back to babies and bottles again – it's a never-ending circle." And off he went to get changed, admiring his tradesmen's quality workmanship as he went into the hall and up the stairs to his bedroom.

Lucy flopped onto the corner couch, the smell of new leather lingering. She pulled her feet up under her, taking a moment to admire the chic décor, her eyes flickering over the cherry-wood furnishings. Stephen and Ellie's wedding photo took pride of place on one side of the white marble mantelpiece, a photo of her tiny grandson on the other. What a year, she thought, a shiver running over her as her mind swept back to the time she'd walked into that exact room, sat on the step and cried. If she were offered a million euro, she wouldn't relive a day of it, having learned the difficult way how materialism comes a very poor second to what really mattered in life – family and friends you can trust. But with a bit of luck (hopefully good luck for a change), it was all behind them now – apart from the impending court case and the fact Jenny was now working as Danny's accountant – far from ideal but better than giving her a payout for free. Allowing her live in one of Ardle Construction's show houses had initially caused friction between Danny and Lucy but eventually – when she'd persuaded him to move Jenny into the smallest one (and the one furthest away from Crosshaven) – she had acquiesced.

Refusing to allow the fire ruin another moment of her life, Lucy pushed all bad thoughts from her mind and went to check on the food sizzling in the oven instead. Humming along to Bagatelle's 'Love Is The Reason' – yet another random selection that suited the occasion perfectly – she took the large joint of roast beef from the oven and set it on the brand-new granite counter-top to cool. "Matt," she called, sticking her head around the door to the games room (a last-minute addition as part of the rebuild), "can you tear yourself away from that snooker table and come and set the table, please?"

"Ah there's a smell I've missed, Mum!" he laughed, sauntering into the kitchen and planting a kiss on her cheek. "It's good to be home!"

Lucy smiled broadly, tears glistening in her eyes. "It sure is, Matt. And I don't plan on leaving it for a very long time again." She wrapped her arms around him and nestled her head in his chest, squeezing him tight. "I'm so glad you've come home for the holidays, love. Having you all under one roof – even if it is only for a short while – is all my dreams come true."

"Don't get soppy, Mum. Give it a day or two and you'll be sick of us making the place look untidy. Have you and Delia organised your tickets for the New York shopping trip you've been talking about?"

"Not yet but it's high on our travel agenda."

He ran his little finger under her eyelashes to wipe away her tears.

Lucy pulled herself together and went back to slicing her meat, instructing Matt to uncork the wine and give another polish to her best goblets. She nibbled a bit of beef, relieved as its succulence melted in her mouth. She had gone all out to impress her visitors, a four-course meal planned to within an inch of its life the first welcome they'd receive. Her stomach flipped over nervously as Danny's voice filtered in from the hallway.

"The Aussies are here, Luce. Come on you too, Matt," he instructed, "there's a load of luggage to be carried in." He made to walk away and then stuck his head back into the kitchen again. "Gloria and Delia have arrived now as well. Travelling together I might add. Maybe I should text Tony to call on some pretence or other?" Danny's green eyes twinkled mischievously.

Lucy laughed. "I don't think today's the day for matchmaking, love, and from what I hear Tony's well able to arrange his own dates!"

Danny grinned and turned his attention to greeting their guests.

Her mother and sister would never be without their arguments but since Gloria had reinstated herself in her own house, relations had improved significantly, distance being the key to their truce. But her mother and sister's relationship wasn't of any major concern to Lucy, unlike another relationship she'd been wondering about but hadn't found the right moment to question. Suddenly she needed to know so that she could enjoy this happy event without any lurking tensions.

"Matt," she said, delaying her son a moment before following Danny outside, "I don't like to pry, but you and Heidi?"

Matt tilted his head sideways, a defensive look in his eye. "We're taking things slowly, Mum. It was complicated to begin with but, wow, it's snowballed since then. And now with Isobel on trial and everything, we've a lot to work through. Being in New York makes it easier to be honest and teaching English to foreign students has given her a new lease of life." He blushed a little, shrugging his shoulders and shoving his hands in his pockets. "I love her, Mum."

Lucy bit her lip, his honest declaration a powerful blow to her private hope that their relationship would fizzle out and they could have a clean break from the Black family. Not wanting to upset or infuriate Matt, she swallowed her maternal instinct to instruct him to be careful. For the millionth time!

"And Alex? How is that going for her?" she enquired, noticing the tension leaving Matt's shoulders, proud of how well she was hiding her grave reservations. So far at least.

"He's a cool kid," he responded, "has a very open relationship with his adoptive parents and is taking things at a relaxed pace with Heidi."

"That's good. Too much too soon seldom lasts. This way, who knows?"

Matt nodded, thinking of the uncanny resemblance between mother and son, the overwhelming change in Heidi since Alex came into her life.

"Lucy? Matt?" Danny's call echoed through the house.

Slipping her apron over her head and placing it neatly over the handle of her AGA cooker, Lucy smoothened her new dress over her slim hips, checked her appearance in the mirror and hurried to the front door to greet her guests.

Her heart hardened when she noticed the *For Sale* sign on Carol's entrance pillar. How she wished it didn't get to her every time she stepped outside. Recent memories continued to rage inside, the cruel way her family had been deceived, manipulated and – in Danny's case – almost sent to their death by the Black family. But in time, despite Carol and Isobel's hasty departure to Galway after Isobel's costly bail release, they would get their comeuppance and pay a high price for their appalling actions.

Stephen noticed the faraway look in his mother's eye and stepped into her line of vision, blocking her view of the house across the road. Wrapping his free arm around her shoulders, he hugged her tightly. "Come on, Grandma, I've carried this little package halfway across the world and he's dying to leap into your arms. Aren't you going to bring him inside and let him see where he's sleeping for the next couple of weeks?"

Lucy let go her resentment and held out her arms for her wriggling grandson, refusing to allow her neighbours ruin another moment of their lives. Enough time had been lost, too much hurt between them to be forgiven. Like an unexpected ray of sunshine, the baby gurgled into Lucy's ear, his innocence lifting the hurt inside her and forcing a broad grin on her face. Exchanging a swift glance with Danny, she and her toasty little bundle led the extended Ardle family into Sycamore Lodge, where empty photo albums and picture frames waited in every room to capture a brand new generation of memories and mementos.

THE END

If you enjoyed *Love is the Reason*
by Mary Malone, why not try
Never Tear Us Apart also published by Poolbeg?
Here's a sneak preview of Chapter One.

mary malone

Never Tear Us Apart

POOLBEG

Prologue

Discovery of Body Upgraded to Murder

The body of a woman discovered late last night when Gardaí were called to an apartment complex in a North Co Dublin suburb has been identified as that of a twenty-eight-year-old employee with Ellis Enterprise.

A postmortem investigation carried out yesterday revealed that the woman had died from head injuries. "Her death is being treated as suspicious," according to Detective Superintendent Karl Wilson who is leading the investigation.

Neighbours describe her as pleasant and polite but refrained from further comment. Detective Superin-tendent Wilson says the Gardaí are gathering evidence and following several lines of enquiry.

Searches by crime officers are continuing in the premises where her body was found. Her name cannot be released until all family members have been notified.

Gardaí are looking for witnesses and would appreciate any information in strictest confidence to Clontarf Garda Station at 01-6664800.

Chapter 1

Four days earlier

Sitting at her office desk on Friday afternoon, Vicky Jones found it impossible to concentrate on her work, an imaginary clock ticking loudly in her head, every passing second adding to her anxiety. She stared at the computer screen in front of her, twisting her blonde hair into a knot around her fingers, holding it tightly in place for a moment before letting it fall in soft waves to her shoulders once more. How she wished she could do the same with the concerns jiggling around in her head.

She glanced at her watch. Fintan should be home by now after the lunch-time stint at the club. She wondered about his afternoon and what he would do to pass the time. She wondered for the umpteenth time what he was hiding from her.

Her fingers itched to pick up the phone and call him. It would be reassuring to hear his voice but she knew after that she'd want more. He could tell her anything over the phone. If he answered the land-line, he could pretend he was sitting at home alone with his feet up. And if she caught him on his mobile, he could say he was in the supermarket picking up some groceries. But she still wouldn't know for sure. She still wouldn't know if he was telling the truth.

She glanced at the door to her boss's office. How long more would the meeting last? Should she dare take a chance? She chewed on her bottom lip as she thought about it but waited a moment too long because right on cue – right when she was on the verge of making a dash from her desk, running all the way to the DART station and grabbing the first train to Malahide to hurry home and check up on Fintan – the door opened and Ariel Satlow burst out.

Her brown eyes were flashing in fury. She pulled the door shut firmly behind her and made a beeline for Vicky's desk, banging the file she was carrying down on the hardwood surface. She barely took the time to draw breath before launching into a litany of complaint.

Vicky exhaled slowly, the confines of the office stifling, Ariel's dramatic entrance overpowering. Reaching for the bottle of water on her desk, she filled her glass and took a long, refreshing drink, forgoing any notion of sneaking away and giving her full attention to her colleague instead.

"Things didn't go well with Ben then?"

Ariel shook her head, her dark hair shining under the bright fluorescent light. "Understatement of the year! I can't get anything right around here any more." She picked up the file with both hands, banging it on the desk once more for effect. "This week is going from bad to worse!"

"I thought you two had a meeting about your accounts

already this morning? Surely Ben's not still harping on about the same thing?"

"Yeah, he did speak to me earlier – just as I was getting ready to leave for that meeting with clients."

"What bad timing!"

Ariel nodded, inhaling a long deep breath through her nose before letting it escape noisily through her lips. "He wasn't one bit impressed with the work I'd handed up. I could barely concentrate on the presentation I had to give to that company afterwards!" She planted her backside on the edge of Vicky's desk.

"I can imagine."

"Nothing I send in is good enough any more. I haven't lifted my head since I got back from my meeting and he's firing accusations at me as though I'm sitting around filing my nails!" She nervously flicked imaginary dust from her fitted black skirt. "I don't have a problem taking correction, Vicky. You know that. But this? This is downright unfair."

Vicky nodded her understanding, trying to think of something to say that wouldn't sound disloyal to either party. Working as Ben's Personal Assistant had its awkward moments. Like the one she was in with Ariel now.

"He's under a lot of pressure with the tax-return deadline only a few weeks away," she ventured.

"And him being under pressure is probably my fault to begin with," the other girl deadpanned.

"But you're only human! And mistakes happen to everyone."

"But these weren't my mistakes! I know they weren't!" Ariel clasped and unclasped the delicate diamond bracelet she wore on her slim wrist. "I've hardly ever made cock-ups in my accounts before and now it's as if everything I

481

touch turns to mush." She lowered her voice, a trace of uncertainty in her eyes as she leaned in closer to Vicky. "That's two accounts I've messed up today. Add them to the other mishaps this week and it makes five altogether! If I'm not careful, I'll be out on my ear. And I won't be able to explain why, which will look great on a job application."

Vicky chewed her lip. "And you're sure they were okay when you finished them?"

Ariel let out a long sigh, flicking absent-mindedly through the pages in her file. "I couldn't be more positive."

"So how do you explain the errors?"

She stared at the ground for a moment and shook her head. "I can't . . . When he called me in just now to go over the mistakes I'd made on the Hennessy account, I felt like such an imbecile. What if he lets me go, Vicky? What if my job is on the line?" She brought her hands to her face and groaned.

"Now you're being silly. He's always held you in the highest regard."

Ariel was one of the most popular consultants within the company, the person with the highest number of requests for repeat business. And the majority of her new accounts came to her on recommendation for a job well done.

"Huh! Not any more he doesn't!"

"As far as I know, he has a video conference with Hennessys later. Maybe that's why he's treating whatever you're working on with such urgency? He's probably under pressure to get things finished. You know what some of these companies are like. Particularly when it comes to making tax returns."

But yet again Vicky's words failed to console.

Ariel fiddled absent-mindedly with the diamond

studs in her ears and stared into the distance, catching a glimpse of the DART as it sped along in a blur of green. "No. Ben doesn't yield under duress. And the clients rely on us to keep an eye on deadlines, not the other way around! No. The only person Ben has issue with at the moment is me. He's like a dog with a bone."

"I hope it's not me you're gossiping about, girls!" Marcus, one of the other consultants, wagged a finger as he approached them, strolling in the direction of the tiny cafeteria, an empty coffee cup in his hand.

"You wish!" Ariel turned to face him, laughing with him when he shrugged and smiled, his warm green eyes twinkling.

"Don't worry, Marcus. We've got much more exciting things to discuss!" Vicky called after him and then turned back to Ariel. "What were we saying? Oh, yes. A dog with a bone. Not very friendly then, I take it?"

"Definitely not. More like the leading husky pulling a heavily laden sleigh!" Ariel let out a long sigh.

Vicky smirked, visualising a team of huskies with her boss barking orders from the front. "Let's hope his bark is worse than his bite then!"

"I won't be taking any chances. At the rate he's checking my work he'd be better off actually doing it himself. He might trust me enough to look over the figures before they're returned to the client." She picked up the file and hugged it to her chest. "I was this close, Vicky," she made a gesture with her index finger and thumb, "to pressing delete on the set of accounts he had open on his desktop. If he's going to treat me like a child, why shouldn't I act like one!"

She delivered her last sentence as more of a statement

than a question, glancing behind her towards Ben's office, opening her mouth wide and letting out a silent scream.

Vicky watched her closely, noticing her flushed cheeks and exasperated expression. She also recognised the hurt and confusion in her eyes.

"It's not like you to let things get you down. You're usually so . . ."

"Usually so what? Calm? Measured?"

Vicky pushed her chair slightly back from her desk. "So in control. I was going to say you're usually so in control."

"But I'm not in control. I can't understand what's happened and none of the others are getting the gruelling he's giving me. Then again, they're all men! I'm the only female on the team." She shrugged indifferently as if she had already given up the race.

"You're not suggesting Ben is sexist, are you?"

Ariel inhaled a slow, deep breath. "It's not something I've noticed before but it has to be more than a coincidence that he's singling me out. What do you think? Could there be a grain of truth in it? Have you ever noticed a chauvinistic side to him?"

"That's a fairly loaded accusation, Ariel." And, after all, the errors in the accounts *did* exist, she thought. Her fingers flew across her keyboard as she clicked on her electronic scheduler and added a reminder entry to the tasks column, her eyes focusing on the screen in front of her. "You're sure you haven't anything else bothering you? Anything distracting you?" She stopped typing and looked up again, assessing the girl sitting at the edge of her desk.

Ariel shook her head. "No. Nothing's distracting me. That's not it." She dropped her gaze to the floor once more.

"Pressure of work?" Vicky prompted.

But she met with another cul-de-sac.

"If anything, I work better under pressure."

"Put it behind you is my advice then."

But Ariel wasn't quite ready to let go. "The only solution I can come up with is that the place must be haunted." She smiled. "Little gremlins living in our computers, dancing around the files when we're not at our desks. Can you imagine them?"

"Do you think they'd show their faces if we asked them nicely?"

Ariel giggled at the absurdity of their conversation "Unlikely," she conceded. "I'd better get back to work or Ben will be shouting for figures." She ran her fingers through her black shoulder-length hair, sweeping it back from her pretty face, then jumped up from the desk in haste at the sound of Ben's door opening.

"Ariel, why are you still here? And was that my name I heard?"

She swung around to face him. "Oh, er, yes, Ben. I'm just discussing some files with Vicky, telling her I needed to get them back to you as soon as possible." Her voice was unsteady, her tone guarded, as if she was waiting for him to fire yet another accusation in her direction.

"Since when did you need Vicky's advice to get things done?"

A deep red blush began in the hollow of Ariel's throat, creeping along her slim neck and into her cheeks, embarrassment spreading all over her face. "Vicky's helping me tidy up a few correspondence lists," she improvised. "That's all."

"I thought I told you I needed that file straight away. You're not going to get it done standing gossiping to Vicky!

Prioritise, Ariel. The correspondence can wait. What about deadlines? Do they mean anything to you any more?" He put his hands in his trouser pockets and stood a couple of feet away from her as he waited for her to respond, the deep-etched lines around his eyes a trademark of his fifty-five years, his broad shoulders and lean physique a testament to regular visits to the swimming pool.

"Yes, of course they do. I'm always working with deadlines in mind."

Dropping her head for the briefest of seconds, Ariel took a few steps away from Vicky's desk. But then she stopped and turned to face Ben again, straightening her posture and pulling herself up to her full five feet, seven inches – five feet, eight and a half including the heels she was wearing.

"If I have to stay up all night, I will sort this mess out. I will get to the bottom of it, Ben," she promised. "Those mistakes weren't my doing." She moved swiftly towards her office, shutting the door quietly behind her.

Once inside the door, Ariel leaned against it, closed her eyes and waited for her heart rate to return to normal.

If you enjoyed this chapter from
Never Tear Us Apart by Mary Malone
why not order the full book online
@ www.poolbeg.com